Finding HOME

USA Today and International Bestselling Author
Lauren Rowe

Copyright © 2024 by Lauren Rowe

All rights reserved.

No part of this book may be reproduced in any form or by any electronic or mechanical means, including information storage and retrieval systems, without written permission from the author, except for the use of brief quotations in a book review.

Published by SoCoRo Publishing

Cover design Shannon Passmore of **Shanoff Designs**

FINDING HOME

By Lauren Rowe

Please check the content warning on Lauren Rowe's website.

CHAPTER 1
CALEB

About a year and a half ago
Santa Monica, California

I turn onto my side and exhale in the quiet darkness of my bedroom. When the change of position doesn't quell my racing thoughts, I turn over and check the time on my nightstand.

4:37.

In less than three hours, my sister will be here, so we can take our mother to her first chemo appointment. It's going to be a long, sleep-deprived day. A whole lot longer for Mom, though, so I shouldn't complain. Not even in my own head.

I turn onto my back this time and try to let the distant sounds of the ocean lull me to sleep; but I can't keep my thoughts from spiraling the same way they did last night. And the night before. Although tonight, I'm back to thinking about my kid—the six-month-old who's out there somewhere, probably in Seattle, but maybe not. Is my kid a boy or girl? What's their name? Do they look like me? I know it's early days yet, but are they showing signs of musicality?

I roll over onto my side again.

I hate feeling like the second coming of my deadbeat father—someone I swore as a teen twenty years ago I'd never become. Granted, I've been sending massive sums of money to my child on a monthly basis, and at a level that's far more generous than anything my baby momma could have hoped to squeeze out of me, if I'd forced her to take me to court. Which I didn't. But the fact remains, I'm not in the kid's life. Never have been. And worst of all, thanks to my own stupid insistence during negotiations, my kid will never know their father is C-Bomb, the drummer from Red Card Riot.

When I insisted on complete anonymity and confidentiality a year ago through my lawyer, I was certain that's what I wanted: zero obligations to my future child, other than sending money. But once the baby was born, and especially after my good friends, Colin and Amy, had a baby only a week after my kid's birth, doubt started creeping in. After my mother's diagnosis, my doubt solidified into regret. And now, after watching a video of Colin and Amy's six-month-old, Rocco, trying apple sauce for the first time today, my regret morphed, once again. This time, into full-blown guilt and shame.

Did *my* baby recently try apple sauce, like Rocco? If so, were *my* baby's facial expressions as funny as Rocco's? Colin and Amy belly-laughed behind the camera in that video today. If I'd been there to witness my own baby making silly faces in a highchair, would I have belly-laughed like they did? It feels like forever since I've done that. *Have I ever?*

I sit up in bed and rub my face. I never imagined myself having these kinds of thoughts when I signed that agreement with Claudia Beaumont. When I first learned of her pregnancy, I didn't even remember her—not until my lawyer showed me a photo of the pretty blonde groupie from Seattle to jog my drunken memories. Plus, Claudia said she didn't want me involved, other than sending child support payments, so why *wouldn't* I agree to oblige her?

Claudia only asked for fifteen grand per month, which my lawyer said was fair, since she'd probably get more in court. But I offered Claudia twice that amount—thirty grand—on two conditions:

One, confidentiality.

Claudia couldn't talk about our agreement or her night with me, and she also had to keep my identity a secret, not only from the kid, but from the world at large. As the "bad boy" drummer for Red Card Riot, I wasn't afraid of the world's condemnation. I knew the world would shrug their collective shoulders to find out C-Bomb had accidentally knocked up a groupie during a casual hook-up.

No, when I demanded confidentiality in exchange for more money than Claudia could win in court, I was actually concerned about my mother and sister finding out my dirty little secret. God help me, I knew if those two ever found out I'd not only fathered a kid without telling them—but worse, I'd also decided not to step up, other than financially—they'd never forgive me. Also, they'd want to forge a meaningful relationship with the kid, which would force me to do the same, and I selfishly didn't want to do that. Or so I thought at the time.

My second condition to Claudia Beaumont was one my attorney, Paula, initially balked at: Claudia could never bring the baby to her hometown of Prairie Springs, Montana. At least, not during summers. Once Paula showed me a photo of Claudia, I vaguely remembered smoking a blunt with her, either before or after sex, and figuring out the pretty blonde from our show in Seattle had coincidentally grown up in the same small town as my mother. The same place where my grandfather—my mother's father, who was still alive at the time—owned a cabin on Lake Lucille.

Back then, I knew my grandfather's health was failing, and that my mother would soon inherit the lake cabin, at which time she'd probably want to start going back to Prairie Springs during summers again, like we used to do when I was a kid. So, I included my second demand to make sure Mom never ran into Claudia and her kid in Prairie Springs and somehow put two and two together.

In the end, much to my lawyer's surprise, Claudia wound up quickly accepting both of my demands without the slightest push-back. Regarding the Prairie Springs thing, she said, through her attorney, "Fine with me. I don't want to go to Prairie Springs, anyway. My monster of a father worked there as a police officer for decades, and he still goes back frequently to visit old friends."

What did Claudia mean when she called her father a monster? I didn't ask, since I've got a monster of a father, too. I simply thought, "Join the club, Claudia." And never looked back. For a while, anyway. In fact, the night I signed the agreement, I played my heart out for seventy thousand people and soaked in their applause like I hadn't just done the shittiest, most despicable thing in my life.

A soft whimper wafts into my dark bedroom and prompts me sit up in bed. Was that Mom crying out in pain like she did the other night? I get up and creep down the hallway, but when I open the door to the guest room, Mom is fast asleep. I stand in the doorway staring at her chest for a long moment, making sure it's rising and falling. When I'm satisfied she's fine, I creep back to my bedroom, slide back into bed, and try in vain to fall asleep, once again.

If Mom weren't here, I'd already have battled my insomnia by taking a handful of gummies and/or smoked a fat blunt or bowl and/or downed a half-bottle of Jack by now. Or maybe I would have gone downstairs to my home studio to bang on my drums. But I can't do any of that with Mom sleeping down the hallway and her first infusion in mere hours. If Mom wakes up in pain, I need to be alert, not dead to the world in a chemically-induced coma or banging on my drums with earphones on.

I hear another whimper and freeze. That sounded like a baby crying. Am I imagining things, due to my guilt, like the guy in the "Tell-Tale Heart" story—the one where the guy who committed murder hears his victim's beating heart from underneath a floorboard?

I head to my mother's room again. Same result.

Fuck.

Fuck it.

I can't live like this anymore.

With determination flooding my veins, I return to my bedroom, grab my laptop, flop into a chair, and quickly find an old email chain between Claudia's attorney and mine. As I recall, Claudia was copied on one of the emails somewhere...

Here it is. Claudia's personal email address. *Bingo.*

My heart thumping wildly, I tap out an email directly to Claudia Beaumont.

. . .

Hey Claudia,

It's C-Bomb. Sorry to come at you out of the blue, but I got some bad news recently about my mother's health. She's got late-stage cancer, and the doc says the odds aren't good she'll make it more than a year. She's starting chemo tomorrow, and we're hoping she'll beat this thing or at least buy herself more time, but these things are unpredictable.

In light of this new circumstance, I'm hoping to introduce the baby to my mother and sister in LA, as soon as possible. I know this is a one-eighty from what we agreed upon, but I'm hoping you'll have mercy on me. Of course, I'll fly you and the baby to LA and put you up for as long as you can stay. I'll pay for a luxury hotel or you can stay at my place. I live in Santa Monica, right on the beach, in a big house with plenty of room.

If the visit goes well, maybe we can talk about amending our contract to include regular visitation rights for me. I've honestly been feeling tons of regret and guilt about—

I abruptly stop typing. What am I doing? For all I know, the visit might only confirm my initial hunch—that the kid is better off without me. With a sigh, I delete that last, incomplete paragraph and begin typing again.

To be clear, I'm not trying to change our financial agreement. No matter what happens, that thirty grand will always hit your bank account every month until our kid turns eighteen. I'm only asking you to have mercy on me in the coming months. My mother is the best person I know, and she sacrificed everything for my sister and me, so I want to give her the best gift imaginable before she passes. My mother's the one who scraped together her pennies to buy me my first drum kit, Claudia. She believed in me, when nobody else did. I'm living my dreams now, because of her.

I stop typing again. Is that accurate? Am I really living my dreams?

As a musician, I am. Sure.

But in my personal life?

No, not at all.

With a long exhale, I delete that last sentence and begin again.

Time isn't on my side here, so I'm pleading with you to say yes, as soon as possible. Please, Claudia. Do this favor for me and I'll be eternally grateful.

Thanks in advance,
   C-Bomb

CHAPTER 2
AUBREY

Present day, Seattle

I wake up to my alarm to find two-year-old Raine snuggled up against me, fast asleep. That's weird. Like clockwork, Claudia always grabs her baby girl out of my bed when she gets home from the hospital. That's been our deal, ever since I showed up on Claudia's doorstep over a year-and-a-half ago, feeling broken-hearted and bruised after my breakup with Trent: Claudia takes care of Raine, once she gets home from work in the wee hours, so I can get up early and head off to work in time for the breakfast rush.

With a yawn, I kiss the top of Raine's soft, blonde curls and grab my phone from the nightstand. Claudia hasn't dated since she broke up with Ricky about a year ago, but if that cute ER doctor she's been drooling over finally made his move, I bet she went for it. If that happened, though, she'd surely text me to let me know the exciting news and also that she might not be home at the usual time.

Nope.

I've got nothing from Claudia.

Did she feel sick when she got home, and now she's fast asleep on the cool tile floor of the bathroom? A tad worried, I slide out of bed, taking care not to wake the cling-on sleeping next to me, and tiptoe out of my bedroom. But there's no Claudia in the bathroom as I pass by. Also, no Claudia in her bedroom. In fact, her bed is still neatly made.

My stomach tightens with concern, but I tell myself not to freak out—that I'll surely find Claudia asleep on the couch. Claudia is sober these days—she went to rehab the minute she found out she was pregnant—so I wouldn't normally jump straight to thinking Claudia might have gotten shitfaced and passed out on the couch. But in this moment, my brain can't come up with any other logical explanations besides that cute ER doc or Claudia falling off the wagon.

My pulse pounding, I stride into the living room, but Claudia's nowhere to be found. Not only that, her car keys aren't in the dish by the door; her purse isn't sitting on the kitchen counter; and there's no jacket slung haphazardly onto the back of the blue chair.

Okay, I'm officially freaking out.

I look at the time on my phone.

5:12.

Claudia knows I've got to be at the restaurant at six, and that it takes me sixteen to eighteen minutes to walk there, depending on lights and weather. She'd never make me late for work, but I suppose there's still twenty-five minutes for Claudia to walk through that door without doing that.

Suddenly, the location app on my phone pops into my head. I never think to look at it, since Claudia's always at work or here, and my parents are always in their usual places in Prairie Springs. But I'm definitely thinking about it now.

I swipe into the app and press Claudia's name . . . and gasp loudly at her location. *Claudia is at the downtown Seattle police station.* At least, her phone is.

Did Claudia lose her phone and someone brought it in? Or was Claudia the victim or witness to a crime last night? Please, God, don't let it be that Claudia fell off the wagon and got herself arrested for drunk driving. If that's the case, I never saw it coming. Yes, Claudia has been grieving her mother's death; but as a general matter, she's seemed happier than ever over the past year or so, ever since she ditched Ricky's ass, and we fell into our happy, peaceful routine with Raine.

My breathing jagged, I smash the button to call Claudia. If she's sitting in a jail cell, she won't be able to pick up, obviously. But if—

"Hello?"

A chill shoots down my spine. That's not Claudia's sweet, kewpie-doll voice. That's the voice of a man—a complete stranger.

"I'm calling for Claudia," I manage to say, despite my somersaulting stomach. "This is her phone."

"We've been waiting for someone to call, since the phone is locked. Who am I speaking with?"

Dread tightens its grip on my chest. "Aubrey Capshaw. I'm Claudia's best friend and roommate. Who's this?"

"Detective Howard of the Seattle PD."

My heart stops. "Is Claudia hurt? Does she need bail money or an attorney?"

The man pauses. "Are you sitting down, Aubrey?"

I clutch my chest and squeak out my affirmative reply.

"Claudia was hit by a drunk driver while crossing the street after work last night. I'm sorry to inform you: she suffered catastrophic injuries and died at the scene."

My brain feels like it's physically melting inside my skull. "If this is a prank," I choke out. "Then you're—"

"This is very real, unfortunately. I'm sorry for your loss."

A strangled wail escapes me—a horrible, tortured screech I've never heard my body produce before now. It's the sound of a heart shattering. The sound of a lifelong soulmate being ripped away from its other half. And worst of all, it's the sound of an innocent, happy two-year-old losing her beloved mommy, in the blink of an eye.

"Maybe it wasn't her," I manage between sobs.

"It was definitely her. She had her ID on her and a coworker identified her. Listen, can you help us contact Claudia's next of kin? The emergency number Claudia listed at work for her mother doesn't work, and—"

"Claudia's mother died a couple months ago." With the phone to my ear, I wrap my free arm around myself and rock back and forth, feeling physically ill.

"Can you confirm we've got the right number for her father, Ralph Beaumont? We left a voicemail for him to call us, but—"

"*You called Claudia's father?*" I scream at top volume. "She never wanted to see him again! She hated him!"

The officer says something in reply, but I don't hear a word of it; because, suddenly, Claudia's tiny, blonde doppelganger is standing in the entryway to the living room with wide, anxious eyes and chaotic bedhead.

"I have to go," I bark into the phone. Without waiting

for the detective's reply, I disconnect the call and stride on wobbly legs to the sweet angel who's got no idea her mommy is never coming home again.

"You not use inside voice," Raine chides me groggily, rubbing her eyes and yawning. "'Member what Mommy said?"

With a loud sob, I pull Raine to me and hold her tightly for a long moment, as she babbles about I don't know what. Finally, when I lean back to look into her eyes, she wipes at my tears with her little hand and says, "You have boo-boo, Auntie Aubbey? You need Band-Aid?"

The two innocent questions shatter the last remaining shards of my heart. That's what Claudia always asks her baby girl, whenever she cries for as-yet unknown reasons.

Without waiting for my reply, Raine adds, "I get Mommy."

She starts to wriggle in my arms, presumably aiming to get down and run to her mommy down the hall, but I keep a firm grip on her and bring her to the couch. "Mommy's not in there, baby. Stay here with me. I need to tell you something important."

I place her on my lap, facing me. For a long moment, I can't get another word out, because my chin is quivering too much. But finally, I manage to pull myself together enough to speak in a tight, halting voice. "Rainey, Mommy went to heaven last night. She didn't want to go. She wanted to stay here with you, forever, but she didn't have a choice. She had to go."

Raine tilts her head and scrunches her itty-bitty eyebrows, looking deeply confused. "Like Gramma?"

I run my fingers through Raine's soft, blonde hair. "Just like Gramma, yes. Mommy's body is gone now—" The words feel like razor blades being dragged across my heart. "But her spirit will always watch over you and love you." I don't mean to do it, but I lose it; and that's when Raine loses it, too.

"I don't want Mommy in da heaven!" she screams. "I want Mommy here *now*!"

"I know, baby. I want that, too. But she had to go."

"Mommy come back here *now*!"

"She can't. But I'm here, and I promise I'll always take care of you."

"I. Want. My. *Mommy*!" Raine wails, huge tears pouring down her cheeks. She leaps off the couch and puts her hands on her little hips. "*You get my mommy now!*"

Raine reminds me so much of her sassy, charismatic mommy in this moment, my body reacts violently. Holding my hand to my mouth, I lurch off the couch, sprint past Raine into the nearby bathroom, and retch out the entire contents of my stomach.

When I'm done, I sit on the floor, crying and whimpering. How the fuck am I going to do this? I'm twenty-four and a waitress. Without Claudia's money from The Drummer, I can't afford to live in Seattle on my own. Although, come to think of it, now that Claudia is gone, I don't even want to live here. Big city life was always Claudia's dream, not mine. I much prefer the quiet pace of our small hometown.

I make a snap decision. I'll go home to Prairie Springs—to the place where my parents can help me—financially, emotionally, and logistically—to the place where I can safely break down and curl into the fetal position for however long, while my parents look after Raine.

As resolve floods me, Raine waddles into the bathroom

doorway and whimpers that she wants her mommy. Realizing I've got to pull myself together for Raine's sake, I force myself off the floor, gulp down water from the faucet, and splash cold water on my face. When I finally feel capable of speaking, I scoop up Raine and take her to my bedroom.

We lie on my bed together for about twenty minutes, with both of us crying our eyes out. But, finally, Raine sits up and announces she's hungry and wants Mommy to come back from "da heaven" to make her pancakes.

There's no point in trying to explain it all to her again. She didn't comprehend the situation when Claudia's mother died a few months ago, so she's not going to understand her mommy's death any better now. Hell, I'm twenty-four, and I don't understand death—especially not when it happens to a gorgeous, vivacious, brilliant twenty-four-year-old who lives and breathes for her baby girl.

I wipe my eyes. "I'll make pancakes, while you stay here and watch a show." I grab my iPad and Raine makes her selection; and when she's calm and distracted, I race into the kitchen with my phone to place a call to my parents.

Thankfully, my mother picks up after only two rings, despite the unusual timing of my call. I never call Mom for our daily chat before work. We always talk while I'm walking home from the restaurant after my shift.

"Are you okay?" Mom asks, her voice on edge.

"There was an accident," I gasp out. "Claudia's gone, Mom. Raine is here with me. She's fine. But Claudia is dead."

The rest of the conversation is a blur to me. Words are exchanged, and my mouth moves, but my brain isn't connected to any of it. By the end of the conversation, the only thing I'm sure about is Mom is sending plane tickets for Raine and me to come home on the next flight out.

Claudia wasn't allowed to take Raine back to our hometown of Prairie Springs, thanks to the horrendous agreement she signed with The Drummer. But *I* never signed that thing. And *I* never took a penny from the asshole and never will. Which means *I* can do whatever the hell I want with Raine—which is exactly what I'm going to do.

CHAPTER 3
CALEB

Three weeks later
A rehab facility in Malibu, California

With sweat beaded on my brow, I bash my toms and kick my bass drum, hard, in time to the song blaring in my headphones—"Bleed" by Meshuggah. It's my go-to whenever I need to sweat and blow off steam. Or, these days, whenever I'm trying to exorcise the grief, guilt, and shame that constantly ravages me, ever since my mother died without knowing she was a grandmother. Not to mention, without me being there to hold her hand, as I'd promised.

I'm clean and sober now, unfortunately, so I can't drink myself into oblivion or smoke a bowl to numb the pain. For well over two months now, and thoroughly against my will, I've been high on nothing but fucking life, man. I don't recommend it.

The door to the small, sound-proofed studio opens without warning and a staffer dressed in the facility's uniform of black scrubs pokes his head into the small space. Breathing hard, I stop banging, slide my headphones down to my sweaty, tattooed neck, and glare at the guy. Everyone knows this hour every day is more important to my well-being than the useless, daily therapy sessions I'm required to attend. Everyone knows not to bother me when I'm here—that this is my version of church.

"Sorry to bother you, Caleb," the staffer says quickly. "You've got a visitor in the lounge."

My eyebrows ride up. "On a Wednesday?"

Once a patient makes it through detox the first week, they're allowed to start participating in Visitation Tuesdays. In my case, that's meant regular visits from my little sister, Miranda, four years my junior, throughout my time here. Also, early on, it meant occasional visits from my longtime attorney, Paula, who had to deal with the fallout of my destructive tantrum at that hotel in New York.

Still breathing hard from my exertion, I ask, "Is my attorney here?" Normally, I'd assume my sister, Miranda, is my visitor, since Paula stopped coming once all legal issues had been resolved. But Miranda flew to Paris with a group of friends yesterday, so it has to be Paula, since she's the only other person on my approved visitors list.

My sister keeps pushing me to add more names to the list—my three bandmates from Red Card Riot, for example. Some other close friends, too. But like I told my sister, I don't want to burden anyone else with my bullshit, nor do I want to deal with my bandmates' rampant anxiety about how my stupid actions have made us temporarily uninsurable for our next tour. If I'm being honest, I'm also not willing to be subjected to my friends' well-intended pep talks.

No, while I'm forced to be here and go through the motions, I simply want to be left alone to bang on my drums, attend all required, useless therapy sessions, work out, play ping-pong with that cool actor dude who's staying here under a fake name, and otherwise keep to myself.

"I don't know who's here to see you," the staff member says. "All I know is I was told to come get you for an emergency visitation."

I walk down the hallway toward the visitor's lounge, shitting bricks.

Emergency.

That's the word the staffer used, a day after my sister boarded a flight.

I swear, if my sister has been ripped away from me, less than three months after Mom, I won't survive it. One way or another, I'll figure out how to end myself, despite the tight security in this place.

I turn a corner and enter the lounge, and when I see my attorney, Paula, sitting at a table in a corner, the dread I've been feeling during my short walk here morphs into downright panic.

"Is my sister okay?" I blurt, as Paula rises and extends her hand.

"I'm not here about Miranda." Paula takes my hand and then motions to a chair. "Please, sit."

I exhale an ocean of relief and settle into a seat across from Paula. If she's here for a legal reason—even one that's an "emergency" in her book—that's something I can handle without breaking a sweat. "Did the hotel in New York decide I caused more damage than initially reported?" I ask with a scoff.

"I'm not here about that. I'm here about Claudia Beaumont." She takes a deep breath. "She's dead." When my jaw drops, Paula adds, "She got hit by a drunk driver a few weeks ago while walking to her car after work. And now, her father is trying to get full custody of her child—*your* child—because, Beaumont thinks, full custody will entitle him to the same thirty grand per month you've been paying to his daughter."

I run a hand over my black, knit cap, feeling sick to my stomach. Of all the scenarios playing in my mind as I walked to the visitor's lounge, this wasn't one of them. "Does he have the kid now?"

"No, Claudia's long-time best friend, Aubrey Capshaw, is with her. She'd been living with Claudia and the child in Seattle for quite some time. I'm told she's taken the child back to Prairie Springs, to her childhood home, where she's living with her parents and caring for the child there."

I stare at Paula in stunned silence for a long moment. I've been enraged at Claudia Beaumont for a while now, ever since she replied to my heartfelt, pleading email about my mother with a concise, "Fuck off, C-Bomb. A deal's a deal. Don't ever contact me again." But even so, I've never wished the woman *dead*. My god, poor Claudia couldn't have been more than twenty-four or -five, and this was how the poor girl went out?

"Is my kid a boy or girl?"

"A girl. Raine Beaumont. That's Raine with an 'e' on the end." Paula hesitates. Assessing me, apparently. Finally, she says, "I've got a photo of Raine, if you'd like to see her."

I nod, too overcome to speak, and a moment later, Paula hands me her phone, its screen filled with the stunning, smiling face of an adorable toddler with big, blue eyes and blonde curls. Also, to my intense fascination, she's got miniature versions of my exact nose and eyebrows.

"*Raine*," I murmur, staring at the smiling photo. "You poor kid." My heart aching, I slide Paula's phone back to her across the table.

Two and a half years ago, when Claudia and I struck our deal through attorneys, Claudia said she had big plans for my money. She was going to rehab before the baby was born to get herself clean and sober and ready for motherhood. She was going to rent a big house in a safe neighborhood in Seattle—a place with a backyard big enough for an elaborate playset. She was going back to school to finish up some remaining credits for a nursing degree and she planned to start a hefty college fund for her child. All of it was well intentioned, but unlikely, I figured. Especially after her terse, cold reply to my heartfelt email, I thought to myself, "This girl is so full of shit."

I haven't given Claudia's lengthy To Do List much thought recently; but now, suddenly, I need to know if Claudia did any of that stuff before her untimely passing, or if, instead, she pissed all my money away on plastic surgery, drugs, and tropical getaways.

"Did Claudia rent a big house in Seattle with a gigantic playset in the backyard?" I ask. "Did she become a nurse, like she said?"

Paula tips her head to the side. "I know Claudia was a nurse. The police report said she was killed right outside the hospital where she worked. I don't know anything about her living situation, other than the fact that she lived with Aubrey Capshaw. Age twenty-four. A waitress." She narrows her eyes. "Why do you ask?"

"Doesn't matter." I hang my head. Tears are unexpectedly pricking my eyes, and I don't want Paula to notice. Thinking about Raine losing her mother is making me think about me losing mine. I can't even imagine how fucked up I'd be right now, if I lost my mother at age two.

Paula touches my forearm and whispers, "We have some time-sensitive things to talk about, Caleb; but if you need a few minutes to collect yourself, I'll take a walk and come back in fifteen."

I take a deep breath, wipe my eyes, and look up. "No, I'm fine. What's the emergency, as it pertains to me?"

"We need to stop Ralph Beaumont, Claudia's father. I've received a demand letter from his attorney, demanding you support his claim for custody and start paying him child support, immediately. As next of kin, he's already swooped in and taken control of all Claudia bank accounts, including the substantial sum she'd set aside for Raine's college fund. But apparently, that's not enough for him. In fact, that's just the tip of the iceberg of what he wants, as Raine's only living blood relative." She levels me with dark, intense eyes. "Other than you, of course."

I sigh. "I signed my parental rights away, remember?"

"Jesus, Caleb, did you not listen to me *at all* back then? No, you didn't. Like I told you at the time, a private custody and support agreement isn't the same thing as a legal relinquishment of parental rights. Luckily, with that positive paternity test on the books, we've already got indisputable proof you're the child's father, so we're ready to roll without delay."

"Ready to roll ... *how*?"

Paula shrugs. "Based on that paternity test alone, you'd

almost certainly win custody over Beaumont. Against Aubrey Capshaw, I'm not as sure, given that she's been in a co-parenting role for most of the child's life. But at the very least, you'd most certainly be able to win regular visitation rights until—"

"Wait. Back up. Is Aubrey demanding money from me, like Beaumont?"

"No, I haven't heard a word from her. I'm only aware of her whereabouts because Beaumont mentioned them in his demand letter. Apparently, he's got lots of spies in Prairie Springs." Her jaw tightens. "Caleb, Beaumont wants you to take the child—*your* child—away from Aubrey—the child's only lifeline—and hand her over to *him*; and then he wants you to support his custody lawsuit against Aubrey and ultimately pay him exactly what you paid his daughter. If we don't act pre-emptively, Beaumont is going to file a petition for custody next week in Montana, against both you and Aubrey. He says he'll spend every dime of Claudia's savings account to get the victory he wants."

I shift in my seat. "What, exactly, do you want me to do about that, Paula?"

"The right fucking thing!"

"Which is?"

"File a custody petition of your own, here in LA, for full custody, before Ralph Beaumont files his petition in Montana. Work directly with Aubrey, instead of Ralph!"

My stomach somersaults. By now, I've thought about my kid more times than I can count, wishing I'd done things differently. But I've never once fantasized about becoming the kid's sole and full-time parent. I mean, Jesus, is that really what Paula's suggesting here—that I drop everything and become Mr. Mom? If so, she's conveniently overlooking the fact that I'd make a shitty parent. "You truly think it's in the kid's best interest to be with *me*, full-time?"

Paula leans back, studying me, intensely. "If you're not willing to seek full custody, then at least meet with Aubrey and throw your money and support behind *her* getting full custody, with regular visitation rights for you. Otherwise, Ralph is going to steamroll Aubrey, thanks to all the money he's gotten his hands on, and we simply can't let that happen." She glares at me. "Don't you remember the word Claudia used in relation to her father? *Monster.* She said not going to Prairie Springs with her baby was fine with her, because she didn't want her *monster* of a father—"

I exhale. "Yes, I remember."

"I did some digging and found out, over the years, neighbors repeatedly called the police to the Beaumont home in Prairie Springs for domestic disturbances. But no matter her obvious, visible injuries, Mrs. Beaumont would never press charges against her husband. In fact, she always claimed she got those bruises and injuries by some freak accident."

I close my eyes. It was the same thing with my own mother, until I finally got big enough to beat the shit out of my father, several times, to protect her.

I open my eyes, suddenly feeling resolved. "Okay."

"Okay what?"

"Okay, I'll go to Prairie Springs on the next flight out and do whatever's necessary to keep Raine away from Claudia's monster of a father."

Paula's face lights up. "I'm glad to hear you're willing to jump in, but you'll have to wait till your mandatory rehab stint is over to do that. In the meantime, however, I'll set up a Zoom call with Aubrey to—"

"No, I'm not going to wait three weeks to meet my

child." I stand. "Now that I know the situation, I'm going to help her, right fucking now."

Paula rolls her eyes. "I love your enthusiasm, but you know full well this rehab was court ordered, and you've still got three weeks left."

"There's got to be a loophole for family emergencies. Especially if I handle this quickly."

"Caleb—"

"No, listen to me. I'll fly to Montana tonight or tomorrow, whichever we can line up; and then, I'll bring my kid back here the following day, stow her with a nanny, and then return here to finish my rehab. On that timeline, I'll be back here on Monday, at the latest."

Paula snorts. "Court-ordered rehab doesn't work like that. You're stuck here, whether you like it or not. So, let's please get Aubrey on the phone and—"

"No, Paula. I'm going to Prairie Springs now to do what I should have done two years ago. Do me a favor and find me a really good nanny while I'm gone, okay?" With that, I start walking toward the door of the visitor's lounge.

"Wait, Caleb!" Paula calls out. "Stop! If you leave without authorization, you'll need to start rehab all over again, from day one, when you get back."

I stop and turn around with a scowl. "I'll be gone for three or four days." When Paula says nothing, I throw up my arms. "We're talking about my *child*, for fuck's sake. She's in peril, and I'm the only one who can save her. That's what you've been saying, right? That I'm the kid's only blood relative, besides a monster of a grandfather who's never met her and is a known wife beater?"

Paula twists her mouth, apparently conceding my point.

"How much do nannies cost? Less than thirty grand per month?"

Paula snorts. "A lot less than that. Mine costs about a hundred grand per year. So, eight or nine grand per month. But that's for two kids."

"That's it? If I'd known that, maybe I would have done things differently, right out of the gate. Jesus Christ." I start heading down the hallway again. After two years of guilt, regret, and shame, after two failed attempts at getting Claudia to bring my kid to LA for a visit, I'm *finally* going to meet my child. My daughter. *Raine*. Granted, this miracle is happening after my mom's passing, which is a gut punch. But even so, better late than never. At least, I can take comfort in the idea that Mom might be smiling down on Raine and me, as I finally do what I should have done, all along.

"Caleb, please, listen to me," Paula calls out. She's scurrying behind me down the hallway, her heels clacking on the linoleum. "You can't show up in Montana, unannounced, rip your daughter out of Aubrey's arms, and fly her off to a whole new life in a brand-new city."

"You said my paternity is already established."

"Would you stop, please? Your legs are long and I'm in heels."

I stop and turn around.

"I'm not talking about legalities," Paula says breathlessly. "I'm talking about what's best for the child. Raine doesn't know you from Adam. You're going to need to build trust with her before taking her away from Aubrey, or you're going to traumatize her, even more. Not to mention, you might also give Claudia's father some hefty ammunition to use against you at the custody hearing."

I quirk my eyebrow. "Ammunition?"

"What father with his child's best interests at heart would solve the present crisis by ripping his child away from the only person she knows and loves? At the custody hearing, we'll need to prove you're a fit father, Caleb. And, frankly, a fit father would never do that."

"Fuck." I look out a window to where that cool actor dude is playing ping pong with a newbie. "Okay, then," I say, returning my gaze to Paula's. "I'll bring *both* Raine and Aubrey back to my place in LA. Aubrey will be Raine's nanny, until Raine has gotten to know and trust me."

Paula pulls a face that suggests she doesn't hate the idea. But what she says is, "You're assuming Aubrey will say yes to that arrangement, and that's not a given."

I scoff. "I'll make her an offer she can't refuse. You said she's a twenty-four-year-old waitress, right? Okay, then I'll offer her more money than she's ever made in her life to take care of a toddler she's already taking care of for free. Who would say no to that?" When Paula doesn't supply an answer to my rhetorical question, I wink and add, "Don't worry about anything except springing me from this jail—I mean, *rehab*—for four days, tops, and filing that custody paperwork. Other than that, I promise, I'll handle everything else like a champ."

CHAPTER 4
CALEB

As I drive in my rental car down Main Street in Prairie Springs, I'm flooded with a thousand childhood memories. I haven't been back here in well over fifteen years, ever since Grandpa fell in love with a woman in Kansas and started renting out the lake house as an Airbnb. And yet, despite the passage of time, driving through this place still feels like coming home.

Well, I'll be damned. The tackle shop is still there, same as ever. The hardware store and that dive bar, too. Same with those two rival diners directly across the street from each other, though it looks like one has a different name now.

It's all the same as it ever was, mostly, with all of it set against a backdrop of purple mountains, leafy trees and pine needles, river valleys, and big sky. In Los Angeles, everybody's always looking for the next shiny, new thing. Trends and "what's hot now" rule the day. But here in Montana—at least, in this small corner of it, there's a sense of time standing still in the best possible way.

Grandpa's lake cabin, which became mine and my

sister's, once Mom passed almost three months ago, is about twenty-five minutes away from the town's main drag. But since everyone who lives on or near Lake Lucille comes into town regularly for supplies and everything else, anyone in the generalized area thinks of Prairie Springs as home.

My phone pings with an incoming text, but I ignore it, since I'm driving and only about a mile from my destination. Hopefully, that was Paula giving me an update on the rehab situation. When I stepped off the plane earlier and Paula hadn't texted yet, I messaged her, only to be met with a curt reply: *"Still working on it."*

I reach a stoplight, the street where the navigation lady has told me to turn left, and wait at the red light. Too curious to wait, I reach for my phone and discover that text from a minute ago, was, indeed, from Paula.

It's good and bad news, but mostly good. Neither the court nor the insurance company will let you off the hook, unless and until you complete the entirety of your three-month rehab stint. However, when I advised them of your family emergency, they said they'll allow you to satisfy the remaining three weeks and two days remotely. You'll need to attend all daily therapy sessions via Zoom. Also, you'll need to get yourself a sobriety coach, basically, someone who'll supervise you around the clock for the next three weeks and confirm, in writing, on a nightly basis, that you successfully remained sober over the prior twenty-four hours. Said coach must be an adult who passes a background check and isn't related to you, and you can pay them a reasonable rate. This is the best I can do.

. . .

"You've gotta be fucking kidding me," I grumble. The stoplight is green by now, but there's nobody behind me, so, as the light cycles back to red, I type a reply to Paula with angry fingers.

I'll do the Zoom thing, and I'll put it in writing myself every night that I'm still sober. But I'm sure as shit not going to hire someone to babysit me, round the clock, for the next three weeks and two days. No fucking way.

If push comes to shove, I could ask my good friend, Amy, to help me out, once I get back to LA. When Amy was my personal assistant years ago on a tour, she kicked ass, after a rough start, so I know she'd do a good job for me. True, Amy is a mother now. But I bet if I were to explain my situation to Amy and Colin, they'd both come and bring their kid, Rocco, too. You know, make a family vacation out of it. My place is right on the beach, after all, while their house is inland on a canyon.

The light turns green, once again, and I make the left turn the navigation lady is insisting upon.

In short order, however, as I'm driving down a quiet residential street, my phone pings with another text. When I glance at my screen, it's Paula again, and the message is long; so I pull over to read.

You have two choices. One, you can accept this generous accommodation from the rehab facility, do exactly what they're requiring, get a certification of completion in three weeks and two days, and move on with your life. Or, you

can refuse their generous terms, thereby officially quitting rehab before completion, and suffer the consequences. It's up to you. Let me know what you decide.

"Fuck, fuck, fuck," I shout into the cramped space of my rental car, while banging the heel of my palm on the steering wheel. I know full well what's at stake here. When I trashed that hotel penthouse in New York three months ago, the night my mother died, I did enough damage to turn my temper tantrum into a fucking felony. Which meant the judge had my nuts in a vise when he ordered me to rehab in lieu of jailtime. After that, the insurance company hopped on board and made completion of rehab a condition of their coverage for any upcoming tour.

With an exhale of exasperation, I press the button to call Paula.

"Are you calling for a reminder of the list of consequences if you quit rehab?" Paula asks calmly, with faux sincerity. "Or are you calling because you finally understand you've got no choice here?"

"You're sure I can't get a couple days reprieve while I'm here in Prairie Springs? I'll hire a sobriety coach, once I get back to LA."

"You need one today. Good news, though. I've already run a background check on Aubrey Capshaw, and she's good to go. You're welcome."

"Aubrey Capshaw?"

"Why not? You're already planning to lure her into becoming Raine's nanny, right? So, fine, pay her a bit more and add babysitting you to her list of job duties for the next three weeks and two days."

"I'm not going to tell Aubrey about my mandatory

rehab, Paula. There's already enough shit for us to deal with, without me adding that to the pile." Aubrey doesn't know I'm coming to see her today, any more than my daughter does. I got the address from Paula, hopped the first flight out this morning to Billings, rented a car at the airport for the hour-long drive to Prairie Springs, and here I am.

"If you've got a better idea than hiring Aubrey to babysit both you and Raine, I'm all ears," Paula says. "Although, before you enlighten me, I should remind you that your sobriety coach will need to certify your sobriety for the first time today, by ten o'clock tonight, Pacific Time, so whatever brilliant idea you're about to spring on me had better be easy and fast to implement."

I feel like a caged animal. But still, I'm not convinced Aubrey is my only option here. "Ten o'clock is still a long way away," I mutter. "I'll let you know what I decide in a bit."

"Suit yourself. How close are you to Aubrey's house?"

"Exactly point-three miles. I pulled over to talk to you on a residential street around the corner from her address."

Paula lets out a little sound of relief. "Now, don't forget, Caleb, you only get one chance to make a first impression. When you meet Raine, remember you're big and covered in tattoos, so you'll want to crouch down to her level and—"

"I'll handle it fine," I bark out, feeling annoyed. "Talk to you soon." Admittedly, I don't know jack shit about kids, but I know enough, at least, not to barrel in there like a bull in a china shop and start barking orders at a two-year-old who lost her mommy mere weeks ago.

After ending the call, I start up the rental car again; and after a couple turns that wedge me deeper into the tree-lined neighborhood, the robot voice on my phone tells me I've arrived at my destination. The Capshaws' house.

The home is a small but welcoming one. A one-story house that's well cared for. Probably a two-bedroom/one bath kind of configuration, by the looks of it. Is my daughter inside that house? Is anyone? If not, Prairie Springs is small enough to ensure I'll meet my daughter, sooner rather than later. Probably, by the end of today, at latest. The thought sends goosebumps rising up on my arms.

I take a deep breath to calm my nerves, shove my phone in my pocket, grab my backpack, and exit the rental car. With long strides, I make my way up the walkway toward the house. But before I get to the porch, the sounds of high-pitched, happy giggling and squealing catch my attention. They seem to be coming from the other side of a wooden fence—from the home's backyard. On instinct, I head over to the fence to take a peek.

I'm six-three and change, so it's easy for me to peer over the upright wooden planks. When I do, my heart stops at the source of those giggles: the little girl from the photo. *Raine Beaumont.* A pint-sized blonde with soft curls that bounce with every step she takes. She's being chased around a lawn playfully by a knockout brunette with legs for days.

"I'm gonna get you!" the leggy brunette exclaims, laughing, and Raine screams with unrestrained joy as she toddles across the grass.

Tears prick my eyes, even as I'm smiling. My god, my kid's laugh sounds exactly like my mother's, albeit at a much higher octave.

Regret and shame slam into me again, this time because I didn't fight Claudia tooth and nail, after getting that curt "fuck off" email from her. I emailed her again after that, a few months later, as well as messaging her on social media; but when all my messages bounced back, and it was clear Claudia had blocked me, every which way, I made the regrettable decision to leave it alone for now. To try again later. Mom was going downhill fast, at that point, and I felt like I had enough on my plate without opening up a can of worms that might not even get the desired result in time. The only thing worse than not telling my mother about her grandchild, I figured, was giving my mother false hope about meeting her grandchild.

But now, suddenly, as I stare at my child, my flesh and blood, I know I made a terrible miscalculation. How did I not understand the unbreakable bond that was forged the instant that little angel came into the world with my DNA enmeshed in every fucking cell in her tiny body? That little person right there is *mine,* goddammit. And nobody, not Ralph Beaumont, or Aubrey Capshaw, not even Claudia Beaumont from the grave, can take her away from me, now that I'm realizing my fucking mistake.

As I'm standing frozen and mesmerized at the scene unfolding before me, the leggy brunette—Aubrey Capshaw, I presume—catches my gleeful daughter, scoops her up, and covers her in noisy, energetic kisses that elicit even more giggles from Raine.

"You're fast, but I'm faster!" the brunette shouts playfully.

"No, *I'm* da fasty!" Raine shouts back, still giggling away.

"Oh, yeah? Show me, then!" Aubrey puts Raine down, and the pair repeats the same chasing exercise I've just witnessed, much to my grinning, teary-eyed delight.

I'm fixated on Raine, initially. For quite some time. But

when my gaze eventually shifts to study Aubrey, it occurs to me she's smoking hot. She's got long, tanned legs. Shiny, flowing, dark hair. Smooth, glowing skin and a fresh-faced, girl-next-door kind of appeal that's insanely attractive to me. I haven't had sober sex yet. No sex at all for at least six months. And I'm suddenly feeling every minute of my celibacy.

Am I allowed to fuck my nanny/sobriety coach, or is that frowned upon?

I've no sooner had the thought than Aubrey's eyes land on me—on the top half of my head that's exposed to her over the wooden fence—and she screams bloody murder at the top of her lungs.

CHAPTER 5
AUBREY

Ralph Beaumont.

Holy fuck.

He's here. In Prairie Springs. Claudia's father has come to take Raine away from me, just like I've been petrified about, ever since that stupid, clueless detective left a message for him about Claudia's accident.

These are my panicked, frenzied thoughts when I notice the top half of a male face—two blazing green eyes topped by a black, knit cap—spying on Raine and me from over my parents' backyard fence. At the sight, a blood curdling scream lurches from my throat, prompting the man's eyebrows to shoot straight to the edge of his knit cap.

As the scream leaves my mouth, it occurs to me the man looks quite a bit younger than Ralph Beaumont. Decades younger. Not to mention, he's quite a bit taller than Claudia's father, too, as I recall; unless that guy is standing on a step stool behind that wooden fence.

The realization that the stranger isn't Ralph, after all, is a massive relief. But not a complete get-out-of-jail-free card for my nerves, since he's still, nonetheless, a complete stranger who's peeping at Raine and me over a fence. Hopefully, he's nothing but a lost delivery guy or a neighbor with some wayward mail. But I pick up Raine, just in case, and hold her protectively to me. For all I know, Ralph sent this guy here to threaten me or otherwise try to pry Raine away from me.

"Didn't mean to scare you," the man murmurs in a low grumble that confirms he's not, in fact, standing on a step stool. "Are you Aubrey Capshaw?"

"Who are you?" I ask defensively, squeezing Raine.

The man pauses. And then, on an exhale, he replies, "Caleb Baumgarten."

My lips part in surprise. Raine's accidental sperm donor, C-Bomb of Red Card Riot, is standing at my parents' fence? Under any other circumstance, I'd probably feel a bit starstruck. But knowing he's the selfish prick who hasn't given a shit about his child for the past two years, makes disgust, rage, and fear my only possible emotions.

Surely, C-Bomb came here to strong arm me into taking Raine away from Prairie Springs, since that was a term of his agreement with Claudia. But guess what? I didn't sign that thing, and I'd never sign a similar one. Prairie Springs is my home; and unlike Claudia, I love it here. Plus, C-Bomb's got absolutely nothing I want, so he's got zero leverage. I don't want this man's money. And I certainly don't want to have sex with him. He was always Claudia's celebrity crush, not mine. As this prick is about to find out, all I want is Raine and the freedom to raise her in Prairie Springs with my parents. *And without him getting in our way.*

"Can you come out here to talk to me?" he asks.

Poor Raine is shaking in my arms, thanks to my blood curdling scream. When the poor kid last heard me screaming, her mommy never came back home. And so, before I reply to the asshole drummer's request, I hold up a finger to him, my body language telling him to hold on; and then, I put my forehead against Raine's and whisper calmly that everything is all right.

"Silly Auntie Aubbey stepped on a rock," I whisper with a smile. Raine's never been able to pronounce *Aubrey* correctly, so Claudia and I latched onto her adorable pronunciation. *Aubbey*. "That's why I screamed," I continue. "Not because of that man over there."

"Who dat man?"

A snarky, vindictive piece of me wishes I could reply, "That's the asshole who pays an ungodly sum every month *not* to have you in his life." But since I can't say that, I reply, instead, "He's a good friend of your mommy's. He came to talk to me about Mommy."

Raine's little face perks up. "Mommy coming back?"

Oh, my heart. Even after three weeks, which is a lifetime to a two-year-old, Raine still asks me that question, every single time her mommy's name is mentioned. Sometimes, unprompted, too.

I stroke her little cheek with my knuckle. "No, love, Mommy's still in heaven with Grandma." As Raine frowns, I quickly change the subject. "I bet the brownies have cooled by now. Should we go inside to see? You can eat one and play a game on your iPad, while Auntie Aubbey talks to Mommy's friend outside."

Thanks to the promise of brownies and some coveted screen time, Raine instantly forgets all about the scary man behind the fence and begs to go inside and get this show on the road. I motion to the rockstar behind the fence to meet me around the corner at the front door, and the top half of his head disappears.

As I guide Raine toward the house, I glance at my

watch. My parents should be home from Dad's doctor appointment in thirty minutes or so, if the doctor wasn't running late today, and the last thing I need is for C-Bomb of Red Card Riot, of all people, to be standing at their doorstep when they pull up.

My parents have no idea who fathered Claudia's little girl. Nobody knows, other than me, C-Bomb, and whoever C-Bomb might have told. So, there's no telling what kind of warm reception my parents would give the unlikely rockstar in their front yard, if they were to drive up before I've shooed him away. Mom is the kind of person who's never met a stranger, and Dad is a massive music fan who considers Red Card Riot one of his favorite bands. Even on pain killers, which he's been taking since severely breaking his leg last week, I'm sure Dad would recognize C-Bomb, thanks to his towering frame and famous tattoos.

When I've gotten Raine situated with her iPad and a brownie and told her to stay put on the couch until I return, I take a big-girl breath and head to the front door. When I step outside and behold the physicality and charisma, in person, of the man I've seen on my computer screen countless times, I feel like I'm getting physically blown back by a massive jet engine.

Holy crap.

Muscles. Ink. Tall. Beard. Scowl. *Hot*.

As to that last thing, I'm surprised to think it. C-Bomb's not *my* fantasy come to life, like he always was for Claudia; but seeing him now, in person, I can definitely understand his worldwide appeal.

The thing Claudia always loved about C-Bomb was the fact that he's the peacock in his band, despite him being the one sitting behind a drum kit. He's the one who never wore a shirt in music videos and during performances; the one who changed his hairstyle frequently, going from a mohawk to long hair to a buzz cut in record speed. But to my surprise, the tattooed Viking standing before me now doesn't look anything like a peacock. More like a deranged, exhausted serial killer on the lam.

"Sorry I scared you," C-Bomb mutters, his low grumble of a voice perfectly matching his mountain-man appearance. I can't help noticing C-Bomb's beard is longer than I've seen in photos and videos online. Also, he's *fully* covered in tattoos these days, from his neck down to his fingers. Whereas, in the "Shaynee" music video from forever ago, he only had a smattering of ink on his arms.

I clear my throat. "I thought you were a Peeping Tom, C-Bomb."

"Sorry about that." He motions to the screen door behind me. "Can we talk inside?"

I cross my arms over my chest. "No. Raine's in there."

C-Bomb shifts his weight. "I know. I want to meet my daughter."

I repress the urge to snort. To scoff. To spit out, "After two years, *now* you suddenly want to meet your daughter?" But, instead, I bite my tongue and calmly ask, "For what purpose?"

C-Bomb's chest heaves. "I heard about Claudia. I'm sorry for your loss. For Raine's loss." When I say nothing, he shifts the backpack that's slung over his broad shoulder and looks around nervously. "Hey, can we talk inside? I don't want to get recognized by a nosey neighbor and have to say no to a fucking selfie right now."

"I don't feel comfortable inviting you inside, unless I know why you're here."

His jaw tightens. "She's my daughter. I have a legal right to meet her, whether you like it or not."

Fuck, fuck, fuck. For three weeks now, I've been having horrible nightmares about Claudia's father showing up, out of nowhere, to rip Raine away from me, when I should have been having them about this man, all along. "Maybe, maybe not," I manage to say, sounding a whole lot more confident than I feel. "Either way, I'm sure you'll agree there's a time and place for a first meeting, and this isn't it."

"Why not? When's the right time, according to you?"

"All I know is you can't show up here, out of the blue, after two years of being a deadbeat dad, and—"

"I'm not a *deadbeat*. I've been paying child support, since day one. Double what any court would have ordered me to pay, plus all Claudia's medical expenses from the pregnancy and birth. I realize it's not much better, but I'm not a deadbeat. I'm an *absentee* father."

I scoff. "Excuse me if I don't rush off to polish your Father of the Year trophy."

"I'm not saying I'm proud of myself. Just saying there's a difference."

I roll my eyes. "Okay, well, pat yourself on the back any way you want, if it helps you sleep at night. But the fact remains you can't just waltz in here and meet Raine, and play daddy for fifteen minutes before disappearing again, mere weeks after she lost her mommy. She still doesn't completely understand Claudia's never coming back, C-Bomb. So, I can't allow you to come here and confuse her into thinking—"

"Caleb." When I pause, he adds, "I'm not here as C-Bomb. I'm Caleb Baumgarten, and that kid in there is *mine*." His green eyes are blazing. "And I didn't come here to play daddy for fifteen minutes. I admit I've made mistakes in the past. I know that. I regret them. So I've come to make things right, as best I can."

Panic floods me. *What the fuck does that mean?* Has this man come to take Raine away from me? I force myself to ask the question I'm not sure I want to know the answer to: "Make things right, *how*?"

"I'm her family," he says, leveling me with hard eyes. "Her *father*. I convinced myself she was better off without me, when she had her mother. But now that Claudia is gone, I can't sit by and let a non-family member—"

"*Non-family member?*" I shriek, anger flashing inside me. "I'm more *family* to that little girl than you'll ever be. While you were busy fucking another groupie, you want to know what I was doing, C-Bomb? Holding Claudia's right hand during Raine's birth, while her mother held her left." I'm gathering steam now. "And only a few months after that, I came back and moved my whole life to Seattle to live with Claudia and Raine, for good. I was there for Raine's first bite of solid food. Her first word, crawl, and step. Her first and second birthdays. And where were you all that time? What were you doing that was so important you couldn't be there for your baby girl? So, don't you dare come here and—"

"Would you calm the fuck down?" he bellows. "Jesus Christ." He roughs a palm down his face and takes a deep breath. "I didn't say 'non-family member' as fighting words, okay? I said it as a neutral, objective fact. Raine is *my* blood, not yours. Raine has *my* genes inside her, not yours. She's *my* family, both legally and biologically. So, while I thank and respect you for being an *honorary* family member to Raine all this time, for helping raise my kid when I was admittedly too big a flop-dick-asshole-loser to do it, the objective fact remains she's *my* kid, and I'm not going anywhere, now that I'm here, whether you like it or not."

I let out a shaky breath and mutter, "If you think telling

me to calm the fuck down is going to calm me down, then you're as stupid as you look."

C-Bomb tilts his head back, so it feels like he's speaking to the blue sky above when he grumbles, "Can we please just fast-forward to the part where we talk like adults about a very difficult situation? Or are you too young to understand what being an adult means?"

"Fuck you. I'm more of an adult than you've ever been in your entire goddamned life."

He sighs. "That's fair."

"And, no, there's no fast-forward button. Not when you've been a dick-headed deadbeat dad. Oh, sorry, absentee father for two solid years." I put my hands on my hips and glare at C-Bomb like I'm ready to throw down if he so much as twitches. I'm not normally combative by nature. In fact, I'm usually quite the friendly little peacemaker. But this asshole's got my momma-bear instincts flaring.

I'm grateful he stepped up financially and without forcing Claudia to go through an exhaustive legal battle to get the money. But there's no amount of cash that can buy my respect. And I adamantly do *not* respect a man who preferred to pay an exorbitant amount each month to keep his child firmly out of his life, forever. Seriously, how has this sorry excuse for a man slept a wink over the past two years? How did he not at least feel the desire, even once, to ask Claudia for a fucking photo of his child?

"We can do this the easy way or the hard way," C-Bomb says evenly, his eyes boring holes into my face. "Talk to me in a civilized manner, or I'll have no choice but to sick my lawyer on you."

A soft whimper escapes my throat, and C-Bomb's features soften, ever so slightly.

"I swear, I didn't come here to threaten you," he says

quickly, one large palm raised. "I didn't come to fight. I came here to meet my daughter and work with you, not against you, so she doesn't wind up in the hands of Ralph Beaumont."

"*Ralph Beaumont?*" I gasp out. He's got my full attention now.

C-Bomb gruffly pulls out a piece of paper from his backpack. "His lawyer sent this letter to my lawyer. Can I step forward to give it to you, or will you scream bloody murder again, if I come near you?"

I roll my eyes. "I screamed when I saw you, as anyone would, because you were spying on me like a creeper, C-Bomb." I march down the porch steps, closing the gap between us. And when we're on the same level on the walkway, I finally grasp how tall he truly is: a full foot taller than me.

"Call me Caleb," he says, as he hands the letter to me.

I don't understand why he cares. I've seen countless interviews where the interviewer and even his own bandmates called him C-Bomb, and that's what Claudia called him, too, even after his dick had been inside her. But whatever. As much as I'd like to continue rankling him, I'm also a firm believer in calling people whatever they've asked to be called.

"Fine. *Caleb.*" I snatch the letter from him and start to read; and with each passing sentence, my heart rate quickens some more. Midway through, I look up, aghast. "Ralph is demanding full custody? We can't let that happen. He's a horrible, violent man. Claudia never once let him anywhere near Raine."

C-Bomb gives me a curt nod. "That's why I'm here. Finish reading."

I do as I'm told and find out Ralph thinks a judge would

side with C-Bomb over him in a custody battle, since both men have never met Raine; but Ralph isn't quite as convinced he'd beat *me,* if push came to shove. His solution? He wants *C-Bomb* to forge an alliance with him to knock *me* out of the picture, at which point, Ralph would then take Raine, through a private, side agreement with C-Bomb, under the same terms as C-Bomb's arrangement with Claudia.

I look up from the letter in my hand, feeling like I'm going to vomit. "The 'loving arms of her grandfather?' Caleb, Ralph is a violent sociopath. As a kid, I personally saw him beat the shit out of Claudia's mother, right in front of Claudia and me, and Claudia said he did it all the time. Please, we can't let that horrible man—"

"We won't. *I* won't. That's what I came to explain to you, Aubrey. I'm not going to let that motherfucker anywhere near my daughter, no matter what."

I exhale in relief. The fact that he called Raine *his* daughter should freak me out, by all rights. But in this one specific context, the word choice is more comforting than threatening to me. If C-Bomb thinks of Raine as his daughter, then hopefully that will make him feel that much more inspired to keep Ralph the fuck away from her.

I feel the nonsensical impulse to throw my arms around this mountain of a man and beg him to keep his promise to keep Ralph away from Raine, no matter what. But, instead, I get ahold of myself, cross my arms over my chest, and ask, "How'd Ralph's lawyer find out you're Raine's father? Claudia told me your identity was a huge secret and I could never tell anyone."

One side of C-Bomb's mouth hitches up, his implication clear: *And yet, Claudia told you.*

I wave at the air. "Claudia told me everything and vice

versa." When Caleb smirks, I add, "She trusted me not to tell a single soul about you, not even my parents, and I never did."

C-Bomb assesses me for a longish beat. "I don't know how Beaumont figured me out. My lawyer thinks someone from the coroner's office with access to the paternity test might have told Ralph or the detective in charge of Claudia's case, who then told Ralph. Either that, or someone from the coroner's office contacted Ralph for a payout, in exchange for the information. You'd be surprised how many people come out of the woodwork, looking for a payday, when they've got dirt on a celebrity with deep pockets."

"Well, I'm not looking for a payday," I snap. "The only thing I want is to raise Raine here, in Prairie Springs, with my family." I look at him pleadingly, but it's clear from his impassive glare the one thing I want is the one thing I'm not going to get. Not if C-Bomb—*Caleb*—gets his way.

My spirit sinks. Is Caleb intending to take Raine home with him to wherever he lives? If so, how can I possibly stop him, when there's no doubt he's Raine's father and he's got all the money in the world to hire the best lawyers? I'm unemployed with about sixteen dollars in my savings account at the moment.

Money has never been plentiful in my family. We do fine. We get by. But Mom only works part-time as a school counselor, and not for a whole lot. And even though dad's construction company does pretty well for him at times, there's always dry spells, due to weather and the smallness of our town. There's only so much work to go around a place like Prairie Springs. Add Dad's broken leg and medical bills to the mix, and I can't fathom how we'd be able to hire a lawyer to try to beat Caleb and Ralph in a custody battle.

Caleb rubs the back of his neck before cutting the thick silence between us. "Listen, Aubrey. I'm filing a lawsuit against Ralph in LA."

"Oh, thank God."

"And also against you, technically. But only because—"

"*You're suing me?*" I scream.

"Would you let me explain? My lawyer says I have to name you as a party, along with Ralph, since you've currently got physical custody. But that doesn't mean we're enemies, okay? We both want what's best for Raine."

"*I'm* best for Raine."

"Would you listen? I want to join forces with you. We'll both go against Ralph in the lawsuit, together, and tell the judge we've agreed to a custody arrangement."

My heart is thrumming. "What kind of custody arrangement?"

"I'll get legal custody, since I'm her father, and you'll get unlimited visitation rights. Forever. My lawyer can explain everything to you in LA. I'm taking Raine back there tomorrow, and I really want you to come with—"

"You're taking Raine to LA?" I scream. "*Tomorrow?*"

"And I want you to come with us. I want to hire you to be Raine's full-time nanny."

My brain is melting. "Raine doesn't even know you."

"Which is why I want you to come with us and be my live-in nanny, at top dollar. Aubrey, I'll pay you a hundred grand per year to do what you're already doing for free." When I stare at him, flabbergasted, he quickly amends, "Okay, fine, one-fifty. That's way above market. A damned good deal, especially since I'm asking you to keep doing something you'd already be doing, anyway."

"But not in LA!" My head is spinning. I need a lawyer. I need my parents. I feel sick. "I'm not Raine's *nanny*," I spit out, like the word is a slur. "I'm her Auntie Aubbey. Her *family*. She loves and trusts me. My parents, too. She calls them Grammy and Pop-Pop."

Caleb exhales. "Okay, so we'll bring your parents to LA, too. I've got a huge house with plenty of room for everyone."

I stare at him, slack-jawed. Is he insane or just stupid?

"My parents have a home here. A life. *Jobs*. They can't just pick up and leave because Mr. Rockstar sauntered into town and dangled some cash in front of their noses." I shake my head. "Raine's having nightmares every night and her potty training has regressed. She's traumatized. And now you want to drag her to a new place *again*, because you can't be inconvenienced to get to know her for a little while on her home turf, first?"

He twists his mouth. "You want me to stay here in Prairie Springs?"

"Of course. Obviously. It's the right thing to do."

He shifts his position and scratches his tattooed arm. "For how long?"

I'm excited he's asked the question. It gives me hope. "Three or four months, at least. While you're here, you can visit her every day. Get to know her. Earn her trust. And if things are going well in a few months, if you still want full custody of her, then I'll come to LA with you, as Raine's nanny, and help her get settled with you there. But only if you swear on a stack of bibles that, no matter what, you'll always give me unlimited access to her. Forever."

He twists his mouth. "That timeline's not going to work for me. My lawyer said the custody hearing in LA will probably happen in a month or so."

My eyes widen. "A *month*?"

"I understand what you're saying, though. It probably

makes sense to transition Raine a bit more slowly than I was initially thinking."

Ya think? "Caleb, listen, my father is injured. He broke his leg badly last week, so he can't travel for a while, and Raine adores him. If you saw them together, you'd never want to take her away from him. Not now, at least. *Please.* This isn't about you or me. It's about Raine. She's got a family here. A new life. Stability, when she needs it most."

As I wring my hands, Caleb ponders my plea for an eternal moment.

Finally, he exhales and says, "I'll stay in Prairie Springs until it's time for us to leave for the custody hearing in LA. That way, Raine can get to know me before then, on her home turf, surrounded by people she loves and trusts."

I exhale an ocean of relief. It's not the length of time I begged him for; but at least it's better than Caleb forcing Raine to come with him to LA *tomorrow*. Plus, a lot can happen in a month. Maybe, when Caleb learns what parenthood actually entails, how hard and thankless the job can be at times, he'll realize he's more than happy to leave Raine with me in Prairie Springs, after all, leaving him free to visit his daughter, whenever the mood strikes him.

Also, by the time the custody hearing rolls around, if I'm not thoroughly convinced Caleb is good for Raine, whether as her full-time father or a regular visitor, I'll be free to tell the judge my honest feelings then, no matter what Caleb currently thinks I'm going to say on his behalf at the hearing.

"Okay," I say, nodding decisively. "Thank you for changing your plans for Raine's sake."

"I only want what's best for her." He begins to say more, but before he gets his next words out, his gaze shifts sharply to a spot behind me and to my left. Instantly, the hardness in Caleb's green eyes vanishes, replaced by something I'd call wonder and awe.

Fuck. I turn around, and, as suspected, Raine is standing behind the screen door, smashing her little face against it like she always does, so her nose rides up and makes her look like Peppa Pig.

"Auntie Aubbey?" Raine squeaks out. "All done."

"Okay, honey. I'll be right in."

I turn back around to address Caleb, but he's fixated on Raine and practically vibrating with excitement.

"Hello, Raine," Caleb coos softly, his deep voice quavering. "I'm Caleb. It's really great to meet you."

CHAPTER 6
CALEB

R*aine.*
    My child.
    My daughter.

She's stunning. Breathtaking. An angel on Earth.

Peeking over a fence at her didn't have nearly the same impact as staring into her big, blue eyes from a short fifteen yards away, even if it's only through a screen door. I feel like I could topple over from the torrent of euphoria flooding me.

She's staring at me. Not replying to my greeting. So, I try again.

"Hi, Raine. I'm—"

Without warning, Raine scampers away from the screen, shrieking like she's seen a velociraptor.

"Nice," Aubrey hisses. "You scared her to death."

"By saying hello?"

"While looking like the Grim Reaper! She's not used to men, Caleb. She's only met two in her life, other than doctors: my father and Claudia's ex. And neither of those guys are covered in tattoos all over their neck and arms."

Aubrey crosses her arms over her chest defiantly, and I can't help thinking it's a good look for her. *Defiance*. Although, honestly, I'm beginning to think there's not an expression in Aubrey's repertoire that could possibly be a *bad* look for her. Up close and standing still, she's even hotter than I realized while watching her in motion from afar.

"You don't need to go to her?" I ask, motioning toward the screen door.

"I can hear her singing in there. That means she's okay and probably playing with her dolls."

I shift my weight. "Okay, so . . . if she's good now, let's go in."

Aubrey shakes her head. "Let's give her a few minutes to process."

I close my eyes, begging the universe for patience. When I open them, Aubrey looks brazenly disdainful of me. "How long was Claudia with her ex?"

Aubrey scowls. "Why do you care?"

"Just wondering if he was good with Raine." I've got no grounds to feel jealous or protective about another man possibly getting close to my kid, but it's what I'm feeling, nonetheless. If this ex of Claudia's treated my daughter like anything other than a princess, I'll hunt him down and give him some free dental work.

"Ricky was fine with her. Not amazing, not terrible. He's irrelevant. All I'm saying is you've got your work cut out for you, if you're serious about becoming a real daddy to Raine because . . ."

I don't hear the rest. Once Aubrey said the word *daddy*, my brain short-circuited. Holy shit. It didn't occur to me Raine might call me daddy one day. But now that Aubrey's used the word, it's all I want. The ultimate goal before this forced month in Prairie Springs is done.

After finishing her rant, whatever it was, Aubrey sighs and says, "I'll go check on her now. Wait here, and I'll call you when it's a good time to come in." She turns to leave but abruptly stops on the porch. "When you say hello to her again, this time smile at her, for fuck's sake."

"I smiled before."

"No, you grimaced like you were about to turn into The Hulk."

I force a smile. "Better?"

Aubrey shudders. "No, that's horrifying. Never mind. The grimace was less scary."

As I roll my eyes, Aubrey swings open the screen door and disappears into the house.

I fidget as I stand and wait for Aubrey to call me inside for what feels like a lifetime. But finally, she calls my name and I head into the house. Once in the living room, I find Aubrey sitting on a couch, its back covered with a crocheted blanket, with my tiny daughter in her lap.

"See?" Aubrey says to Raine, her temple resting on Raine's head while looking at me. "Mommy's good friend Caleb is just a normal, nice man with silly scribbles all over his body and funny hair all over his face. Isn't he silly and funny?"

Aubrey fake laughs, and my little daughter joins her nervously, but even as Raine laughs, she's gripping Aubrey with her tiny, splayed fingers like a lifeline.

"Caleb, did you get into Raine's box of markers and draw all over yourself, you naughty boy?" Aubrey asks breezily. "If you did, that's not allowed. Is it, Rainey?"

Raine shakes her head.

"Remember when you did that, Pooh Bear?" Aubrey coos, poking Raine's belly playfully. "Remember how Mommy laughed and gave you a bubble bath?"

Raine frowns. "Mommy said, 'You not allowed do dat, Rainey.'"

"She did say that, but gently. Mommy wasn't mad at you, Boo. Mommy thought everything you did was the cutest, funniest thing, ever. She loved you so, so much." Aubrey chokes on her last few words, causing her to stop and inhale deeply before starting again. "Remember Sully in *Monsters, Inc.*? Caleb is like him. He looks scary and big, but he's really silly and funny."

As Raine considers this new bit of information, I make a mental note to watch *Monsters, Inc.*, as soon as possible.

"Can you say hi to him?" Aubrey prompts softly, poking Raine's belly again.

Much to my thrill, Raine waves shyly at me and squeaks out the tiniest, "Hi."

That's it. Put a fork in me, I'm done. My heart is a puddle. My fate sealed. Come hell or high water, no matter what it takes, I'm going to do whatever it takes to become the father this cutie pie deserves, so I can hear her calling me "Daddy," as soon as possible.

"Hi, Raine," I reply softly, even though I want to scream it out of excitement. "I'm Caleb."

"Say, 'Hi, Caleb!'" Aubrey prompts cheerfully.

"Hi, Coobie."

Aubrey and I exchange a small smile at her adorable pronunciation. Aubrey's grin wasn't a wide one, like mine, by any stretch, but it nonetheless feels like progress.

Aubrey calls to me, "Hey, Caleb, what's all that scribbling on your skin? Did you do that with markers?"

My heart is pounding. "No, they're tattoos. Body art that never goes away."

"Never?" Aubrey whispers. "Did you hear that, Pooh Bear?"

"*Never?*" Raine whispers, looking up at Aubrey with astonishment.

"Ask him."

Raine shakes her head, so Aubrey presses forward.

"Only adults are allowed to get tattoos, right, Coobie?"

I look at Aubrey like, *You're not seriously going to adopt that nickname for me, are you?* And Aubrey smirks her reply. Clearly, yes, she is.

"Yeah, that's right," I say to Raine. "Tattoos are only for adults, since they never go away."

"Can you say tattoos, Pooh Bear?"

"Tatta."

"That's right," Aubrey says, giggling. "How about body art?"

"Bobba art."

Aubrey chuckles again, as I bite back a smile.

"Perfect," Aubrey coos with a kiss to Raine's head. "Good job."

Feeling emboldened, I hold up my arms and interject, "Yup. No bubble bath in the world will take any of these bad boys off. That's why I had to be sure I loved every single one." It suddenly occurs to me I'll need to find room on my body for Raine's name somewhere, once I get back to LA and get with my usual guy. I'm pretty much out of real estate on my skin at this point, but I'm sure he'll figure something out.

"Guess what?" Aubrey says, drawing me out of my thoughts. "Caleb doesn't know how to color in a coloring book!"

"I know how!" Raine blurts, like it's a crazy coincidence.

"Maybe you can be a good friend to Coobie and teach him how."

Damn, she's good. I was already hell-bent on hiring

Aubrey as Raine's nanny, out of convenience and continuity. But now that I've seen Aubrey in action with my daughter, I bet I would have hired her, regardless, even if she were a total stranger applying for the job and using this interaction as her interview.

"I teach?" Raine asks Aubrey.

"I bet Caleb would really like that. Why don't you ask him to find out."

"I'd love to be your student, Raine," I say eagerly. Too eagerly, probably, given the scowl on Aubrey's face.

"*Let her ask you*," Aubrey scolds quietly.

"Oh. Sorry."

"Go on, Pooh Bear. Ask him."

Raine levels me with the two most beautiful eyes ever created in the history of eyeballs. "I teach?"

"Yes, please. I'd love that. Very much. Thank you."

With a determined little nod, Raine slides off Aubrey's lap and sprints out of the room, presumably to get the tools of her trade.

"She's so predictable," Aubrey says with a soft chuckle. "Teaching and coloring: the two best ways to her heart. Pancakes, too. That's the trifecta." She makes a face that plainly says, *All of which you'd have known if you'd bothered to meet your child before today.*

I exhale. "Can we please just turn the page and—" I stop talking and slap a smile on my face when Raine returns to the room, excitedly carrying a box of crayons and a coloring book.

In the cutest voice ever, she commands me to sit on the floor next to her for my first lesson. So, of course, I comply, as butterflies ravage my stomach. Once we're situated on the carpet, Raine proceeds to open a coloring book and babble happily, frequently in words I can't understand, as she shows me the do's and don'ts of creating a colorful masterpiece.

"Okay, I think I understand," I say. And to my delight, she hands me a crayon and motions to the page before us.

"We do togedder," she announces with authority. And a moment later, we're jointly working on coloring a page featuring a mouse in a ballgown who's throwing a lavish tea party for a big group of her forest-critter friends.

As I color on the floor next to Raine, I feel intoxicated by her. By the flowery scent of her shiny hair. By the fact that her little fingernails are the same shape as mine and my mother's. I can't help smiling at every tiny squeak of pride she makes in her student's progress, every little grunt as she works on her own art. The buzz I'm feeling right now is better than any drug or booze. It's better than playing a show for thousands. Better than winning a Grammy. Better than banging on my drums or riding my motorcycle up PCH on a perfect California day.

When I make a mistake of some kind, according to Raine, she touches my hand to correct me; and when I feel my daughter's tiny touch, I'm flooded with an intense sensation of love and protectiveness that shocks me to my core. The sensation is so overwhelming, in fact, I quickly bow my head and pretend to be furiously concentrating on my work to hide the moisture forming in my eyes.

With my head still bowed, I say a little prayer. *Please, let my mother see this moment.*

I don't know if I believe in an afterlife. I go back and forth on that. But in this moment, I desperately *need* to believe in one, for the sake of my soul. To be able to forgive myself for fucking things up, so badly. To be able to get a good's night sleep, ever again. Being here now, I understand how profoundly I've fucked up in the past.

Not only in relation to my mother, but in relation to myself.

"Dat good!" Raine says brightly, patting my hand. "Good job, Coobie!"

I'm forced to look up before I'm ready to do it—when I've still got tears in my eyes. Fuck me. Aubrey is clocking my tears. In fact, the second her eyes meet mine, tears spring into her dark eyes, too.

I hang my head again, feeling embarrassed. And before another word is exchanged, the sound of the front screen thwapping draws my attention, and an older man and woman enter the house, with the man on crutches.

"How'd it go at the doctor?" Aubrey calls out, as I covertly wipe my eyes and take a deep breath to get ahold of myself.

"It's gonna be a long haul, Shortcake," the man on crutches replies, before coming to a stop alongside his wife in the entryway to the living room.

"Hello," the woman says tentatively. She stares at me with deep confusion on her face before turning to Aubrey for an explanation.

Aubrey motions to me. "Mom, Dad, this is Claudia's good friend, Caleb. He came over to learn how to color with Raine."

"Hi," I say feebly, getting up from the floor.

"Claudia's good friend?" Aubrey's mother echoes, looking even more confused.

I shake Aubrey's parents' hands. But when I start to explain my presence, Aubrey immediately stops me with an authoritative wave of her hand.

"Continue your coloring lesson with Raine," she commands. "While I talk to my parents in the kitchen." Aubrey smiles at Raine. "We'll be right back, Rainey."

"Mm hm," Raine says absently, while coloring up a storm.

With my heart pounding in my ears, I watch Aubrey and her parents head into the adjacent kitchen, all of them moving at Aubrey's father's slow pace. But just before the trio disappears into the next room, Aubrey's father blurts, "I swear to God that guy looks *exactly* like the drummer for Red Card Riot!"

CHAPTER 7
AUBREY

Dinner is underway and going pretty well, surprisingly. For the past half hour or so, my parents, Caleb, and I have been eating together at the small table adjacent to the living room. Raine's not here anymore. She started the meal with us, but she's now lying on the carpet nearby, working on a new page in her coloring book.

Dad has dominated most of the dinner conversation thus far, by asking Caleb endless questions: about Red Card Riot, the art of drumming, the music industry in general. I'm grateful for Dad's chattiness, since it's given me the chance to stare at Caleb and assess him. Can I trust this man? What's his real end game here?

Once again, my eyes rake over Caleb's tattooed forearm as he lifts his fork to his mouth. And as he chews, my gaze remains, once again, fixated on the movement of his lips. Those are some damned fine lips, especially when framed by that beard. It's a weird thought, since I don't normally like beards. It's a thought that makes me remind myself, yet again, that the physical attraction I'm feeling for this man isn't something I could ever pursue. Obviously.

When Claudia told me about her shocking encounter with C-Bomb after his show in Seattle, she lamented that she never got to kiss those lips. Apparently, C-Bomb fucked her from behind while gripping her hips with those two, big, tattooed hands right there; and he did it without ever kissing Claudia or looking into her eyes. Claudia said the sex itself was super-hot. *It was the hottest, most animalistic sex imaginable*, she told me. *Ten out of ten*. But even so, she admitted she still felt a touch disappointed she didn't get to taste the lips she'd been fantasizing about kissing since middle school.

Frankly, I've never understood Claudia's fixation on C-Bomb. Truly, never.

But I get it now.

I still despise the man for the way he's neglected Raine. Also, because he never asked for Claudia's phone number after their encounter, which deeply disappointed her. But now that I'm seeing the guy in person, I can't deny I finally get his worldwide appeal. At the very least, I can understand why hate sex is a thing. In a flash, I see Caleb gripping *my* hips from behind and having animalistic sex with *me*, while I shout epithets at him and swear I hate his guts for never once coming to meet Raine.

Dad laughs at something Caleb says, jerking me from my mortifyingly horrendous thoughts, and Mom and I exchange a withering look about his happy guffaw. We'd both normally be happy for Dad to get to meet the drummer from one of his favorite bands; but in this moment, we're both far too wary about Caleb's intentions to feel anything but unsettled and cautious. If Caleb gets custody of Raine, will he keep his word and always give us full access to her, or will he eventually ice us out, once we're no longer useful to him?

In the kitchen earlier, when I rapidly explained Caleb's unexpected presence in our house, I expected both my parents to express the same unadulterated indignance I felt. But even though both seemed highly protective of Raine, and even though they both expressed the need for us to always keep a skeptical, watchful eye on Caleb, they both also expressed deep joy about Raine finally getting to meet her daddy. My father, especially, was willing to help Caleb get to know Raine, for her own good, far more so than Mom and me.

"Would you forget he's C-Bomb from Red Card Riot for a minute," I whisper-shouted angrily at Dad in the kitchen earlier. "And focus on the fact that he's an absentee father who's shown up, out of the blue, to take our baby girl away from us?"

"Then why agree to stay in Prairie Springs for a month, if his only goal is to take her away?" Dad countered. "Look, honey, a child needs her father. Yes, C-Bomb's made mistakes in the past, but he's come to correct them. That's a good thing. So, I vote we try to help him do that."

When I grumbled, Mom said, "Even if we don't trust him completely, the fact remains there's no way we can defeat Ralph Beaumont on our own. So, what choice do we have but to align ourselves with Caleb, at least, at first? Your dad is right. We can pull a whammy on Caleb in court, if it comes to that. But for now, let's help him with Raine, and get on his good side, so he'll keep his promise and keep us in her life."

"How'd you two meet?" Caleb asks my parents, drawing me back to the dinner table.

"I grew up in Prairie Springs," Mom replies. "And Joe

grew up two towns over. He played football for the rival team—"

"Go Red Devils," Dad interjects.

"And I was the head cheerleader for mine. Go Spartans." She giggles. "It was quite the scandal, actually."

"Barb was forbidden fruit," Dad says with a wink at Mom. "Irresistible."

Caleb glances at me. "Forbidden is the best kind of fruit, if you ask me."

I look away, blushing. I'm sure it was a coincidence Caleb looked directly at me when he said that, but my body reacted like he'd just used a Taser on me, just the same.

"After thirty years together," Mom says, "I think everyone in Prairie Springs has finally forgiven my traitorous betrayal. The people in Joe's town? Not so much."

Dad laughs. "They've more than *forgiven* you, Barb, or else they wouldn't have put you in charge of the summer festival for the past ten years."

Caleb asks what that means, and Dad proudly launches into explaining that for the past decade, my mother has been in charge of the elite committee that meticulously plans our town's biggest, annual fundraiser/community event: our beloved summer festival.

"That's impressive, Mrs. Capshaw," Caleb says.

Mom bats at the air. "It's really not. I'm the only one willing to do it, basically. And, please, call me Barbara or Barb."

"And call me Joe," Dad chimes in.

Caleb asks the timing of this year's festival, and Mom tells him the date: a Saturday that's about two months away in mid-August.

"Every year," Mom says, "the festival raises money for the school and some other local causes. And do you know what the committee did behind my back this year? They added *Joe* to the list of recipients because of his broken leg! I told them, no, no, we'll manage. But wasn't it sweet of them to want to do that for us?"

I shift in my seat, feeling annoyed with Mom for rejecting the committee's generous offer to help us out this year. Dad's surgery was expensive, even with insurance; and Dad's going to be out of work for at least four months. Probably longer. And now, we might have to scrape together money for a lawyer, too? As hard as it might be for my proud parents to accept, we really could have used that donation, however small it might have been.

Caleb's forehead creases. "If you need money, I've got a lot of it."

"No, no," Mom says quickly, blushing a deep crimson. "Joe will be back to work in no time, and I've got my job to pay the bills in the meantime."

It's total bullshit. Mom's job will cover only a fraction of our living expenses, and she knows it. And it won't make a dent in Dad's medical expenses.

I address Caleb, eager to change the subject. "We'd love a donation from you for this year's live auction. It's always the biggest moneymaker of the entire festival."

"Oh. Yeah, sure, I can do that. You mean, like, signed band memorabilia and merch?"

"Exactly. That'd bring in a pretty penny, I'm sure."

Caleb looks at Mom. "When do you need it by?"

"A week or so before the festival would be great. That'll give me enough time to post the list and finalize the auction programs."

"Plenty of time," Caleb murmurs with relief. "I'll figure something out and let you know."

"Thank you so much. That's very generous of you."

"I'll come up with something good."

Caleb smiles at me, like he's expecting a pat on the back; but I give him nothing. For all I know, this man will be back in LA in two months with Raine, after winning custody of her at the hearing in a month, and the promise he just now made to donate to the auction will be a distant memory.

Caleb shifts his attention to my father—the friendliest face at the table. "So, Joe, how'd you break your leg?"

Dad motions to his propped-up leg in a cast and frowns. "Oh, man, C-Bomb, it was a pisser." And away he goes, launching into the same story I've heard on repeat, since the accident last week. If I were telling this story, I'd simply say, "Dad fell off a roof while fixing it with a newbie who made a big mistake and accidentally knocked Dad to the ground." But Dad being Dad, he spins a yarn like he was the main character in a two-hour action flick that day.

"Oof," Caleb says with a wince, once Dad gets to the part of his story where he's writhing in pain on the ground.

"Oof is right," Dad says with a chuckle. "Thirty years working construction, twenty of it as the owner of my own company, and it was my first broken bone."

"Too bad you're out of commission for a while," Caleb says. "I just inherited an old cabin on Lake Lucille, and I'm predicting it's going to need some major upgrades and repairs."

"Give me six months, and I'll fix anything the place needs."

"I'm not sure if I can wait that long."

"You're aiming to sell the place?"

Caleb shrugs. "Not sure yet. I haven't been back here in over fifteen years, ever since my grandpa moved away and turned the cabin into a short-term rental. Once I see the place again, I'll have a better idea about what needs to be done, and if I want to keep it or sell it."

"Is that where you'll be staying while you're in town?" Dad asks.

"Yeah, I had a service go in there and clean it for me this morning, so I'm good to go."

"You said you inherited it?" Mom asks tentatively.

A look of deep sadness flickers across Caleb's face. "From my mother, about three months ago. She got the place when my grandpa died a couple years ago, but unfortunately she never made it up here to see the place again."

We all express our condolences, and Caleb thanks us and takes a long guzzle from his water, like he's throwing back a tall whiskey. I noticed Caleb turned down a cold beer earlier when offered one, and that surprised me. Normally, a person turning down a beer doesn't register with me. Who cares? But the online version of C-Bomb I've studied relentlessly over the years seems like the kind of guy who'd never turn down a beer.

After supporting Claudia on her sobriety journey, I have a sixth sense about people turning down alcohol—when it feels meaningful and when it doesn't. And in this instance, it felt meaningful. Like Caleb very much wanted to say yes to that drink, but he forced himself to refuse it.

My eyes rake over Caleb's large, tattooed hand wrapped around his water glass; and my mind conjures to the vision of that hand gripping Claudia's hip as he fucked her from behind. I can't believe this famous man's dick was inside my best friend, right after he'd played a sold-out show in Seattle . . . and that now, he's sitting at my parents' dinner table in Prairie Springs, eating my mother's famous chicken pot pie. It's boggling my mind to try to reconcile the peacock of a man I've seen online with the quiet, understated man sitting across from me.

Dad's voice interrupts my thoughts. "If you want to FaceTime me in the light of day tomorrow and show me around the cabin, I'd be more than happy to give you my professional opinion about what upgrades and fixes the place might need."

"I'll definitely take you up on that," Caleb says. "Thanks. I worked construction myself in my teens, and I've always enjoyed working with my hands. Depending on your advice, maybe I'll tackle some of the projects on my own, since I'm gonna be stu—While I'm here."

Stuck here. That's what he was going to say. *While I'm gonna be stuck here, anyway.*

I exchange another look with my mother. One that says, "*I don't like him.*"

"Aubrey will be a good pair of eyes, too," Dad says, oblivious to the nonverbal exchange happening between Mom and me. "She used to work for me during summers in high school, and she's always had a great eye."

I pat Dad's hand on the table. "Don't oversell me. I know how to use power tools and follow your explicit instructions to a T, and that's about it."

"Don't sell yourself short, Short Cake," Dad replies. "By the end of every summer, you were better at supervising projects than my best project managers."

Caleb smiles at me. "A woman of many talents."

Once again, my body jolts at Caleb's eye contact, the same way it did when Caleb looked at me while counting himself a fan of "forbidden fruit."

Mom looks between Caleb and me. "Aubrey, honey, will you help me clear the dishes?"

"Let me do it," Caleb says, rising from his chair.

"No, no. You're our guest. If you want a job, keep Joe company, since he's stuck there."

I smirk. I'm not sure if Mom purposefully used the word "stuck" to let Caleb know *she* knows he stopped himself from using that exact word a moment ago in relation to himself; but if so, I'm deeply impressed by her subtle sassiness.

Without daring to look in Caleb's direction, I grab all the plates off the table, while Mom grabs the serving platters, and with items in hand, we both quickly scamper into the kitchen.

The minute we're out of earshot of the men, Mom whispers, "Stop flirting with him, Aubrey."

"*What?*" I gasp out.

"You heard me. It won't end well for us, if you keep doing that. So, don't."

"I'm . . . Mom, I haven't been flirting. If anyone's been doing that, it's *him*."

Mom looks unconvinced. "You might think it'll help our cause for you to cozy up to him. But when he inevitably loses interest, then what? We'll be screwed."

I roll my eyes. "I'm not even remotely attracted to him. And even if I were, which I'm not, I wouldn't act on it. Give me some credit."

After one last, lingering look of warning, Mom starts loading up the dishwasher with an assist from me. Once that job is done, I grab the brownies from earlier today and head out to the table with them, while Mom stays behind to wash some pots and pans. But when I get back out to the dining area, Caleb and Dad are no longer sitting there. I walk into the living room and discover Dad is nowhere to be found, while Caleb is lying on the floor next to Raine, helping her color another page from her coloring book.

"Oh, dat good!" Raine squeaks out, leaning her cheek against Caleb's massive bicep. And just like that, my left ovary feels like it's rupturing.

"That's because I have the best teacher in the world," Caleb replies happily.

"Who?" Raine asks innocently.

"You," Caleb replies with a chuckle.

"*Me*?"

"Who else?"

They both giggle uproariously, and, suddenly, I'm hit with two competing sensations: one, my right ovary joining my left in total obliteration; and, two, the sensation of foreboding descending upon me. Suddenly, I know my parents were right earlier in the kitchen: I need to get on Caleb's good side, rather than trying to fight him, or I'm likely to get screwed.

Feeling overwhelmed, I put the brownies down on the table with a loud *thunk*, prompting Caleb to look up at me. When his green eyes meet mine, and I can plainly see the look of pure joy on his face, the foreboding I was feeling a moment softens a tiny bit. Obviously, this man screwed up by not wanting to know Raine till now. Obviously, this man has missed out on getting to know the best person in the history of the world. But he's here now. And it's in our baby girl's best interests to have him here, assuming he's genuinely going to commit to becoming her father. Time will tell. But in the meantime, my only path forward is to help Caleb succeed. Not for his sake, but for Raine's. And, ultimately, for my own, too.

Mom comes out of the kitchen and gasps when she beholds the happy scene on the floor of the living room. She silently watches Caleb and Raine for several minutes, while exchanging looks with me. But, finally, Mom says, "Rainey, honey. It's bathtime. Say goodnight to Caleb and thank him for coloring with you."

Raine loves bathtime, thanks to the colored, foamy soap Mom bought for her to paint with on the tile walls, so it's a brilliant maneuver. In lightning speed, Raine ditches Caleb like a hot potato, hops up from the floor, and takes my mother's offered hand.

"Thank Caleb for coloring with you," Mom says as they depart.

"Tank you, Coobie," Raine calls to Caleb, batting her eyelashes.

"No, thank *you* for teaching me," Caleb says, and I let out a sigh of relief that's his reply. Mom's call to action to Raine *assumed* our girl would be bathing and *sleeping* here tonight, at our house, as usual, rather than going to Caleb's lake cabin with him for the night. So, it's a huge relief he didn't correct that assumption and ask us to pack an overnight bag for Raine.

When Mom and Raine are gone, I sit on the couch with my heart pounding in my ears.

"She's incredible," Caleb says, taking the arm chair across from me.

Yes, I want to say. *A fact you would have known already, if you'd bothered to meet her, even once, over the past two years.*

I take a deep breath. "She's really warming up to you."

"You think?" Looking pleased, Caleb leans back and spreads his muscular thighs. "So, let's talk some more about that nanny job."

Crap. I can't let him dictate the narrative here. I need him to understand *we're* holding the power here, not him. Because *we're* the ones who already know and love Raine.

"Here's what I think we should do," I say, trying to sound casual and unbothered. "You don't really need a nanny while you're here in Prairie Springs, because Raine will be staying with us, and you'll be visiting her every day, either here or at your cabin. Why don't we wait to find out the result of the custody hearing before we—"

He leans forward. "No, I need you and Raine to stay with me at my cabin, actually. The whole time I'm here in Prairie Springs."

Fuck, fuck, fuck. I didn't see that coming. "But Raine is happy and settled here with my parents and me. So, I propose we—"

"It's non-negotiable. You're both coming to stay with me."

My brain feels like it's melting. Grasping for words. "But why? It makes much more sense for me to take care of Raine here, like always, while you—"

"The truth is I need to hire you as my sobriety coach for the next three weeks and two days, Aubrey. In addition to hiring you as Raine's nanny during that same period of time."

My brain freezes. "I-I . . . *What?*"

With a long exhale, Caleb leans back again and explains the entire situation to me. When he's done speaking, I remain silent for a long moment, trying to process.

Finally, I say, "I'm not qualified to be a sobriety coach. I have no idea how to do that."

"You're over eighteen, right?"

"Twenty-four."

"Are you capable of abstaining from alcohol and drugs for the next three weeks and two days?"

I scoff. "I haven't had a drink in over two years, and I've

never done any kind of drugs. I quit drinking for Claudia and never looked back."

"Congratulations. You're qualified."

"But I don't want to live with you," I insist. "I want to stay here with Raine and my parents and—"

"It's non-negotiable, Aubrey." When I say nothing, he throws up his hands in frustration. "It's not like I'll be holding you prisoner at my place. You can see your parents every day, if you want. But you and Raine absolutely have to come live with me for the next three weeks and two days. *Non-negotiable.*"

I rub my neck, feeling a bit hot and dizzy. "How much will you pay me to do both jobs—sobriety coach and nanny—for the next three weeks and two days?"

Caleb pauses. "Five grand."

My heart stops. Holy shit. Five grand for only three weeks of work is more than I've ever made in my life! But even so, he's clearly desperate, so I think I can get even more, if I push back. Six grand, maybe? Two grand per week, to make it a round number.

I open my mouth to suggest the new, higher number, but Caleb speaks first.

"I think that's fair for now, considering you're doing both jobs," he says. "But once the sobriety coach portion of your job is over, and once we know the result of the custody hearing, we'll re-negotiate your full-time nanny salary, For now, though, while I'm staying here in Prairie Springs, I think it's fair for me to pay you five grand per week to do both jobs."

Per week?

Wait.

Did Caleb just say he's willing to pay me five grand . . .

per *week* . . . and not five grand . . . *total*? I feel like I'm going to faint.

"Come on, Aubrey," Caleb huffs out, when I'm too shocked to speak. "Don't play hardball with me. You'd be taking care of Raine for the next three weeks, anyway, for free. Granted, I realize I'm also asking you to babysit me, on top of that, but that's why—"

"No, no, I . . ." I take a deep breath to steady myself. "Five grand per week is fine. For now." Holy crap, this is a godsend. With an easy fifteen grand in my pocket, I'll be able to help my parents put a major dent in their medical bills! Do I want to spend the next three weeks and two days living under the same roof with a pathetic man-child who's got the fate of my happiness in the palm of his hand? No. I'd rather eat rusty nails. But what choice do I have? At least, this living arrangement will afford me the chance to help my parents while *also* trying to influence Caleb before the hearing. If I play my cards right, maybe I can make him see it's *me* who should get custody of Raine, while *Caleb* gets unlimited visitation rights.

"So, we've got a deal?" Caleb asks, a hint of annoyance in his tone.

I clear my throat. "Yes. For now."

I take Caleb's offered hand, but when electricity courses between us at the point of contact, I release his palm like I've touched a hot stove.

"*What, uh* . . ." Damn. Come on, Aubrey. *Focus*. "What time do you want me to bring Raine over to your cabin in the morning?"

"Raine can sleep here tonight, but you're coming with me to my place."

"No, Caleb. Let's start this arrangement tomorrow. Give me a day to—"

"I can't do that. As my sobriety coach, you'll need to submit a form certifying my sobriety, starting tonight."

My jaw hangs open. "*What?* But, Caleb—"

"Whatever you're about to say, don't bother. Like I keep saying, it's non-negotiable." He smirks at whatever he's seeing on my face. "Go on, Aubrey. Go pack a bag and say goodbye to Raine and your parents. Whether you like it or not, you're coming home with me."

CHAPTER 8
CALEB

I glance over at Aubrey's stunning profile in my passenger seat again. Same as before, she's silently staring out the windshield of my rental car like an annoyed, kidnapped robot. Although come to think of it, I doubt a robot could be programmed to pout that much. Or look that fucking hot.

Man, it's too bad Aubrey hates my guts. Given that we're going to be stuck under one roof for the next three weeks and two days, it would have been an unexpected silver lining of our forced living arrangement to partake in a little carnal fun every night after Raine's bedtime.

With a sigh over what could have been, I shift my eyes off Aubrey's pouting profile and take the next curve on the winding road leading to my family's cabin on the lake. After a bit, I get to the next curve, the one with the big fir tree at its apex that got slightly singed in a fire when I was ten or so. My stomach flutters with butterflies at my destination's proximity. Only this time, unlike when I was a kid, those butterflies bring with them nostalgia and uncertainty, rather than unadulterated excitement.

When I used to come here as a kid, the sight of that big fir tree meant imminent independence. A carefree escape from homework, chores, and all the screaming back home. Now, as an adult, however, I understand *why* Mom sometimes abruptly packed up the car without warning to come here in the middle of the night. *Why* Grandpa would give Mom such a big bear hug when we arrived on his doorstep. *Why* Mom always shed those big, soggy tears into her father's chest. So much so, they'd soak Grandpa's flannel shirt. And most of all, I now understand the happy smile Mom wore for Miranda and me was a mother's gift to her children. A ruse that allowed us to cluelessly enjoy our little vacation and conveniently forget about the latest bruises on our mother's arms and neck.

Thankfully, Dad knew he wasn't welcome at Grandpa's cabin. Grandpa once told my father, "I've got a locker full of rifles, Greg, and I know exactly how to make anything look like a hunting accident." We all knew he wasn't kidding.

After another turn in the winding road, I spot the two black cottonwoods that mark the small dirt road leading to our family's cabin, and a moment later, there it is. The small house on the lake I used to visit frequently as a kid, although it looks quite a bit bigger nowadays. Also, much nicer than I remember it, thanks to some massive, modern windows installed on its front facade. Did Grandpa renovate the crap out of this place before putting it up on that short-term rental site?

I slowly drive my car across some noisy gravel on the side of the house and park the car, and Aubrey immediately unbuckles her seatbelt. Without a word or even a glance toward me, she grabs her overnight bag and exits the car. When I don't follow because I'm studying the new, modernized look of the house, Aubrey stands near the front of the car and awaits me, her arms crossed and her body language bursting with impatience and disdain.

By my late teens, I'd become too obsessed with my band and chasing girls to come along whenever Mom came here. And once I successfully started flaking on coming here, my sister, Miranda, four years my junior, took it as her cue to start following suit, since she never liked coming here, anyway. *Too many bugs*, Miranda always said. *Nothing to do.*

All of a sudden, Miranda started sleeping at her best friend Violet's place, whenever Mom came here. And a few years after that, Grandpa got himself a girlfriend from Kansas—a pretty widow with a cool house and some kids she didn't want to uproot. And that was that. Mom started visiting her dad in Kansas without Miranda and me, since we'd become "too busy" for family outings like that; and I lost access to this magical place in Montana, without ever knowing my final visit here had been my last.

Aubrey's arm waving at me in my peripheral vision catches my attention, and I slowly turn my head to stare at her in a daze.

"Are you coming?" she mouths on the other side of my windshield, her eyebrows raised with annoyance.

With a long exhale, I unbuckle my seatbelt, grab my backpack from the backseat, and amble toward Aubrey at the front of the car. As I approach, a crease splits her otherwise smooth forehead.

"Are you okay?" she asks. "You look pissed off."

"That's just my face, sweetheart. I've got resting 'pissed off' face."

The slightest twitch of a smile plays at Aubrey's pouty lips, but she manages to suppress it before returning her attention to the house. "You kept calling this place a cabin, so I pictured a little log cabin in the woods. But this is a proper lake house, Caleb. A vacation home."

I shrug. "It started out as a little cabin in the woods, so that's what we've always called it. My grandpa must have expanded and renovated the place over the years, without me knowing it." I point. "Those big windows there are new to me. And that whole side of the house is an addition. A third bedroom, maybe?"

"Cool." She's practically tapping her toe. "Can we go inside now? I need to pee."

I shift the backpack slung over my shoulder and lead the way. But as we walk toward the front of the house, I remember something I want to see along the side of it. I don't say a word to Aubrey about my divergence from the route to the front door, but she follows me, anyway, probably figuring there's some preferred side entry into the house.

When I get to my destination—the big black cottonwood my grandpa planted to mark my birth over thirty-five years ago—I run my fingers over the ridged, rough bark, searching for the symbol I carved into it during my childhood: a letter "C" for "Caleb" with a lit fuse attached to its top for "Bomb." *Baum*-garten.

"Did you carve that?" Aubrey asks, leaning in close to peer at the symbol. Surely, the design is self-explanatory to her, since she knows my full name.

I nod. "When I was twelve or thirteen."

"I didn't realize you've been C-Bomb for so long. I thought you adopted that as a one-name celebrity thing. You know, like Prince or Shakira."

I shake my head. "Dean started calling me C-Bomb in middle school, when we first learned about the A-bomb." I can't fathom I need to explain the identity of Dean to her. Surely, Aubrey knows I'm talking about Dean Masterson, the insanely talented lead singer of my band who's easily ten times more famous than me. "Once the band took off," I add, "the nickname took on a life of its own in pop culture; but before that, I was always Caleb and C-Bomb, interchangeably, with my closest friends. Still am. Some of my best friends still call me C-Bomb, as often as they call me Caleb."

"I noticed that on your neck earlier." Aubrey points at the side of my neck. Specifically, to the spot where I have this exact same "C-Bomb" symbol inked into my flesh.

"Mm hmm." Now that she's brought up one of my tattoos, I'm fully expecting the conversation to take the usual course. Namely, for Aubrey to ask me the meaning of this or that other tattoo. Or maybe to compliment her favorite design. But to my surprise, Aubrey doesn't follow the usual script.

With her fingers brushing over the carving in the tree, she murmurs, "Seems like there's a lot of memories in this place for you, huh?"

My chest tightens. It's an understatement. Being here is like visiting a ghost of my prior self: a younger version of Caleb Baumgarten who loved coming here to escape and forget about the stress caused by my turbulent father back home. "Yeah, lots of memories," I mutter vaguely. I shift my backpack and clear my throat. "Come on, babysitter. You need to pee, right?" I stride away from the tree without looking back. "We'll go in through the back door. We've probably got mud on our shoes now."

"Love the rustic vibe," Aubrey murmurs, looking around the living room. She motions toward the ceiling. "Those exposed beams are gorgeous."

"They're new from when I was here last."

She motions across the room. "Love that stone fireplace, too."

"When I was a little kid, we used to make s'mores in that fireplace."

"Ooooh, we should do that with Raine."

Raine. My heart rate quickens at the mention of my daughter's name. I can't believe her little feet are going to pad across the same wooden planks my own two-year-old feet traversed thirty-plus years ago. "Great idea. Before we pick her up tomorrow, let's stop by the grocery store for supplies."

For the first time since our eyes connected over that wooden fence, Aubrey looks semi-tolerant of me. At least, she doesn't look nearly as much like she wants to slide her hands around my neck and *squeeze*.

"Should we take a look around the place?" I ask.

"Let's do it."

We wander through the house and confirm my grandfather did, indeed, add a third bedroom on the west side, as well as all new windows and several upgrades to the cabin's only bathroom.

"Do you have any thoughts, in terms of upgrades and fixes?" I ask, as we return to the living room.

"It depends on what you plan to do with the place. If you want to spend the money to make this place your own personal haven, you'd probably want to do more than if you're aiming to turn a maximum profit on a sale, you know?"

I look around, my mind buffering. If I wind up with full

custody of Raine, I'd likely want to keep this place, so I can bring my daughter here, now and again, the same way I used to come as a kid. If I *don't* get custody of Raine, however, I'm certain my sister will want to sell the place and split the proceeds, since she's never liked coming here, anyway. If that scenario faces me, I think it's possible coming here will feel too painful for me to fight my sister's wishes on the matter.

"Not sure yet," I say vaguely, averting my eyes from Aubrey. The last thing I want her detecting is my present state of uncertainty about the outcome of the custody hearing. I'm mostly confident and determined, but I'm a bit out of my depths here, frankly; but, of course, I want Aubrey thinking I've got this situation completely under control.

Aubrey says, "I think you should figure out your intentions for the place before you do too much to it. Either way, I'd recommend replacing the rotting deck for safety reasons. Later, if you decide to keep the place, I'd also upgrade the kitchen and add a second bathroom."

It's the same list I came up with during our short tour, other than adding the second bathroom. I can't argue with that additional idea, however, now that Aubrey's raised it. If this place becomes a vacation home for my growing daughter and me, I'm sure Raine would appreciate her own bathroom, as she gets older, so she doesn't have to share one with her old man.

"I think I'll take on the deck by myself, while we're staying here," I say. "And figure out the rest after the custody hearing."

"As long as you're going to rebuild the deck, can I suggest a whole new design for it?"

I ask her what she's got in mind, and Aubrey holds up a palm and uses her index finger to visually explain what she means. By the time she's done walking me through it, I'm thoroughly impressed and sold on the idea. In fact, it feels like a no-brainer to follow Aubrey's vision to a T.

"You're good at this," I say.

Aubrey blushes. "I worked every summer for my dad in high school. I guess I learned a thing or two."

"Clearly." I flash her a small smile, but she doesn't return the gesture. *Again.* With a sigh, I add, "Okay, thanks. I'll get the lumber tomorrow and get started."

"I know my dad is presently out of commission, but I'm sure he could wrangle a small crew to help you finish the deck as quickly as possible."

I shake my head. "Getting the project done quickly isn't the goal. I like working with my hands and feeling pride in a job well done. I'll take your dad's supervision and advice, though."

The slightest hint of a smile plays at Aubrey's lips. "My father is the exact same way, and I learned it from him. We both take pride in a job well done, too."

I try my damnedest not to smile at her again, since my prior attempts at warming things up between us haven't been well received. But it's hard not to smile with my eyes, at least. Aubrey's so damned cute and sexy, all rolled into one. Also, so damned *likeable,* even though she obviously can't stand me. "If I decide to go forward with the other projects you suggested," I say, "I'll hire your father to do them, whenever he's feeling up to it."

Aubrey's cheeks visibly bloom. "Really? Thank you. I know my father would appreciate that. By the time he's cleared to work, he'll be in a pretty deep hole, financially. Don't tell him I told you that. But it's the truth, unfortunately."

My stomach tightens at the worried look on her pretty

face. I noticed Aubrey looking the same way earlier at dinner, when her mother said she'd turned down the festival committee's offer to send financial assistance the Capshaws' way.

Aubrey rubs a palm down her bare arm and clears her throat. "So, what's your timing on going to bed? As your sobriety coach, I feel like I should know your schedule every day."

"I'm pretty wiped. I was thinking I'd take a hot shower and get into bed pretty soon."

"That works for me. I'm tired, too. Raine woke up with another nightmare last night, so I didn't get a good night's sleep again."

My eyebrows cinch together. "Raine's been having nightmares?"

"Every night since . . ." Aubrey doesn't finish her sentence, but she doesn't need to: her crestfallen expression and moist eyes have finished it for her.

I have no idea what to say in this moment. Whenever people have tried to say something comforting about my mother's passing, their words have always fallen flat, like lead balloons, no matter how good the person's intentions. So, in the end, I ignore the obvious emotion washing over Aubrey's pretty face and stay on topic. "You never need to stay up on my account. If you're wiped out for whatever reason, you can always go to bed first, whether I'm still awake or not."

Aubrey looks at me like I'm crazy. "Every night at ten, I need to send in that form certifying you've been a good little boy all day, remember? And I can't do that, if I've been sleeping on the job."

I scoff. "I don't think the job requires you to match my sleep schedule, Aubrey." I motion toward the moonlit lake and surrounding cluster of trees immediately outside the large windows across the room. "Not here, especially, when there's nothing around for miles."

Aubrey shakes her head. "I'm getting paid to do this job, so I'm going to do it to the best of my abilities." She raises an index finger. "Speaking of which, I'd better do a quick sweep of the house before we head to bed for the night."

"A sweep of the house?"

"For alcohol. In case someone who stayed here left something behind."

I roll my eyes. "I can't imagine that's necessary."

Aubrey, looking around, ignores my comment. "I'll start in the kitchen, unless you'd prefer me to start in your bedroom, so you can get in there now."

I release a loud exhale. "Kitchen is fine."

"Awesome." She turns on her heel and strides into the adjacent kitchen, leaving me gawking involuntarily at the swishing movement of her hot little ass for a moment, until, finally, I pull myself together enough to amble into the kitchen after her.

When I enter the room, Aubrey is already bent over and peeking into a low cabinet, so I lean my ass against the kitchen counter and watch the show.

"You didn't happen to have an alcoholic beverage at the airport or on the plane today, did you?" she asks, her gaze trained on her next opened cupboard. "Because the email I got explaining my job duties said you'll need to co-sign onto today's certification only, under oath, due to the hours you spent alone and unattended during your travels." She bends over again, giving me another lovely view of her ass.

"On my honor, I've had nothing but coffee and water all day long."

Aubrey straightens up from the latest cabinet she's

been inspecting to shoot me a pointed look that says, *Your honor means nothing to me, motherfucker.*

I chuckle. "Do you want me to swear it on something sacred to me?" With a dramatic hand to my heart, I declare, "Aubrey Capshaw, I swear to you and the god of rehab I've stayed sober all day. I swear it on my love for my mother, sister, and bandmates, and on every dime in my bank account."

Aubrey rolls her eyes. "Your money is 'sacred' to you? Nice, C-Bomb."

It's the first time she's addressed me that way, since she made the switch to Caleb at her house. But it seems fair in this context. Sassy and teasing, even. Is the ice thawing a bit? "The money part was a joke," I say with a smirk. "Although it certainly doesn't suck to have money."

Aubrey pulls an adorable face. One that says, *I wouldn't know.* But she doesn't say a word before moving on to the next cabinet.

"I realize you're going to have to take a small leap of faith today," I say to her bent-over backside. "But after today, I promise you'll quickly find out I'm sincerely determined to stick with the program. It's in my best interest to do that, for a variety of reasons."

Aubrey stops what she's doing and flashes me an earnest look. "I'm proud of you for working to get sober. I know from watching Claudia it's a difficult thing to do."

"I didn't do it of my own free will. I had an expensive meltdown at a hotel in New York the night my mother died, and a court ordered me to go to rehab to avoid jailtime. And then, the insurance company that insures our tours piggybacked on the court's decision, so now I have to stick with my program, if I want my band to be insurable for tours again."

Aubrey shrugs, looking unfazed. "Whatever got you here, you're still the one doing the work. As far as I'm concerned, the praise is still well deserved."

"The crazy thing is I don't even need a formal program to quit drinking. I've quit before, whenever I've wanted to. Just to prove I could."

"But you always started drinking again?"

"Yeah, whenever I felt like I'd proven my point to myself."

"Or maybe you've actually needed a program, without realizing it."

I pull a face. "No, before now, my goal was never to stop drinking, forever."

"Is that your goal now: to stop drinking forever?"

"Yeah," I say slowly. Begrudgingly. "I guess it is."

Before now, I hadn't consciously formulated a goal for my sobriety, and I certainly hadn't thought the word "forever." But now that we're having this conversation, I'm realizing there's no other path forward for me, assuming I win custody of Raine.

Whenever I drink or smoke weed, I wind up giving myself permission to do whatever the fuck I want, without a shred of accountability. And that's obviously not going to work in my new role as a father. I've never laid a finger on anyone I care about when drunk or high. Never would. So, thankfully, in that way, I'm nothing like my father. But I definitely let some major guardrails down, whenever my brain is in a fog, and that's simply not going to be an option anymore, in my new life as a father.

When it's clear that's all I'm going to say on the subject of my sobriety, Aubrey turns and resumes her work. Feeling a bit exposed and vulnerable, I open the cabinet nearest to me and scope it out, figuring the sooner Aubrey finishes her ridiculous task, the sooner I can go to bed.

When I finish scanning the empty cabinets closest to me, I turn to tell Aubrey it's all clear over here. But when I see her bent over and peeking into a low cabinet, when I get yet another glorious eyeful of her incredible ass, my words lodge in my throat. *Damn. That's an ass I'd love to mark with my teeth.* The thought sends tingle shooting into my dick. Yes, Aubrey's a thorn in my goddamned side. But hot damn, she's one hell of a sexy thorn.

As I'm still ogling Aubrey's backside, she straightens up and checks a high cabinet, causing her to reach up and strain on tiptoes. As she stretches, her tank top rides up from the top of her shorty shorts, treating me to a delightful peek of her belly. It's only a tiny swath of bare flesh. But it's enough to send another round of tingles shooting between my legs.

I haven't had "clean and sober" sex yet, but I've certainly thought about sex a hell of a lot the past few months, ever since my sex drive came roaring back after detox the first week of rehab. I suppose it's possible I'm feeling this intense sexual attraction to Aubrey, simply by virtue of her being here with the right body parts for my innately wired sexuality. I can't deny I'm a horny motherfucker right now. But I don't think that's it.

On the contrary, I'm pretty damned sure my body would be craving Aubrey's with feral force, even if I had a world of women to choose from. Even if I'd had sex with someone, other than my hand, every night for the past few months. Even before rehab, with Mom living with me for so long, and with my focus on her and her downward spiral, I put my entire life on hold for quite a while, including performing and going out with friends. Which meant, for months, I was no longer engaging in the activities that most typically led to me meeting women.

"A little help, please?" Aubrey says, drawing me from my sexual thoughts.

I sidle over to her and easily reach the high shelf she's struggling to sweep with her hand; and to my surprise, my knuckles clank against something hard toward the back of the shelf. When I grasp the object, I pull down a half-empty, cheap bottle of tequila. "Well, I'll be damned."

It's a brand of tequila I wouldn't dirty my mouth for, under normal circumstances. But I can't deny, in this moment, the sight of the liquid sloshing around against the bottle is making my mouth water. Just this fast, after two months of daily counseling sessions and everything else, I'm suddenly feeling the primal urge to throw away all my progress by twisting off that cap and taking a long, thirsty guzzle, whether it's the cheap shit or not.

"I had a feeling," Aubrey says. "With this place being a short-term rental, the odds were high *someone* brought alcohol here to party with and forgot to take it home with them."

She puts her hand out, and, much to my chagrin, I hand over the bottle; at which point, Aubrey strides to a window on the other side of the kitchen, twists opens the cap and pours every drop of liquid gold into the bushes below.

Fuck me. As I watch the stream of booze disappearing into darkness, my taste buds conjure the flavor of tequila. The unmistakable smell of it, too, even if I'm only imagining both sensations from this distance.

"I think I'll head off to bed," I blurt, my pulse quickening.

"Okay, let me do a quick sweep of your bedroom first."

I rough a hand down my face, feeling like a trapped animal. Shit.

"You've got this, Caleb," Aubrey says warmly. She places the empty bottle onto the counter and walks over to me. To my surprise, she places a reassuring palm on my forearm and squeezes. "I'm not your enemy, okay? When it comes to your sobriety, I'm your teammate. I swear, I'm in your corner on this. Not only for your sake, but for Raine's."

Raine.

It's the magic word. The "why" my counselor, Gina, is always yammering on about.

Before now, I've admittedly been a distant, disinterested shithead in all my counseling sessions with Gina, since simply avoiding jailtime wasn't enough of a why for me. Neither was the insurance thing. Same with *not* pissing off my bandmates. But Raine? She's more than enough of a *why* for me to see this thing through now. I don't know my daughter yet, thanks to my own terrible choices. But I don't need to know her to love her, just this fast, and to decide I'm now going to do whatever it takes to become the father she deserves.

"I appreciate that," I reply softly to Aubrey. With her hand still on my bare forearm, I hold her gaze. The air suddenly feels like it's crackling between us. At least, that's how it feels on my end.

With flushed cheeks, Aubrey removes her hand from my forearm like it's on fire. "I'll go check your bedroom, so you can get to bed."

Her chest heaving, Aubrey turns on her heel and strides away, giving me yet another lovely view of her swishing ass as she goes.

Suddenly, I know two things to be true, with total clarity:

One, I'm going to fuck Aubrey in this house, sooner rather than later. It's fucking inevitable. Unavoidable, like gravity.

And two, from this moment forward, I'm going to stick with my sobriety and do whatever it takes not to fuck up this second chance at a new beginning with my daughter. *No matter what.*

CHAPTER 9
AUBREY

I wake up in a cold sweat, gasping for air and feeling like my heart is being scraped by a spiked, metal rake.

Claudia.

She was screaming in pain in my nightmare. Falling down a well. She cried out for me, desperately. Reached for me, her blue eyes wide and full of terror. But I couldn't help her. On the contrary, I watched in horror as my best friend since fourth grade fell into a deep, dark abyss and, eventually, disappeared from sight.

I reach for Raine next to me, frantically, and whimper when she's not there. But when my brain orients, I remember Raine is safe at my parents' house. That Claudia is gone and at peace now, and I'm sitting in a dark bedroom in Caleb's lake house. With a shudder, I bow my head, rest my forehead against arms on my knees, and sob like a baby.

I was so exhausted when I finally slid into bed in this cute little rustic bedroom, and honestly so excited to finally get to sleep without Raine's warm body draped all over mine for a night—also, to get to sleep without ministering to Raine after a nightmare—I thought for sure I'd sleep blissfully till morning for the first time since Claudia's death. But no such luck. Apparently, in the absence of Raine's nightmares, my brain conjured one of its own to fill the void.

When my tears subside, I check the time on my phone. It's just past three. Too early to get up for the day, so I get up to pee and get a quick drink of water from the faucet.

In the hallway, I tiptoe past Caleb's closed bedroom door and head into the small bathroom. After doing my business in there, I creep back out into the dark hallway and immediately bump smack into something hard and totally unexpected: Caleb's bare torso.

"Gah!" I blurt, as I bounce off his naked chest. "I didn't see you!"

"I thought you were in your room," he mutters, stepping backward and raising his large palms in a show of harmlessness.

Shit. I'm wearing nothing but panties and a tank top, due to the heat, and Caleb's wearing nothing but briefs that make the large package behind them easily identifiable. It's the first time I'm able to confirm the extent of his tattoos. They're everywhere. Covering every inch of his body, other than a few small patches on his thighs.

Yum.

That's my body's involuntary reaction to the nearly naked, muscled and tattooed man standing mere inches from me. Obviously, my conscious brain doesn't respect or like this selfish, entitled man-child. Also, I've never been attracted to inked bad boys with demons. That was always Claudia's thing, not mine. But my body in this moment is having a primal, visceral reaction, whether it makes sense or not.

Caleb's broad chest heaving, he turns sideways to let

me pass in the narrow hallway, at which point I can plainly surmise he's hard as a rock behind his briefs. Blushing as I pass, I wrench my gaze off his bulge, but when my eyes land on the lustful, greedy blaze in his green eyes, I quickly look down at my bare feet and blush.

"Well, goodnight," I choke out, as I reach my bedroom door.

"Goodnight," he replies smoothly, no hint of flustered distress in his tone. "Sweet dreams, *babysitter*."

Damn. That boy's got some serious swagger. Clearly, Caleb knows he's a sight to see. A worldwide sex symbol. I wish that obvious, hard bulge didn't affect me in the slightest; but it did. *A lot.* In fact, thanks to that brief encounter, I'm now short of breath and pulsing in my panties.

Inside my bedroom, I lay a hand on my chest and feel the fast drumbeat of my heart. I haven't had sex since breaking up with Trent almost two years ago, and, suddenly, my body is feeling every minute of that drought.

With a long exhale, I turn on my side in bed and tell myself to calm down. To forget what I saw. But visions of Caleb in that hallway keep slamming into me, unbidden, making it impossible for me to fall asleep again.

Eventually, I give in, reach underneath the covers, and give myself a lovely orgasm. Normally, I'd need my trusty vibrator to reach the finish line. But I didn't bring it with me, so I don't have a choice. Although, even if I had it with me, there's no way I'd use it and risk Caleb overhearing that tell-tale hum.

To my surprise, my fingers accomplish the task, pretty easily, for the first time in a very long time. And shortly after that small victory, I'm finally able to shut down my brain enough to drift off to sleep.

FINDING HOME

Something awakens me. A low creak of a sound. I open my eyes to early morning sunlight peeking through my window. *There it is again.* Did someone take a step across a loose floorboard in the hallway? Was that Caleb . . . or someone else? *Is Ralph Beaumont here?*

My heart stampeding, I look around, feeling disoriented and panicky, and quickly decide I must have dreamed the sound. Except, no, there it is again, and I'm now wide awake. Shit. That wasn't a floorboard creaking. That was definitely Caleb from across the hallway. Was he groaning or wincing in pain? Throwing up, maybe?

Fuck, fuck, fuck. I just realized I didn't check Caleb's backpack when I did my sweep last night, which means he could have smuggled in drugs or booze, without my knowledge; and now, for all I know, he's overdosing and choking on his own vomit across the hallway.

In a frenzy, I lurch out of bed and barrel into the hallway, and when I hear the pained groan from Caleb again, I rap on his closed door and call out his name.

"*Aubrey*," he chokes out in reply, his strained tone making it clear he's in some kind of distress. Without hesitation, I swing open Caleb's door and take two steps inside the room, worried I'm going to find him seizing and frothing at the mouth. But, instead, I get an eyeful of something totally unexpected: Caleb, fully naked on his bed, his extremely large, and very hard, dick in his extremely large hand.

"Aubrey," Caleb groans out again, his eyes shut tight and his features contorted.

Quickly, I flee the room and carefully shut the door behind me, praying he was too distracted to notice my presence in his doorway. Back in my room, I stuff in my earbuds, click play on my "favorites" playlist on my phone, and try to drown out the sounds of Caleb's groans. Unfortunately, however, the second random song that comes up is "Shaynee" by Red Card Riot. Their smash-hit debut single. The song that first introduced Claudia to the band when we were in middle school, which then prompted her to introduce the band to me.

Crap. The sounds of Caleb's crashing drums on the track makes me think of Caleb's muscled body. His hard dick in his huge hand. The sound of my name lurching from his tortured, groaning lips.

Fucking hell.

I should change the song.

Right away.

I really should.

But instead, I listen to the whole damned thing, three times through, while touching myself during the second cycle and making myself come during the third, the same way I did in the middle of the night. Two orgasms in a matter of hours? It's a record for me.

When I'm done pleasuring myself, I pull an earbud out and listen for any signs that Caleb is still jerking off. But the house is silent, the only sounds coming from the lake and the breeze outside.

I throw on some clothes and head to the bathroom. Thankfully, Caleb's door is still closed when I pass by, which I'm hoping means he drifted off to sleep after getting himself off.

From the bathroom, I head into the kitchen, where I make myself some jam and toast from the few supplies we brought over from my parents' house last night. I'm pretty sure Caleb didn't notice me bursting into his bedroom, so at least there's that. But, still, Caleb not knowing what I witnessed doesn't mean I didn't witness it. And, unfortunately, I'm not sure if I'll ever be able to eradicate that insanely hot image from my mind.

Movement in the doorway catches my attention. It's Caleb striding into the kitchen in gray sweats and a dark T-shirt.

"Good morning, babysitter."

"Good morning, babysittee. How'd you sleep?"

"Like a baby who's being babysat." He chuckles. "You?"

"Not great. But I never sleep well in a new place."

He indicates the half-eaten toast and jam sitting on my plate. "That looks good. Where's the bread?"

"You want the rest of mine? I took a couple bites and realized I'm not hungry."

"You sure?" When I nod, Caleb plops into a chair across from me, slides my plate to him, and takes a huge bite of toast. "Is it too early to FaceTime your dad to show him around the house? I'd love to get his take on what the place needs."

I sigh with relief. Clearly, he doesn't know I witnessed him jerking his salami this morning while groaning out my name. *Thank God.*

"My dad's an early riser," I say. "And so is Raine, so I'm sure he's up with her." I jut my chin toward his plate. "Finish eating, and we'll make the call." With that, I get up and pretend to concentrate on the business of making coffee, even though I can physically *feel* his eyes on my ass the entire time.

CHAPTER 10
CALEB

"Take my truck into Billings," Aubrey's father, Joe, insists. "Rather than your rental car. They probably won't have all the lumber you need in stock, so you'll probably have to order it. But take Big Betty into Billings, just in case."

"Big Betty?" I ask.

"That's what my father lovingly calls his truck," Aubrey interjects behind me with a laugh.

"She's my pride and joy," Joe says, matching his daughter's chuckle. "Other than you, of course, Shortcake."

I'm on a FaceTime call with Joe, standing on a patch of grass in front of my rotting deck, with Aubrey standing nearby. We've just finished giving Joe a visual tour of the place, from top to bottom, and he wound up independently confirming all his daughter's suggestions from last night. Although Joe added a suggestion of his own: replacing the roof, if I decide to keep the place. I can't fault Aubrey for not including the roof on her list of suggested fixes, though, since we didn't climb up there last night in the dark. If we had, I'm sure Little Miss Meticulous Aubrey Capshaw would have mentioned that idea, too. As I'm beginning to learn, Aubrey is nothing if not thorough.

Joe says, "If you send me the dimensions of the deck you're planning to build, I'll write up a list of materials you'll need to show the lumber guy in Billings."

"Thanks, Joe. I appreciate that. I'll take you up on Big Betty, too. Even if it turns out I can't get all the lumber in Billings today, I'm gonna get myself a drum kit and some workout gear today, so I'll definitely put your truck to good use, either way."

"You're gonna buy a whole new drum kit for a three-week stay?" Aubrey asks.

I shrug. "At home, I play drums every day. I'm already going batshit crazy, after only one day of going without."

"Man, I wish I could be a fly on the wall when you play," Joe says wistfully.

"Come watch me, anytime."

"Really? Okay, I will!"

I chuckle at his exuberance. "Do you play?"

"I wish. I've always loved live music, though. Especially classic rock."

"That's my jam, too. I tell you what. Whenever you're feeling up to it, I'll give you a drum lesson to thank you for loaning me Big Betty. Pick your favorite song, and I'll teach you how to drum to it."

Joe gasps. "Seriously? Holy shit, C-Bomb! Thank you. But only if you promise to call me, anytime, whenever you need help with the deck."

"Deal."

"Well, isn't this a lovefest," Aubrey teases. "Hey, Dad, does Mom work today? How long can we stay in Billings before you'll need us to come back to pick up Raine?"

"Stay as long as you like, Shortcake," Joe replies. "Yeah,

Mom's working today, and then she's got a committee meeting for the festival. But I've gotten pretty good on my crutches, so I can watch Rainey on my own, just fine." After we thank Joe, he adds, "When will you be coming by for Big Betty? I'll make sure Raine's had breakfast by then, so she's not cranky when you come."

Aubrey giggles. "Thank you. God knows, Caleb doesn't need to meet Hangry Rainey any time soon."

"I'll take her, any way I can get her," I say.

Aubrey looks unconvinced. But what she says is, "When will you be done with your counseling session?"

"Ten. It starts at nine and lasts a full hour."

Aubrey returns to her father on my phone. "Caleb has a Zoom call he needs to do till ten, Daddy, so we'll be there around 10:30 or so to pick up Big Betty."

"I'll have the munchkin ready to say hi to you."

"Make sure to tell her Mommy's nice friend, Caleb, who colored with her yesterday, will be coming over again. You know how shy she can be. Let's get her primed and ready for him."

"Got it."

"Thanks, Joe. I appreciate that."

"Oh, Rainey just walked in and heard your voices. She wants to say hi."

My heart rate quickens. But when Raine's big, blue eyes appear on my screen, it's instantly clear she only wants to say hi to her "Auntie Aubbey," and not to me.

"Hey, baby girl!" Aubrey coos to the little face on my screen. "Did you have fun with Grammy and Pop-Pop last night?"

"We pwayed Hungwy, Hungwy Hippos!"

"You did? I *love* that game. Do you remember my friend, Caleb, here?"

"Hi, Raine," I say, my heart hammering, as I try to flash her my least scary smile.

Raine doesn't reply to me, so Aubrey quickly says, "Maybe Caleb can play Hungry, Hungry Hippos with us sometime soon." But Raine is already gone—headed off to wordlessly follow whatever muse has diverted her two-year-old mind.

"She can't get enough of me," I deadpan, making Aubrey and Joe chuckle in concert.

"It's going to take some time," Aubrey says, patting my forearm. And just like that, the same electricity I felt last night at Aubrey's touch returns with a vengeance.

As Aubrey wraps up the call with her father, I hand the phone to her and move a few steps away, in case my body reacts the same way it did in that hallway last night. And a few minutes later, when Aubrey returns my darkened phone to me, I say, "I've got an hour before my Zoom call, so I think I'll take a walk while making a couple important phone calls."

"Give me a second to throw on my sneakers, and I'll be right back to walk with you."

"That wasn't an invitation. My phone calls are of a personal nature."

Aubrey shrugs. "For the next three weeks, I go where you go."

I look at her incredulously. "I'm going to walk the dirt path around the lake. Last time I checked, there weren't any liquor stores or weed dispensaries on the trail."

Aubrey shakes her head. "I took your word for it last night, by necessity, but that was the last time. When I send in that form every night, swearing under oath you were in my line of sight all day and never had access to drugs or alcohol the whole time, I want to be one-hundred-percent certain my statements are the absolute truth."

"This is overkill, Aubrey."

"You're famous, Caleb. For all I know, you might walk past some rowdy bachelor party, or maybe a group of women having mimosas on their deck, and when someone recognizes you, they'll invite you to join their party."

I exhale in frustration. "You're not going to let me out of your sight, even once, for the next three weeks?"

"I mean, you can go to the bathroom on your own. But only if I'm sure you're not smuggling something in there. You can also go to bed on your own every night, but only after I've done a sweep of your room and confiscated your car keys."

"*My car keys?*"

"After we said good night last night, I realized I should have done that. I blew it."

"You don't need my keys."

"What if you get the bright idea to wait for me to fall asleep, so you can drive into town? It's in your best interest for me to have your keys, just in case."

"Jesus Christ."

"To answer your question from before, yes, Caleb, I'm going to be stuck to you like glue at all waking moments, other than the scenarios I've mentioned, including trailing you on your little nature walk this morning. Don't worry, I'll stay far enough back not to overhear whatever you're saying to your girlfriend or whoever. In fact, I'll put in my earbuds and listen to loud music, if you like. But you can't get rid of me, whether you like it or not, so you might as well stop fighting it."

Aubrey rambles on for a bit longer, but I tune her out and let my thoughts spiral, the second she uses the word *girlfriend*. Maybe I'm reading too much into that word, but I can't help thinking that was Aubrey's subtle attempt, whether conscious or not, at finding out if I'm single. Now, why would Aubrey want to know about that? Could it be, when she barged into my bedroom and gaped at my hard dick in my hand this morning, I made an unforgettable impression on her? That was my plan, of course, when I purposefully groaned out her name, loud enough for her to hear. Did my diabolical plan work like a charm?

"I don't have a girlfriend," I say evenly, trying not to accompany the comment with a smirk. "Haven't had one for a very long time."

"Not that I care."

My smirk breaks free. *Sure, Aubrey*. "If you must know," I say, my skin tingling at the blush in her cheeks, "I need to call my sister and let her know I've got a toddler I've never bothered to tell her or my mother about. And after that hard call, I'll need to call my attorney and get an update on the lawsuit."

Aubrey perks up. "Can I listen in on the phone call with your lawyer?"

"No. But I'll give you a recap afterwards about anything that affects you."

"Everything regarding Raine affects me, Caleb. I'm the closest thing she's got to a parent."

The comment stabs me in the heart; but I can't deny the truth of it.

"I promise to tell you everything you need to know. But you can't listen in, or else the attorney-client privilege goes up in smoke."

Aubrey narrows her eyes. "Don't screw me over, Caleb. I swear to God, if you make me regret helping you get close to Raine—"

"I won't screw you over, Aubrey. I promise on my mother. I've seen how much Raine loves you and your family. I understand that fucking you over would mean fucking Raine over, and I'd never do that."

Aubrey assesses me with dark, piercing eyes for a long beat, before finally murmuring, "If I find out you're not telling me the truth, if you're simply using me with the intent to discard me later, then I'm going to fight you tooth and nail, when the time comes."

"I'm telling you the truth."

Aubrey gnaws at her lip for a long moment while assessing me. Finally, she says, "If you're gonna make your Zoom call, you'd better get walking. Can we make it around the entire lake in time for your counseling session?"

"Not even close. I'll turn around and head back at the right time."

"I'll set a timer and let you know when it goes off." She presses a few buttons on her phone, her tongue jutting to the side with concentration, and when she looks back up, she frowns at whatever she's seeing on my face. "What?" she barks out. "Why are you smiling at me like that?"

I didn't realize I was smiling, so I don't know how to answer the question, other than to say, "I'm just amused by what a little rule follower you are." Is that really the source of my grin, though? More likely than that, I think I'm just impressed with this woman, period. She's a force of nature, wrapped up in the hottest little package I've ever beheld. Who wouldn't smile at the sight of her kicking ass and taking names?

"Please, stop fighting me, Caleb," she says on an exhale. "If I don't follow the rules, the rehab center won't certify your rehab, and the judge—"

"I know all that, Aubrey. No need to say it out loud." I

make a shooing motion. "Go on. Get your shoes on, babysitter, or I'm leaving without you."

With a little gasp of excitement, she turns and bounds away, her hot little ass a work of art as she goes; and a moment later, she reappears in white sneakers, workout shorts and a tank top, with her dark hair pulled back into a ponytail. When she reaches me, Aubrey stuffs earbuds into her ears and makes a big show of turning on a playlist on her phone.

"Ready," she chirps. "Lead on."

With a deep sigh, I grab my earbuds from my pocket, slide them into my ears, and head to the dirt trail that follows the lake's shoreline; and when I've checked behind me and confirmed Aubrey's indeed trailing behind by about twenty yards, I place a FaceTime call to my sister, Miranda —a call I'm deeply dreading. She's undoubtedly going to ream me. And when she does, I'll one-hundred-percent deserve it.

CHAPTER II
CALEB

France is eight hours ahead of Prairie Springs, so I texted my sister yesterday evening, while she was fast asleep, that I'd be FaceTiming her around 4:00 pm Paris time to get her up to speed on something important.

"Hey," Miranda says, answering my call. She's got a full face of makeup and the top of whatever she's wearing is sparkly. Clearly, she's dressed to paint Paris red with the group of girlfriends she flew there with the other day. "Is this about selling the cabin?"

"No. I haven't decided about that yet."

Concern flickers across Miranda's face. "What, then?"

I flap my lips together. "I'm just gonna cut to the chase, because there's no easy way to say this." I inhale deeply. "I've got a two-year-old daughter named Raine. I came to Prairie Springs yesterday to meet her for the first time, and I found out she's incredible, Miranda. An angel on Earth."

I've done the impossible: rendered my chatty, vivacious sister speechless. After a moment, however, Miranda gathers herself enough to express confusion and shock about my revelation. She demands details, which I provide in a long ramble. And by the time I'm finished talking, my sister is no longer shocked and confused. She's flat-out *enraged* by my secrecy before now.

"You're telling me Mom died without knowing she had a granddaughter?" Miranda shouts at top volume. "Caleb Baumgarten, how could be so heartless and selfish?"

I try to explain myself, as best I can, but even as I try to defend myself, my sorry excuses sound hollow and insufficient, even to me. "If it matters," I say, "I reached out to Raine's mother, Claudia, about six months after Raine's birth, asking to fly both of them down to my house to meet you and Mom, but Claudia told me to fuck off. When I reached out again a few months later, it turned out she'd blocked me."

"And that stopped you?" Miranda bellows, tears streaming down her cheeks. "If you really wanted to meet your child—Mom's *grandchild*—you could have flown to Seattle to try to convince Claudia in person."

"You're right. I should have done that. In my defense, Mom was really sick by then, and I didn't feel like I had the emotional bandwidth to try and possibly fail. I didn't want to give Mom false hope, if things didn't work out." When my sister glares at me, I rough a hand down my face. "I'm sorry, Miranda. I fucked up. When I found out she'd blocked me, I decided to leave it alone till Mom got better and try again later." I swallow hard. "But, of course, Mom never got better, so . . ."

Miranda bursts into sobs, and the already jagged pieces of my heart scraping inside my chest cavity shatter a bit more. "All those times I visited you in rehab," she says, "you never once thought to mention—"

"I'm sorry, Miranda. I was selfish and stupid."

"No, you were beyond selfish and stupid. You were cruel and heartless. An asshole-douchebag!"

"I don't know if you'll ever be able to forgive me, but I promise I'll never lie to you again."

Miranda wipes a tear. "If you do, you're fucking dead to me, Caleb."

"I understand." She's said that before, but she's never once followed through with it. For reasons I'll never understand, my sister always defends me. Always supports me. No matter what bullshit I put her through.

Miranda inhales deeply and wipes her eyes. "How'd the meeting with Raine go yesterday? Did she like you?"

I can't help smiling at the memory. "Like is too strong a word. But she warmed up to me by the end of our first meeting." I tell my sister the whole story about Raine teaching me to color, and how brilliantly Aubrey drew Raine out of her shell, and Miranda cries throughout my entire telling.

"Goddammit, you prick," she murmurs. "You've ruined my makeup. Now, I'm gonna make all my friends wait for me, as I redo it."

"Where are you going tonight?"

"Some fancy night club. I don't know." She wipes her eyes again. "Should I cut my trip short and come to Prairie Springs?"

"No, stay there. Have fun. Once I've made some progress with Raine on my own, you can come meet her."

"Can I at least see a photo of my niece?" Miranda asks.

"Of course. I'm sure Aubrey has one. Hang on. She's walking twenty paces behind me."

"*Huh?*"

Without explaining, I turn around and discover Aubrey's kept her distance on the dirt trail, as promised.

But she's not walking calmly behind me, as expected. She's performing some kind of dance routine back there to the beat of whatever song is blaring in her earbuds. In fact, she's going all out back there: throwing up her hands, shaking her ass, performing choreography as enthusiastically as any dancer in a music video.

I wave my arm above my head to get Aubrey's attention, and when our eyes meet, she abruptly stops dancing, bursts out laughing at herself, and pulls out an earbud.

"Come say hi to my sister, Miranda!" I call out.

I don't need to ask her twice. With a huge grin on her face, Aubrey bounds happily toward me. When she comes to a stop next to me, I pull out my own earbuds, in order to put the call on speaker mode. I make all necessary introductions, and both women quickly launch into an enthusiastic conversation about how great it is to meet the other.

"Caleb said you might have a photo of Raine?" Miranda asks hopefully.

"Oh, I've got a million of them." Aubrey swipes on her phone and holds it up to display a heart-melting photo of Raine in fairy wings, and Miranda gushes and coos at the beautiful sight. Rinse and repeat. Clearly, Aubrey wasn't exaggerating when she said she's got a million photos.

"Oh!" Aubrey says, selecting another shot. "This one was taken at a pond we always went to in Seattle. Rainey loves feeding ducks." She displays the photo, eliciting predictable coos from my sister, before returning to her phone again.

Suddenly, Aubrey's vibrant smile turns wistful and sad. She looks up, her dark eyes pained. "Would it be okay if I show you a shot of Raine with her mother?"

"Please do."

Aubrey holds up the shot, and I'm met with the smiling,

pretty face of Claudia Beaumont, pressing her cheek happily against her daughter's tiny cheek.

"Claudia was my best friend since grade school," Aubrey says softly. "We grew up together in Prairie Springs."

"She was beautiful," Miranda says. "I'm so sorry for your loss, Aubrey."

"Thank you. No matter what, I want Raine to grow up knowing she had the best mommy in the world."

"She will," Miranda says. "Right, Caleb?"

"Of course. Absolutely." I've been angry with Claudia for about a year and a half now, thanks to her curt, dismissive response to my heartfelt email. But now, thanks to that smiling photo of her with her beloved toddler, my anger has given way to grief for Aubrey and Raine. Can I really blame Claudia for telling me to fuck off, after the way I'd basically told her unborn child to fuck off from day one?

I look at my sister, and the tears in her eyes reflect my own feelings back to me. I blew it. Epically. And I'll never fucking forgive myself for it.

Aubrey clears her throat. "Here's a brand-new shot. The first photo ever taken of father and daughter."

My breathing halts as I behold the stunning image of me coloring on the floor with Raine, totally unaware Aubrey was snapping a photograph. "I had no idea you took that."

"I figured you'd want to memorialize the once-in-a-lifetime moment."

I can barely breathe. "Thank you for thinking to do that, Aubrey."

Aubrey blushes and shrugs.

"Will you text that photo to me?" I choke out, feeling like my throat is closing up.

"Of course. If you don't piss me off too much before

then, I might even put it on a coffee mug for you for Father's Day."

Miranda chuckles. "I already adore you, Aubrey."

As the ladies continue talking, I stare, transfixed, at the sacred photo. But a moment later, my sister interrupts my trance by telling me she's got to go to fix her makeup, so she and her friends won't be late for their big night out.

We say our goodbyes to Miranda, and through it all, it's clear my sister's not yet ready to forgive me for keeping her niece a secret. But at least, she tells me she loves me in parting, as always, before hanging up.

After Miranda disappears from my screen, Aubrey says, "Your sister is amazing."

"Yeah, she's awesome."

My phone buzzes with a text. When I look down, it's from my sister:

Hey asshole, don't forget you're there to get to know your daughter, not to fuck her nanny. If you fuck Aubrey and then break her heart, where will that leave poor Raine? Without the one person she's got left in this world. So, please, think with your head and your heart, and not with your dick, you horny-ass motherfucker!

Jesus.

I have no idea what compelled Miranda to shoot off such an unhinged text within seconds of hanging up. Yes, I'm a horny-ass motherfucker, and my sister knows that about me. But I'm positive I didn't make my intense physical attraction to Aubrey obvious during the call. Did I?

"Oh! The timer just went off," Aubrey announces. "Time to turn around."

"Perfect timing."

Aubrey motions to the dirt path we've just traversed. "After you. And yes, I'll hang back again and listen to music."

"Actually, walk with me at first. When I texted my attorney about our arrangement yesterday, she said she wanted to meet you."

I make the call on speaker phone, and right out of the gate, Paula and Aubrey connect in a way that kind of irks me. My attorney is never warm and sweet like this to me. What the fuck?

After a bit, when the Paula-Aubrey portion of the phone call has run its course, Aubrey drops back to walk—or dance—about twenty yards behind me again, and I resume talking to my attorney in private.

"She's fucking adorable," Paula says. "Also, completely credible. At the hearing, I'm sure the judge will believe every word she says, which means you'd better make sure Aubrey likes you and believes you've got nothing but Raine's best interests at heart."

"I do."

"Good. Let's keep it that way."

At my prompting, Paula gives me an update on the lawsuit, letting me know it's going to be filed in Los Angeles before the end of the day. "As we discussed," Paula continues, "we'll ask for sole legal and physical custody for you, with full visitation rights for Aubrey. That's what you still want, now that you've met Raine?"

"Now more than ever."

"If you're not positive about that, tell me now, so I can amend the suit to support *Aubrey* having physical custody, while you get legal custody and visitation rights."

"I want my daughter, Paula, and I want Aubrey and her family to be a part of her life, forever. I don't have any doubts about that now."

Paula smiles broadly. She rarely does that, when we're talking business. But this time, my trusty attorney can't keep her excitement from lighting up her face. "Okay, I'll get the paperwork filed. In the meantime, your job is to bond with Raine before the hearing in a month. You'll need to convince the judge you're a fit father, Caleb. Your sperm fertilizing an egg isn't nearly enough to establish that."

"I know that better than anyone, thanks to my own fucking father." I glance back at Aubrey. Once again, she's in her own little world back there. "Luckily, I've got Aubrey helping me learn the ropes. She's incredible with Raine and patient with me. She really understands how to—"

"Fucking hell, Caleb. *No*. You can't have sex with Aubrey."

I'm floored. "What are you talking about? What made you say that?"

"When you said her name, you looked like a goddamned wolf in heat. Don't even try to deny it. I'm an expert at reading body language, and yours screamed, 'I want to fuck my kid's nanny!'"

I roll my eyes.

"You deny it?"

"Completely. One question, though." I smirk. "Would it fuck things up, from a legal standpoint, if I did fuck Aubrey?"

"I knew it!"

I chuckle. "Just answer the question, counselor. That's what I pay you to do."

Now it's Paula's turn to roll her eyes. "A custody hearing is like a mini-trial, Caleb, except the judge is the one who makes the decision, rather than a jury. The last thing we need is for the judge to think Aubrey's testimony has been compromised by you giving her orgasms and/or whispering sweet nothings into her ear for the past month, in order to manipulate her testimony. She's quite a bit younger than you, remember? We don't need the judge wondering if—"

"So, are you saying it'd be a bad idea because the optics wouldn't be good, or are you saying it'd be illegal?"

"It wouldn't be illegal, no. But it'd be a bad idea."

I glance back again. "Well, you'll be happy to know the odds of it happening are low, anyway. Aubrey hates my guts, so I don't think she'd say yes to me, even if I tried."

"If that changes, if Aubrey decides she can overlook her hatred of you for some meaningless fun in the sack, then, please, resist the temptation and keep your dick in your pants. This hearing is going to be contentious, and we both know you've got a horrible track record with women."

I've reached the patch of shoreline that's directly in front of my house, so I stop walking and turn to look at Aubrey on the path behind me. She's not dancing like she's in a music video any longer. She's now gazing out at the lake as she moves, looking contemplative and hot as hell.

"I've got a counseling session to attend," I say to Paula. "Keep me posted on the lawsuit."

"You and Aubrey will need to sign declarations in support of our pleadings, by the way. I'll email them to you to look over and sign today."

"I'll let Aubrey know."

"She really should have her own attorney to help her understand her rights and the process. If I find someone to represent her, will you foot the bill?"

"Why would I do that?"

"Because it's the right thing to do. Because helping Aubrey will ultimately help Raine, and you're a fit father who'll do anything to help your child and the people she loves. But also because, if Aubrey has her own legal counsel, she'll be even more credible in court, which will ultimately help your cause."

I exhale. "Fine. Do it."

"Thank you, sir. Enjoy your Zoom call."

"Can't wait."

We say our goodbyes and hang up, at which point, I beckon to Aubrey to come close. With each step she takes toward me, the more my body starts buzzing with my intense, undeniable attraction to her.

I know what Paula said about fucking Aubrey, but I can't imagine the threat of *potentially* "bad optics" keeping me from shooting my shot with her, should the opportunity arise. Last night, Aubrey brazenly stared at my hard-on, when we crashed into each other in the cramped hallway, supposedly by accident. And this morning, Aubrey rushed to my room the minute she heard me groaning out her name, exactly like I was hoping she'd do.

Sorry, Paula. If my next ploy to get Aubrey's attention, whatever it turns out to be, works out even better than the first two, I can't imagine *not* at least trying to ride that wave as far as Aubrey will let me take it.

CHAPTER 12
AUBREY

"Hey, Dad," I say, as Caleb and I walk into my parents' house to borrow Dad's truck for our drive to Billings.

"Hey," Dad replies. "The keys are on the hook." He's sitting on the couch with his leg up. In front of him, Raine sits with her dolls, stuffed animals, and plastic tea set strewn across the carpet. When she sees me, however, she gets up and bounds over.

"Hi, sweetie," I say, scooping her up and giving her a squeeze. "Remember Mommy's good friend, Caleb?" When I put her down, Raine clings to my legs and stares shyly up at Caleb's towering, tattooed figure.

To his credit, Caleb crouches down low, all the way to Raine's eye level, before greeting her softly with, "Hi, Rainey. I hope you'll color with me again soon. You're an excellent teacher."

Raine shakes her head and digs her tiny fingers into my bare thigh.

"Okay, if you don't want to color," Caleb says quickly,

"we can do anything else you want." He motions to the toys on the carpet. "We could have a tea party, maybe?"

Raine looks up at me for reassurance and I express my encouragement.

"We pway bawn?" she squeaks out.

Caleb looks simultaneously elated and confused. Happy Raine's addressed him, but baffled because he's obviously got no idea what the heck she just said to him.

"You want to play *bomb*?" Caleb asks, his brows cinched together. "Did Aubrey tell you my name is C-Bomb?" He gasps excitedly. "You want to play *drums* with me, Raine?"

Raine shakes her head and repeats herself in frustration, to no avail; so I finally decide to act as Raine's interpreter, more to ease the poor girl's frustration than Caleb's obvious cluelessness.

"She wants you to play *barn*," I clarify. "As in, barn animals."

"*Oooh*," Caleb says. "Sure. Yes. Anything you want." He cocks his head. "How, exactly, is that game played?"

Raine motions to the ground. "Get down."

When Caleb looks at me, at a loss, I snicker and explain, "She's commanding you to get down on your hands and knees, boy, and oink like a pig or moo like a cow for her pleasure."

The look of repulsion on Caleb's face makes both Dad and me cackle with laughter.

"You're jerking my chain," Caleb says.

"I'm not. If you prefer, you can bleat like a sheep or cock-a-doodle-doo like a rooster. Bonus points for oinking like a pig, though. Raine loves pigs the most, for some reason, even more than ducks."

Dad chimes in, "Probably because I always sing her the little piggy song about her toes."

"That's got to be it," I agree. I return to Caleb with a grin. "How much do you want to bond with her, Caleb? It's time to walk the walk, babe."

"I tell you what," Caleb says to Raine. "We'll play barn at my house tonight. There's a lake there, with a nice little shoreline, so maybe we can also play with your tea set and make cakes in the sand. My little sister, Miranda, used to love doing that when she was little."

Caleb looks at me for reassurance, but I give him nothing. I've agreed to help him, yes; but I can't *do* it for him. Sooner rather than later, if this man truly wants to become a father—a real daddy—then he's going to have to learn to humble himself in all new ways.

"Pway bawn *now*?" Raine asks, looking up at me.

I pat her head. "No, love. Caleb and I have to go shopping now, while you stay here with Pop-Pop. But guess what we can do after we come back? *Feed ducks at Caleb's house.*"

Raine gasps. "*Duckies?*"

"I saw some on the lake this morning, so we'll be sure to bring duck food for them, when we go back there tonight."

Raine's suddenly all-in, and Caleb looks relieved and grateful for my intervention.

We say our goodbyes to Dad, who insists on Caleb driving Big Betty throughout the entirety of his stay in Prairie Springs. "I can't drive for several months," Dad says. "No need for you to keep paying for a rental car." Dad says he's got a buddy who works near the airport with his adult son, so returning Caleb's rental car will be easy enough. And just like that, it's settled. Caleb will be driving Big Betty for the foreseeable future.

After we grab the car keys off the hook, Caleb says goodbye to Raine, far too enthusiastically, and Raine reflexively cowers next to my father, rather than returning his enthusiastic sentiments.

"Shit, I suck at this," Caleb murmurs, as the screen door *thwaps* behind us.

"She's just really shy."

"Hey, guys!" Dad yells from inside. "Come back in here! Raine wants to say something to Caleb!"

We barrel back inside, wide-eyed, and stare expectantly at Raine.

"Go on, cutie pie," Dad prompts. "Say, 'Bye-bye, Caleb,' like you just did. Only a little louder this time."

"Bye-bye, Coobie," Raine says, so quietly, we almost miss it; but based on Caleb's over-the-top reaction, she might as well have just screamed the words, thrown her little arms around Caleb's neck, and laid a big fat kiss on his bearded cheek.

"Bye-bye, Rainey," Caleb chokes out with a tight little wave. "See you later. Can't wait to feed those duckies with you."

"Come on, Coobie," I say, pulling on him. "She can smell the desperation on you."

We head outside again.

"*Desperation*?" Caleb asks.

"Yes."

He scoffs. "In the beginning, I didn't try hard enough, and now I'm too desperate?"

"Don't hate the player. Hate the game."

"Seriously, I don't understand what I'm supposed to do here."

"Just, you know, be yourself and keep showing up. I know you want this, but you can't act like you're desperate for her to like you, or she'll sniff it on you and get the ick."

Caleb exhales. "I *am* desperate for her to like me, though."

We stop in front of Dad's truck and he motions to the keys in my hand.

"Can I drive?"

"Please do. I hate driving." I toss him the keys and walk around to the passenger side.

"Seriously, Aubrey. Tell me exactly what I'm supposed to do here."

"Just show your authentic personality a bit more, or else she'll know you're kissing her little ass and she won't respect you."

"She's *two*."

"Which is old enough to lose respect for you, if you kiss her ass."

We slide into our respective seats, with Caleb sighing and exhaling in frustration.

When we're both situated, he grumbles, "The truth is, the most authentic version of me is desperate for Raine to like me."

It's the most vulnerable he's looked in my presence. Feeling a touch of compassion for his plight, I pat his tattooed forearm. "I know, Coobie. I'm sure you feel like you're between a rock and a hard place."

He nods. "Time is ticking. The hearing's in a month."

"I know, but Rome wasn't built in a day. Keep showing up and being yourself, as best you can, and soon, she won't be able to resist you."

The vulnerability he displayed a moment ago evaporates, replaced by swagger. "Tell me, babysitter," he says, his tone flirtatious. "Does that same strategy work on big girls, too?"

I roll my eyes. "Just drive, Coobie. It takes an hour to get to Billings, and that's the maximum amount of time I can sit next to you in a locked car without giving in to the impulse to strangle you to death."

Caleb chuckles. "You know the expression, 'The lady doth protest too much?' That's you, *Aubbey*."

"You know the expression, 'Shut the fuck up and drive, motherfucker?' That's you, *Coobie*."

He guffaws. "That's no way to talk to your boss, Miss Capshaw."

"You're not my boss. You're my . . . what's the name for someone I'm required to watch over?"

"Your hostage?"

"My *ward*. You're my ward, and I'm your guardian. We're emphatically *not* boss and employee."

"No? I'm paying for services rendered."

"If you paid someone to give you piano lessons, would they be your employee? No, they'd be your *teacher*. That's me, except I'm giving you *Raine* lessons. Becoming-a-good-daddy lessons. *Being-a-good-and-responsible-person-instead-of-an-entitled-rockstar-manc-child* lessons."

To my surprise, Caleb cracks up again. "Glad to hear it. That's a huge relief, honestly."

I turn to look at him, confused. I just insulted the man, after all. Why isn't he mad at me? "What's a relief?"

"That you don't consider me to be your boss." He flashes a wicked grin. "I'm pretty sure it's a no-no for a *boss* to want to fuck his *employee*, after all."

My jaw hangs open as my cheeks burst into flames. "In your dreams, Coobie."

"Yeah, literally, in my case." He winks. "Last night, as a matter of fact." He leans toward me. "Want to hear about my sex dream? It was scorching hot and about *you*."

Holy shit. Does this mean Caleb saw me when I barged

in on him, stroking his dick and groaning out my name? Or is it pure coincidence he's bringing up having a sex dream about me now?

I scoff. "No, I don't want to hear about that, even a little bit." It's a bald-faced lie, but a necessary one. No matter what, I'm determined not to give in to my shocking, detestable impulse to tackle this man and do every imaginable thing with the hard dick I witnessed him stroking this morning.

He winks. "Okay, well, if that changes, let me know."

"It won't." I've said that with more confidence than I feel, but there's no way I'm going to let this egomaniac know his magnetism is working on me. I motion to the dangling keys in the ignition. "Are you going to drive us to Billings, or am I going to spend the rest of the day, sitting in my parents' driveway, trying my damnedest to overcome the urge to strangle you?"

With another chuckle, one that makes me feel certain Caleb knows his charisma is working its magic on me, Caleb turns the ignition and pulls out of my parents' driveway. And the moment we break eye contact and I'm no longer required to maintain the mask of disdain I've been wearing throughout this entire back and forth, I turn toward the passenger-side window and let loose the beaming smile I've been holding back through sheer force of will—the grin that's been threatening to break free, ever since Caleb admitted he thinks of himself as a *boss* who wants to fuck his *employee*.

CHAPTER 13
AUBREY

"Now, *this* is a truck," Caleb says. We've made it to I-90, the interstate that leads straight into Billings, and Caleb can't stop talking about how much he loves driving my dad's old tank of a truck.

"Isn't she great?" I tap on Big Betty's dashboard with my knuckle. "Dad's had her forever, and she just keeps on chugging."

"They sure don't make 'em like this anymore."

"Dad always says the same thing. Whenever he needs to buy a new truck, he's going to get the brand-new version of this one."

"How soon is he planning on getting a new truck? Whenever he does, I'd be tempted to buy this one off him and pay whatever it takes to get it refurbished." He pauses. "I mean, assuming I've kept the cabin, of course."

Crap. Why hasn't Caleb made up his mind about that, when it would be in everyone's best interest for him to keep the lake house? There's no place quite like Prairie Springs, especially for raising a kid. Why can't he see that? "I don't know when Dad will be able to afford a new truck, now that he's injured. I guess we can cross that bridge, if you decide to keep the lake house."

A short silence looms between us.

Caleb adjusts his hands on the steering wheel. Clears his throat. "So, tell me, Aubrey, do *you* have a boyfriend?"

I snort-laugh. "You said that like we were in the middle of a conversation, and I'd just asked you the same question in reverse."

"You did ask me the same question. Earlier today, right before our walk around the lake. Remember?"

I pull a face. "And you're only now getting around to throwing the question back at me?"

"I had some phone calls to make, remember? Also, you were annoying the fuck out of me with your goody-two-shoes routine, so I didn't feel like talking to you anymore."

I scoff. "If not being willing to lie under oath makes me a goody two shoes, I'll wear that as a badge of honor."

Caleb rolls his eyes. "Do you have a boyfriend or not?"

"Why so testy?"

"Just answer the question."

"Why do you want to know?"

"Why did you want to know the same thing about me?"

"I didn't. Don't."

"Then why'd you ask me the question?"

"I don't think I did. I think I assumed one of your calls might be to a girlfriend, and you corrected me."

"Same thing."

"Not at all."

"Just answer the fucking question, for fuck's sake. Jesus Aubrey. Whether you asked me directly or not, you still got the information out of me. Fair is fair."

I release a dramatic sigh, even though I'm feeling nothing but amused by his ornery tone. "No, I don't have a boyfriend. I broke up with the only boyfriend I've ever had coming up on two years ago."

Caleb looks pleased. "How long were you with him?"

"From our junior year of high school to almost two years ago, so you do the math."

Caleb smirks. "Young love. It hardly ever lasts."

"Especially when your boyfriend smacks you hard across the cheek during an argument."

Caleb's lips part. He looks from the highway to me again. This time, with blazing green eyes. "Your ex *hit* you?"

"Slapped me. With an open palm."

"Did he do that regularly?"

"Just the once. But that was enough for me."

"Damn straight, it was."

"I broke up with him that same night and never took him back, despite him groveling and begging for months."

Caleb lets out a slow exhale, like he's trying not to flip his lid. "I'm sorry that happened to you, but I'm proud of you for not giving him a second chance. Those types never change, no matter how much they promise they will."

"That's why I left Prairie Springs and went to live with Claudia in Seattle. I wanted a fresh start."

Caleb's face goes dark. "He lives in Prairie Springs?"

I can't help smiling. Caleb suddenly looks like a bomb-sniffing dog on a scent. "He used to. He moved away, shortly after I did. He worked construction for my dad while we dated, so when he slapped the boss's daughter, he needed to find a new job, *pronto*." Trent moved to Billings, actually. The city we're driving toward right now. Or so I've been told by Trent's sister. But based on Caleb's murderous expression, I'm thinking it's probably not the best idea to tell Caleb that additional fact.

"I bet your dad wanted to fucking kill him."

"He sure did."

"Were there any red flags? Or did the smack come out of nowhere?"

"There were red flags, yeah; but I ignored them. Little by little, Trent kept crossing lines and pushing the envelope; until one night: *bam*. I tried to grab his phone out of his hand because I thought he'd been texting with another girl, and he slapped me across the face so fucking hard, I stumbled back and fell to the ground."

"Jesus fucking Christ. Did you press charges?"

I shake my head. "I was too embarrassed. Prairie Springs is a small town, and everyone loves Trent and his family."

Caleb releases a long, slow exhale through his nose. "That's how it was with my mother. My father smacked her around for years, and she never reported him."

"I'm so sorry."

"When I started making good money, I told my mother, 'No more excuses. It's time to leave him for good.' And she finally did."

My heart squeezes at the look of pride on his face. Clearly, this story—the fact that he was able to help his mother get away from her abuser—means a lot to him. "It sounds like you were a great son."

Caleb glances at me, his green eyes pained. "Not when it mattered the most, unfortunately."

I should probably leave it alone and not ask for details, due to the tortured expression on his face. But I can't help myself; I'm too damned curious. "What does that mean?"

Caleb takes a moment to collect his thoughts, his eyes trained on the highway. Finally, he says, "After my mom got cancer, I moved her into my place, and I was by her side through everything. The band took a hiatus, since I didn't want to travel. We said no to everything." He sighs. "But when we were offered a performance slot at a big awards show in New York, my mom told me to go. She said she'd be fine. She wanted to watch me on TV. So, off I went. And it was that very night when Mom unexpectedly took her last breath, while I was three thousand miles away and couldn't hold her hand, like I'd promised to do."

My heart is hammering. "You couldn't have known."

Caleb turns from the road to me, his green eyes tortured. "It wasn't a one-off, Aubrey. Me, not being there for someone I love." He returns his gaze to the road. "Honestly, it was the latest in a long line of fuck-ups."

"She told you to go. It's what she wanted."

His jaw clenches. "Doesn't matter. I promised I'd be there when she took her last breath, and I broke that promise to her and to myself. Unfortunately, it was totally on-brand for me, though." He swallows hard. "Before that, I didn't step up to become a father to Raine. I hid her existence from my family and friends. Before that, I pissed off my bandmates, time and again, in ways big and small, because I didn't give a shit about anyone but myself. Before that, it was betraying the only girl I've ever truly loved. Before that..."

The only girl I've ever truly loved. Caleb is still talking, but those words suddenly have my undivided attention.

"So, you see," Caleb says in wrap-up. "My fuck-up with my mother, my fuck-up with Raine . . . It's all consistent with my lifelong MO of letting people down."

I take a deep breath. "Humans aren't perfect. We make mistakes. The good news is you came here to correct your mistakes with respect to Raine. Let that be the beginning of a new era for you."

Caleb silently takes the exit off the freeway for Billings,

and we're both quiet for several minutes, during which my mind races about that same item on Caleb's long list of mistakes. *Before that, it was betraying the only girl I've ever truly loved.* Who was she? How and why did he betray her?

Finally, as we're driving down a major street in Billings, I gather the courage to ask about the titillating topic. "How'd you betray the only girl you've ever truly loved? Did you cheat on her?"

"Yes, but it was worse than that."

I gasp. "*You hit her?*"

Caleb abruptly swivels his face toward me, his green eyes flashing. "Absolutely not. I'd never do that."

I sigh with relief. "What's worse than cheating? Did you cheat with her sister or best friend?"

Caleb stops the truck at a red light and stares ahead through the windshield. When he doesn't speak, I prompt, "How long ago was this?" Still no reply. "Come on, Caleb. I already hate you, so this couldn't possibly change my already horrible opinion of you."

To my relief, Caleb smirks at my comment. If I'd said the same words to him yesterday, I'm not sure they would have come across as a joke. Today, however . . . I'm not sure "hatred" still exists in this space, and I'm sure Caleb can feel that. Do I respect this man to my left? No. Do I like him? Not quite. But now that I've seen glimpses of actual vulnerability and humanity in his eyes, I have to admit I've softened toward him a teeny-tiny bit.

"When did it happen?" I prompt softly. "Let's start with that."

"When I was in my early twenties."

"So, like, well over a decade ago? That's a long time, Caleb."

"And yet, I think about it almost every day."

The light turns green and we're off again; and a moment later, Caleb is parking the truck in front of our first destination of the day: a big-box home improvement store. Conveniently, it's located kitty-corner from the music store where Caleb plans to buy himself a drum kit, so we'll quickly be able to check off our first two errands before piling back into the truck to drive across town to the sporting goods store.

"Will you tell me what happened?" I ask, as Caleb turns off the truck, making its big engine falls silent.

Caleb sighs. "There's no point, Aubrey. All you need to know is I've hurt anyone who's dared to love me, other than the guys in my band and a small handful of good friends." He scoffs. "Although I guess I've fucked over my bandmates now, too, with my stunt in New York. Thanks to me, we can't get insured for a tour, till I complete rehab."

"Which you're working on."

"We had to cancel some really big things, thanks to me."

"You'll do them another time." I touch his arm. "Addiction isn't voluntary or spiteful. It's a disease. I'm sure your bandmates understand that."

He shakes his head. "The thing is, I'm not an addict. I could see the difference between myself and other people in rehab. To some degree, I've *chosen* to be a dick. *Chosen* to let people down. *Chosen* to be out of control and selfish." Emotion washes over his rugged features. "That's why I'm so determined to make things right with Raine. This is my big chance to finally do something right and good. To become the man my mother thought I was, all along."

I bite the inside of my cheek, feeling touched by his vulnerability. "How have all the rest of your romantic relationships gone for you, since that one in your twenties?

Have you cheated on all your girlfriends, ever since, or have you grown and matured?"

"I've only ever had the one girlfriend."

My lips part in surprise. "You haven't had a single girlfriend in over a decade?"

"I mean, I've dated, sure, but I've never promised anyone exclusivity again. My word is worth shit, so why bother?"

Does that mean he's only ever *loved* that one time, too? That'd be a shocking thing for a man of thirty-five. Add to that, the fact that he's been traveling the world with his band all that time, probably doing what he did with Claudia on a running loop, and I suddenly feel like I've got a much better understanding of this man. The rockstar who didn't bother to ask for Claudia's phone number or to meet with his child before now.

Caleb looks out his side of the truck. "I've always known I'm no good at giving love," he says softly. "And that I'm not a good bet for anyone giving it to me. So, why bother and waste everyone's time, you know?"

Oh, my heart.

I touch his tattooed arm, making him look at me. "My mother is a school counselor, and she always says, 'If you keep telling yourself something, then it becomes the truth. And then, it stays the truth, until you start telling yourself something different.'" He seems receptive, so I add, "Since your brain is always going to tell yourself stuff, because that's how brains work, then why not *choose* to tell yourself something good? Something productive? 'I've turned over a new leaf. I'm committed to becoming a better man, a great father. A great friend, bandmate, and brother.' Maybe even a great boyfriend or husband one day. Why not? Everyone deserves love,

Caleb." I grin sympathetically. "Even someone as horrible as you."

Caleb can't keep himself from returning my smile, though he's clearly trying not to do it.

"Manifestation," he says softly. "My sister believes in that shit, too."

"So did Claudia. And look what she accomplished. With the help of your money, she manifested a whole new life for herself and Raine. Plus, she got her mother away from her abusive father."

He lights up. "Seriously?"

"And before that, Claudia finagled her way backstage at her favorite band's show and wound up having sex with her biggest celebrity crush. So, seriously, don't knock manifestation till you've tried it." Thick silence fills the cab of the truck, and it occurs to me I totally ruined the vibe by mentioning Caleb having sex with Claudia. But if Caleb truly is planning to raise Raine for the rest of his life, then, sorry, he needs to understand how amazing and wonderful Raine's mommy really was. "I don't know how much you remember about Claudia," I begin. "But she was—"

"Nothing much," Caleb interrupts. "I was shitfaced when I hooked up with her. Honestly, it's all a blur." He pauses, apparently lost in thought. "I remember smoking a blunt with a pretty blonde in Seattle and talking about Prairie Springs, though. When my lawyer showed me Claudia's photo, I remembered that part. But that's about it."

I should feel offended on Claudia's behalf. Or maybe vicarious disappointment for her. And yet, the overwhelming emotion I'm feeling is relief that Caleb doesn't stroke that big dick of his while fantasizing about Claudia, the pretty blonde he banged in Seattle. Claudia, the girl all the boys wanted when we were growing up together in

Prairie Springs. Surely, Caleb groans out a different name, every time he strokes that big, thick dick of his; but I can't deny, as I'm sitting here next to him, it's a massive relief to find out he groaned out *my* name before ever groaning out Claudia's.

"Listen, about Claudia," Caleb says. "I know she was your best friend, and you feel loyalty to her; but you have to understand, to me, she was—"

As he's talking, my eyes happen to lock onto a figure exiting the music store across the street; and the moment my eyes relay the man's identity to my brain, I gasp loudly, interrupting Caleb, mid-sentence. Throwing my palm over my mouth, I slump down in my seat to avoid being seen.

"What?" Caleb blurts. "What's wrong?" He turns his head to follow the trajectory of my gaze, to where my ex-boyfriend, Trent, has now stopped a few feet away from the music store entrance to tap out something on his phone. Caleb motions to Trent. "That guy there?"

I nod and whimper. "That's Trent. My ex-boyfriend."

Caleb practically snarls. "*The one who punched you?*"

"Slapped me, yes. Very hard." I slump down even more and a little squeak escapes my throat. What are the odds in a city of a hundred thousand? Although Trent loves music and plays guitar, so I guess—

Without warning, Caleb unfastens his seatbelt and swings his car door open with a kind of ferocious, alpha-dog energy that makes it clear he's not planning to invite Trent for a friendly beer.

"Where are you going?" I blurt, causing Caleb to lower his face into the opened door frame.

"I'm going to teach our buddy Trent a much-needed lesson about karma." With that, he slams the door and marches across the street, while I inch up higher in my seat, enough to peek over the dashboard and watch whatever's going to happen next.

With my heart going a mile a minute, I watch Caleb, a man on a mission, stride over to Trent. When Caleb reaches his destination, he says something that makes Trent look up from his phone and instantly go wide-eyed. It wouldn't surprise me if Trent has instantly recognized Caleb. He's a musician himself who loves music and music pop culture; and I know for a fact Red Card Riot is one of his all-time favorite—

Holy fuck! Out of nowhere, Caleb just slapped Trent, hard, across the cheek, making him recoil, stumble back, and drop his phone!

I yelp in shock. But only a fraction of a second later, my shock morphs into glee, which prompts me to laugh out loud, involuntarily, at the sheer absurdity of the delicious moment. Seriously, if I'd taken a sip of water immediately before that slap, I would have done a spit-take.

Without another word being exchanged, Caleb trots back to the truck with a wicked grin on his face that makes me guffaw again. This time, he comes around to my side of the truck. After opening the door, he leans his full head into the opening and flashes me a beaming smile that takes my breath away. "You're welcome." He winks.

"You shouldn't have done that," I blurt, even though I'm elated he did. I peek toward the scene of the crime again, and thankfully, Trent is scurrying away at a hurried clip, rather than coming over here to do God knows what in retaliation. "Caleb, you can't walk around slapping people on the street." I don't know why I'm flogging him, when all I want to do is high-five him. But that's what my knee-jerk reaction is, so I guess I'm committed now.

Caleb looks at me like I've got two heads. "That

douchebag slapped you, Aubrey. He deserved that and more."

I can't suppress my smile, even though I don't want to give Caleb a free pass for what he did. Was it delightful? Yes. But it was also a totally unhinged thing for him to do, especially considering his celebrity status. Has he forgotten about Ralph Beaumont and the custody hearing in a month? "What if Trent sues you?"

"He won't."

"You don't know that."

"Yes, I do, because suing me would require him to admit what he did to you. And I assure you, he doesn't want to do that." Caleb smirks. "Either way, it was totally worth it. If he sues me, I'll pay him off, like all the rest."

"*All the rest*? How many people have you slapped on the street like that?"

"Nobody. Not like that. But over the span of my life, I've definitely beaten the shit out of more than a couple people who totally deserved it."

I hate myself for it, but my body is having a tingling, physical reaction to that revelation. I'm never attracted to bad boys. Loose cannons. Men with anger management issues. But, damn, I'm finding it difficult not to be attracted to *this* one.

I bite my lower lip, trying to stifle my satisfied smile. "What'd you say to Trent, right before you slapped him?"

Caleb chuckles at the memory. "I said, 'Hey, *Trent*.' And he goes, '*C-Bomb*? Whoa!'"

Caleb mimics Trent's starstruck facial expression, and there's no doubt in my mind Trent's brain melted into a puddle of goo in that moment.

With a snicker, Caleb continues, "When he put out his

hand to shake mine, I said, 'This is for Aubrey Capshaw, you little bitch.' And then, I bitch-slapped him."

I burst out laughing, along with Caleb. What must Trent have been thinking in that shockingly outrageous moment? I'm sure he felt thoroughly disoriented and confused.

"Man, I wish you could have seen the look on his face when I slapped him," Caleb says with a chuckle. "It was . . ." He makes a classic "chef's kiss" gesture.

On a personal level, I'm feeling nothing but delighted by this unexpected gift of sweet revenge. But in the context of the impending custody hearing, his behavior was totally unacceptable. "Sorry to seem ungrateful," I say. "But with Ralph coming after Raine, you can't do that kind of thing. In a month, you have to convince the judge you're a fit father, remember?"

"Don't you think a fit father would defend his daughter, if some guy smacked the shit out of her?"

"In the moment? Yes. But two years later, that's cold-hearted revenge, Caleb."

"Justified, though."

"I'm not your daughter. You don't even know me."

He's not persuaded by my logic. Clearly, he thinks what he did was totally in the right. But after a bit, when I maintain stern eye contact and don't back down, his gleeful smile slowly fades. "He won't come after me. But your point is well taken. I'll be much more careful next time, in light of the hearing."

"There can't be a next time! That's my entire point!"

Caleb shakes his head. "Sorry not sorry, Aubrey. If I find out a guy has laid hands on one of mine, then there's gonna be a next time."

One of mine. Not gonna lie, his word choice makes my ovaries vibrate with lust. Nevertheless, I still manage a stern facial expression when I say, "That's all well and good under normal circumstances. But not when you're in the middle of a custody dispute for Raine. Prioritize and channel your anger, for her sake. *Please.* You're not some random guy. You're a celebrity with deep pockets. You attract attention, Caleb."

"No need to beat a fucking dead horse, Aubrey. I heard you. I get it."

"Do you?" My amusement vanishes. "We won't get a second chance to convince the judge you're worthy of Raine, and I can't beat Ralph on my own. I can't let you fuck this up for me. Fuck it up for yourself, all you want, since that's your *brand*. But don't fuck it up for me."

We stare at each other, both of our chests heaving.

"*I won't fuck this up*," Caleb grits out, his green eyes flashing. "Like I said, Trent won't come after me, 'cause he won't want to admit he slapped the shit out of you. Why would he ever want to admit he assaulted the sweetest, hottest girl in the entire fucking world? It's not gonna happen, Aubrey. I'd bet my life on it. So, give it a fucking rest."

My heart stops. Sweetest? *Hottest? Entire world?*

I should be pissed about his certainty. His grouchiness. His loose-cannon behavior. But I'm suddenly feeling nothing but electrified.

"You saw the way he skittered away like a cockroach, rather than staying to fight back?" Caleb says, apparently unaware he's unleashed a torrent of energy coursing through my veins. "In my vast experience with this sort of thing, that's a dead giveaway he knew he had it coming."

I feel the urge to exit the car, bridge the gap between

our bodies, and smash my mouth and body against Caleb's —and then drag him to the closest hotel and get him to groan out my name again, this time with that big dick of his inside me. Somehow, however, through sheer force of will, and also because I've never done anything that wild and crazy in my life, I keep my butt in my seat and calmly say, "I appreciate you wanting to avenge me when the opportunity fell into your lap. But, please, promise me, it won't happen again, at least not before the custody hearing."

"I can't promise you that, because I don't know what the next dickhead might do to deserve whatever I'm going to do." Smiling wickedly, he leans farther into the doorway, bringing his face, and his lips, mere inches from mine. I could be wrong, since I've only ever dated Trent. But it sure feels like he's non-verbally asking for permission to kiss me.

Goddammit. My body wants to give him the green light, but my brain knows it's a terrible idea. And so, I lean back, abruptly, causing Caleb to straighten up and clear his throat.

"So, uh, which do we want to do first," he asks. "Order the lumber for the deck or buy a drum kit?" It's an unnecessary question. We've already talked about ordering the lumber first, and then crossing the street to go to the music store.

"Lumber."

He opens the car door wide for me, inviting me to step out. "Did you get that list of materials from your dad?"

"I did." *I already told him that.* I pile out of the truck, averting my eyes, in case I'm visibly blushing. "I also made a list of all the errands we talked about, so we won't forget anything."

"I'd expect nothing less from you." Caleb shuts the car

door behind me and gestures to the home improvement store. "Come on, babysitter. Let's have some fun boosting the local economy of Billings."

CHAPTER 14
AUBREY

Caleb and I are back at the lake house now, after a long, decadent—and, yes, incredibly fun—day in Billings of shopping, hanging out, and goofing off. For the past few minutes, we've been going back and forth between the loaded truck and the house, hauling in today's massive haul. Once we're finished setting up here, the plan is to drive to my parents' house to pick up Raine and bring her back; so, of course, we're both eager to make everything perfect and inviting for Raine's imminent arrival.

Caleb wasn't kidding about boosting Billings' local economy today. We scratched off every item on our To Do List, and more. Besides ordering the lumber needed for Caleb's deck project, he also snapped up a professional-grade set of fancy tools at our first stop of the day. My father already owns tools, by the dozens, so I told Caleb he could borrow them. But Caleb insisted on having his own set for the project.

After I'd balked at his expensive and unnecessary purchase, Caleb insisted, "When I'm done building the deck, I'll give all these tools to your dad as a thank-you gift for helping me with the deck. I'm sure they won't go to waste."

After the home-improvement store, we headed to the music store across the street, as planned, where Caleb got himself a sparkling new drum kit. Of course, he had to sit down to try the kit out before making his selection, which meant, in no time flat, a crowd gathered to watch him. Phones came out. Selfies were requested and given. Baseball caps and T-shirts were signed. Two arms, too, on two different people. Both guys said they planned to get Caleb's signature tattooed over.

It was crazy getting to witness Caleb being C-Bomb, live and in person, versus watching him on my computer screen. I hate to admit it, but it was also delightful knowing everyone standing around assumed I was C-Bomb's girlfriend. I'm not proud of the jolt I felt in that music store; it was predictable, basic, and stupid of me. But in that moment, I admit I felt special to be the one C-Bomb kept smiling at when he played. The one he called over, when it was time to leave. The one he whispered to, when he tried to pay for that drum kit. Ultimately, the music store insisted on gifting the kit to him, in exchange for permission to post videos of today's unexpected visit.

So, anyway, yes. I fully admit I was lame and weak today, and I'm pissed at myself for it. Sorry, Claudia. I know you would have given your left arm to get to cosplay C-Bomb's girlfriend for a day, the way I did today. But for me, even as I was doing it, and tingling from head-to-toe from the whole experience, a piece of me knew I was being a basic bitch. One of the herd. Not to mention, breaking girl code by spending such an amazing day with my best friend's man.

With Caleb's new drum kit loaded into the back of Dad's big truck, we then headed to a big-box sporting-goods store across town, purportedly to buy a set of dumbbells for Caleb and nothing else. But once we were there, Caleb basically bought out the entire store.

He snapped up clothes, first. T-shirts and sweats, a bathing suit, etcetera, since he'd only packed for a two-day trip to Prairie Springs. And then, cornhole and bocci ball sets. A deluxe barbeque for the new deck he's yet to build, although it's true we can start using it now, even before his project is completed.

Caleb also bought a metric ton of stuff for Raine. Noise cancelling headphones, in case his drumming becomes too loud for little ears. Clothes, shoes, frilly bathing suits. A tiny life jacket, arm floaties, and sand toys. The cutest little donut-shaped floatation device with a built-in seat. A kiddie-sized golf set. And on and on.

Surely, we're done now, I thought, once he'd filled our shopping cart to the brim. But nope. When he noticed me covertly peeking at a tag on some expensive, designer yoga pants, simply because I was curious, Caleb sprang into action, suddenly hell-bent on showering *me* with gifts, in addition to Raine. Ignoring my protests, Caleb grabbed a second shopping cart and started filling it with expensive work-out gear for me, a yoga mat, several sets of light dumbbells, a fancy water bottle that cost too much for what it is. And on and on.

As we headed to the check-out area with our *two* shopping carts, I thought for sure we were finally finished with the madness. But Caleb had one more trick up his sleeve: he asked a worker to grab two mountain bikes for him, plus a kiddie seat and three appropriately sized helmets, and meet us at the registers.

When I saw the final total, I practically fainted on the spot. But it was nothing to Caleb. In fact, he handed over his gleaming black credit card like he was buying a couple frozen yogurts. I tried not to swoon. Tried not to blush. Money can't buy integrity or good character. That's what my parents always say, and I agree wholeheartedly. But, still, I'm ashamed to say it, but it's true: shopping with an extremely wealthy person was damned fun.

After the sporting goods store, we headed to a burger place for lunch next, since we'd both worked up an appetite spending all that money. And that's where the budding friendship that felt like it was forming during our drive to Billings really started to flourish. During our meal, Caleb and I chatted easily. We swapped stories and laughed frequently. Notably, Caleb not only asked questions about Raine, but also about Claudia, too, which I greatly appreciated. So, of course, I returned the favor by asking Caleb lots of questions about his closest family and friends.

When the check for lunch came, Caleb said, "I'm having too much fun to leave yet. Show me something a tourist should see in Billings."

I knew exactly where to take him. The Yellowstone Museum. It's not a world-famous attraction, by any stretch. Certainly not a "must-see" for a guy who's traveled the entire world. But still, we had a blast walking around the exhibits for an hour and a half, chatting and laughing and building on the conversations we'd had over lunch.

From the museum, we went for ice cream. And it was while we were enjoying our cones at an outdoor table that Caleb spotted our next stop of the day: a nearby toy store.

Toys.

My god, Caleb Baumgarten bought a mountain of them for his daughter. He actually wanted to buy out the entire toy store for her. One of everything, to be shipped to his lake house. But I told him, no; he could pick out *three* gifts for Raine and leave it at that.

"*Six*," Caleb countered.

"You already bought her a bunch of sand toys and a floatie at the sporting goods store," I reminded him.

"I'm turning the third bedroom into a kick-ass playroom for her," he fired back. "So, that means I need to get her lots and lots toys."

"Pick four," I compromised, using the same voice I always use with Raine when she requires a firm boundary, at which point Caleb pouted the exact same way Raine always does when she doesn't get her way. It was the first time I could see Caleb's features in Raine, clear as day, rather than only seeing Claudia's. It was a jarring moment for me: confirmation, in a visceral way, that Caleb is half responsible for the existence of my favorite person in the world.

Thankfully, Caleb ultimately took my advice about the toys. Sort of. He bought five toys, instead of buying out the store. Although I think that had more to do with the lack of room left in the truck than anything else.

Finally, after loading our toy purchases into the truck bed, we made our way back onto I-90 and into Prairie Springs, where we stopped at a grocery store on Main Street for a few supplies before heading to Caleb's house to unload and prepare for Raine's imminent arrival. Which is what we're still doing now.

With a soft exhale, I place the last bag of toys in the third bedroom—Raine's new playroom—and begin unboxing and setting up a bunch of stuff. When that task is completed, I head into the hallway, intending to head outside again for another load of whatever. But when I reach the living room, I stop dead in my tracks. Across the room, Caleb is taking a seat, shirtless, behind his new drum kit, drumsticks in hand.

The sun is setting behind Caleb through large, floor-to-ceiling windows, bathing the room in glorious, golden light that only enhances the "golden god" aura wafting off his muscled frame. Yes, I watched Caleb playing drums at the music store today. But he wasn't shirtless back then. And we weren't alone. Also, we hadn't yet spent the whole day together, talking, laughing, and becoming increasingly comfortable with each other. So, to put it mildly, I'm now experiencing extreme anticipation and excitement about what's about to happen.

Before Caleb begins playing, he notices me standing in the doorframe watching him. He flashes me a cocky wink. One that reminds me he's not only Caleb Baumgarten, but also C-Bomb from Red Card Riot. And then, with a sharp rise of his tattooed chest and a twirl of a drumstick, the rockstar begins to play.

With each strike of his sticks and each thump of his foot, it becomes more and more obvious to me: this is what Caleb Baumgarten was born to do. He's a work of art when he plays. Indeed, the colorful tapestry of his tattoos on his skin seem more vibrant when Caleb plays, like the lines and swirls on his flesh are pulsing in time to the music. Or maybe that's my clit pulsing, because I'm definitely feeling highly aroused. Damn.

I shouldn't let myself feel this way. Sexually attracted to him. He's slept with my best friend, for crying out loud; and, even more importantly, he didn't want Raine for two solid years. And yet, I can't stop raw, undeniable yearning from coursing through me.

As if sensing my lascivious thoughts, Caleb shoots me a

white-hot smolder, without missing a beat in his playing. I look away, feeling like my clit is going to explode if I maintain eye contact. But looking away doesn't solve the problem: that pulsing between my legs persists. In the end, I force myself to do the only thing that will save me from this rising urge I'm feeling to tackle him. I stride out the front door of the house on unsteady legs, determined to grab some more stuff from the truck and forget what I've just witnessed.

When I get to the truck, however, I discover it's empty. Caleb must have taken everything else inside, while I was busy setting up the playroom.

I can't go back inside yet, though. I'm still too worked up. It won't end well.

As Caleb's drumming wafts through the evening air, I stroll toward the shoreline and gaze out at the sun-kissed, serene lake. But when I notice a strange man on a rowboat, I take a reflexive step backward. *Is that Ralph Beaumont?* The man isn't close enough to identify, and the lighting isn't good. Also, I haven't seen Claudia's father in years, so my recollection of him might not be accurate. But something about that guy on the boat reminds me of Ralph.

Last I heard, Claudia's horrible father moved to Great Falls, after his wife finally left him and Claudia refused to speak to him. But Great Falls is only about three-and-a-half-hours away by car. Was Ralph already served with the lawsuit? When I spoke to the attorney Caleb hired for me this morning, he said they'd filed the lawsuit in LA and that Ralph would probably be served tomorrow. Did they wind up serving Ralph today? If so, would that turn of events have pissed off Ralph and inspired him to immediately hop into his car, drive his ass to Prairie Springs, and then hop into a rowboat to spy on us?

A chill races down my spine. Claudia's father is evil incarnate. The kind of man who doesn't know how to turn the other cheek. So, I honestly think that scenario is possible. Is it *probable*, though, considering the timeline of everything? Probably not.

With a shudder, I tell myself I'm being paranoid. But just in case, I turn on my heel and sprint back into the house.

CHAPTER 15
AUBREY

"No, no, no!" Raine shouts, shaking her little head. "*No, tank you.*"

Caleb looks up at me, crestfallen, his expression asking, *Now what?*

We're at my parents' place to pick up Raine for the night, now that Caleb's house is ready for her. When we arrived an hour ago, Mom had dinner almost ready, so we sat down and enjoyed a wonderful meal with my parents and Raine. One that seemed relaxed and comfortable, in terms of Raine's interactions with Caleb.

After dinner, I bathed Raine and put her into a comfy pair of footy pajamas, thinking she might fall asleep on the drive to Caleb's house; and throughout the entire process, I chatted up the lake and the ducks and all the new toys waiting for her over there. She seemed excited then. So what gives now? Out of nowhere, when I tried to carry Raine outside to Big Betty for the drive to Caleb's house, she started screaming and refusing to go.

With her little hands on her hips and her face twisted into the same scowl I've seen on Claudia's face, countless times, Raine shouts, "I no go Coobie house! I stay Grammy 'n' Pop-Pop!"

"I'll be there with you," I coo. "I'll even sleep with you there, like we always do here. And in the morning, we'll find some ducks to feed."

Dad chimes in, "I bet Caleb will make pancakes for you in the morning, like I always do."

"Absolutely," Caleb confirms.

"No, no, no!" Raine screams, her face as red as a beet. "*Mommy* make da pancakes! No Coobie!"

Fuck. This is a disaster. I cover my face with my hands, so Raine won't see the tears that are stinging my eyes. Every time I think this poor child's grief is fading somewhat, something like this happens to remind me she's lost her entire fucking world, and that's not something she can bounce back from in a matter of weeks.

While my face is still buried in my hands, there's an unmistakable sound from across the living room: the *thwack-thwack* of our front screen being opened brusquely and then slamming shut.

He didn't. He *wouldn't*.

I look around, and, yep. As suspected, Caleb is gone. Fucking hell. "Can you handle her?" I murmur to my mother, before flying out the front door.

Once I'm outside, it doesn't take long to spot my runaway charge bounding up the street at a fast clip, his powerful legs making long strides and his muscular arms swinging at full throttle. "Caleb!" I shout at top volume. "You can't go anywhere without me!"

Caleb doesn't stop running. In fact, the motherfucker picks up his pace.

Begrudgingly, I take off running after him, but thanks to our vast height differential, I can't close the gap. "Caleb

Baumgarten!" I scream, my voice breaking. "If you don't stop, I won't certify your sobriety today, and you'll have to start over!"

Caleb stops running, so I do the same, while squeezing the sharp ache in my side.

He turns around about forty yards ahead of me, breathing hard. And when his eyes meet mine, he shoots daggers at me, like he thinks it's *my* fault Raine won't come home with him. With a visible exhale, he rips the black knit cap off his head, causing his dark blonde mop to fall and run wild.

Fuck. That's the word Caleb just now muttered. I can't hear him from here. But it was clear enough from the movement of his lips.

I motion. *Come here.*

He pauses. Scowls. Kicks a rock in the street. But, finally, he starts slowly sauntering toward me.

"You can't do that," I snap, when he's close enough to hear me speaking at a normal volume.

"I needed a minute to myself," he snaps back, coming to a stop in front of me.

"I can't let you out of my sight, unless you're in a controlled environment, or else I can't certify your sobriety—"

"Fucking hell, Aubrey. Give it a fucking rest, would you?"

My eyebrows shoot up. "Excuse me? You're the one who begged me to be your babysitter, Caleb, the last thing I ever wanted to be; so, please, feel free to find someone else to—"

"Would you stop breathing down my neck all the time? This isn't about you. I just needed a goddamned minute to myself."

I cross my arms over my chest. "Tell me something. Do

you think running away from Raine is more or less likely to make her trust you? Hmm?"

Caleb exhales a long, exhausted breath. His shoulders sag. He looks up at the sky. "Why doesn't she like me? How long am I supposed to keep banging my head against a fucking wall?"

My jaw hangs open. "You can't be serious."

He returns his gaze to me and stares with hard eyes, letting me know, yes, he's dead fucking serious.

"You've been at this for less than forty-eight hours," I remind him with annoyance. "And you're *already* ready to give up?"

"I didn't say that."

"Your actions did. And actions speak louder than words. You ran away, when the going got tough, Caleb. *Again.*"

"I took a break."

"Call it what you want, but what *I* saw was you making a choice to abandon Raine, yet again."

He scoffs.

"Fathers don't get to take breaks whenever they please, Caleb. Sometimes, they have to stick around and be the adult in the room, even when it's frustrating. Even when they feel rejected. Even when they're a rockstar who's used to constant adulation and fucking pandering."

He scoffs again, except this time he also adds an eye-roll into the mix.

"She was having a *tantrum*," I persist. "Not only because she misses Claudia. Not only because she doesn't know you from Adam. Not only because she's testing you. But because she hasn't learned to regulate her emotions yet. Because she's *two* and therefore doesn't always have the right words to express her big feelings." He finally looks like he's listening now, so I add, "You'll be happy to know Raine has tantrums with me, too."

He looks surprised. And, yes, happy about the revelation.

"And if Claudia were still here, she'd be having tantrums with her, too." I narrow my eyes. "You asked what it's going to take? *Consistency*. Sticking with it. Proving to Raine you won't run away, no matter what, no matter how much she screams or tests you. Guess what you just taught her, Caleb? 'When I'm sad and scared, Coobie abandons me.' Is that the lesson you wanted her to learn about you today?"

Throughout my speech, Caleb keeps wincing, repeatedly, like I've been stabbing him in the chest with an ice pick. But he says nothing.

"Parenthood is a show-me-don't-tell-me kind of thing," I huff out. "Show Raine she can trust you, and she will. Maybe not today, but soon. But run away when the going gets tough, and she'll never trust you. Keep doing that, and I'll be forced to tell the judge I don't think you're up to the job of fatherhood. That, instead, *I'm* the one who should be awarded full custody."

I wasn't planning to reveal my Plan B to Caleb. I figured, if I wind up feeling the need to pivot at the hearing and fight for myself, I'd ambush Caleb by doing that. But in this moment, I can't think of a better way to light a fire under Caleb's stubborn, stupid ass than explaining all possible consequences of his choices.

When Caleb doesn't speak, I forge ahead and fill the thick silence. "If you've realized being a father isn't what you want, then stop wasting my time and Raine's. Stop confusing her and giving her false hope, because she's already been through enough, and I'm not going to let you traumatize her further."

Caleb's intense, green gaze bores into me for a long moment, during which I feel physical heat wafting off him. Plainly, he hates my guts now. It's written all over his—

Without warning, Caleb slides a big, calloused palm onto my cheek and leans in to kiss me. And even though I've been fantasizing about him doing this exact thing, all day long, I summon otherworldly willpower, put my palm against his chest, and turn my head. "We shouldn't, Caleb. We can't."

Caleb drops his hand from my cheek and steps back. "Sorry," he mutters. "It won't happen again."

Shoot. I'm the one who stopped him, so why do I feel so disappointed he's respecting my wishes? "Let's go back into the house," I whisper hoarsely.

He takes a deep breath. "Okay."

"But only if you're positive you're going to stick it out. If not—"

"I'll stick it out."

"You're sure?"

"Let's go."

I turn around and start walking on wobbly legs toward my parents' house. *Crap*. His lips were *this* close to mine. So close, my entire body felt like it was short-circuiting.

"No more slamming doors," I mutter, as we walk shoulder-to-shoulder down the quiet street. "When I heard that slam, I flinched, so I'm guessing Raine did, too. Is that what you wanted? For the women in your life to flinch and be scared of you?"

Caleb looks decimated. Sick to his stomach. "No. That's the last thing I want."

"Then you have a fucked-up way of showing it."

"I slammed the door because I was pissed at myself. Not at Raine."

"You think she knows that?"

He exhales deeply.

"Look, you're not a robot, okay? You're going to have normal, natural feelings during frustrating experiences. But as a father, you can't lose control of your *behavior* in response to those feelings. Do you understand what I mean?"

"I'm not an idiot, Aubrey. Yes, I understand."

He glares at me, but I don't care if he's pissed. If this were about him being a dick to me, I'd forgive and forget and leave it alone. But this is about Raine, and I can't let her bear the brunt of his inability to control his impulses.

We've reached my parents' porch, so I stop and stare him down before entering.

"You're going to act like a parent now?" I ask, holding his pained gaze.

He nods slowly, looking like he's physically biting his tongue; so I swing open the front screen, and step inside the house.

"Everything okay?" Mom asks, as we enter the living room. She's sitting in an armchair with Raine on her lap and a cartoon show on the TV, while Dad sits on the couch with his leg up.

"Everything's fine," I say brightly. "Caleb just needed a breather."

"Sorry about slamming the screen," Caleb mumbles. "It won't happen again."

Mom smiles reassuringly, with far more compassion than he deserves, if you ask me. "Emotions are high," she says. "This is a tough situation."

"That's no excuse," Caleb says. "I'm the adult." He looks at Raine. "The parent. I can't do that sort of thing, ever."

Mom shoots me a look that says, *How did you do that?* But to Caleb, she says, "You're still learning, honey. Nobody's perfect." She kisses the top of Raine's hair, but Raine is too sleepy and cozy against her chest to react.

"I think you should keep her here again tonight," Caleb says. "Baby steps. We'll try again tomorrow."

Mom nods and replies, "I think that's for the best. You two come back bright and early in the morning for breakfast, and we'll try again."

Caleb scratches his inked bicep. "Would it be okay if I slept here tonight, too? I don't need a bed. I can sleep on the floor."

Mom looks confused. "Why do that, when you can drive twenty-five minutes and sleep in your own, comfy bed?"

Caleb's soulful eyes are trained on Raine's groggy face, as she watches the cartoon and ignores the world around her. "If she wakes up with another nightmare, I want to be here."

My parents and I share a look. Clearly, we're all equally touched by Caleb's request.

"Of course, you can stay," Mom says softly. "Our home is yours, Caleb."

"Thank you so much, Mrs. Capshaw."

"Barbara. You're part of the family now."

Caleb's Adam's apple bobs. "Thank you, *Barbara*."

With a little wink at Caleb, Mom turns her attention to Raine in her lap. "Guess what, Pooh Bear? Coobie is going to stay the night, so he's here if you have a nightmare. Isn't that sweet of him?"

Raine nods her head, but it's clear she's not listening.

"Hey, Rainey," Dad interjects softly. "How about Coobie reads your bedtime story tonight, instead of me?"

"No. No Coobie," Raine says sleepily. "Pop-Pop."

"I'll read to you tomorrow night," Dad says.

I glance at Caleb. He's looking at Raine like he wants to fall to his knees and beg her to love him. Accept him. *Forgive* him. But when he speaks, it's in a calm, patient tone. One that doesn't hint at the internal turmoil he's surely feeling.

"Pop-Pop can read to you tonight," he says. "I'll read to you another time, maybe. Whenever you're ready."

I exchange another look with my mother, this one conceding I'm impressed, before Mom shifts her gaze to Caleb and flashes him a sympathetic smile. "I'll fetch you some pillows and blankets, honey. The couch is kind of lumpy. But at least, it's better than the floor."

CHAPTER 16
AUBREY

I wake up in my childhood twin bed with a big yawn and pat the bed next to me for Raine. She's not there. After a trip to the bathroom, I pad down the hallway on my way to the living room, waving to Mom on her stationary bike as I go.

In the living room, the couch is empty, other than a neatly folded blanket and pillow stacked to one side of it. No Caleb.

A cute giggle reaches me from the next room, the kitchen. So, that's where I go next.

When I arrive in the doorway, my father, Caleb, and Raine—the little one standing on a chair next to towering Caleb—are in the midst of whipping up breakfast with enthusiasm. While Caleb supervises Raine, who's mixing something in a bowl at the counter, Dad stands at the stove on one crutch, manning the griddle. All three backs are facing me, so I lean my shoulder against the door jam and take in the heartwarming scene.

"I had no idea you could mash up bananas to put into the batter," Caleb says to Dad.

"It's so much better than slicing bananas and putting them on top," Dad replies. "Rainey loves it this way."

"I *luh* it," Raine confirms.

"And *I* love *you*," Dad retorts.

I grin. That's a classic Dad-ism. Any time I've ever said I love anything in this world, big or small, he always shoots back, "And I love you." It's lovely to watch my father getting to pour his love into another little girl. Also, to know Caleb is watching him, and, hopefully, learning the tricks of the trade from the best.

"Banana pancakes are actually Rainey's second favorite," Dad explains to Caleb. To Raine, he says, "Tell Coobie your favorite kind of pancakes, Rainey."

"Chocky chip!" she answers proudly, still stirring whatever's in her plastic bowl.

"Make a note of it, Coobie," Dad says. "One day soon, you'll be in charge of the pancake-making."

"Got it," Caleb says. "We'll make sure to buy plenty of chocolate chips, the next time we go to the store."

I smile again. *We*. It was a small word, and perhaps it meant nothing. But Caleb's use of it makes me think he's surrendered to the reality that, at least for the next three weeks, wherever he roams, he'll always be a "we."

"Yummmm," Raine purrs.

"Oh my goodness," Dad says. "Did you taste the batter, you little sneak?"

Raine squeals with delight, giving herself away, and all three break into happy guffaws.

"Okay, my little *chef de partie*," Dad says to Raine, once his laughter subsides. "Let's see if you're done mixing." To Caleb, he explains. "That means pastry chef in French." Dad worked in fast food as a teenager. Apparently, he got the bright idea to assign everyone in the kitchen a fancy title, the same ones assigned in the fanciest French restaurants, and he's been tossing out the verbiage ever since. With no hint of an actual French accent, by the way.

"Good?" Raine asks Caleb, looking up at him expectantly.

"Yup. Great job. Wait a minute, is that a finger-sized hole in there? That looks suspiciously like a *Raine*-sized finger hole to me!"

The trio breaks into happy guffaws again.

"It me!" Raine says gaily, and the trio cracks up, once again.

I clutch my heart. Is there a better sound in this world than a child belly laughing? If so, I haven't discovered it yet.

"Okay, team," Dad says. "Let's make some batter with blueberries in it now. Grammy and Auntie Aubbey both love blueberry pancakes the most."

"Yum," Raine murmurs.

"Really?" Dad says. "I thought blueberry is your third favorite."

"Tird," Rainey confirms.

"But it's still worthy of a *yum*?" Dad asks, laughing.

"Yummm," Raine replies, with extra gusto, and the trio laughs together again.

"Can you hold up three fingers?" Dad asks Raine.

When she tries, and fails, Caleb maneuvers her little fingers to help her out. It's a small thing, I know, the way Caleb's massive, tattooed hands look while gently moving Raine's little fingers into place. But it's enough to send my heart beating in an irregular rhythm.

"There you go," Caleb coos. He rustles Raine's blonde hair. "Okay, *chef party*." He looks at Dad. "Chef party?"

"Chef de partie."

Caleb returns to Raine. "Hold tight onto the counter,

chef de partie, while I get the blueberries from the fridge. Hold tight now. Good girl." With Raine's palms laid flush on the counter, Caleb turns toward the refrigerator and immediately discovers me standing in the doorway with my hands on my chest and moisture in my eyes.

He shoots me an excited grin. One I'd caption, *Do you see how great it's going?* But before an actual word is exchanged, Dad calls out something to Raine, with his back facing me and his eyes on the griddle, that instantly commands my full attention.

"Hey Rainey, did you know Coobie is your *daddy*?"

At Dad's question, Caleb's eyes go wide and my jaw drops. Shit. I never would have introduced that concept to Raine this early on. For all we know, Caleb isn't going to stick around until the custody hearing in a month, let alone for the rest of his natural life. Did Dad consult Mom before revealing that shocking bit of news to Raine? Mom is the school counselor in this family. The expert who's read books on child psychology and development. So, *she's* the one who should lead the charge on when and if Raine finds out Caleb's identity.

"Rainey dadda?" Raine asks, looking at Caleb, who looks deeply tongue-tied.

"Yep," Dad says breezily, still facing away. "Caleb is Rainey's daddy, just like I'm Auntie Aubbey's daddy."

Crap. If Dad's going rogue here and introducing this concept without Mom's blessing, this could end badly for poor Raine. "Hey, Dad," I blurt, my voice tight. "Maybe let's not—"

"Good morning, Shortcake!" Dad bellows happily. "Coffee's made. Blueberry pancakes on the way. Is Mom still on her bike?"

"Yeah. Can I speak to you for a minute in private?"

"Can't right now, honey." Dad motions to the griddle full of pancakes. "The executive chef of the team—that's me—" He winks at Raine. "Can't fall down on the job."

"Dadda, dadda, dadda," Raine sings, shaking her little booty, as she continues gripping the counter, as instructed; but it's not clear if she's singing the word as a simple earworm or if she's specifically calling Caleb the moniker.

"That's right," Dad replies smoothly. "Coobie's Rainey's dadda." He winks at Caleb, who's still standing stock-still at the refrigerator with the door wide open. "Hey, *sous chef*. That's you, Coobie. Get those blueberries and shut the door already. Electricity is expensive."

"Oh. Sorry." Caleb follows instructions, but it's obvious he's not thinking about pancakes any longer. On the contrary, he's clearly bursting with excitement about this unexpected turn of events.

"Now go ahead and measure out another batch of ingredients for the *chef de partie* to mix up," Dad instructs. "Let's get some blueberry pancakes into the assembly line."

"Yes, sir."

"Yes, chef."

"Yes, chef." Caleb returns to Raine, where he slides a protective arm around her again and does as he's told. But through it all, he keeps glancing at me, like he's awaiting my reaction.

Finally, when it's clear I'm at a loss for words, Caleb says to Raine, "Just so you know, you can keep calling me Caleb or Coobie."

"Or Dadda," Dad chimes in.

"Whatever you want to call me is okay."

Dad chuckles. "You can even call him Coobie Dooby Doo, if you want. You know, like Scooby Dooby Doo?"

Raine laughs uproariously. She's watched that cartoon,

I think; but surely, she's simply laughing at Dad's silly inflection, rather than understanding the pun.

"Coobie Dooby Doo," Caleb echoes. "I like that."

"Coobie doo doo," Raine tries, and everyone laughs.

"Hey, I think my daughter just call me poop!" Caleb teases, and Raine screams with laughter, causing the rest of us, even me, to laugh, too.

"Okay, team," Dad says. "The executive chef is ready for some more batter and blueberries. *Chef de partie*—that's you, Rainey—do you have some more batter for me?"

Raine tries to pick up her plastic bowl to show him, but in doing so, she knocks over a coffee mug sitting nearby.

"Uh oh!" Raine says sheepishly, her big eyes widening. "It thpilled."

"No worries," Caleb says, as I say something similar.

I dart toward a drawer to grab a towel, but Caleb beats me to the punch by grabbing a nearby paper towel. After mopping up the spill, Caleb places his large, inked hand on Raine's head and says. "Don't worry, party chef. We all make mistakes. I sure do. All that matters is you keep your cool, fix the mistake if possible, and keep going. Right, Auntie Aubbey?"

My heart skips a beat. "That's right."

Warmth oozes into my core. I'm not sure what spell has been cast on Caleb, or if it will last, but it's clear he's undergone some kind of metamorphosis overnight.

"Auntie Aubbey!" Raine calls to me. She pokes Caleb's forearm. "Dis Coobie Dadda. Dadda clean up. Dis dadda."

Caleb's chest expands and freezes that way. Did she just call him Daddy? It's hard to say. But it certainly felt that way. Shit. If it turns out Mom thinks it was a bad idea for Dad to reveal Caleb's identity to Raine this soon, we're clearly not going to be able to stuff this genie back into the bottle.

"Yup," I choke out. "Dadda cleaned it up for you. Because that's what nice daddies do."

"Dadda, dadda, dadda," Raine sings out, as she happily shakes her little tush and mixes the contents of her bowl.

"I'll, uh, tell Mom breakfast is ready," I murmur, before turning from the doorway and bolting across the living room on rubbery legs.

When I get to Mom, I tell her everything that just transpired in the kitchen.

"You don't seem happy about this," Mom observes.

"I'm wary. What if Caleb doesn't make it to the custody hearing, and then Raine feels like she's lost her daddy on top of losing her mommy?"

Mom smiles. "I think this is a chicken-egg kind of situation. Would I have done it this way? No. But I have to think Raine learning to accept Caleb as her daddy will only strengthen the bond and motivate Caleb to keep going, even more."

"So, you think it'll be a good thing, in the end?" I squeak out.

"I do. I think it'll be a great thing. The best thing." She chuckles. "Your father isn't right about everything, God knows. But about this one thing? I think he was exactly right."

CHAPTER 17
CALEB

We're back at my cabin now. Or, rather, my lake house, as Aubrey keeps calling it. I concede that's a more accurate description nowadays, given Grandpa's upgrades.

The lumber for the new deck was delivered about an hour ago, while I was on today's Zoom call with my rehab counselor. And now, Joe and I are getting everything measured and set up for my big project, while Aubrey and her mother throw a beach ball around with Raine at the shoreline.

"I was thinking the fire feature would go there," I say to Joe, gesturing to the spot. "Do you think I should tap into the gas line or go with a propane tank?"

As Joe explains the pros and cons of each respective approach, my gaze drifts to movement on the quiet lake. There's a guy sitting in a rowboat about a hundred yards out, and something about him doesn't feel quite right to me. Is it my imagination, or is that guy staring at the women and Raine on the lawn?

The hairs on the back of my neck go up and my protective instincts flare. *Could that be Ralph Beaumont?* I haven't seen a photo of the guy, so who knows; but I'm not willing to take any chances.

"I'll be right back," I mutter to Joe, before beelining toward the water's edge. When I start walking, however, the guy in the small boat grabs his oars and starts paddling away, which only makes me even more suspicious. Paula said the custody lawsuit was filed yesterday, but she hasn't confirmed whether Ralph's been served. Did someone from the courthouse give him a heads up? Maybe someone in law enforcement, since Ralph's a retired police officer?

My heart thrumming, I pull out my phone and tap out a quick text to Paula, asking if Ralph got served already, and also asking her to send a photo of him. As I press send on my text, Aubrey comes to a stop next to me.

"I saw a guy watching the house from a rowboat yesterday, too," Aubrey says.

"Same guy?"

"Not sure. Yesterday's guy was wearing a hat and mostly looking away. He was far out, too, like this guy, and the lighting wasn't good."

"What about the rowboat? Same one?"

"I don't remember details about the boat from yesterday. I was more fixated on the guy who was inside it, giving me chills up my spine."

"You think this guy or yesterday's could be Ralph Beaumont?"

Aubrey shrugs. "The guy yesterday looked like every other old white guy, same as this guy. Same as Ralph. For all we know, that's just a well-known fishing spot on the lake, and we're being totally paranoid."

I consider that. "Maybe. Either way, though, let's bring Raine inside for a bit. I'm not taking any chances."

FINDING HOME

"Goodnight, love," Barbara says to Aubrey, giving her daughter a tight squeeze.

All four of us adults—Joe, Barbara, Aubrey, and I—spent the whole day with Raine at my house, and it went better than my wildest dreams. Raine hasn't called me "Dadda" again, not since this morning in the Capshaws' kitchen; but at least now I've got a mini-goal to work toward, as I continue working toward the larger one of getting Raine to trust me, completely.

After Aubrey completes her goodbyes to her parents, she turns to Raine, who willingly let me pick her up a moment ago. "Say goodnight to Grammy and Pop-Pop," Aubrey says. "They're going back home to sleep, while we stay here with Caleb—your daddy."

"I go home sleep?" Raine asks.

"No, we're both staying here with Coobie. Your *daddy*. But in the morning—"

"I go home," Raine says. This time, it's not a question. It's a command. She wriggles in my arms, so I set her down onto her pajama-clad feet, and the second she's free, she toddles to Barbara's legs and holds tight.

Aubrey crouches down. "Sweetheart, I'll be here with you, all night, and—"

"It's okay," I interject. "If she's not ready to stay here yet, let's not force it. It's a marathon, not a sprint." I look at Barbara. By now, it's clear she's the true leader of the Capshaw household, at least when it comes to decisions about Raine.

Barbara looks thoughtful. "I think she could handle it, if we insist."

"I don't want her to handle it. I want her to *want* to

stay." My decision made, I continue with, "We'll come get her in the morning, after my Zoom call."

"That's probably for the best," Barbara agrees. She gently taps Raine's soft hair. "Come on, love. Let's get you into the car and into bed."

"Auntie Aubbey." Raine reaches for her.

"No, honey," Aubrey says. "I'm staying here."

"You want to stay here with her?" Barbara asks hopefully.

Raine looks at Aubrey, and then at Barbara, like she's tempted to change her mind and stay. But ultimately, Raine murmurs something I can't make out. Something the rest of the adults who know her better interpret as a firm decision to join Joe and Barbara for their drive.

I thank Joe again for all his help with the deck today and walk the Capshaws to their car, while Barbara carries Raine. Before she straps Raine in, I pat my daughter on the cheek and wish her goodnight, and then stand next to Aubrey and wave goodbye with a fake smile on my face as the Capshaws drive away with my daughter nestled safely in their backseat.

"Today was good," Aubrey says, as the car's taillights disappear from sight down the dirt road.

"No, it was amazing." I take a deep breath. "I need to go for a walk to clear my head. By myself." I'm elated about today's progress with Raine; but also disappointed today wasn't enough to make Raine trust me. Both things can coexist, it turns out. Elation and disappointment.

"Sorry, I can't let you walk alone," Aubrey says.

I grunt in frustration. "You still don't trust me?"

"It's not a matter of trust. It's a matter of what I've promised, in writing, to do."

I run a hand through my hair. Man, I could use a

fucking drink right about now. Either that, or a really good fuck. But since neither option is available to me, I'll settle for being alone on a long walk, followed by jerking myself off to fantasies of Aubrey Capshaw sucking my cock.

"I'll put on sneakers, real quick," Aubrey says, motioning to the flipflops on her feet.

"Never mind," I grumble. "I'll play my drums, instead. The whole point is for me to be alone, not to walk."

"Suit yourself." She frowns. "Actually, it's pretty late for you to play your drums, don't you think? If someone in a nearby house has a small kid to put to bed, they'll be pissed off at you. Might even call the police."

I stare at her, incredulously. I can't drink. Can't smoke a blunt or a bowl. Can't fuck. Can't walk alone. And now, I can't even play my fucking drums to let off steam? Sounds like the only thing left, literally, is working out, taking a hot shower, and then getting into bed to jerk off to fantasies of Aubrey.

Unless . . .

My eyes shift to Joe's parked truck on the side of the house. Prairie Springs is a ghost town after eight, but I bet the bars and liquor stores in Billings are open till much later, especially on a Saturday night. Billings is only about an hour away, after all. It'd be easy enough to go there and return before Aubrey wakes up, without her ever finding out what I did.

The idea rapidly gains steam inside my head. Yes. This could work. I'll drive away tonight, after Aubrey falls asleep, with Big Betty in neutral and the headlights off. I'll find myself a dive bar in Billings where I can relax and play some pool or darts. Nothing too crazy. And I won't get shitfaced, obviously. Of course, not. I'd simply have one tall whiskey to unwind and recharge my batteries, and then I'll come back here without anyone ever being the wiser. Frankly, I don't see how this brilliant plan could possibly fail. *Unless someone takes a photo or video of you tonight and posts it for the world to see, dumbshit.*

Fuck.

What are the odds of that happening, though? People don't recognize me nearly as much, when I wear a hat, for some reason. So, I'll wear a hat and keep to myself in the bar. And if I happen to get made, nobody will know, for sure, what's in my glass. If shit hits the fan later, I could tell Aubrey and my counselor, Gina, I was drinking a simple Coke. As a matter of fact, I'll order a Jack and Coke, which isn't my usual drink, so it'll look the part.

"Caleb?" Aubrey says, her head tilted and her eyes boring into me. "You okay?"

My mind made up, I force a casual smile. "Yeah, I'm great. I think I'll head straight into a shower and to bed. It's been a long, exciting day."

"Sounds good to me," Aubrey says. "I'm in the middle of a good book."

As we start walking toward the house, my skin is buzzing and my heart pounding. I shouldn't do it. My brain knows that. But the plan is foolproof, really. And I'll be more relaxed tomorrow, if I do this, which will be better for everyone.

"You were great with Rainey today," Aubrey says. "I'm really proud of you."

Guilt rips through me. Adrenaline. Doubt. Maybe I shouldn't go, after all.

"Thanks. Couldn't have done it without you."

I open the front door for Aubrey, and she steps inside the house.

"Keep it up," she says. "As long as you remain

committed to Raine and to your sobriety, I have complete faith everything will go your way at the hearing in a month."

Fuck. Can she read my mind, or was it sheer coincidence Aubrey mentioned my sobriety at this precise moment?

"Well, goodnight, Caleb," Aubrey says. As she says it, my gaze drifts to her lips. To the curve of her neck. To her tits. Frankly, I'd much rather stay here and fuck Aubrey all night, than embark on some kind of nefarious field trip. But I feel like I've got no choice, given the situation. I need to do *something* to let off steam, and I'm gonna jerk my dick raw at this rate.

"Goodnight," I manage, as tingles shoot through me. *Again.* It's a constant occurrence by now. Unfortunately, it happens pretty much every time I think about kissing or fucking Aubrey, which I do constantly. Countless times per day, as a matter of fact.

Aubrey begins walking down the hallway ahead of me, but she abruptly stops and faces me before reaching her room. "Almost forgot." She puts out her hand. "Car keys, please."

Fucking hell. She's relentless. And also, quite possibly, psychic.

"Aubrey, come on," I say with a smile. "What am I gonna do? Sneak away under the cover of darkness and drive into town? Everything in Prairie Springs is closed by eight."

"True, but everything stays open till much later in Billings, especially on a Saturday night."

Jesus Christ. She's scary.

I force a fake chuckle of indignation. "You think I'd risk all the progress I've made today and at rehab by secretly driving all the way to Billings for a stupid, fucking drink?" I chuckle again at the craziness of the thought. "I know full well someone might post a video of me, Aubrey. I'm not dumb." I am dumb, though. Saying this shit out loud is making me realize just how fucking dumb.

"I don't know what you might do, Caleb," Aubrey shoots back calmly. "But if I have your keys tonight, then I won't have to wonder."

I've never felt more attracted to her or more grateful for her presence. Her intuition. Her smarts. I imagine myself marching over to her, taking her into my arms, and kissing that sassy, infuriating, brilliant mouth of hers, and then dragging her into my bed and fucking her to within an inch of her life, all night long.

That's all I want. The chance to fuck this gorgeous woman. I'd take that over whiskey and weed, a hundred times out of a hundred. Why doesn't she want that, too? It's killing me to know my fierce attraction to her is one-sided. That never happens to me. When I want someone, I get them. Easily. So why the fuck isn't Aubrey falling at my feet, like everyone else?

Aubrey waggles the fingers of her extended hand. "*Keys*, Caleb. Come on. Don't make me come over there and grab them out of your pocket."

The thought makes my dick begin to harden, against my will. Suddenly, that's all I want: the feel of her hand in my pocket, brushing against my growing hard-on. But, of course, I can't force her to do that. She already told me no, clearly, when I tried to kiss her in the middle of her parents' street yesterday.

With a sigh, I pull out the keys from my pocket and hand them to her. And then, mostly to keep Aubrey from seeing the bulge that's now pressing against my jeans like a motherfucker, I turn and stomp down the rest of the hallway to my bedroom.

With each step I take, I feel more and more pissed off about the situation. More restless and rejected. Which is why, when I get to my door, I swing it open fiercely and barrel into the room in a huff, fully intending to slam the door behind me to communicate my displeasure. But when I'm just about to release the door, I hear Aubrey's words from yesterday and stop myself.

No more slammed doors, Caleb.

You can't control your emotions, but you can control your behavior in reaction to them.

Fucking hell.

More to prove I'm not the man-child Aubrey thinks I am than anything else, I gently close the door behind me with a soft and civilized *click*, despite how much I want to feel the satisfaction of a good slam. The door closed, I peel off my clothes, slide into bed, and deal with my raging hard-on; once again, while fantasizing about little miss rule-follower, Aubrey Capshaw, having a squirting orgasm all over my face.

CHAPTER 18
CALEB

"Yes, you *wanted* to sneak away last night, but you *didn't*," my counselor, Gina, says on my computer screen. "That's all that matters. Thoughts aren't actions, Caleb. Actions are what matter."

I've never been as honest with Gina, as I'm being during this Zoom call. Up till now, I've viewed myself as an unwilling hostage of rehab. A victim. And so, I've acted accordingly. Remained tight-lipped. Made Gina pull teeth to get anything out of me. But this morning, for some reason, I woke up wanting to try something new—to give today's session a genuine effort. And so, right off the bat, I admitted the bad thing I was planning to do last night. The thing Aubrey sniffed out and thwarted, thereby saving me from myself.

"You should tell Aubrey the truth about last night," Gina, my counselor, says. "The more honest you are with her, the more she can help you."

I lean back in my chair, twisting my lips. I can't believe how close I came to disaster last night. I haven't wanted to admit it to myself, but maybe I need rehab, after all. "I'll think about it."

When the counseling session ends, I close my laptop, get up from the kitchen table, and look for Aubrey in the living room. When the room is empty, I look for Aubrey in the workout/playroom, figuring she might be doing yoga in there. But when she's not there, I head outside and discover Aubrey sitting on a workout mat on the patch of grass in front of the shoreline. She's dressed in workout gear, but she's not presently doing yoga. She's got her knees up and her forehead pressed against them, and her shoulders are shaking with sobs.

Shit. I rush to Aubrey and dive onto the ground next to her. "What's wrong, sweetheart? What happened?"

When Aubrey lifts her head, my heart cracks at the sight of her sad little face. I open my arms to her, reflexively, inviting her to turn to me for comfort; but she only lowers her head again and sobs into her arms.

Not knowing what else to do, I rub her quaking back. "Tell me, baby. *Please*." I look around, my hackles up. Did the guy on the rowboat come back? Was he Ralph Beaumont, after all?

Aubrey lifts her head and sniffles. "I don't know how to do this."

"Do what? Babysit me? Because you're doing a great job of that. In fact—"

"I'm only twenty-four!" she shrieks, her dark eyes rimmed with tears. "Less than a month ago, I lost my lifelong best friend, and now, suddenly I've got to be a full-time, single mother who also has to babysit your ass, while also helping you transform into a model fucking father, while also learning to be a good parent myself, even though I don't know what the fuck I'm doing!"

I rub her back. "It's okay, baby. You're doing great."

"I'm faking it! I don't know what the fuck I'm doing, Caleb!"

"Take a deep breath, sweetheart. Breathe, Aubrey. You're a superstar."

Aubrey hiccups and wipes her eyes. "I had another nightmare about Claudia last night. The worst one yet. She begged me not to let her father take Raine away and do to her what he did to Claudia as a child."

My heart stops. Aubrey has told me about Ralph beating Claudia's mother. But she hasn't said a word about Ralph beating Claudia, too.

"Ralph used to hit Claudia?"

Aubrey's nostrils flare. "He did something worse than that. The worst possible thing, over and over again, beginning when she was around nine or ten."

My stomach revolts. "Jesus Christ."

"Claudia confessed it to me when we were twelve. But she told me he'd kill her and her mother if I told anyone, so I never did. And now, she's gone, and I have to live with my mistake forever." She wipes her eyes. "My parents would have helped Claudia and her mom, if I'd been smart enough to tell them the truth. I should have known that."

"You were a kid."

Aubrey shakes her head woefully. "Ralph told Claudia nobody would believe her, because he was a police officer, and she believed him. So, I did, too. But now, as an adult, I can plainly see we simply played into his hand." She puts her hands over her face. "And now, thanks to me, it's going to be my word against Ralph's at the hearing, because Claudia isn't here to tell the judge the truth, and I don't know if my word will be enough to keep Raine safe."

I gently remove her hands from her face and look deeply into her soulful, tormented eyes. "I won't let Ralph get her. Baby, take a deep breath for me. That's it, baby. Breathe. It's gonna be okay." When Aubrey's chin trembles, I open my arms to her again, purely on instinct; and this time, she falls into them and lets me hold her sobbing frame for several minutes.

When Aubrey calms down enough to speak, she says, "When I moved in with Claudia in Seattle, we talked about everything as adults for the first time. She'd started going to therapy by then, and she was having all kinds of breakthroughs about her childhood and the abuse. She was even working up the courage to report her father to the police in Seattle. But now, she'll never get the chance to do that."

My heart squeezes. "Poor Claudia."

"She was amazing, Caleb. The best mother to Raine. The best friend to me. I wish so badly you could have actually known the real her. She was so much more than the fangirl groupie you met."

My heart feels like drumsticks are banging on it. "If only she'd taken me up on my offer to fly her and Raine out to LA to meet my family and me, I would have had the chance—"

"*What?*" Aubrey's flabbergasted expression makes it clear my revelation is news to her.

"I . . . Yeah. I offered to fly Claudia and Raine to my house in LA."

"*When?*"

"About six months after Raine was born. I sent Claudia an email, directly, not through our attorneys, pleading with her to bring the baby to my house in Santa Monica. I told her about my mother's diagnosis and explained time was short for her, but Claudia turned me down."

"Are you sure? Maybe—"

"Her exact words to me were, 'Fuck off.'"

Aubrey gasps. "I don't believe it."

"I've still got the email."

"But . . ." Aubrey rubs her forehead. "I was living with Claudia by then, and she told me everything. Caleb, Claudia constantly talked about you and what a shame it was that Raine's 'asshole sperm donor' had zero interest in getting to know his beautiful child. Why would Claudia say all that to me, but not bother to mention you'd offered to fly her and Raine to your house in LA?"

"Maybe she was too embarrassed about shutting me down to admit the truth to you."

Aubrey's clearly not buying that explanation. "Can I see her email to you?"

"Sure." I scroll on my phone to find it.

As I'm searching, Aubrey murmurs, "Why on earth would Claudia turn down the chance to come to your house? I would have thought she'd be giddy to get to do that. You were always her celebrity crush, even after she'd had sex with you." She looks out at the lake. "Claudia was a compassionate person. That's why she wanted to be a nurse." She returns to me. "Surely, she would have said yes to you, solely based on the situation with your mother."

"She didn't want me in her child's life out of the gate, remember?"

"Because you demanded she get an abortion! And when she said no to that, you made it abundantly clear you wanted nothing to do with the baby. So, of course, she agreed that was for the best. But trust me, if she thought for a second you'd had a change of heart, or even that there was a possibility of you having one, Claudia would have jumped on the first flight to LA."

I understand Aubrey now wants to think of her best friend as some kind of a saint. It's understandable, in light of her premature departure from this world. But once she sees the email exchange, I think she'll realize Claudia wasn't quite as perfect as Aubrey believes.

"Here it is." After locating the emails, I hand my phone to Aubrey to read them.

For a long moment, Aubrey stares at my screen with tears in her eyes. When she finally looks up from my phone, she's pale. Like she's seen a ghost. "There's no way Claudia wanted to write that reply to you. I don't know if her mother or boyfriend influenced her to write that to you, but the Claudia I knew never would have sent that response. At the very least, she would have let your mother meet Raine. Of that much, I'm sure."

I take the phone back and set it down next to me on the yoga mat. Poor Aubrey. This must be a tough pill to swallow. Clearly, Claudia didn't want to look like a cold-hearted bitch to Aubrey. And I can't blame her for that. Aubrey is such a warm, loving person, I also want her to think highly of me. "Either way," I murmur, "the end result is the same. My mother died without knowing she had a grandchild, and it's all my fucking fault."

"Was that the only time you contacted Claudia?"

"I tried again a couple months later, after my mom's health took a sharp turn, and found out Claudia had blocked me. Not only my email address, but on social media, too. I should have created a new email address and tried again, or maybe hopped a flight and begged Claudia in person, but my mother was in bad shape, and I wasn't in the right headspace to take that on. I thought I still had plenty of time to try again later, once my mom got better. But unfortunately . . . " I look out at the lake. "She never got better."

Aubrey places a hand on my back. "I owe you an apology. This whole time, I've been thinking you never gave a fuck about Raine. Never asked to meet her. Never even asked for a photo or update. I misjudged you. I'm sorry."

Her apology, our proximity. Her touch on my back. It's all filling me with the thumping desire—the *need*—to lean into her and kiss her. But since that's not an option, I swallow hard and whisper, "You might as well keep thinking the worst of me. One pathetic email doesn't change the fact that I wasn't there for my child. For all her firsts. That's something I'll have to live with forever."

Aubrey rubs my back. "Raine is only two. She's still going to have lots of firsts, and you'll be there for all of them."

I bow my head, too overcome to speak. I didn't expect the conversation to take this turn. I'm overwhelmed.

"Don't beat yourself up too much," she whispers softly. "Only a tiny bit." I glance at her to find her smiling. "Honey, Raine won't start logging long-term memories for another three or four years. Soon, she won't even remember a time before Coobie—Dadda—came into her life."

I smile through my emotion, and she rubs my back again.

"When she called me Dadda, it was the best moment of my life."

"One of the best of mine, too. Once my mother told me it was all for the best."

My eyes drift longingly to Aubrey's lips. I want to kiss this woman more than I want to breathe. More than I want a drink or to play drums. More even, than I want my solitude and freedom. But, of course, I don't act on the impulse; but instead, resolve to do the thing my counselor, Gina, instructed me to do: tell Aubrey the truth about last night.

"You were right to take my keys away last night," I whisper. "I was planning to sneak off and drive to Billings."

Aubrey frowns. "I had a feeling." She swats at my shoulder. "Don't you know that would have been catastrophic?"

"I wasn't thinking clearly."

"I would have had to report you! You would have had to go back to square one at rehab."

"I know.

"And then, who knows if the judge—"

"Aubrey, I know. I didn't tell you to get yelled at. I told you to let you know you kept me from self-sabotaging last night, like I always do. I told you, so I can thank you for saving me from myself. So you know, even if you feel like you're faking being a kickass sobriety coach, you're doing one hell of a job."

Her cheeks bloom. "I only want to help you."

"I know, and I'm grateful for it."

My lips are mere inches from hers, as we sit, shoulder to shoulder on the yoga mat, facing the lake. But a promise is a promise. From this day forward, I'm hereby committed to my word being my bond, no matter what. That's going to be my commitment, whenever I give my word; but it's going to be especially true when I give it to Aubrey Capshaw.

Aubrey bumps her shoulder against mine and grins. "I can't believe you almost did that."

"I'm a dumbshit. What can I say?"

Before she replies, the sound of a car traversing the gravel next to the house causes both of us to turn our heads to look. It's Aubrey's mother, Barbara, parking her car on the side of the house. When she stops, Barbara swings open her car door and pops her head out, her face beaming.

"Raine wanted to come over!" Barbara shouts excitedly. "She opened her eyes this morning and immediately asked to come over here to make pancakes—*with her dadda!*"

CHAPTER 19
AUBREY

I finish up the yoga session I didn't do this morning because I wound up having a mental breakdown during my first downward dog and turn off the yoga app on my phone. After Mom dropped off Raine this morning, Caleb took his daughter, "the party chef," inside to make pancakes, while I remained outside with my book. And from that point forward, the morning has felt natural and right. Joyful. Serene. Indeed, the whole time I've been doing yoga, Caleb's been in front of me in the shallows of the lake, enthusiastically giving his daughter her first-ever swimming lesson, and Raine's been having a blast with him.

As I'm turning off the yoga app on my phone, Caleb calls out to Raine, "Great job, Shortcake! Kick, kick!"

I look up, surprised. Shortcake is what Dad has always called me, so my brain assumed Caleb must have been talking to me for a second there. But, nope. He's holding Raine's two little hands, while teaching her to kick her legs and dunk her face into the water.

"That's it," Caleb says, his tone gentle and brimming with encouragement. "You're doing a great job!"

It's a beautiful thing to behold a big, brawny man carefully leading his tiny baby girl around a lake. I'm transfixed by the sight.

After a few more kicks and dunks of her face, Caleb pulls Raine to him, and she sputters and blinks in his arms.

"You want to keep going or stop for now, sweetheart?"

"Thtop."

"Okay, Shortcake. Good job. We'll go again tomorrow, okay? Great job for today."

Caleb begins striding out of the water toward me, with Raine clinging to his massive frame like a wet baby monkey.

"Did you see her?" he asks, stopping in front of me with a handsome smile on his face.

"I sure did. Great job, Rainey."

"My grandpa taught Miranda and me to swim that same way, right there in the exact same spot. I've seen it in home movies."

"I'd love to see them."

Caleb scratches his bearded cheek. "Not sure where they are. I'll ask Miranda."

"Please do." I bite my lip and look away. Since our conversation on the yoga mat earlier, something has shifted between us. *Something big.* In fact, if my mother hadn't driven up when she did, I think I would have thrown caution to the wind and kissed Caleb before our conversation was over.

"Pway bawn?" Raine asks Caleb.

Caleb's eyebrows ride up. "You said you wanted to play with sand toys."

"*Bawn.*"

I chuckle. "Looks like she's changed her mind." When

Caleb frowns, I motion to the grass in front of me. "Go on, *Dadda*. Oink like a pig for your daughter's pleasure."

Raine giggles. "Oinky, Dadda!"

Caleb visibly melts. "You already know how to get anything you want from me, don't you? All you have to do is call me Dadda, and I'm at your service."

Caleb sets Raine down and gets down on all fours in front of her. And then, man, oh man, the brawny, tattooed rockstar starts oinking like a pig with abandon for his baby girl. So well, in fact, Raine and I can't stop laughing with glee at the ridiculous sight.

"Is that good?" Caleb asks. "Can I get up now?"

"Cow!" Raine commands, and to his credit, Caleb doesn't hesitate to moo like a cow. And then, to cock-a-doodle-doo like a rooster. And on and on, as Raine, with a snarky assist from me, goes through every conceivable farm animal.

"Okay, Rainey," I finally say. "Let's let Dadda take a break. It's time for lunch."

Caleb falls onto his back and splays his arms like a dead body, making Raine giggle uproariously. "Thank God," he murmurs. "Playing barn is exhausting."

I laugh. "Thank *me*."

Caleb turns his head and flashes me a panty-melting smile. "I do thank you, Goddess Aubrey. Thank you from the bottom of my heart."

Butterflies whoosh into my belly. "You're welcome." Clearing my throat, I offer Raine my hand. "Come help me make sandwiches for all of us, Boo. Let's give Dadda a second to himself."

"That's okay," Caleb says, sitting up. "Raine and I will make lunch together, while you read. We've got this." He gets up, scoops up Raine, and heads toward the house without looking back at my shocked face. "Come on, Shortcake. We'll make a picnic for Auntie Aubbey."

"A *picnic*?" Raine gasps out excitedly in his arms. "What dat?"

Caleb begins explaining the concept of picnics to Raine, but he disappears before he's finished his explanation. I stand frozen for a moment, trying to wrestle with the yearning I'm feeling. The all-consuming attraction for Caleb that's been wracking my body all morning. But finally, I settle into a beach chair with my book.

A couple pages in, music starts blaring from inside the house, followed by the unmistakable sounds of Caleb banging on his drums. I close my book, feeling annoyed. It's too soon for Caleb to be finished making lunch, so he must have gotten distracted. Or worse, maybe Raine had some kind of meltdown, so Caleb plopped her in front of a cartoon, so he could bang on his drums to let off steam.

I head through the front door, fully expecting the situation to be problematic. But when I step into the front room, I'm met with the sight of Caleb sitting at his drum kit with tiny Raine propped on his lap. Raine's got noise-cancellation headphones on, the ones Caleb bought for her in Billings, and she's banging on a metal cymbal thing, not sure what it's called, with a solitary drumstick, while Caleb keeps a steady beat with the other drumstick and with his foot below.

"Good job," Caleb coos, his sparkling eyes trained on his daughter. "You're a natural."

He hasn't noticed me yet. He's only got eyes for Raine. So, I remain in the doorway.

"Like *dis*, Dadda?" Raine asks.

"Just like that. You want to play a song?" When Raine expresses enthusiasm, Caleb says, "I know the perfect one.

Something with both our names in the title." He pulls out his phone and begins to scroll. "It's called 'Fool in the Rain.' Get it? I'm the *Fool*, and you're the *Raine*."

Raine squeals and bops up and down in Caleb's lap, making Caleb laugh. And a second later, a song begins wafting from Caleb's phone.

I've heard it before, I think. Maybe? Although I'm not sure who plays it.

"Keep the beat now," Caleb instructs. "Like this. Good. Just like that. Without someone to keep good time and lay down a really good groove, a band will always suck. No matter what anyone else might tell you, the drummer is the most important musician in the whole band."

Raine is going for it now, causing Caleb to chuckle at her exuberance. "That's it, Shortcake. Do you like playing the drums with Dadda? That's 'cause it's in your blood, kiddo. You want to know who's playing this song?"

"Me!"

He laughs. "Yes, but I meant who's playing the song on my phone. It's a band called Led Zeppelin. One of the best rock bands in the history of music."

"Oooh."

"Can you say Led Zeppelin?"

"Blebedah."

Caleb hoots with laughter, as I do the same. I've never heard Caleb belly laugh quite like this. It's a magical, glorious sound. Quite possibly, the sexiest thing I've heard in my life, even sexier than the sound of Caleb gritting out my name while jerking himself off.

At the sound of my laughter joining his, Caleb's eyes shift to mine at the door. He beams a glorious smile at me, one that sends butterflies whooshing into my belly and warmth oozing between my legs, before returning gleefully to his daughter in his lap.

"Let's try that again. I'll break it down. Say Led."

"Leb."

"Zep."

"Zep."

"Uh."

"Uh."

"Lin."

"Lim."

"Led Zepp-e-lin."

"Leh Boopoodah!"

Caleb howls with laughter from the depths of his belly, as I do the same. Since there's no reason for me to remain in the doorway any longer, I drift into the room and take a seat on the couch to watch the show.

"I'm going to teach you all about Led Zeppelin, and other bands too, including my own," Caleb says to Raine. "And when you're old enough, you'll come on tour with Dadda and play a song for the crowd. Would you like that?"

"Yeah!" Raine shouts, even though she has no idea what the fuck any of it means.

When the Led Zeppelin song ends, Raine bops around on Caleb's lap, screaming, "Again!"

"*Again*?" Caleb says excitedly. "Okay, cutie. You're the boss. We'll play our song again."

Raine cheers.

"Only this time, now that you're all warmed up, you have to let loose and really go for it, okay? Don't hold back." He presses a button, and the same song starts again, followed by another round of encouragement and instruction from Caleb.

"That's it," Caleb says. "*Feel* the music in your soul. Let it move you."

"She's definitely letting the music move her," I joke. As far as I can tell, Raine's banging her drumstick, willy nilly. Most definitely *not* to the beat of the song. But she's absolutely giving it her all.

"Right?" Caleb says proudly. "The kid's a damned prodigy."

"A *dang* prodigy," I correct. "*Darn* prodigy. Flippin'. Freakin'."

"Oh yeah. Sorry." Caleb grimaces, making me giggle at his adorableness.

Eventually, the song reaches its homestretch again, for the second time, and the singer begins repeating a refrain about the unexpected love he's found. As he sings, it hits me I'm feeling exactly what he's crooning about: *love*. For Raine. For Claudia. For my parents. *And for Caleb, too.* For the obvious effort he's been exerting today. For the unexpected tenderness and pride he's showing toward Raine. And most of all, for the email he sent to my beloved Claudia, begging to meet his daughter, mere months after her birth.

Nobody's perfect. The man fucked up. But now I know, at least he tried to fix his mistake, much earlier than previously known. Not because Raine had been orphaned. Not because he'd received a demand letter from Ralph Beaumont. Not to save thirty grand a month. But simply because he desperately *wanted* to right his past wrongs and forge a relationship with his baby.

To be clear, I'm not falling *in love* with Caleb in this moment, obviously. I'm simply feeling *love for him*, thanks to our shared love of Raine. It's important for me to remember that, so I won't confuse the feelings gripping me for something else. Yes, I desperately want to kiss Caleb. Also, to rip his clothes off and make him groan out my name again, only this time into my ear. But the fact remains—

"Look, Auntie Aubbey!" Raine calls out, ripping me from my lascivious thoughts. "I play drums with Dadda!"

I clear my throat, hoping my lustful thoughts aren't written all over my face. "Yes, you are. You're great at this!"

"Of course, she is. She's *my* kid."

I can barely look at him. The lust I'm feeling is too intense. "Rainey, did you know your daddy is one of the most famous drummers in the world?"

Raine gasps and her blue eyes widen. "He *is*?"

"People pay lots of money to see your daddy playing his drums."

Raine stops drumming and frowns. "I don't have money."

Caleb and I both crack up.

"Don't you worry, Shortcake," Caleb says. "You've got a lifetime backstage pass."

As Raine processes that confusing word salad, my eyes lock with Caleb's. It'd be foolish to let myself fall for someone like Caleb. He's told me, explicitly, he doesn't know how to love. He lets everyone down. He cheated on his only girlfriend.

And yet, sitting here now, I can't deny it: I'm falling hard for this man, whether it's a downright foolish thing to do or not.

CHAPTER 20
CALEB

"*Aubrey.*"

I can't keep myself from groaning out her name, again and again, loudly, as my hand works my aching shaft. And this time, it's not a ploy to get Aubrey to come to me, since I've accepted that's not going to happen. It's an involuntary prayer to the universe to have some mercy on my throbbing cock and aching balls.

Everything about Aubrey turns me on. Every look. Every touch. Even the tongue lashings she delivers so deftly. Always, deservedly, by the way. Fucking hell, no matter what that woman says or does, she lights a forest fire inside me. One I can't extinguish, no matter how hard I try. I'm a ball of flames in Aubrey's presence. A forest fire, whenever I even think about my cock burrowed deep inside her. It's something I think about a lot these days. On a running loop. God help me, the woman is lighter fluid. Fuel to my raging flames.

I groan out Aubrey's name, again, as my pleasure spirals and threatens to consume me, body and soul. And, suddenly, without warning, my bedroom door flies open and Aubrey magically appears in the doorframe. Only this time, unlike before, she doesn't turn and run away. She strides toward me, breathing hard, like her hair's on fire and I'm the cool lake she's intending to plunge herself into to save herself.

"I'm here to take over that job," she murmurs, her dark eyes trained on my dick. "If you'll let me."

Am I dreaming? Am I dead? "Yes," I choke out, elated to realize this is very, very real.

She pulls off her top as she moves, revealing the two most exquisite, perkiest tits I've ever beheld, and by the time she reaches me in my bed, her shirt is on the ground and my lust is a pyre that's consuming every available drop of oxygen in the room.

As I pull her lips to mine, I'm a human back draft. A wall of flames singeing the walls and scorching the ceiling. My fingers dig greedily into Aubrey's bare back as my lips collide with hers. I've waited ten lifetimes for this kiss, waded through dense jungles and traversed steep mountains for it; and now, every cell in my body, every drop of blood in my veins, is exploding with intense yearning, relief, and euphoria.

My tongue greedily finds Aubrey's, and every nerve ending electrocutes at the burst of sensations. She's sweet to the taste. Honey mixed with vanilla. Her lips are as soft as they are hungry. Her skin beneath my fingertips, warm and smooth.

Our kiss is an atomic bomb going off, an all-consuming frisson that rattles my bones and burns away every last remaining drop of restraint. I curl my fingers into her soft hair as I deepen the kiss, and she responds in kind, her fingers tightening in my hair on the back of my head.

Aubrey's hand finds my hard shaft as our mouths

continue their mutual assaults. I groan loudly at her unexpected touch—her greedy, fucking glorious touch—and she whispers hoarsely for me to keep it down.

"Raine's across the hallway," she reminds me, her breathing labored.

It's yet another turn-on. A reminder that we *shouldn't*. That Aubrey's contraband to me. Contraband pussy, as my friends and I call all manner of forbidden fruit. She came to me against her better judgment. Because she couldn't stay away. Couldn't resist me, any more than I can resist her.

"Do you have a condom?" Aubrey grits out.

"I bought a pack in Billings," I confess, grinning like a shark. "When you went to grab those nighttime pull-ups across the store."

"You presumptuous bastard," Aubrey whispers with heat, pressing the crotch of her panties against my hard, aching bulge. But it's clear enough from her facial expression, she's damned glad I presumed.

"I'll get them soon," I say. "First things first, I'm hungry for some contraband pussy."

"*Contraband?*"

I don't explain myself.

I guide her onto her back and pull off her panties like a starving man unwrapping a cheeseburger, and then shudder violently when her deliciousness is revealed to me in all its glory. I've dreamed about eating this pussy. Fucking this pussy. Jerked off to fantasies of this pussy sitting on my face and squirting with pleasure. And now, this pussy is mine for the taking—and even hotter than I imagined it.

Watering at the mouth, I widen Aubrey's thighs, opening her up to me like a blooming flower, and then groan much too loudly at the sight.

"Not so loud," Aubrey whispers, her words coming out between pants of anticipation.

I'm dizzy with lust now. Breathing hard, I stroke the outside of her pussy gently, feeling desperate to lick her. Taste her. Fuck her. *Claim* her. And Aubrey writhes and moans loudly at my touch.

"What happened to 'not so loud?'" I tease.

"Fuck off."

We both laugh.

I begin stroking her with one hand, while caressing one of her perfect tits with the other. And when my mouth is watering too much to resist, I take her peaked, hard nipple into my mouth and devour her, prompting Aubrey to loudly lose her fucking mind.

I dip two fingers inside her, and my dick jolts with pleasure to discover she's already ready for my cock, just this fast. Soaking wet, warm, and swollen. But I'm not going in yet. I've got a meal to eat, first.

With a low moan, I crawl between Aubrey's legs and begin voraciously kissing and licking the sensitive flesh surrounding her bullseye without ever hitting the mark, while sliding my fingers in and out. When it feels like she's reached the peak of this particular mountain, I move on to the next. Devouring her bullseye. My breathing loud and ragged, I zero in on her swollen, pink bud while stroking her G-spot with two precise fingers.

Instantly, she goes nuts on me in the best possible way. In fact, only ten seconds into my new tactic, Aubrey releases a groan that's so fucking loud and tormented, it's my turn to remind her about Raine across the hallway. Only this time, in earnest. Not as a tease.

When another loud moan escapes her, Aubrey squeaks and grabs a pillow, which she promptly shoves over her face. As she growls and roars into the pillow, I double down on what I'm doing between her legs, until she's writhing and gyrating so damned much, it feels like she's having a seizure.

As my tongue laps and lathes, I feel blissed out. Drugged. Shit-faced. Black-out drunk. Far more so than when I've ingested actual chemicals into my body. For months now, I've been craving my favorite whiskey and tequila. Itching to smoke my favorite strains of weed. Hell, during rehab, I've regularly had dreams about snorting mountains of coke, and that's not even my thing. Anything I could imagine that might transport me to another dimension—one where grief, regret, and shame aren't ravaging my soul at all times. But now, come to find out, there's something far better than all of it. Light years better. *Aubrey Fucking Capshaw.*

My eyes roll back, as I revel in the sweet juices covering my lips, tongue, and beard. A second later, Aubrey digs her nails into my bare shoulders with force, arches her back, and releases an orgasm that practically vibrates against my mouth on her clit while squeezing my three fingers inside her.

I rip the pillow off her face, desperate to see Aubrey's expression when she comes; and the "O face" she serves up doesn't disappoint. In fact, it exceeds my wildest fantasies.

My god, Aubrey's moonlit face as she comes is a work of art. The most beautiful thing I've seen in my life, made extra special by the knowledge that she's coming for me. Because of me. Because she came to me, against her better judgment. I've always believed drumming for thousands of adoring fans was the ultimate high. But then Aubrey came along and proved me dead wrong about that. *This.* This is the ultimate high.

As Aubrey's moans subside, I turn her sweaty body onto its side and do something I've been wanting to do for quite some time: I bite her fucking ass cheek. Not too hard. This isn't an assault. Just a little nibble. Enough to make her gasp in surprise and brand her ass as *mine* and make her giggle and sigh.

I'm feral now.

Losing my goddamned mind.

I grab a condom from the nightstand, get my aching cock wrapped up in record speed, and return to Aubrey's naked, slack body on my bed. With a shaky exhale, I crawl on top of her, rest her calves on my shoulders, feel for my target, and burrow myself deep inside her, all the way.

As my body fills Aubrey's, we both moan at the delectable sensation and collide in a deep, hungry kiss as I begin thrusting, in and out. I fuck her without holding back. Deep. Until my balls are flush with her body with every stroke. She feels divinely designed for my body. Created specifically for me. She's fucking perfect.

Our bodies synch up into a grunting, frenzied rhythm; and soon, we're both out of our heads. Setting fire to the bedsheets and to the crescent moon and shimmering lake outside my bedroom window. We're moving as one. *We're in the zone.*

I didn't know it was possible for me to want someone like this, ever again. The last time it happened, the only other time, was fifteen years ago, when I was a dumb, selfish kid. A dumbass who didn't grasp the rarity of it. The preciousness. I assumed it'd happen, again and again, over the course of my long lifetime, as easily as snapping my fingers or calling room service. I assumed it'd be that easy again, simply because I'd been lucky enough to stumble cluelessly into true love, so fucking young, despite myself. But when I never felt that way again, not even close, and the years dragged on, I accepted my fate. No more love for Caleb. Never again.

But now, suddenly, here I am at thirty-five, after a lifetime of being alone and lonely, after a decade and a half of being everyone's third wheel and plus-one, I'm finally feeling that same kind of electricity again. That same kind of magic. Only better this time. So much fucking better. Because I'm not taking it for granted.

Fifteen years ago, I carelessly threw my ex's love away with both hands, in favor of fulfilling my stupid rockstar fantasies. I figured she'd be waiting for me, when I got back from tour. Or if not then, when I was finally ready to commit, whenever that might be.

This time, though, I'm not going to make the same mistakes.

Wait.

Shit.

So, that's it? I'm officially falling in love with Aubrey?

Yep.

I am.

I can't deny it.

Don't even want to deny it.

I'm falling for her, hard. Mind, body, heart, and soul. And it feels so fucking good.

As the truth settles into my chest, I begin fucking Aubrey, even harder, with even more fervor, which then causes our mutual pleasure to spiral even higher, into the stratosphere.

I fuck her till she's growling and gripping my shoulders. My neck. Chest. Hair. Beard.

I fuck her till a torrent of whimpers and moans pours

out of her mouth, till a stream of hoarse whispers escapes mine.

I fuck her till she's running her hands feverishly over the planes and grooves of my back, shoulders, and arms. Till she's gripping my bare ass and digging her fingernails into me and begging me not to stop.

I fuck her till I'm on the cusp of losing it, till I'm whispering into her ear that she's perfect and feels like heaven. I tell her I've waited a lifetime to feel this fucking good. "You've ruined me for anyone else," I confess. And a second later, Aubrey unleashes an orgasm with my cock burrowed deep inside her, all the way, thereby hurtling me into a blissful release of my own.

As I come, I snap my hips forward, driving myself as deep inside her as I can get. So fucking deep, I'm surprised I'm not physically splitting the poor girl in two.

Streaks of light.

Stars.

They're lighting up my blurred vision like a fireworks display, as my body empties itself into her. Well, into the condom, anyway. I swear, I've never regretted wearing a condom more in my life. After news of Claudia's pregnancy reached me, I swore I'd never have sex again without a condom. But in this moment, the idea of making a baby with Aubrey doesn't freak me out. It thrills me.

When my body stops shuddering, I pause to catch my breath, while Aubrey does the same underneath me. That was the most intense, outrageously addicting sexual experience of my life. Hands down. I don't know if I'm truly falling in love with Aubrey, like my body's telling me. It's distinctly possible the intensity of my feelings is purely situational. The product of my blooming love for Raine mixed with my gratitude to Aubrey for making that love possible. But lying here now on top of Aubrey, it sure feels like it.

I guess the only thing I know for sure is I want to have sex with Aubrey again and again. Tonight. Tomorrow night. The night after that. As much as humanly possible, every chance I get, while my brain figures out if my body's telling the truth about my feelings . . . or if it's simply hopelessly horny and deeply confused.

CHAPTER 21
AUBREY

"*I love you*," I murmur.

Caleb is softly kissing every inch of my naked body, from head to toe, making me swoon and sigh along the way.

He taps my cheek with his fingertip. "Auntie Aubbey."

"Caleb," I purr. "I didn't mean to fall in love with you, but I couldn't help it."

Caleb smiles like a demon. "Good to know I've got another person to fuck over." He taps my cheek again. *Tap, tap, tap.* "I use my inside voice like a big girl, Auntie Aubbey. 'Ake up."

What the fuck? I open my eyes and find a pair of blue eyes staring at me from an inch away.

"I smell pancakes," Raine whispers excitedly, delivering another set of taps to my cheek.

I sniff the air and return her smile. "I smell them, too."

Raine squeals. "Pop-Pop?"

"Or maybe Caleb—*Dadda*—got up early to make them for you."

"Let's go see!" Raine scrambles out of bed excitedly and

then jumps around from foot to foot, when I'm not nearly as fast-moving. "Come on!" she shrieks at me, wriggling and waving her arms. "Let's go!"

Cut me some slack, kid. Auntie Aubbey got the living hell fucked out of her last night. Three times. And now, my most intimate muscles feel like they've been put through a meat grinder—in the best possible way, of course.

I place my feet on the floor with a big yawn, which Raine takes as her cue to sprint the door. "Rainey, wait," I call out. "Check your nighttime panties, honey." I've learned not to call her nighttime pull-up a *diaper*. Raine the Big Girl only wears *panties*.

With a little huff of impatience and an eyeroll that reminds me so much of Claudia, it hurts, Raine yanks down her disposable, big-girl diaper to her knees and takes a peek at its crotch. "I did it!" she announces proudly. "No pee-pee!"

"Great job!" I motion toward the door. "Now go to the bathroom like a big girl, and we'll go to the kitchen after that to see if it's Pop-Pop or Dadda making you breakfast."

Raine squeals with delight, and off she waddles toward the bedroom door with her pink pull-ups still at her knees and her tiny, naked butt on full display.

Raine was doing fabulously well with potty training before Claudia's accident, other than a few occasional mishaps at night. But since her entire world came crashing down less than a month ago, the poor girl started having regular accidents again, which means our regular routine now includes lots of reminders and pull-ups at night.

As Raine does her thing in the bathroom, I wait at the door holding a sundress and a pair of panties for her to slide into when she's done. When she emerges, however, I tell her I didn't hear the faucet and turn her around to wash her hands for the full length of "The Birthday Song."

When that bit of business is done, Raine throws on the clothes I've picked out for her in the hallway, while I use the bathroom myself. Due to Raine's intense separation anxiety since Claudia's death, I'm expecting her to be waiting at the bathroom door for me when I come out. But to my surprise and delight, Raine is long gone when I emerge.

I follow the sounds of Raine's happy squeals toward the kitchen. And while I'm still in the hallway, her squeals become mixed with the delectable sounds of Caleb's deep rumble of a voice, saying something I can't quite make out. Whatever it is, it's obvious he's cheerful. Enthralled, I'd even say. And a second later, the same song Caleb played yesterday for Raine—the one he said is called "Fool in the Rain"—begins blaring.

I enter the kitchen and discover the pair bopping in place to the song while making breakfast together.

Caleb looks up with a smile when he notices me. "Good morning," he says brightly. "How'd you sleep, beautiful?"

"Beee-yootiful!" Raine echoes, making Caleb laugh.

"Yes, she is." Caleb's green eyes are positively sparkling. "Very, *very* beautiful."

Fuck. I thought having sex with Caleb—*three times*—last night would get him out of my system. Help me resist him, once and for all. But no such luck. He's even hotter today than last night. Especially when he calls me "beautiful," while dancing with Raine to an absolute bop of a song.

"I slept great," I manage. "For the few hours I got, anyway."

Caleb snickers, knowing full well *he's* the reason I barely got a wink of sleep.

His incredible mouth. Those talented fingers. That

relentless dick. All of a sudden, all of it is flickering across my mind.

"What about you?" I ask. "How'd you sleep?"

Caleb pops a blueberry into his mouth and winks. "Aubrey Capshaw, I can honestly say I got the best damned sleep I've ever had in my entire bleeping life last night."

"Best *darn* sleep."

"Oh yeah. Shoot." His chuckle rumbles through the kitchen. "I made a stack of blueberry for you, by the way." He points to a plate of pancakes on the counter. "A little birdie told me that's your favorite, Auntie Aubbey."

"A *birdie*?" Raine says, looking around.

"A birdie named Pop-Pop. It's a joke."

"*Oh*." Raine laughs uproariously, and Caleb chuckles and pokes her belly. "Don't worry, Shortcake. The same birdie told me you love chocolate chip pancakes. I waited to make a batch of those with *you*."

"Dat my favorite," Raine confirms. "Best damn."

I palm my forehead, as Caleb cracks up.

"See how that works?" I tease. But he's howling with laughter. Not worried in the slightest he's taught Raine a bad word. "She's a sponge, Caleb," I say. But as much as I want to continue chastising him, I can't. His laughter is too cute. Too irresistible. And soon, I'm laughing, too. When I'm finally able to control myself again, I say, "I admit it's hilarious, but don't curse around her again. A social worker is going to interview her in LA before the hearing, remember?"

Caleb's smile fades. Reality sinks in. Our little bubble is popped. Shoot. Why'd I say that?

"Yeah, okay. I'll be more careful." Caleb takes a deep breath and returns to Raine, his jaw tight. "Ready to add the chocolate chips to the bowl now?"

"Ready!" To emphasize her readiness, Raine shakes her little booty with glee, causing me to reflexively lurch toward her, since she's now standing atop an old wooden chair. I needn't worry, though. At the first shake of Raine's little body, her big, strong daddy is there to slide a muscled arm around her and keep her safe.

Swoon, swoon, swoon.

And fuck, fuck, fuck.

I feel exactly like I did last night, when Caleb had Raine on his lap in front of the drum kit. Like a goner. Like a flock of bald eagles has landed inside my belly and started mercilessly flapping around. Like clouds are parting and sunshine is streaming in and rainbows are filling the air all around me. Is this ridiculous swoon of euphoria going to happen to me every time Raine and Caleb have an adorable moment together? If so, I'm in trouble, because falling in love with Caleb simply isn't an option. I mean, come on. Sex was one thing. But pinning my actual hopes on the man being a long-term partner is something else entirely.

"Okay, that's enough stirring, party chef," Caleb says. "All good."

Still bopping in place, Raine abruptly raises the wooden mixing spoon as part of her choreography, but because she's been stirring the contents of her bowl with it, she unintentionally flings pancake batter across the countertop, a cabinet, and the floor.

"Uh oh," Raine says, grimacing. "I make mess." She looks up at Caleb with wide, blue eyes, awaiting his reaction. And much to her relief and mine, Caleb reacts the same way Claudia always did. With laughter and a gentle hug.

"It's okay," Caleb coos to his daughter. "We all make mistakes. Even me. Especially me. Hey, Aubbey, will you come over here and stand next to our girl, while I grab a rag?"

Our girl.

Why is that phrasing hitting me so hard?

My heart stampeding, I head over to Raine and keep her stable on her chair while Caleb cleans up the mess. When he's done, he pinches my ass behind Raine's back and says, "Thanks, Aubbey. You da best."

"Da best!" Raine echoes.

"After my Zoom call, I'm gonna give Raine another swimming lesson, and then I told her we'd watch *Monsters, Inc.* together; so feel free to take a long nap today, if you happen to need to catch up on sleep for any reason." With a grin, he leans in to kiss my lips, like it's the most natural thing in the world for him to do. But I jerk back, reflexively, not wanting Raine to witness our physical connection and get the wrong idea about what it means. Hell, I'm not sure what it means, so how can I expect Raine to understand it? All I know is the poor girl's already had one happily ever snatched away from her. She doesn't need to get her hopes up about another one, and have that one snatched away, too, when Dadda and Auntie Aubbey don't become a couple, after all.

When I reject his kiss, Caleb furrows his brow in confusion, so I jut my chin toward Raine by way of explanation.

"Seriously?" Caleb murmurs. With a sigh, he guides Raine off the chair. "Go change into your swimsuit, Shortcake. I'll have breakfast waiting for you, when you get back."

With a little hoot of excitement, Raine runs off, and the minute she's gone, Caleb folds his arms over his broad chest, leans his ass against the counter, and asks, "Why can't I kiss you in front of her?"

"Because I don't want her feeling confused or upset, when things don't pan out the way she's hoping."

"*When?*"

I bite the inside of my cheek. If my word choice is a surprise to him, then he's the least self-aware human being on Planet Earth.

Caleb sighs. "She's two, Aubrey."

"Old enough to get her hopes up. You don't think she's already been bombarded with happily ever afters in all her cartoons?" I run a hand through my hair. "Look, last night was amazing, but the chances of this thing working out between us, long-term, are slim to none, and we both know it."

"We do?"

"We're going to be in each other's lives for a very long time, thanks to our mutual love of Raine. So, let's be smart and not do something to make it, you know, awkward for us in the future, when things don't . . ." I stop talking when I realize Caleb looks pissed as hell. "You disagree?" I ask hopefully.

His jaw muscles pulse. "Doesn't matter what I think. You're the one with all the answers, apparently. We'll do whatever you want, Aubrey."

"I never said I have all the answers or that this is what I *want*. The only thing that matters is that hearing in a month, Caleb. We can't screw that up. Plus, I'm in charge of your rehab, remember?"

"No, I'm in charge of that. That's on me."

"You know what I mean. I'm in charge of *overseeing* it. *Managing* it. So, it's obviously in everyone's best interests if we keep certain things on the down low, until we're done with rehab and the hearing. If you're still interested in kissing me when Raine is watching, when we're not required to live under the same roof anymore, then, okay, maybe we can—"

"I get it, Aubrey." He throws up his hands. "You want me to be your dirty little secret."

I'm shocked. That's what he thinks I'm saying? "That's not what I meant."

"Whatever. It's fine." His green eyes bore into me. "Just so I understand, you're saying you're open to doing what we did last night again . . . as long as nobody knows you'd stoop that low?"

Is he fucking kidding me? *What the fuck is wrong with this man?* "I'm not *stooping* to anything," I reply calmly, even though I want to scream at him and throttle him. "I'm saying we don't want the social worker or the judge to sniff us out. Not to mention, I'm guessing sobriety coaches aren't supposed to fuck their . . . wards. Clients. Charges. Whatever the fuck you are."

Caleb subtly licks his lower lip. "Just tell me this. Do you regret what we did last night?"

Regret? Again, he's so off the mark, I could slap him. How could he possibly think that, after the way my body reacted to his—not once, but *three* times? "I don't regret anything. Wanting to do the best thing for Raine isn't the same thing as regretting what I did with you. It's not always about you."

Caleb's eyes flash with anger, and I know I've messed up. Why'd I say that? Why am I pushing him away like this?

"Yeah, it's always about me," he spits out. "That's why I'm here in Prairie Fucking Springs for three fucking weeks, when all I want to do is sleep in my own goddamned bed in Santa Monica. That's why I took the risk of leaving rehab early, even before I knew if—"

Raine barrels into the kitchen wearing the hot pink,

ruffled bikini Caleb bought for her in Billings, and he smashes his lips together. Although "wearing" is a stretch in this instance, since Raine's got the top on backward and upside-down and the frilly bottoms inside-out.

"Great job, kiddo!" Caleb bellows, just as I'm about to head over to Raine to help her put everything on correctly.

"You ready for some pancakes, Rainey Baby?" Caleb booms, scooping her up.

"Yessss!" she shrieks.

As Caleb gets Raine situated in a chair, he glares at me like he wants to strangle me. Or is that fuck me? Maybe both.

I take a seat next to Raine, figuring Caleb is right: it's better to support her independence than correct her messed up bathing suit. I mean, whether the thing is on correctly or inside-out and backwards, it's still functional, right?

The thing that's not quite as functional, though? Caleb and me. Clearly, neither of us knows how to navigate this new, physical stage of our forced situationship. That much is now abundantly clear to me. And I'm not sure how to get clarity, going forward.

CHAPTER 22
CALEB

The front door opens.

Two white sneakers enter my peripheral vision.

I look up at Aubrey from the wooden plank I'm attaching to the growing deck. "Hey."

She bites her lower lip. "Hey. Looking good down there."

Now that we're finally alone, I can't resist flirting with her, even though I still don't know what the fuck happened in the kitchen this morning. Why we had that weird tiff, when last night was supernaturally incredible. "Me or the deck?"

Aubrey slides into a nearby Adirondack chair. "Both."

I look down to hide my smile. That was the first time Aubrey's even *flirted* with *flirting* with me today. Now that she's put Raine to bed, does that mean it's game on again? I sure hope that's what's she's thinking, because I've been craving a repeat of last night, all damn day. Except that this time, I'm planning to fuck Aubrey *four* times tonight, just to teach her a lesson about coming at me, when I least expect it. True, she said the word like she's making a major concession. Like the last thing she wants to do is compliment me. But she did. Which means it's full steam ahead, as far as I'm concerned, whether I'm still confused about this morning or not.

After wrangling my smug smile, I look up at Aubrey again. This time, with wanton lust in my eyes. "Lookin' good up there, too. Really, really good." Truth be told, she looks a whole lot better than good; she looks like a goddamned wet dream in her shorty-shorts and cropped tank top that bares a delightful slice of her midsection. I put down the tool I've been using and rearrange myself to sit squarely on my ass. Forearms on my knees. "Is Raine asleep?"

"She was out like a light by page two of her picture book."

I take off my work gloves, my fingers tingling with the desire to touch her. To make her come again, like she did last night. "The kid played hard today."

"She sure did." Aubrey smiles. "She adores you, *Dadda*. You did a great job today."

My heart skips a beat. I had a fantastic day with my girl and Aubrey today. One that made it clear I'm making major progress. With Raine, anyway. I don't know what the fuck Aubrey is thinking. But at least in relation to Raine, today was so damned good, it felt like one of my own idyllic days on the lake during my childhood.

I'm still rankled as shit about the thing Aubrey said in the heat of battle this morning: *It's not always about you.* Yeah, no shit, Sherlock. I wouldn't be here in Prairie Springs, if it was always about me. Even after twelve hours, that bullshit comment still pisses me off. But even so, after thinking about it all day, I've realized Aubrey was right to remind me about the hearing. Also, to insist we keep things a secret, at least from Raine, until then.

Aubrey motions to my phone next to me on the deck. It's blaring a song from my Zepp playlist. "What song is this?"

"'Kashmir.'"

"Led Zeppelin again?"

"Yep. This is one of their most famous songs." I guess we're not going to fuck any time soon. We're going to talk. Not about what's been on my mind all day, though. Not about what the hell happened in the kitchen this morning and why it feels like Aubrey's suddenly pushing me away, despite our amazing night together.

Aubrey taps one of her white sneakers onto the wood below her chair, in time to the music. "I recognize his voice. What's his name?"

Seriously? "Robert Plant. He's got one of the best, most distinctive voices in the history of rock." It's true. Robert Plant's a rock god. But he's not what I want to be talking about in this moment. Honestly, I don't want to be talking at all, unless I'm talking dirty into Aubrey's ear while fucking her raw.

Aubrey gnaws at her lip, like she's trying to work up the courage to say something. I lean back onto my palms and wait. Hopefully, she's finally going to explain what crawled up her ass this morning.

"Do you only listen to Led Zeppelin?" she asks. "Or do you ever listen to, I don't know, girlie pop or dance music as a palate cleanser?"

I grimace. "Ugh. No, Aubrey."

She giggles. "Hey, don't knock it till you've tried it."

"No, thanks." I motion to my phone. "I put on my Zepp playlist, whenever I'm working on the deck, in tribute to my grandpa. Led Zeppelin was his all-time favorite band, so listening to them while I'm working on a deck at his house makes me feel like he's here with me in a small way."

"That's sweet." She pauses. Her shoulders soften, like she's making some kind of internal concession. "It was really sweet when you played that song for Raine. Watching you giving her drum lessons melted my heart. Exploded my ovaries, too."

My eyebrows quirk up. Okay, that was definitely flirtatious. A step in the right direction, for sure. "You told me to be myself with her. So that's what I did. There's nothing more 'me' than playing drums to a Zepp song."

"Besides playing to a Red Card Riot song, of course."

I shrug. "I didn't write all of our songs, so they're not all 'me,' you know? But Zepp? I swear, it's like those dudes somehow cracked the code inside my head." Why are we talking about Led Zeppelin, instead of what happened in the kitchen this morning? Or better yet, now that Raine's asleep, why aren't we inside the house, *not* talking, but banging like animals, instead?

"If you ever teach Raine to play drums to 'Shaynee,'" Aubrey says, "you can tell her Dean is singing 'Rainey' in all those choruses.'"

"Great idea. I'll definitely do that." I wait. Stare at her, silently coaxing her to spit it out, whatever it is. Surely, this isn't what Aubrey wants to be talking about, either. It's written all over her pretty face.

The next song on my Zepp playlist comes on. "Since I've Been Loving You." As it gets going, Aubrey taps her sneakers in time to the music and looks down at her hands in her lap.

"I've never been into classic rock," she says. "My dad's

tried to get me into it, but I've always been more of a pop girlie myself."

I say nothing. Whatever's on her mind, she's going to have to nut up and say it. I'm not willing to try to pry it out of her.

"What's this one called?" she asks.

"'Since I've Been Loving You.'" Heat rises in my cheeks. It's just a song title; so, why did I blush from saying it?

"I like it."

I bite my tongue, very much wishing I could reply, "I'd very much like to fuck you to this song, Aubrey."

"Now that I know you hate girlie pop so much," Aubrey says, "I know exactly what to play to torture you, whenever you piss me off again."

"*When* I piss you off again, not *if*? Maybe there won't be a next time."

Aubrey snorts. "Haven't you been trying *not* to piss me off this whole time, *C-Bomb*? And look how that's turned out. I'm sure I've ripped you a new asshole by now, thanks to all the times you've pissed me off."

I smirk. She only calls me C-Bomb when she's playfully putting me in my place. It's a good sign, I think. "I'll take your word for that, *A-Bomb*, since you're more of an expert than I am about what's between my ass cheeks." Several times last night, Aubrey groped every last inch of real estate back there, while she was in a fugue state of pure ecstasy. "Also, for the record," I add, "I've *mostly* tried not to piss you off. A few times, however, I admit I've actively *tried* to piss you off, for the sheer fun of it."

She gasps. "*Why*?"

"You're hot as fuck when you're angry."

Aubrey rolls her eyes. "Well, that's not toxic or anything."

"Never said I'm not toxic. Only that I haven't tried my best, at all times, not to piss you off, so it's possible I'll be able to avoid doing it in the future, if I decide to give it my best shot."

"Forgive me if I don't hold my breath."

"I didn't try to piss you off this morning, to be clear. I still don't know what the fuck I did to set you off. I mean, I get that we shouldn't get handsy in front of Raine. I'm on board for that. But it seemed like more than that to me." There. I did it. I opened Pandora's Box. But, shit, if we're not going to fuck any time soon, then we might as well get to the bottom of whatever made Aubrey go off on me this morning.

"I think I just . . . Panicked, a little bit."

"About what?"

"Where this might lead. Where it won't." She opens her mouth to say more but closes it abruptly.

"And . . .?" I prompt.

"Nothing. Never mind. It doesn't matter."

It does matter, though. Clearly. There's something more she's not saying. I don't know how to get her to say it, though. I've never been good at expressing my own feelings with words, so I'm the last person who's going to pull something out of someone else.

I've been working on the communication thing with Gina in our counseling sessions. But it still doesn't come naturally to me, especially when I'm dealing with a whole bunch of feelings that have been hitting me like a Mack truck, all at once. I've got new, big feelings for Raine. New, big feelings for Aubrey. A rising feeling of joy and hopefulness that's brand-new to me, too. Or at least, I haven't felt this way in a very long time.

Aubrey clears her throat. "It's not just me who loves

girlie-pop music. Raine loves shaking her booty to a good dance beat, too."

I stare her down. *Come on, Aubrey.* "Maybe we could give each other music appreciation lessons. I'll show you my favorites—the best of rock, decade by decade—while you show me your favorites."

"You'd listen to all my pop favorites?"

I shrug. "Fair is fair."

Aubrey flashes me a beaming smile—one that makes me feel like my haphazard attempt at reconciliation has made a dent in whatever's making her skittish. "Okay, great. Let's do that."

"I'm down to try any strategy that will help me bond with Raine." *And with you.*

"Would you mind if I put on my all-time favorite song now?"

"Go for it."

I stop the song on my phone, and Aubrey starts one on hers. One I recognize instantly, since it's part of the very fabric of pop culture by now: "Pretty Girl" by Aloha Carmichael.

"Ugh, Aubrey. Not this. Anything but this."

She giggles. "Come on, Caleb. This is the best song, ever. My top favorite. My desert island pick."

"Please. I beg you. My ears are bleeding."

"Oh, calm down." She gets up and begins dancing to the song, doing choreography like she did the other day when we walked around the lake, and her perky little tits start bouncing with her effort, making me realize she's braless under there.

"I take it back. The song is a banger," I deadpan, leaning back onto both palms and smiling up at her dancing frame.

"See? Told you it's a great song."

"The best," I say, enjoying the sexy view. "Was this playing in your earbuds the other day, when we walked around the lake?"

Aubrey laughs at the memory and nods. "Whenever it comes on, I feel compelled to do the choreography from the music video. I can't help myself."

"I'm not complaining."

Aubrey catches on to my ogling and adds an extra jiggle to her movement; and, slowly, my dick begins thickening in response.

"Did you know Aloha's signed to my band's label?"

Aubrey gasps and stops dancing. "Does that mean you know her? Are you *friends*?"

"Our paths cross, now and again, at parties and industry events. But, no, I wouldn't call us friends."

Aubrey's face is glowing with excitement. "What's Aloha like? Is she as nice as she seems?"

"She's nice, yeah. To people she likes. But if you're angling for an introduction, don't bother. I'm not someone she likes."

Aubrey gasps again, this time dramatically feigning shock. "*What*? Who on Earth could resist your cheerful, charming personality, *C-Bomb*?"

By all rights, I should be laughing with her right now, since she's adorable and funny. But I can't laugh because I've just realized my mistake. Surely, the odds are high my ill-advised disclosure about Aloha will lead to Aubrey asking me—

"Why doesn't Aloha like you? What'd you do?"

Yup. That.

"Nothing too egregious. She's good friends with some people who think I'm an immature, hotheaded little prick."

"Why do they think that about you?"

"Because I was an immature, hotheaded little prick to them." I manage a tight smile, but Aubrey frowns. Fuck. Why'd I lead the conversation down this path, when it will almost certainly lead to me being asked to explain my bad behavior? Aubrey of all people—the woman I'm trying to get into my bed again—the woman I might even be falling in love with—doesn't need to know about that whole saga. Not now. Not ever.

"What'd you do, Caleb?" Aubrey prompts, her dark eyes wide. Suddenly, it's clear she's not being playful anymore. She's not flirting. She's locked in and dead serious.

I scratch my arm and try to look unbothered. Neutral. Like it was no big deal, rather than the thing that still haunts me, to this day. "Nothing too terrible. I was just being my cheerful, charming self. Apparently, I'm not everyone's cup of tea." Averting my eyes, I decide I'm done with this conversation now. All conversation, in fact, for the rest of the night. It's high time for me to fuck Aubrey Capshaw or jerk off to fantasies of her, if she's not down.

I turn off the putrid song blaring on Aubrey's phone and grab both phones off the deck. With a loud sigh, I get up and put away my tools, signaling to Aubrey I'm done here for the night. And not only in relation to the deck.

"I'm going to bed," I announce, when my clean-up is done. "Am I going there with or without you, babysitter?" I didn't plan to put it so bluntly. Didn't plan to force the issue. And I certainly didn't plan to call her "babysitter" while inviting her to get fucked. But the Aloha thing's got me stressed—worried Aubrey's going to somehow find out about what happened between me and Violet—and me and Dax. And now, my brain's hurtling into a bit of a tailspin.

"Wow, what a romantic invitation," Aubrey deadpans.

"You want romance, baby? Then C-Bomb's not your

man. You want orgasms? Come to papa." Why am I acting like this, when all day long, it's become painfully obvious to me how much I desperately want to give Aubrey both romance and orgasms? Why, why, why can't I simply tell her how I'm feeling about her?

"Well, first of all, I don't want to have sex with *C-Bomb*," Aubrey huffs out. "And second of all, ideally, I want both. Romance and orgasms, whenever I find my person. Don't worry, I know he's not you. Obviously. But, yes, I definitely want and deserve *both* in my next relationship."

Fuck me. The thought of her with someone else makes me homicidal. And yet, this is a self-imposed wound, isn't it? I practically forced her to say that shit to me. *Why*? Why am I pushing her away, when all I want to do is take her into my arms and confess I'm starting to feel something amazing for her. Something that makes *me* want to be her next relationship?

"Why are you suddenly acting like a caveman?" she asks. "I don't understand you."

That makes two of us, baby. "There's not much to understand, Aubrey. I want to fuck you. Not talk about fucking Aloha Carmichael."

"Jeez, Caleb. Sorry. She's my all-time favorite artist, so I was excited to find out you've met her." She's standing now. Her hands on her hips. "What the fuck is your problem? Tell me what's going on in your head."

"I'm horny. That's my problem. That's the sum total of what's going on in my head. The desire to fuck you. So, are you in or out, babysitter? If you're out, tell me now, and I'll go take a cold shower."

Aubrey rubs a palm down her face. "God, I hate myself for this, given how rude you're being; but, yes, I'm in. Only if you promise not to be a jerk while fucking me, though."

"Deal."

"Also, only if you ask me nicely."

"I just did."

Aubrey scoffs. "If that was your idea of nice, then my answer is no."

"You already said yes."

"With a caveat."

I roll my eyes and take a deep breath. "Aubrey Capshaw, please come to bed with me."

"Come on, Caleb. You can do it nicer than that."

Fuck it. I take a few steps, till I'm standing directly in front of her, and slowly sink to my knees before her. "Please, Aubrey. If I don't fuck you tonight, I'm not sure I'll survive till morning." She laughs, thinking I'm joking around. But, sadly, I'm not.

"What, exactly, will kill you, if I say no?"

"My aching balls will most likely explode, and I'll bleed out."

Aubrey laughs again. "Well, jeez, now that I know it's a matter of life and death, how could I say no?"

Relieved, I stand up, take Aubrey's face in my hands, and pull her mouth to mine for a passionate, hungry kiss. And just like that, we're both on fire again, every bit as much as last night. Even more so, I'd say, now that we both know what awaits us.

As our kiss deepens, I feel a shockwave of greed scorch through me. It's beyond something physical. Far beyond lust. Just this fast, I'm pretty sure I literally *need* this woman in my life. And, honestly, if that's the case, that scares the shit out of me.

I lift Aubrey up by her ass and press her center into my steely bulge, and Aubrey responds with a soft moan and grinding motion that sends lust rocketing through me. Fuck me. She already owns me, this woman. I don't want that to be true. It's thoroughly inconvenient for a guy like me. But this taste of her is confirming it. *I'm a fucking goner.*

Still holding her by her ass cheeks, I carry Aubrey inside the house, and she wraps her legs around me and grinds herself into me while running her hands greedily through my hair.

Quickly, I realize my bedroom is too far away for me to survive the journey without my balls exploding before arrival. *I need to get my mouth on Aubrey's perfect tits right fucking now.*

CHAPTER 23
CALEB

I lay Aubrey down on the couch and begin furiously peeling off her clothes. "I've been drooling over your perfect tits all day," I confess, as I toss her crop top to the floor. To emphasize my point, I lean in and suck on a peaked nipple, and she moans softly and writhes at the sensation.

After devouring both Aubrey's tits with fervor, I slide off her shorts, murmuring about how much I've been dying to eat her pussy again. "Hate me if you want, if it gets you off, but nobody can give you orgasms like I can."

"I don't hate you," she whispers hoarsely, her eyes closed and her head slung back. "I'm just . . . Let's not talk."

"Fine with me."

I've got her naked now, so I get myself the same way, and then kneel on the floor in between her bare thighs, eager to bury my face in her contraband pussy.

After kissing her inner thighs, I go after her sweet spot like a man on death row scarfing down his last meal. And only a few minutes later, I've got Aubrey coming hard against my mouth and fingers, even more forcefully than last night.

"The condoms are in my room," I gasp out. I rise from my knees, breathing hard, and stare down at her naked, sweaty figure in the moonlight. "Stay put, baby, and I'll—"

"I put a condom in the pocket of my shorts." She points to the crumpled item of clothing on the floor. "I had a feeling we might not make it to your bedroom."

Euphoria slams into me. All day, I've been wondering if she wants me the way I want her. If my torture is a mutual thing. But now I know: no matter how much she second-guesses me or pushes me away, no matter how much she tries to play it off like she could take me or leave me, the truth is she can't resist me, any more than I can resist her.

Panting, I grab the condom and get myself covered in record speed. And by the time I'm all wrapped up and ready to go, Aubrey's bent over the back of the couch, like she's offering her backside to me on a silver platter.

"Do it like this," she purrs, looking at me seductively. "I want it hard."

It wouldn't have occurred to me to fuck Aubrey from behind, since that's the sexual position I've always used when fucking a stranger. A groupie. A fan. A reporter who's hit on me. Basically, anyone I'll never see again who's made it abundantly clear they're down to fuck. Why would I want to fuck *Aubrey* like this, when all I want to do is look into her big, brown eyes and kiss her lips, while my body impales hers? I'm already addicted to seeing Aubrey's "O" face. It's better than any drug or booze. And I can't see it, if she's faced away while she comes.

"Come on, *C-Bomb*," Aubrey coos. "Fuck me hard like this."

I'm confused. Mere minutes ago, Aubrey said she had

no desire to fuck *C-Bomb*, only Caleb. But now she's using that nickname while offering her naked ass to me? Make it make sense.

It occurs to me I've got a split-second to make this decision, or she's going to pull away. Revoke her offer. Feel rejected. So, I quickly decide, fuck it. I'll fuck Aubrey Capshaw any way I can get her.

"Whatever you want, *A-Bomb*," I murmur. When she snickers, I add, "You're hotter than an atomic bomb, baby." I stride to her, my cock leading the way, and press myself into her while kissing her neck and groping her tits from behind. After a bit, I reach around and finger her, and when she's as wet and ready for me as can be, I grab her hip with one hand while gently gripping the back of her hair with the other, and sink my cock deep, deep, *deep* inside her.

As my body fills hers, all the fucking way, Aubrey cries out; and as I begin to fuck her without mercy, she groans loudly, prompting me to move my hand from her hair to her mouth to stifle all forthcoming noises. She asked for hard, so hard is what I give her. Until, eventually, we're going at it with so much animalistic fury, I have to grip Aubrey's hips with two hands to keep our pounding, slapping rhythm.

Looking at the back of her head isn't what I want, though, And I can't pretend otherwise. Maybe one day, I'll get to a point where I'm so sure of our connection, I'll enjoy switching things up and using her body like this. Like she's just another groupie. But for now, it's the last thing I want, honestly. I don't want a warm body; I want *Aubrey*. I don't the back of her head; I want Aubrey's beautiful face. Her deep brown eyes lighting a fire inside me, the likes of which I've never felt before.

"Not like this," I gasp out, as clarity slams into me. *I love Aubrey Capshaw.* Holy fucking shit. I love this woman. I'm not falling for her. I'm already there. And not because of our shared love for Raine. Not because I'm stuck with her in this house. But because she makes me feel with my whole heart, not only a mere fraction of it, for the first fucking time in my whole life.

"I need to see your face," I grit out. "I need to kiss you, baby. Turn around." Without waiting for her to comply, I pull out and abruptly turn Aubrey's lithe body around to face me; and the sight of her flushed face and sparkling eyes almost brings me to my knees. And not as a bit this time.

I slide my hands to her rosy cheeks, pressing the tip of my straining cock into her belly, and kiss her with more hunger than I've ever felt for anyone in my life. This woman has awakened something inside me. She makes me want to be a better man. Not only for Raine. Not only for myself. But to be worthy of her.

As a firestorm of hunger engulfs me, I lift Aubrey up and set her onto the back of the couch. When she's perfectly aligned to receive me, I cradle her back in my forearms and fuck her with rhythmic, deep, slow thrusts, kissing her voraciously as I fuck her. Murmuring into her ear about how good she feels. And to my extreme pleasure, Aubrey gets wetter and wetter with each slow thrust, until she's audibly sloshing with each movement of my cock. She plainly enjoyed getting fucked from behind like a groupie earlier, but this is different. I can feel it. She's *enraptured* now. Euphoric. Ecstatic. Transported. The same as me.

Without warning, Aubrey lets out a low keening whimper, followed by a guttural groan, and my eyes roll back into my head.

As she comes with my cock buried deep inside her, balls deep, the sensation of her body milking mine is too much for me to withstand. I'm only human, after all, no matter what the internet says about me. I snap my hips forward forcefully, impaling her violently with the full length of me, and come with a loud groan. With my orgasm complete, I slide a hand to her extended throat and kiss her jawline, her cheek, her temple, reveling in her. Savoring the moment. Claiming Aubrey Capshaw as mine, all mine.

Sadly, the time for me to pull out and disentangle my body from hers arrives, far too soon. So, we slide onto the couch and cuddle with our naked limbs intertwined, staring at the moonlit lake through the large windows installed by Grandpa at some point over the past fifteen years.

"That was even better than last night," Aubrey whispers. "I didn't think that was possible."

I caress her back. "Why'd you call me C-Bomb when you asked me to fuck you? On the deck, you said you don't want to fuck C-Bomb. I'm confused."

She sighs. "I'm sorry. That was cruel of me."

"I wouldn't say cruel. Just confusing."

"No, trust me, it was cruel. A defense mechanism. A way to push you away and punish myself."

"*Punish* yourself? For *what*?"

Aubrey sighs again. "All day, I've been struggling with something, Caleb. Waging a tug of war inside my head about you."

I hold my breath. "What'd I do?"

"Nothing. It's all in my head. I wanted you so much last night, I convinced myself it didn't matter that you'd already slept with my best friend. But today, I couldn't stop feeling guilty about what I did."

"*Guilty*?"

"For stealing my best friend's crush."

It's the last thing I expected to hear. Absolute horseshit.

"Claudia always had a huge crush on you," Aubrey explains. "Even after she had sex with you. In fact, her crush only got bigger after that."

Jesus Christ. No wonder Aubrey's been wigging out today, if this is the kind of batshit-crazy bullshit she's been thinking about. I put my finger underneath her chin. "Aubrey, listen to me. Claudia didn't know me. She had a crush on an idea. On *C-Bomb*. A fantasy she'd built up in her head. And I didn't know her, either. To me, she was just another pretty face. A groupie who threw herself at me, and I accepted the invitation."

"How do you know she threw herself at you, if you don't even remember having sex with her?"

"Because I know I never have sex with anyone, especially on tour, unless it goes down that way." Aubrey looks skeptical. "It's true. Whether I'm high, drunk, or sober, I always know not to put myself in a position where someone can claim there was any kind of coercion or persuasion. I'm a high-profile person, Aubrey. I'd rather party with my friends after a show or go back to my room and drink myself into oblivion than mess around with anyone who might claim I did something wrong later on. Unless someone basically throws themselves at me—and I'm talking about them *telling* me, clearly, they want to fuck me—then I'm never gonna do it."

Aubrey considers that for a long moment. "Your life sounds really lonely."

It's an understatement. "All I'm saying is you've got nothing to feel guilty about. No fucking way."

Aubrey looks out at the lake. "If Claudia were here, I think she'd be furious with me for having sex with you."

"She's not here. And if she were, she'd have no claim on me."

"I'm her best friend, though. There's this thing called girl code. And I've broken it."

I never saw this coming. Not in a million years. Does this mean Aubrey might put an end to things between us because I fucked someone else, almost three years ago—someone who's now dead—and I don't even remember doing it?

I look down at my hands, feeling unexpectedly emotional. For the first time in so long, I actually *feel* something; and now my past is going to fuck it up for me? "Claudia had sex with my body, once," I whisper. "Almost three years ago." I look up. "But you're the first person to have sex with *me*, the real me, in almost fifteen years."

Her lips part in surprise.

"Aubrey, you're the first person in a very long time to actually make me feel something, and I'd honestly be heartbroken if a few minutes with Claudia, a woman who wanted me as a bucket list item, winds up fucking up my chances with you."

Aubrey holds eye contact, her chest heaving. "Claudia said you fucked her from behind and never kissed her. That's why I asked you to do it that way. I wanted to experience you, the same way she did. I wanted to understand how she felt with you, compared to the way I did last night. I wanted to see if I could feel a difference."

"And?"

Her chest heaves, but she says nothing.

"Look," I say. "No matter what position I fuck you in, you're always gonna be Aubrey, and I'm always gonna be Caleb. Which means, no matter what, it's always gonna be different than anything and everything that's come before. For me, anyway. That's the truth." I didn't mean to admit all that to her. Didn't mean to show my cards, this quickly.

But something inside me knows, without a doubt, if I don't fight for Aubrey in this moment, if I don't tell her the truth about how I'm feeling, I'm going to lose her forever.

"Tell me," I whisper. "Please, Aubrey. What was the result of your little experiment? Was there a difference when I fucked you from behind?"

She swallows hard. "A big difference. When you were facing me, when you kissed me and looked into my eyes, I felt ... electricity. Like you truly wanted *me*. Not just sex."

I exhale with relief. "I do want you. I feel addicted to you." I also dream about her. Ache for her. *Love her.* But the rest, I couldn't possibly say out loud. "If you don't want me," I add, "if you're too hung up on what happened between Claudia and me to—"

"No, I do want you," she says, placing a palm on my cheek. "I feel addicted, too. That's why I've been feeling so guilty. If I didn't feel anything for you, I wouldn't feel this conflicted."

I let out a long breath. "The past is the past. We can't change it, so let's not dwell on it."

She chews her lip and nods.

"Will you do me a favor? Don't call me C-Bomb during sex. Everyone calls me that, even my best friends, so feel free to call me that, any other time. Just not during sex."

Nodding, she leans down and kisses me, but abruptly pulls back. "Will you do me a favor, too? Please, call me A-Bomb during sex, as much as possible." She giggles. "That was so fucking hot."

I laugh with her. "Deal."

And just like that, I feel like we've had a breakthrough, Aubrey and me. A meeting of the minds. Without needing to say it out loud, it's now settled we're not drawn to each other merely because we're stuck together, anyway. We're not a fire storm, simply because our bodies happen to fit together like they were made for each other. Or because of our shared love of Raine. No, something bigger is at play here. Something that might alter the course of my life, forever, if I don't fuck it up. The only question, at least in my mind, is whether I'm even capable of *not* fucking it up.

CHAPTER 24
AUBREY

Warm wind is whipping my hair.

Loud music is blaring.

Caleb and I are driving my father's truck down I-90 toward the airport in Billings, on our way to pick up Caleb's sister, Miranda. And I can't remember the last time I felt this happy. This alive. This . . . *in love.*

A moment ago, Caleb put on a song by a band called Pink Floyd—something he really wanted me to hear—and it's emphatically *not* my jam. But even the weird music can't dampen my mood. I'm floating on a cloud today. Eager to meet Caleb's sister. Thrilled to celebrate the official completion of Caleb's rehab tonight. But most of all, I'm excited that Caleb and I have had so much fun together over the past weeks, both as a trio with Raine and also as a passionate duo by night. I haven't told Caleb this, but the weeks I've spent with him and Raine at the lake house have been the best of my life. Even better than the time I spent in Seattle with Claudia, and that felt like heaven on earth.

I look over at Caleb's profile as he drives Dad's big

truck. He's got one hand on the steering wheel and the other clasped loosely with mine. He's singing along to the weird song and looking gorgeous while doing it.

Butterflies whoosh into my belly. My heart goes pitter-pat.

We haven't labeled this thing we've been doing for weeks now. I think we both realize that wouldn't be wise, until we know the outcome of the custody hearing next week. But secretly, I already know I've fallen in love with Caleb. How could I not?

Caleb's phone buzzes and he looks over at it. "Miranda's landed."

"I can't wait to meet her."

"She said the same thing about you."

I pick at a little piece of fuzz on my jeans. "I know you're not technically done with rehab until tonight, but if you want to take your sister for a walk around the lake when we get back, I'll bend the rules and let her babysit you for a while."

Caleb rolls his eyes, making me laugh.

"That won't be necessary. But thanks."

"Seriously, though, I won't be offended, if you want to ditch me for a while. After all the time you've been forced to spend with me, I'm sure you're chomping at the bit to *finally* get some time away from me. While your sister is visiting, I'm sure you'll want to spend some alone time with her and Raine. Or maybe just the two of you. Whatever you want to do, it's great with me."

Caleb looks over at me like I've got three heads, and I await his reply with bated breath. I've grown to love our forced living arrangement; honestly, I'm sad it's ending. Yes, I'm thrilled for Caleb to complete his rehab requirement, and I fully understand, logically, that human beings need solitude and independence at times. But at this point, I fear I'm physically addicted to this man's constant physical presence, and I'm not quite sure how I'm going to handle being away from him for hours or days at a time. Sure, I'll still be Raine's nanny for the foreseeable future. Technically. Assuming things go well at the hearing. So, I'll still be in close proximity with Caleb for that reason. But with the end of rehab, and the upcoming hearing in LA, I'm beginning to feel anxious about what our future together might look like.

Caleb adjusts his grip on the steering wheel. "My sister is bringing my mom's ashes for us to scatter on the lake. So, we'll definitely go off to do that alone. I might also want to go for a walk or run on my own, now and again, without needing to worry about your short little legs keeping up with me." He stifles a grin. "But if I'm being honest, I don't feel the need or desire to change our living arrangement at all."

My heart flutters. "Oh."

"Yeah, we'll no longer be *required* to be stuck like glue after tonight . . ." Caleb's green eyes fine mine. "But, honestly, I don't feel the urge to get myself. . . *unstuck* . . . any time soon."

Elation floods me. "I don't feel the urge to get myself unstuck, either. I like being stuck to you. I'd miss you, if you were gone too long."

A smile splits Caleb's rugged face. "Yeah?"

I blush. "Yeah."

"Okay, then, sounds like we're in agreement to keep everything pretty much the same."

"Sounds like it," I agree, even though I want to squeal and hoot with glee.

"Cool."

"Cool."

We share a huge, goofy, blushing smile, and then ride in thick, electrified, giddy silence for the next several minutes.

Two uneventful songs pass on Caleb's "Songs Aubrey Needs to Hear" Playlist, but when the third one begins, and the lead singer starts singing, I gasp out, "Led Zeppelin!"

"Look at you! You're getting good at recognizing them now. This is a top favorite of theirs."

I pause to listen. "What's it called?"

A deep crimson overtakes Caleb's face. "'All of my Love.'" After the words leave his mouth, he returns to the road ahead of him in a way that feels forced and unnatural. Like he's actively *not* looking at me. Am I imagining that... and also the blush that's still consuming his features?

"I can see why you love this band so much," I say. "Every song slays."

"They're the best band, ever."

"Not RCR?"

Caleb scoffs. "My band isn't even in the top 100 of the best bands, ever."

"I'm sure a large segment of your fanbase would disagree."

"If so, they haven't educated themselves on the history of rock 'n' roll."

I smile to myself. After weeks under Caleb's passionate tutelage about music, I've got a whole new appreciation for rock; and to his credit, Caleb's learned to appreciate my pop-girlie favorites, too. Most of them, anyway.

As the song blares, I glance out my side of the truck and notice a minivan in the next lane. Its back is stuffed to the gills with little kids; its front is occupied by a young, nerdy man and a cute woman in glasses.

All of a sudden, I find myself imagining Caleb and me

sitting in the front of that minivan, driving a car-full of kids. Caleb and me, living the rest of our lives, exactly as we've been doing these past weeks. Together. As a real family.

That's not what we've been calling ourselves, obviously. A family. But isn't that what we've become? I'd say yes, without a doubt, if only we didn't have the uncertainty of the custody hearing looming.

Depending on what happens in court, this fairytale family we've been creating—*cosplaying*?—might disappear in the blink of an eye. The truth is, no matter how real this all feels, or how intense my feelings for Caleb have grown, it's still distinctly possible Caleb might blame me—and therefore drop me like a hot potato—if things don't wind up going his way at the hearing. I take a deep breath and remind myself to remember that.

CHAPTER 25
CALEB

A banner hangs above the front door of my house, imprinted, in all caps, with: "CONGRATULATIONS, CALEB!" Strings of white lights twinkle above our heads. Outdoor speakers I installed last week are currently pumping out a playlist of Aubrey's pop favorites at low volume. Most of which, I've honestly learned to like. It's my "rehab is my bitch!" party on my new deck, attended by the people I now consider my family: Aubrey, her parents, my sister, and Raine.

After eating a dinner that was cooked to perfection on my new barbeque, we're now sitting at the patio table I picked up in Billings the other day, finishing up the delicious dessert—apple pie with homemade vanilla ice cream—made by Barbara. And every single time I look around the table at the chatty, happy faces around me, I can't stop thinking the same thing on a running loop: *Man, I love these people.*

"It sounds straight out of a Hallmark movie," my sister says, referring to Prairie Springs' Summer Festival. At my sister's urging, Barbara's been telling Miranda all about the festival for the past several minutes.

"That's a perfect description," Barbara agrees. "That's what everyone loves about it. We keep it simple and old fashioned and lean into our small-town vibe."

"What, exactly, happens at this adorable festival?" Miranda persists, placing her elbow onto the table. "Are there, like, events and games, or . . . ?"

"Oh, yes," Barbara says. "We have all kinds of fun stuff, culminating in a live auction at the end that raises money for the school and various local causes."

My sister nudges me. "You've donated to the auction already, right?"

"I'm going to. I haven't figured out my exact donation yet."

"There's still plenty of time," Barbara assures me with a wink.

"Come on, you loser-procrastinator," Miranda says. "Let's figure out your donation now, so Barbara can run with it." She taps a manicured finger onto the wooden table. "Four tickets to your next show with backstage passes? That's a no-brainer. Also, a bunch of signed merch." She drums her fingers. "What else? It needs to be something people can't get on the open market."

I shift in my seat. "The thing is, my band doesn't know when we'll be playing next. We had to cancel our tour when I . . . messed up in New York." I glance at Aubrey and she smiles sympathetically. I've already told her about how I epically trashed my hotel suite in New York after finding out about my mother's passing three thousand miles away.

"How about a one-on-one drum lesson taught by you, here in Prairie Springs?" Miranda suggests. "I bet that would bring in big money."

I shift in my seat again. Doesn't Miranda realize I can't commit to anything, especially not in Prairie Springs, until I know the outcome of the fucking custody hearing? The closer it gets, the more nervous I become that the judge is going to destroy the happiness I've found with Aubrey and Raine. Have I done enough to win custody, or is my entire life about to get decimated in that courtroom in LA? My insomnia has been coming back to haunt me the past few nights, as the custody hearing draws ever closer.

"Maybe," I say vaguely, just as the latest song on Aubrey's playlist ends, and Aloha Carmichael's female-empowerment anthem, "Pretty Girl," begins.

At the sound of her favorite song, Raine slides off her chair and starts dancing for the group on the deck, much to everyone's delight.

"She's doing the dance from the music video," Aubrey explains to Miranda with a chuckle.

"I know that dance!" Miranda shouts excitedly. "I'll do it with you, Rainey!"

"My Aubbey!" Raine shrieks, pointing at Aubrey. And in short order, both women—my sister and the woman I can't get enough of—are standing on either side of my baby girl, performing the choreography as a trio. Sort of. Truthfully, Raine is a shit show, in terms of her ability to keep up with the dance. But she's damned cute while trying.

Of course, Joe, Barb, and I cheer the performance enthusiastically. But midway through the song, Raine points at me and shouts, "Dadda dance!"

My eyes find Aubrey's. She's smiling. Egging me on.

"You heard your daughter," Aubrey teases.

"Come on, Caleb," Miranda adds. "Dance, *Dadda*."

Fuck it. I'm so fucking happy these days, I'll do pretty much anything to make my daughter smile. I rise from the table, scoop up my baby girl, and dance around the deck with her in my arms to the beat of the song, while Raine laughs like a hyena in my arms.

When the song ends, Raine throws her head back and belly laughs, making me do the same. And when she tilts her head back up, she does something amazing. Something she's never done before. Something that rocks my fucking world. She grips both sides of my beard in her tiny hands, kisses me square on the mouth, and says, "I luh you, Dadda!"

My heart explodes. "I love you, too, Shortcake," I choke out. "So, so much."

Euphoria. Relief. They're slamming into me like a hurricane. Making me physically dizzy.

For weeks, I've worried I haven't been doing enough to win Raine over. To impress the judge when the time comes and prove I'm a fit father. For weeks, I've worried the unthinkable might happen. That the judge might award Raine to Ralph Beaumont, instead of me. In fact, I've started having nightmares about that scenario.

But now that I know Raine loves me, and that she'll likely tell the social worker that, I feel invincible. Like nothing and nobody can stop me now. This little girl is mine, and I'm hers. And nobody will ever break that bond, ever again. Not even me and my usual self-sabotaging bullshit. I'm done being unreliable and selfish. I'm done being a dumbass. From this moment forward, as long as I live, I'm going to be the best father to Raine, as humanly possible.

I pull my baby girl close and squeeze her tight, feeling like my heart is going to physically burst and splatter all over my newly finished, pristine deck. But after a moment, I realize our embrace is missing something essential. *Someone* essential. *Aubrey*.

Wiping my eyes, I find her beautiful face over Raine's head and beckon to her; and when she joins our family hug, the words *I love you, Aubrey* crash into me, unbidden.

As we break apart, I avert my eyes from Aubrey, so she won't detect the truth in my eyes. Paula told me Ralph's lawyer will probably ask me about my relationship with Aubrey in court, in an effort to prove I've improperly influenced her testimony. When that happens, Paula said, I'll need to be ready to answer with a straight face, "Aubrey Capshaw is my nanny and friend; also, Raine's beloved auntie." So, I can't tell Aubrey the depths of my feelings for her now. But the minute all the bullshit with the hearing is behind us, however, I swear I'll say everything that needs to be said, without holding anything back.

I put Raine down, and she immediately begins twirling and dancing to the next song on Aubrey's playlist. When my hands are free, Miranda steps up and wraps me in a warm hug.

"I'm so happy for you," she murmurs.

"I wish Mom were here to see this," I choke out.

"She's watching right now and smiling."

After one more tight squeeze and an exchange of "I love you's" with my sister, we decide the time has come to scatter my mother's ashes on the lake, as planned. Due to my tantrum in New York and subsequent, court-ordered trip to rehab, we never got the chance to properly mourn our mother together. So, this evening, we're finally going to give Adele Hayes Baumgarten the memorial she deserves.

I call to Aubrey, "Would it be okay if we take Raine with us on the rowboat for the ashes thing?" True, Raine's my kid, so I don't technically need Aubrey's permission to take her anywhere, especially now that I'm free of all those pesky rehab requirements. But by now, I trust Aubrey's judgment. Not only about what's best for our sweet girl, but also about what's best for me. For all of us. In fact, I think it's fair to say, just this fast, Aubrey's become my North Star. My moral compass. My guiding light.

"If Rainey wants to go, and as long as you bundle her up and she wears a life jacket, I think it's a great idea." She calls to Raine who's still twirling and dancing. "Rainey, do you want to go on a rowboat with Auntie Miranda and Daddy to say goodbye to their mommy in heaven?"

Raine stops twirling. "Me, too?"

Every adult exchanges an apprehensive look.

"No, not to you, honey," Aubrey says gently. "Your daddy is never going to say goodbye to you."

"Not ever," I add quickly.

Raine looks puzzled. "*Me, too?*" she repeats. "I say bye-bye to *my* mommy in da heaven, too?"

This time, every adult collectively wilts for the poor kid. Aubrey told me they had a small memorial for Claudia here in Prairie Springs, a few days after she and Raine arrived. But I can't imagine Raine remembers that or even understood what it meant at the time. Surely, only the passage of time and the continued absence of her beloved mommy have helped her begin to comprehend the absolutism of it all. The hard, cold reality that Mommy's not at work. Mommy's not at the store. Mommy is simply gone, forever.

I touch Raine's soft head. "Of course, you can say goodbye to your mommy in heaven, while Auntie Miranda and I say goodbye to ours. I think that's a great idea."

"And den Mommy come back?" Raine asks hopefully, looking up at me.

My shoulders droop, along with my spirit. "No, my love. Your mommy and mine are both in heaven, forever. But they still love us and watch over us, all the time."

"Oh," Raine says sadly, bowing her little head.

"You know what I think?" Aubrey interjects. "I think your mommy and Daddy's mommy are having fun together in heaven. I think they have tea parties together, and they feed ducks and play barn all the time. But only when they're not busy watching over you from a cloud and giggling about how much fun you're having down here."

Raine contemplates that briefly, before murmuring softly, "I luh Mommy."

The comment isn't accompanied by tears. It's not the catalyst for a meltdown. It's a simple, and heartbreaking, statement of fact.

"I love your mommy, too," Aubrey says. "So, so much."

"So do I," I say. "We all do." I've never thought that before, let alone said it. But suddenly, I realize something big: if Raine loves someone, then I do, too. It's as simple as that.

The sound of tires traversing nearby gravel attracts everyone's attention; and when I turn my head, I clap my palms in celebration. The sparkling new truck I ordered from Billings has arrived with a sedan trailing behind, and now it's coming to a stop alongside the house.

As I head over to Joe at the table and grip the top of his shoulder, everyone around me, including Joe, says some version of "Who's that?"

"You like that new truck, Joe?" I ask. "It's pretty cool, eh?"

"Looks like Big Betty's great grandchild."

"It is. The exact same make and model, only new and shiny, with all the bells and whistles."

"You've got good taste. You're gonna love driving it."

"Oh, it's not for me," I say with a smirk. "It's for *you*, Pop-Pop."

Joe's jaw drops. "*What?*"

"To thank you for helping me with the deck."

Joe shakes his head, flabbergasted. "Caleb, *no*."

"I won't take no for an answer. You wouldn't take my money, so you're getting a brand-new truck, and that's that."

"I can't—I can't accept it."

"Shoot. I guess I'll have to donate it to a charity, then, because I can't return it and I certainly don't want it." I chuckle at the tortured expression on Joe's face. "Come on, Joe. Let's go check it out, at least. You can do that for me, right?"

Joe looks at his wife, and she moves her head as if to say, "Go on."

As Joe gets situated on his crutches, I say, "I wouldn't have finished the deck without you. And even more importantly, I wouldn't have known how to be a good father to Raine, if it wasn't for you. The way I see it, a new truck was the least I could do."

"Aw, Caleb." Joe's eyes have filled with tears. He motions to me like a toddler begging to be picked up, and I give him a bear hug, taking care not to topple him over on his crutches.

"Thank you so much," Joe says into my shoulder. "But I'll only accept the truck, if you agree to take Big Betty in exchange. Aubrey told me you love driving her."

He's not wrong about that. I love driving that big, old truck. It makes me feel like a real Montana Man, just like my grandpa. "I tell you what," I say. "If I wind up keeping this place, then I'll absolutely take Big Betty off your hands. Come on now. Let's go check out your new wheels." I call to Aubrey. "A-Bomb, will you do me a favor and bundle up Raine for the boat? This will only take a couple minutes."

Aubrey looks a bit deflated, and I'm not sure why. But when her father speaks, I think I understand.

"You *still* haven't decided to keep this place, huh?" Joe asks, as we slowly make our way toward the truck. "I'm surprised. Seems like you're right at home here."

The comment shocks me. But one look at Aubrey, and I can tell she shares her father's sentiment. Barbara, too.

Seriously? I don't have the heart to tell any of them this, but even if I keep the lake house after the custody hearing, it'd only be a second home. A vacation retreat from my real life in LA. How could this place ever be anything else, considering what I do for a living? "I'm waiting till after the custody hearing to make any firm decisions about my future," I reply to Joe, just as Aubrey bustles Raine into the house.

"I guess that makes sense," Joe says.

"Yeah, I don't feel like I can make any decisions about anything other than my pursuit of Raine till then."

"Gotcha."

Truthfully, I don't know what I'll do if winning at the hearing somehow causes me to lose Aubrey. For instance, if Aubrey decides moving to LA for good to be with Raine and me isn't in the cards for her. I've been assuming that's what Aubrey would do, if the judge grants me full custody. I've taken it for granted Aubrey would set everything aside to move to my city—Raine's new home with me. But the look Aubrey flashed me before heading into the house? Yeah, it's calling my assumptions into question. Reminding me of the old adage about what happens when you *assume*. And now, suddenly, I'm scared shitless that the price of me becoming the father Raine deserves will be me losing the woman who's made that possible.

CHAPTER 26
CALEB

D*amn.*
Aubrey is on fire tonight.
That would be a true statement every night, of course. The woman's an atomic bomb. But tonight . . . Jesus fucking Christ. Is this white-hot blowjob Aubrey's gifting me her way of thanking me for the truck I gave her father earlier tonight? If so, I'll gladly buy the man a fleet of trucks every week. A fleet of yachts, airplanes, and helicopters, too.

Was it watching me dancing around with Raine to "Pretty Girl" that got Aubrey's motor running so hot tonight? If so, I'll dance with my daughter to every girl-power anthem in the world, every night of my life.

I tilt my head back on my pillow and sling my forearm over my eyes, trying to withstand the insane pleasure Aubrey's giving me. It feels so good, it's blurring with pain. Catapulting me into a state of delirium. Does this woman's mouth have a personal vendetta against my cock or what?

As Aubrey's mouth takes me higher and higher, I start shaking and shuddering, like she's using a Taser on me.

And when my loud groans threaten to wake up the Munchkin across the hallway, she hands me a pillow for my face.

After the crestfallen look on Aubrey's face earlier tonight—the one she wore when her father expressed surprise about my current state of indecision regarding the cabin—I thought Aubrey might want to skip sex tonight, in favor of talking about my vision for the future.

But the opposite happened. When Aubrey came to my room tonight, not only did she want sex, as usual, she attacked me like never before and told me some good news: she'd brokered a deal with Raine to sleep with my sister, Auntie Miranda, for the whole night. Which means Aubrey can stay in my bed the entire night, for the first time, ever, without needing to sneak back to Raine by sunrise.

Aubrey tries a new angle with her mouth, and my eyes suddenly roll back into my head. What kind of sorcery is this? I've had more blowjobs than I care to admit; but not a single one has ever made me feel like I'm being physically electrocuted by pleasure.

"*Aubrey*," I grit out from behind the pillow smashed over my face. "What are you doing to me, baby?" If I knew this was waiting for me every night, I'd never need another drop of alcohol or hit of weed. I'd never suck on a vape again or pop a gummy. Hell, I'd never even take a fucking Tylenol, if I knew this drug of a woman was all mine, forever.

Forever.

It's the first time I've thought the word in relation to Aubrey. But the minute the word strikes me, it feels natural and right. Like a no-brainer. In fact, thinking about Aubrey being mine forever only turns me on, even more.

As another shockwave of arousal rockets through me, I buck my hips and grip Aubrey's hair, trying to hang on.

My balls tighten, and a growl hurtles out of me from the depths of my soul.

Aubrey lets out a low, ragged groan that matches my own desperate sounds; and a second later, a tsunami of ecstasy slams into me, throttling me with a release that's so fucking body-quaking and head-spinning, I can't keep myself from writhing on the bed like a goddamned marlin hauled onto a fishing boat.

I'm expecting Aubrey to pull away and let me come all over my stomach. But, instead, she shoves my cock down her throat like a champ and enthusiastically swallows every drop of me. So fucking hot.

It's not the first time I've been swallowed down. Not even close. But it's the best time, by a long mile. Although everything Aubrey does at this point, both in and out of bed, is the best time. A godsend. Another reason to fall even more deeply and madly in love with her. I've entered The Promised Land. Sheer Nirvana. A place no drug or booze or any other woman could possibly take me.

When my quaking orgasm ends, I slide the pillow off my face and inhale deeply. "Jesus, Aubrey," I mutter on my exhale. "That was incredible." I raise my head to look at her. And what I behold is damn-near the sexiest thing I've ever seen. Aubrey looks shit-faced drunk. So, full of lust, she's seeing stars.

"Here, kitty-kitty," I coo in a low grumble. "Come sit on my face, baby."

With a greedy smile, she lets me guide her onto my face; at which point, I grip her hips firmly and fuck her with my tongue and lips like a man possessed. As her pleasure ramps up, and her movements become more and more heated and desperate, I get into it more and more. Until soon, I've got Aubrey writhing and gyrating on my face like she's on the brink of total and complete obliteration.

A string of expletives pours out of Aubrey's mouth. Suddenly, she begins snapping her hips back and forth on my face with even more fervor, like she's a sprinter who's lunging forward toward the finish-line tape.

With a fierce grip of my forearms and a long, low growl, she freezes, stock-still, on top of me. And a second later, every inch of flesh in contact with my tongue and lips begins pulsing and throbbing rhythmically.

I grab Aubrey's ass as she comes, reveling in every sensation. The sweet taste of her. Her intoxicating scent and sounds. Until, finally, Aubrey's body stops rippling and her loud groans subside.

Purring, she breathlessly slides off me and flops onto the mattress next to me, a satisfied pile of flesh and bones. "I've never come that hard in my life," she gasps out between pants. "I thought I was going to pass out." She turns her sweaty face toward me and beams a smile at me that quickens my heart rate. "Did I hurt you?"

I snicker. "If that was you hurting me, then call me a masochist, baby."

"Seriously, though. Tell the truth. I feel like maybe I was too rough on your face."

I laugh. "Baby, no, you didn't hurt me at all. That was the hottest thing, ever, and I can't wait to do it again."

Relieved, she throws her forearm over her forehead and giggles. "You're amazing at sex."

Well, yeah, I've had a lot of practice, I think. Although, come to think of it, I'm not normally much of a giver, when it comes to sex with someone I don't give two shits about. So, in that sense, I can't honestly say I've had much practice doing what I just did to Aubrey. I've done it before, obviously. But not for a very long time.

Aubrey snuggles close, interrupting my thoughts. "Before I came to you that first night, I didn't expect you to be all that great at sex. You've really surprised me."

"Excuse me? What about me made you think, even for a minute, I'd suck at sex? Also, why come to me at all, if you expected me to suck?"

She's giggling uproariously. "I wanted to find out for myself. Honestly, I wanted you so badly by that point, I didn't care if the report card on you turned out to be true or not."

Shit. I don't need to ask who supplied the "report card" to her. *Claudia.* Surely, Aubrey's bestie had already told her every fucking detail about our brief encounter, so Aubrey assumed I'm always a wham-bam-thank-you-ma'am kind of guy. "Is Claudia always going to be lying here in bed with us?" I ask, feeling annoyed. "No matter what I do or say, am I never going to be able to shake my past sins, when it comes to you?"

Aubrey looks up at me, her features stricken. "No, I . . . I shouldn't have said that. I'm sorry."

I close my eyes. "It's fine."

"No, it's not. You're right. That was out of line." She pauses, apparently waiting for me to say something. When I don't, she traces a fingertip down my bare chest and whispers, "If it makes you feel any better, Claudia also said you've got a massive dick."

"It helps a bit."

Aubrey giggles. "She also said she had the time of her life with you, despite you not giving a crap if she got off, too. So, at least, it wasn't all bad news."

I rough a hand over my face, realizing I've got to

confront this latest ghost of my past, head-on, or I'm never going to stand a chance of leaving the past behind me, once and for all.

I tug gently on a lock of Aubrey's hair. "Unfortunately, there are probably lots of women out there who'd give me the same report card as Claudia." I sit up onto my elbow and look down at Aubrey's moonlit face. "I've been pretty jaded about sex for a long time. Pretty jaded about women, in general. Once I got famous and rich, it felt like . . . I don't know. It wasn't possible to find someone who wanted me for me, so why bother? I'd already blown it with the only girl who'd ever loved me for me. The only girl I'd dated seriously before the band took off. Once I got famous, I knew I'd never have another chance at connecting with someone on a deeper level again, so I embraced that fact and accepted that I was now a trophy. A bucket list item. A story to tell friends. I know the world thinks it sounds fun to fuck a different woman in every city—"

"Who thinks that? That sounds gross."

"It is. That's my point. Sex for me hasn't been fun or fulfilling for a very long time, so I'm not surprised my partners, including Claudia, were less than impressed."

Aubrey processes that for a moment. "Remember when you wouldn't tell me what you did to the only woman you've ever loved? I did some internet sleuthing to try to piece it together, and I think I've figured out the story. Is she Violet Morgan, the wife of the lead singer of 22 Goats?"

Welp, here we go. I didn't mean to lead the conversation here, but that's exactly what I did. "The internet's got the story mostly wrong," I say. "There was never a love triangle between Dax, Violet, and me. Violet had already broken up with me, long before she met Dax. Dax never 'stole' Violet from me, and I never horned in on his relationship with her."

"Did Dax really write that song 'Judas' about you—in response to your 'Fuck you, Judas' tweet? You posted it around the same time photos of Dax and Violet were first splashed all over the gossip blogs."

"You've done your homework."

Aubrey shrugs. "Seems like it was big news, at the time."

I roll my eyes. "It was huge news, unfortunately. At least, in my corner of the world." I gather my thoughts. I never envisioned myself telling Aubrey this story. Not in a million years. But suddenly, it seems necessary, if I want to have any hope of forging a relationship with her in the future. "I was never pissed at Dax for stealing Violet away from me, because he didn't. It was more that I was pissed he stole the *opportunity* for me to try to win Violet back, which was never going to happen, anyway. It was that Dax hid his relationship with Violet, while our bands were on tour together, after Dax and I had grown super close. I trusted him like a brother during that tour. Confided in him about a bunch of stuff, including Violet. So, when I found out what was going on behind my back, I felt betrayed."

"Understandably."

"Not really. Looking back, I acted like an immature little prick. A big baby."

"No, you trusted Dax, and he didn't tell you the truth about what he was doing."

"How could he? His band was the opener. It was their big break. Their first tour. And Dax knew I was an unpredictable, immature hothead. Was he really supposed to risk me kicking his band off the tour? He's got two bandmates who would have fucking killed him if he did that and blew their big break over a girl. He was stuck between a rock and a hard place. Looking back, I can't blame him for choosing his bandmates, his career, and his new girlfriend over the feelings of his new, hotheaded, immature friend."

Aubrey runs her palm across my naked chest. "Have you told Dax all that?"

"Mostly. Not with that much clarity, though. I apologized to him and Violet at a wedding about five years ago, but I don't think I said everything to them, quite as well as I just said it to you."

"Maybe you should contact them and say it again. Only better this time."

"Nah. Everyone has moved on. I'm sure they never want to hear from me again." I twist my mouth. "I believe Violet came into my life to teach me how awful it feels to betray someone who trusted you completely, and I came into hers to teach her what a walking red flag looks like, so she could avoid someone like me the next time. And then, years later, Dax came into my life to deliver some much-deserved karma."

"You should tell them that, Caleb."

"Nah. They're happily married with a kid now. In the end, we all got exactly what we deserved."

Aubrey strokes my chest. "For what it's worth, I don't think you're a walking red flag anymore."

"I was for years, though." I gnaw at the inside of my cheek. "When I found out about Dax and Violet, I punched him in the face so hard, I almost broke his jaw. And for what? Because he fell in love with his future wife—a woman who rightly didn't want me anymore? A woman who'd loved and trusted me, so I treated her like shit in return? Honestly, Dax is the one who should have punched *me* for the shit I pulled with Violet."

"What did you do to her, exactly? You never told me what's worse than cheating."

Shit. All of a sudden, it occurs to me Aubrey is going to be the most important witness at the custody hearing. Shouldn't I be putting my best foot forward with her, so she can credibly try to convince the judge I'm a fit father to Raine? On the other hand, though, I can't keep this from Aubrey any longer. I love her. I want to be with her, always. Which means she deserves to know this story, in full, without me editing or spinning it. How else will she be able to decide if she truly wants to be with me?

I inhale deeply, feeling like I'm standing on the edge of an abyss. But really, I've got no choice in the matter, do I? I need to take this leap of faith. "Violet is four years younger than me," I begin. "Same as my sister. They grew up together, so Violet used to come around all the time. For years, Violet was nothing but a starry-eyed kid to me. Miranda's sidekick." I smile. "Or maybe it was the other way around. Hard to tell with those two." I pause to gather my thoughts. "Anyway, Violet was always around. Sometimes, she and Miranda would watch my band rehearse. Occasionally, they'd come get burgers or burritos with us after a jam session. And I thought nothing of her. But then, one day, right after Violet graduated high school, right before she went off to college across the country, she and I were alone in Dean's garage for some reason. Can't remember why. We were sitting on this raggedy couch together, just talking. And the next thing I knew, I was kissing her, and she was telling me she'd always loved me." I pause, as memories slam into me. "We wound up having this kind of magical summer together. From that kiss forward, we were joined at the hip. We never even dated. It was like, we kissed and that was that. We both just assumed we were end game."

My heart thundering, I peek at Aubrey to see if I've said too much. Pissed her off. Freaked her out. But she's poker-faced. Listening intently.

"By the end of that summer, our song 'Shaynee' was gaining traction online and in our hometown. We started getting some cool local gigs. And Violet came to every show, without fail. She even started marketing the band and getting us more gigs. She was all-in, you know? She believed in us, even more than we believed in ourselves." I gnaw at my lower lip. Saying all this shit out loud, especially to someone I want to think highly of me, is harder than I thought it'd be. "So, anyway," I continue. "Violet had an older brother, Reed Rivers, who lived in LA and had just started an independent record label there."

"You grew up in San Diego, right?"

"Yeah. So, without telling my band, Violet *commanded* her big brother, Reed, to drive down to San Diego to check out our band at a gig. He didn't want to come, apparently. Only did it as a favor to Violet, because she said she'd never talk to him again, if he didn't." I chuckle. "So, Reed came, and wound up signing us on the spot, and the rest is history. We became River Records' first huge success story."

"From what I've read, you guys took off like a rocket."

"We did. All of a sudden, everything changed. We were on a world tour, performing our songs in front of thousands of screaming fans at sold-out shows. Our debut album skyrocketed to the top of the charts. We were nominated for awards, and on and on. And I let it all go to my head. I convinced myself my 'rockstar life' wasn't real. That my 'real life' would be waiting for me, unchanged, when I got back home."

"So, you cheated on Violet, while you were on tour?"

Every fiber of my body wants to lie and say, "Only once, when I was drunk and high and didn't know what I was doing." But the truth is, I got drunk and high with the intention of cheating on Violet, over and over again. Because I'd convinced myself, as long as I wasn't sober, it wasn't real. "I cheated on her, yeah. Multiple times. And it was the worst thing I've ever done." I take a deep breath. "I've done worse things, since then." My Adam's apple bobs. "Not stepping up to be a father to Raine, for instance. But, still, to this day, what I did to Violet is on my Mount Rushmore of the shitty things I've done." I swallow hard. "I know the world thinks I've been on top of the world, since my band hit it big. But looking back, I was much happier in the months leading up to my band's big break, than in the years that followed."

Aubrey is silent for a long time. "Are you happy now, Caleb?"

I lift my head and look into her dark eyes. "Happier than I've ever been in my entire fucking life."

Her chest heaves. "Happier than during your 'magical summer' with Violet?"

"Aw, baby." I pull her to me and kiss her gently. "Sweetheart, there's no comparison. This is the most magical summer I've ever had. Trust me on that." I kiss Aubrey again, this time passionately, to keep myself from saying the words on the tip of my tongue: that I know now what I had with Violet was simply puppy love, whereas what I feel for Aubrey is adult love. True love. The kind that stands the test of time. "I'm ready to be a good man, Aubrey," I murmur. "I'm ready to be worthy of complete trust. You can trust me, baby. I swear it. I'll always tell you the truth. Good, bad, or ugly."

Aubrey bites her lip but says nothing for a long moment. Finally, she asks, "What did your sister think about you dating, and then cheating on, her best friend?"

"Oh, man, Miranda was *pissed*. I don't think she's forgiven me for what I did to Violet to this day."

"Are they still friends?"

"Best friends. Like sisters. If all three of us were stuck on a sinking boat—Miranda, Violet, and me—and there were only two life jackets left, I know for a fact Miranda would let me drown."

"That's not true. I saw the way she looked at you tonight. She worships you."

I shake my head. "No. She loves me, but she loves Violet more. I don't blame her for that, by the way, after all the bullshit, big and small, I've put her through over the years. And not only in relation to Violet. I don't respond to her texts. I ghost her for months at a time. I say I'll come to this or that thing, and then I miss it. And now, on top of everything else, there's the thing with me not telling her and our mother about Raine. I think that stunt brought me *this* close to losing Miranda forever."

Aubrey pulls a face. "Why have you been such a shitty brother?"

"I don't know. It's nothing personal to Miranda, you know? I've always been a shitty everything to everyone. It's like, the minute someone gets too close, I find a way to push them away. To prove I'm not worthy of their love, like I've known all along. Either that, or I get to drinking and smoking and simply forget where I'm supposed to be."

"You think that's because of the stuff with your father?" When I look at her blankly, Aubrey adds, "He beat your mother. He abandoned you. He convinced you you're not worthy of love, so you've continuously proved him right."

I'm floored. Rendered speechless.

"You disagree?"

"No, I . . . I was silent because you just blew my fucking mind."

Aubrey runs a fingertip across my bare chest. "The great news is you've now got the chance to prove your asshole father wrong about you by becoming an amazing father to Raine."

My heart is thumping. "Thank you for spelling it out like that to me. I've never thought about it like that."

"You haven't talked about your father in therapy all this time?"

"I haven't taken therapy all that seriously."

"Maybe it's time to start."

"Yeah, maybe."

Aubrey grins. "You've got this, Caleb. I have total faith in you."

I can barely breathe. I pull her to me and squeeze her tight. I don't know what I did to deserve this gift from the universe. This woman who's teaching me new things about myself every day and helping me become the best version of myself; but, just like Aubrey said, I've got a huge opportunity here. One I won't fuck up.

Aubrey touches my face. "The past is the past. Decide who you want to be and will him into existence. That's all you've got to do."

"I will," I whisper. "Thank you, Aubrey." I kiss her passionately, and soon, my cock has turned to steel, once again. I slide my fingers between Aubrey's legs, getting her primed for round two, eager to get inside the woman who's surely going to become the great love of my life.

CHAPTER 27
CALEB

I *can't sleep.*

Not because I'm lying here stressing or feeling shame, as I've done in the past. Not because Aubrey's body is entangled with mine, and her body heat is like a furnace. Although it is. No, tonight I've got insomnia simply because I'm too damned happy to sleep. Because the honest conversation I had with Aubrey earlier tonight about Violet and Dax and my long history of being a selfish shithead blew me away and took the weight of the world off my shoulders. Add to that how thrilled I am to get to sleep next to Aubrey for the entire night for the first time, and falling asleep is a pipe dream.

A rustling sound from outside catches my attention. I'm not too worried, though. There are lots of animals that come out at night, so I'm sure it was—

There it is again. Only this time, the sound strikes me as manmade. The movement of two human feet taking steps, one after another. *Is someone walking out there in the bushes surrounding my house?*

I gently disentangle Aubrey from my body and slide out

of bed; but when I peek out my bedroom window, I don't notice anything out of the ordinary. The moonlit lake is serene and the firs, black cottonwoods, and thick shrubbery in all directions are still and quiet.

A bush in the lower right of my vision appears to shimmy against the stillness of the night, drawing my attention. *Holy fuck.* Is that a man, dressed in black, crawling on the ground on all fours like a military operative, or is that an animal, scurrying to safety under cover of darkness?

My heart hammering, I throw on a pair of jeans, a sweatshirt, and shoes, and head to Grandpa's gun locker in the hallway closet. I turn the combination lock left, right, and left again, hoping the numbers are still the same as always—the digits of Grandpa's birthday; and to my relief, the lock immediately opens with a soft click.

I swing the door open and discover Grandpa's three hunting rifles lined up on a rack, like always. I've never personally enjoyed hunting, but I've never once turned down the chance to shoot bottles and cans in a field.

Shit. There's no ammunition in any of the three rifles and no box in the locker, either. It's probably for the best. I'd rather not die from an old, misfiring gun tonight, while shooting at phantoms in a fit of paranoia.

Paranoid or not, though, it's always better safe than sorry. I close and lock the gun locker, grab a flashlight from the kitchen counter, and head outside into the cool night air.

Slowly, I creep around the corner of the house, past the big, black cottonwood with my childhood carving etched into its bark, as leaves and pine needles noisily crunch underneath my work boots. Barely breathing, I turn another corner, toward the spot where that bush seemed to ripple in the darkness. But I see nothing.

I stop and listen. Hold my breath.

Wind is whipping the green canopy of pines and leaves above my head. Insects are chirring. My pulse is pounding loudly. But that's it. Other than those sounds, plus the ragged whoosh of my fitful breathing, I detect nothing. Either I've imagined danger lurking in the darkness, or whatever danger was actually here took off at the sound of my work boots moving toward it.

Either way, this is a good reminder for me to remain vigilant. Keep myself on high alert. Even if I imagined danger lurking tonight, there's still evil out there. A monster of a man who's hell-bent on taking my daughter from me and then almost certainly doing to her what he did to his poor daughter.

I take a deep, steadying breath and start marching toward the house, as one thought plays in my head on a running loop: *God as my witness, I'll do whatever it takes to protect my family from Ralph Beaumont or anyone else who tries to harm them.*

CHAPTER 28
AUBREY

"Holy guacamole, Coobie," I say, looking around Caleb's sprawling living room.

"*Gooby-gabby-momo*," Raine echoes in front of me, attempting to mimic my exclamation. Of course, Caleb and I guffaw at her attempt.

The three of us, sans Miranda—we parted ways with Caleb's sister at LAX—have just stepped inside Caleb's sprawling, modern beach house in Santa Monica, and it's beyond anything my feeble mind could have conjured. As it turns out, Caleb lives his "real life" in LA as the wealthy rock superstar he is, not the wood-working, drum-banging, mountain man I've come to know and love in Montana. As I'm now seeing, he's a man who prefers sleek lines and modern glass in his chosen living accommodations, rather than cozy, rustic wood, stone fireplaces, and exposed beams.

I should have predicted this. Caleb only *inherited* his grandpa's cozy wooden lake house, whereas he *bought* this home, out of all the options available at his hefty budget. If I'd been thinking clearly, I would have expected Caleb to choose to live in luxury like this. The man loves spending money, after all. I found that out during our first shopping spree in Billings. And he's had a lot of it for a very long time. For almost fifteen years now, Caleb's been accumulating insane amounts of wealth while living a "single rockstar" lifestyle. One unfettered by typical adult responsibilities and the usual guard rails that keep the rest of us in check.

When Caleb told me about his house in LA during our flight today, I pictured him living in a cute little beachside bungalow, since he only described his place as being "right on the beach." Caleb explained, "There's a little staircase from my property down to the beach below, so, it'll be easy to go back and forth all day long, just like we do back home at the lake."

Yep. Caleb used the word *home* in relation to his lake house in Montana today on the plane. And don't think I didn't feel giddy about it, even though I knew his word choice might have been a simple slip of the tongue.

"Do you see the ocean, Shortcake?" Caleb asks Raine, gesturing to floor-to-ceiling windows on the opposite side of the expansive room. "We can swim in it, just like we do in the lake back home."

There it is again! *Home.*

"Dat *ocean*?" Rainey asks with wide-eyed astonishment, even though Claudia and I—sometimes, with Claudia's mother, before she got sick—used to take Raine to the ocean all the time in Seattle. Apparently, Raine doesn't remember those beach days now; or if she does, the grey, tumultuous version of the sea she visited in Washington doesn't bear enough of a resemblance to the glittering, sapphire-blue ocean in California to trigger her rapidly vanishing memories.

"Would you ladies like a tour?" Caleb asks, an adorable grin on his handsome face.

"Right after I take Little Miss Can-I-Have-a-Second-Juice-Box-in-the-Car to a potty."

Caleb chuckles and points toward a hallway. "Right through there on the left."

"Dadda do it?" Raine asks to my surprise. I'm always the one who deals with Raine's potty breaks, not Caleb.

"You've got it, kiddo!" Caleb booms. "I'll race you there!" He takes off running. Or, at least, he pretends to. And Raine toddles gleefully after him.

I'm now alone in Mr. Rockstar's living room, surrounded by photos and memorabilia: the artifacts of Caleb's superstar life away from Montana.

Slowly, I amble around the room perusing everything like there's going to be a pop quiz later. It's all deeply fascinating to me. Like seeing another version of Caleb on a different timeline. There are framed platinum records, album covers, and memorabilia; photos of Caleb with smiling people who seem to be other famous musicians, based on context clues. There's a pair of framed drumsticks bearing a signature I can't read. A signed guitar, too. Several framed magazine covers.

I lean in close to study one magazine in particular: a copy of *Rock 'n' Roll* that features Caleb as its cover model. He's got a mohawk in the photo, which normally wouldn't be my thing, but on Caleb it's a damned good look, especially when paired with the over-the-top snarl he's wearing. He's flexing his muscular arm in the shot—showing off a tattoo on his bicep: a classic cartoon bomb emblazoned with a "C."

I've seen that same tattoo countless times in person. Every day for the past month. I've even kissed it, many times. But, somehow, seeing the tattoo on the cover of a wildly popular, iconic music magazine and presented as pop culture iconography is making me see Caleb through a whole new lens. No wonder Claudia was always so infatuated with him. He's one hell of a sexy beast. Dangerous. Wild. Hot as fuck.

I continue my tour of the room, feeling a bit off-kilter and confused. I knew this side of Caleb's life exists. The fame and money. The rarified, celebrity air he's been breathing for well over a decade. But, still, the simple life we've shared for the past month is so far removed from this stuff, I'm finding this slingshot back to reality a bit jarring.

"I went poopie in da potty, my Aubbey!" Raine screeches happily, as she runs back into the room. For a while now, Raine's been calling me "Aubbey" and "my Aubbey," rather than "Auntie Aubbey." Not sure when it started, exactly, but it feels natural and right at this point.

"Yep, she pooped like a champ," Caleb declares with a laugh, entering the room behind his daughter. "Never let it be said my daughter sucks at anything, even pooping."

I snort-laugh.

"And yes, I made sure she washed her hands for the full length of 'The Birthday Song,'" Caleb says with a wink. He claps his palms together. "So, ladies, are we ready for that house tour now?"

"Ready!" Raine shrieks at the top of her little lungs. To emphasize her readiness, she performs an enthusiastic shimmy that makes her look like an upright worm on a hook. Does that child even know what a house tour is? More likely than not, this is yet another case of Raine buying whatever her brawny Dadda is selling, whether she understand it or not.

"Hop aboard the tour bus, Shortcake," Caleb says,

crouching down to offer his back to Raine. When she's safely cleaved to his backside, and his strong hands are firmly holding her tiny legs in place, Caleb begins showing us around his gorgeous home.

The kitchen is filled with endless white cupboards, gleaming steel, and stunning tile accents. On the way out, I make a mental note to do a sweep for booze when the tour is over.

Next up, we're treated to a music studio featuring an elaborate drum kit, a vocal booth in the corner, and even more framed platinum records and memorabilia. There's also a fully stocked bar in the corner of the room, I can't help noticing. One I'm going to clear out, immediately after my sweep of the kitchen.

"I'll get all that stuff cleared out and replaced with seltzer water and juice," Caleb murmurs, reading my mind. "I went straight to rehab from New York, so I haven't been home and had a chance to—"

"It's all good, honey," I say reassuringly. "I'll clear out everything for you, just like I did back home." *Fuck*. It's one thing for Caleb to say that, but he might feel pressured by *me* saying it.

"Thanks," he says, seemingly unfazed by my word choice. In fact, he's smiling from ear to ear. Is that because I offered to help? Because I called him honey? Or is he happy to discover, somewhere along the line, I've grown to consider the lake house my home?

"It's a good thing we came home two days before the meeting with the social worker, huh?" Caleb says. "It would have been terrible, if she saw this place, as it is."

"We definitely dodged a bullet there."

We share a smile, but I'm honestly feeling a bit stressed. In Montana, I had no doubts about Caleb's readiness to take on Raine, forever. But here, I can't help wondering if he's truly ready for a job that big. If he's got any doubts about his commitment to fatherhood, he'd better tell me soon, because in a matter of days, I'm going to testify in support of his bid for full custody, with full visitation rights for me, rather than the other way around. And I can't do that, if he's not one-hundred-percent committed.

I keep telling myself Raine belongs with her father. That it's the best thing for her, even though I want her for myself. But the more I fall for Caleb—or *think* I'm falling, anyway—being here is making me wonder if I've been falling for the fantastical *Montana* version of him—the more I'm worried my judgment has become hopelessly clouded by my feelings. Has Caleb been playing me, this whole time? I don't think so. *But what if I'm wrong?*

We continue the tour and visit a game room next, one featuring a pool table, foosball table, several pinball machines, and, surprise, surprise, an astonishing array of bongs, ashtrays, and booze bottles.

"Shit," Caleb says, when he beholds the vestiges of his past life all around us. "I mean, *shoot*. Sorry, Shortcake."

"Shit," Raine echoes.

"*Shoot*," Caleb corrects. "Shoot, shoot, shoot."

"Shit."

"Just leave it, and she'll forget."

With a sigh, Caleb moves to the next room—a space filled with comfy sitting areas and a big-screen TV; and not surprisingly, another round of ashtrays, bongs, and papers used to roll joints.

Caleb slides Raine off his back, looking distraught. "I should have had someone check the whole house before we got here," he murmurs. "Sorry. I didn't think to do that."

"It's fine," I say. "After we have some lunch, you can take Raine to the beach while I clear out the house."

Caleb looks stressed. "Thanks, Aubrey. I appreciate that."

I lay a palm on his forearm and smile reassuringly. "I think it's good you're seeing the house with sober eyes. If this place had already been cleaned out when we got here, maybe the new you wouldn't have realized just how much the old you probably needed mandatory rehab."

Caleb contemplates that. "Yeah, I think you're right. I probably needed it, without realizing it." He looks beautifully vulnerable in this moment. So much so, I'd kiss him right now, if Raine weren't here.

Off we go again, this time into a long hallway. As we walk, Caleb motions to a passing guestroom. "That'll be your room, A-Bomb." He winks. "As far as the social worker will know, anyway."

We enter a room at the end of the long hallway. Caleb's bedroom. The primary suite, featuring the same spectacular ocean views as the living room. Not surprisingly, given the rest of the house, Caleb's bedroom is a beautiful space. One that's fit for a king and decorated by a pro. There's an attached bathroom that's bigger than my parents' living room. A walk-in closet that's bigger than my childhood bedroom. A fireplace, sitting room, and more framed memorabilia. And best of all, there's a small shelf in a corner filled with framed family photos.

I study Caleb's collection of family photos, as father and daughter chatter about the ocean view in another corner of the room. Suddenly, I notice a framed photo that makes me gasp and clutch my heart. Somehow, Caleb managed to add a photo of Raine to his collection—a smiling shot of her sitting on the shore of Lake Lucille with her beloved sand toys strewn around her. I didn't take the shot. In fact, I've never seen it before. Which means Caleb must have snapped it and asked someone here in LA to frame it for him.

"What is it?" Caleb asks, reacting to my audible gasp.

"This photo of Raine."

Caleb and Raine join me at the photo collection.

"Dat me!" Raine says, pointing.

"It sure is," Caleb says. "And you know why? Because this shelf is for photos of everyone I love most in the whole world. That's why you're there, front and center. Because I love you so, so much."

"Who dat?"

"That's two of my best friends, Colin and Amy, and their little boy, Rocco. He's the same age as you. You're gonna meet him soon."

"Who dat?"

"That's my grandma and grandpa. And that's Auntie Miranda there. And my mother."

Raine looks up at her daddy. "Where my mommy and Aubbey and Grammy and Pop-Pop?"

Caleb's face bursts into shades of crimson. All of a sudden, he looks tongue-tied and nauseated. "That's a great question, Rainey. They should be here, because they're our family, too. You're absolutely right about that." He flashes me an apologetic look while talking to Raine. "For now, we'll put their photos in *your* room, though, so you can start a family photos shelf of your own. Would you like that?"

"Yass!" While Raine squeals and dances around excitedly about the idea, Caleb looks at me, sweating bullets. Clearly, he thought the addition of Raine to his shelf would be a praiseworthy surprise. But now, it's turned into a fuckup.

"That photo of her is really sweet," I whisper. "Don't stress, Caleb. She's your daughter,. She belongs there."

He smashes his lips together, looking pained. And you know what? I feel pained, too. Logically, I know I shouldn't. I don't belong on that shelf, and neither do Claudia or my parents. But I can't deny my heart feels excluded in this moment. If I needed a reminder that I've been getting swept away by my feelings for Caleb, this is probably it. Clearly, I need to cool my jets and keep my heart guarded, just in case the custody hearing doesn't go, as planned.

Caleb clears his throat. "I figured with the social worker coming on Thursday—"

"Yeah, that makes sense," I insist. "It was the right call. We don't want the social worker digging too deep into what's been going on between you and me." I force a smile. "Is there a bedroom for Raine?"

Caleb looks deeply uncomfortable, but he forces a smile, the same as me, and says, "Of course. I saved the best for last." He scoops up his daughter and holds her like a football as he marches out of his bedroom, while I tear myself away from the shelf of photos and follow him.

"Wowee!" Raine chirps, as Caleb enters her room. I can't blame the kid. I'm feeling pretty *wowee'd* myself. The room is Girlie Heaven. A pink-and-purple Shangri-La that's been decorated to perfection and stuffed to its rafters with every manner of toys, dolls, and stuffed animals.

In a corner, there's a colorful, plastic kitchen, bursting with accessories. In another, there's a dress-up station filled with all manner of glittering costumes and props. There's a dollhouse, complete with furniture and people; a Barbie area, too, chock full of everything our plastic heroine needs to live her best life. There's a fluffy, pillow-covered bed, and purple bubble letters above it, spelling out Raine's name on a pink wall.

My eyes train on a framed photo below Raine's name, and I step forward to get a better look. When I get closer, I realize it's a shot of Caleb and Raine—the photo I snapped at my parents' house while father and daughter colored together for the first time.

My heart hammering, I motion to the framed shot. "When and how did you do this?"

Caleb bites back a shy smile. "My friend Amy did that for me last week." He looks around proudly. "She did this whole room for me."

"She did a great job. Isn't your room amazing, Rainey?"

"Mayzinggg!" Raine holds up her arms and shimmies. "Dis for *me*?"

"All for you," Caleb confirms. "See those letters there? That spells Raine."

"Dat me!"

"It sure is. And you see that photo there? Who's that?"

Raine centers her attention and gasps. "Raine and Dadda!"

"That's right, love," Caleb chokes out. "The Fool and the Raine. You and me."

Caleb and I never interact romantically in front of Raine. But this one time, I can't keep my hands off him. As Raine runs around the room, checking everything out, I hurl myself at him and burrow my face into his massive chest. "You did so good," I choke out. "You're such a sweet daddy."

Exhaling with relief, he kisses the top of my head. "I'm sorry about the photo shelf in my bedroom. With the social worker coming, I freaked out about—"

"No, you did the right thing. Please, stop feeling bad about that. Revel in your triumph here, instead." I wrench myself away from his warm chest and motion to the room around us. "The effort you've put in to make Raine feel at home is really impressive and special."

"But I want you to feel at home, too, Aubrey," he says, his green eyes pleading with me.

I don't know what to say, so I simply press my lips together. This place is gorgeous, but it's going to take a long while for me to feel at home here, if ever. That doesn't mean I'm not willing to try. But I can't even think about *starting* to try, until I know the results of the damned custody hearing.

"Is anyone else hungry?" I ask enthusiastically, feeling eager to change the subject.

"I sure am," Caleb replies. "Rainey?"

She doesn't reply. She's already deep in play mode at her little kitchen, whipping up an imaginary, culinary delight.

"Rainey," I ask, "are you hungry for lunch?"

"Mm hmm," she replies absently, not bothering to look at me.

I return to Caleb. "Why don't you play with her, while I figure out ordering some lunch. When we're done eating, I'll get started on clearing out the house, while you take her down to the beach. She'll be good and ready for a nap after that."

"Sounds like a plan."

I turn to leave, but Caleb stops me. "Hey, baby," he whispers, making me stop in the doorway. "Thank you. For everything. I'll never be able to thank you enough for what you've done for me. I hope you know that."

My heart is exploding with love for him. But somehow, I manage to say, "I only want what's best for Raine." It's a true statement. But it's also a withholding one, in context, when the full truth is that I'm bleeding out with love for the man.

As Caleb's smile fades, I turn on my heel and march into the hallway, saving myself from admitting something I shouldn't. That I love him. If I stay in Caleb's presence any longer, I'll tell him so. And I can't do that until after the hearing, if ever. Not until I know, for a fact, the feelings I've been experiencing are real, mutual, and, most importantly, strong enough to withstand the ruling from the judge, whatever it might be.

CHAPTER 29
CALEB

"This is where you plan to live with Raine for the foreseeable future?" the social worker asks.

I clear my throat. "Yes, ma'am."

With pursed lips, she jots a note on her pad. She's got quite a poker face, this woman. Not to mention, dark, piercing eyes that remind me of the sixth-grade teacher who hated my guts.

"The school district is excellent here," I add, even though she didn't ask, and she jots another note. "If that changes, I'll send Raine to the best private school in the area. There are a lot of them to choose from." Another note. "But I'm thinking public school is a good idea to start with, so she's surrounded by all kinds of people, you know?" Fuck, I'm stressed. I never babble like this.

Aubrey is playing with Raine in the backyard, while I've been guiding this court-appointed social worker around my house. If Aubrey were here, I wouldn't be this nervous. She'd calm me down. But that's not an option, apparently. The social worker wants to talk to her, separately.

After her close inspection of the main living areas, all of

which are now squeaky clean and family friendly, thanks to the Amazing Aubrey, the social worker asks to see Raine's bedroom.

"Right this way," I say, trying, and failing, to sound relaxed and casual. Man, I'm sweating bullets.

"I noticed the Volvo in the driveway," the social worker says behind me, as we head down the hallway. "Is that your car or Miss Capshaw's?"

"Mine. I bought it yesterday, specifically for transporting Raine. If Aubrey—Miss Capshaw—drives Raine, I'll make sure she uses that car, too." When the woman jots another note, I add, "My sister sent me an article about how Volvos are one of the safest family cars, so that's what I got."

"Is your sister coming here today?"

"Oh. I . . . No. I didn't know she was supposed to come. I can call her now, if you—"

"No, no. That's fine. Your sister won't be living here with Raine, correct?"

"No, ma'am. Just Aubrey and me. Miss Capshaw. My sister lives nearby, though. I can call her to come, if you'd like to meet her."

"Do you plan for her to interact with Raine regularly?"

"Yes, ma'am. She loves Raine, and Raine loves her."

"Then, yes, I'd love to meet her, if she's available."

"Yes, ma'am. I'll text her right now and call if she doesn't reply quickly." I pull out my phone with a trembling hand and shoot off a text to my sister in all caps that begins with "URGENT!!!" before returning to the social worker with a tight smile. "Okay, so, this is Raine's room here." I motion to the doorway, but the woman doesn't step inside. She's too busy taking a note, apparently.

"What do you normally drive, when you're not driving Raine?"

Why is that relevant? I'm deeply annoyed by the question, but I answer calmly, in a neutral and non-defensive tone, hopefully, listing off the three other cars and one motorcycle sitting in my garage.

"Do you wear a helmet when riding your motorcycle?"

"It's required by law." My heart rate quickens. Is my motorcycle a strike against me? Do good fathers not ride them? My own father rode one, but he was a horrendous father. Fuck. Maybe I shouldn't have mentioned the motorcycle, although the way this is going, she'll probably ask to see my garage, anyway. "I don't ride it very often," I blurt. "The motorcycle. And I'd be willing to get rid of it, if that would make a difference in the outcome. I certainly don't want a motorcycle more than I want custody of my daughter."

Seriously, I need to shut the fuck up now. It's written all over this woman's stern face: my babbling isn't helping my cause. In desperation, I motion to Raine's doorway, and thankfully, this time, she enters the room.

"It's fit for a princess," she murmurs, looking around. Is that a compliment or a dig? Damn, she's got a better poker face than my buddy, Colin, and he's the only one who can always beat me in cards, thanks to his stellar poker face.

I look around, trying to see the room through this social worker's eyes, and, suddenly, it looks criminally over-the-top to me. Like I'm trying to buy my daughter's affections. "I wanted Raine to feel safe and happy here."

"I'm sure she loves it." It's the first kind words she's uttered to me today. But then again, for all I know, she's thinking, "Because little kids can be easily bribed." So, I tell myself not to read into the seeming vote of confidence.

"If there's anything you'd suggest to make this environment better for Raine, I'm all ears."

The woman looks up from her pad and smiles politely. "I'm not here to make suggestions to you, Mr. Baumgarten. It's my job to report whatever I see, and what I've concluded about it, and then to report my expert findings and opinions to the judge."

My stomach somersaults. "Yes, ma'am."

She scribbles a note onto her dreaded pad again, and I can't help feeling like I'm sixteen and just failed my first driver's test again. It was nerves that tanked me then, the same way nerves caused me to flunk every math test in middle school, even after I'd studied really hard. Frankly, the only times nerves have ever helped me is when I'm sitting behind a drum kit, getting mentally prepared to play for tens of thousands of people. Other than that, I swear to God, my nerves have always been my worst fucking enemy.

"How many nights has Raine slept here?"

I shift my weight. "Three. We just got in from Montana. She loves the beach here. Loves her room. She's been sleeping like a rock."

"For three nights."

"It's a big deal. She never had three nights in a row without a nightmare before we got here."

The woman's eyebrows ride up, and I know I've fucked up. "Raine has frequent nightmares?"

Fuck. "She just lost her mother. We comfort her as best we can. Aubrey's mom is a school counselor, so she knows what to do. We're doing everything she's told us to do."

The woman motions to the photo of Raine and me above the bed. "This is sweet."

"Aubrey took that shot." I'm about to add, "It's from my first meeting with my daughter." But when I realize the comment would only emphasize the short amount of time that's passed since that magical moment, I shut the fuck up about that and, instead, offer, "I'm going to get some framed photos of Raine's mother for her room. Photos of Aubrey and Aubrey's parents, too. I have a shelf of family photos in my room, and Raine liked that, so I told her I'd make a shelf like that for her, too."

"Is Raine included in your collection of family photos?"

I breathe a sigh of relief. It's the first answer I feel great about. "She's front and center. Would you like to see?"

"Yes, please."

As the woman follows me out of Raine's bedroom, I babble, "I'm always going to honor Claudia's memory, and so will the Capshaws. And, of course, no matter what happens, the Capshaws will always be a huge part of Raine's life. She loves all of them, and so do I."

I didn't mean to say that last part. It just slipped out. And now, I don't know if I've fucked myself over or helped my cause. Either way, the truth is the truth: I love Aubrey and her parents. Not because I've been forced to hang out with them for the past month. Not because of our shared love of Raine. But because they're my family now, every bit as much as Miranda. And so is Claudia, I suddenly realize, through all the people I love who loved her.

When we get to my room, the social worker leans down to study the photo of Raine. "What an adorable shot. She's beaming with happiness."

My heart flutters hopefully. "That was taken at my lake house in Montana. Raine loved playing with her sand toys there. I bought her a set for this house, too, so she can continue making mud pies for everyone."

The woman seems like she's trying to suppress a smile. But she says nothing as she makes another note. When she looks up again, all traces of her smile are gone; she's all business again. "All right, Mr. Baumgarten. I think I've got what I need, in terms of the environment. Let's bring in Aubrey and Raine for their interviews now. I'll talk to Aubrey first; and then to Raine in her bedroom. And then, hopefully, your sister, if she makes it here before I'm done."

"Miranda's on her way now." I hold up my phone by way of explanation.

"Wonderful."

I swallow hard and shift my weight. "I didn't realize you'd be talking to Raine separately. I thought I'd get to be there. She's really shy."

"I promise it'll be painless for her. We'll play dolls in her room, or maybe draw or color; and while she's playing and distracted, we'll chat. I promise, by the end, she won't even realize she's been interviewed."

"She's really, really shy, and I don't want her feeling stressed."

"Neither do I, I assure you. I promise I'll be very gentle with her. I've been doing this for twenty years, Mr. Baumgarten. She's in good hands."

I wipe my sweaty palm against my sweaty forehead, feeling like I'm going to shit my pants or puke. If ever there was a time to throw back a stiff drink or inhale a fat, juicy blunt, this is it. "Just don't push her too hard, okay?"

"I won't. I promise."

I exhale. "Okay, then. I guess I'll go get Aubrey and Raine."

"I'll wait here. Mr. Baumgarten?"

I turn in the doorway.

"Take a deep breath. You're doing great."

CHAPTER 30
CALEB

I triple check the straps on Raine's car seat in the back of my new Volvo. "This is gonna be so much fun, Rainey. You're gonna love feeding the ducks."

"Duckies!" Raine shouts, fist pumping the air.

My stomach twists again. Little does she know, she won't be feeding them with me.

When the social worker revealed I'd have to do this unthinkable thing—namely, bring my sweet angel of a daughter to meet the devil himself—granted, under the watchful eye of the social worker—I tried to refuse. Pleaded my case. But apparently, the exercise is court-ordered and non-negotiable. And so, after some major reassurances from the social worker and a very long conversation with Aubrey last night, here I am, strapping my baby girl into my car to do something I don't want to do. I wanted Aubrey to come with me for the hand-off today, but the social worker said things will go more smoothly for Raine, in terms of her separation anxiety, if she only has to say one goodbye.

"It's going to be okay," Aubrey says behind me, as I shut the back door of the car.

"If he lays a finger on her, I'm pulling the plug."

"He won't. The social worker said she's instructed him not to touch her at any time."

"Just saying, if he does, I'm taking her away."

"We have to follow the judge's order, Caleb. Keep your eye on the forest, not the trees here. *Please*."

The meeting spot for today is a neighborhood park with a duck pond that's only about five miles away from my house. As I park the Volvo in the parking lot, the social worker waves in greeting. A moment later, a white-haired man exits a car that's already parked nearby.

Ralph Beaumont.

By now, I've seen him in photographs. But now that I'm seeing him in the flesh, I'm even more convinced he was the fucker on the rowboat. Unfortunately, Rowboat Guy was too far away to know for sure, though.

"Duckies!" Raine shouts from the back seat, kicking her legs happily, and a spear of guilt impales me. My shy, skittish daughter trusts me completely now. How can I betray her trust by handing her off to two strangers, even if only for a few minutes? The social worker handled Raine perfectly the other day, as promised, so I guess it's possible she'll work miracles with her again today, even in Ralph's presence. But there's something about Ralph's demeanor that sends a chill down my spine, and I'm worried Raine will sense it, too.

"Lots of duckies," I mutter. "You're going to have so much fun."

With a crashing heart, I exit the car, unstrap Raine, and

carry her in a tight embrace toward the social worker and the devil himself.

"Hello, Mr. Baumgarten," the social worker says politely. To Raine, she says with a smile, "Remember me? We played dolls together in your room."

Raine nuzzles shyly into my chest and doesn't speak.

"Hi, Raine," Beaumont says. He takes a step forward, so I take a step back, much to his obvious annoyance. "I'm your grandpa," he adds. "Your mommy's father."

I bite my tongue. *You're not Raine's grandpa. And you weren't poor Claudia's father, either. You were her fucking rapist.*

"I heard you like to feed ducks," Beaumont continues. "I was thinking we could feed them together and talk about your mommy."

The social worker says something about me putting Raine down, but I reflexively squeeze her tightly against me, like I'm protecting her from shrapnel from an explosion.

"Mr. Baumgarten, she'll be fine," the social worker says. "I'll be here the whole time."

"You want to feed ducks with this nice lady?" I choke out.

"No," Raine says into my chest, and my heart feels like it's physically cracking.

"You love feeding ducks, Shortcake."

"Dadda feed ducks."

The social worker tries to coax her, but Raine digs in her proverbial heels.

I'm at a loss.

Unwilling to set her down, now that she's clinging to me for dear life.

But like Aubrey said, this isn't optional. I'm required to do this by court order.

Shit. If I come home and tell Aubrey I never handed Raine over today, she's going to lose her shit. "Just for a few minutes," I coo to Raine. "It'll be fun." I start to put her down again, but she clings to me even more fiercely and screams, "No, Dadda! No, no, nooooo!"

My heart feels like it's shattering into a million pieces. No is her favorite word these days, but her normal protestations don't sound anything like this. In this moment, my baby sounds genuinely terrified. Like she's seen a ghost. Does she have a sixth sense about this dangerous, soulless man, or is my body language somehow setting her off?

Stuffing down tears, I tell Raine I'll be nearby. That this will only take a few minutes. That this is the same nice lady she played dolls with the other day. But reasoning with a toddler is a fool's errand, and my words have zero impact.

Finally, the social worker tries her hand at coaxing Raine. And just as she seems to be softening a bit in my arms, maybe even warming to the idea, Ralph starts barking at her to be obedient and do as she's told, and my baby bursts into tears and clutches me for dear life.

Fuck it.

He might not have touched her, but his harsh tone clearly scared her shitless. Whether I'm under a court order or not, I'm going to do what's best for my daughter and get her the hell out of here.

Holding Raine firmly against my chest, I coo, "It's okay, baby. You don't have to go. Dadda's got you." As Ralph loses his shit, I glare at the social worker, daring her to contradict me. "Either I'm staying here with her, or I'm taking her away now."

"He can't do this!" Ralph barks. "Make him give her to me!"

"*Sir*," the social worker says to Ralph. "Take a step back and keep quiet."

"I will *not* keep quiet. He's violating my legal rights!"

"*Sir, step back*. I won't warn you again."

I've heard enough.

With my arms wrapped securely around Raine, I say to the social worker, "My daughter is obviously terrified of this man, and for good reason. He's a stranger to her."

Beaumont scoffs. "Says the guy who only met her a month ago."

I have no comeback for that, unfortunately, so I turn and stride silently to my car, as Beaumont screams bloody murder behind me and the social worker yells at him to calm down and remain quiet.

"You're okay, baby," I whisper soothingly to Raine, as I strap her into her car seat. "Dadda's got you. I'm taking you home now, baby."

Raine wipes a tear. "To Mommy?"

The last remaining, dangling shard of my heart splinters and crumbles. "No, love, to our house at the beach."

I shut the door on her tear-streaked face, quaking with adrenaline. As I head to the driver's door, Ralph shouts, "Thanks for violating the court's order, asshole! That's only going to help me and hurt you, dumbass!"

I slide into the driver's seat, feeling sick to my stomach. Is he right? Am I screwing myself by walking away? Am I too focused on a specific tree, rather than the forest?

I pull my car out of the spot, as Ralph charges at my car, his face as red as a beet.

As he approaches, I roll down my window. Not to hear the string of expletives he's shouting at me, but to shout something I probably shouldn't: "See you in court, motherfucker! And after that, in fucking hell."

After leaving the park, I'm tempted to drive around aimlessly for an hour or so. Long enough for Raine to fall asleep and for me to act like everything went according to plan, when I return home to Aubrey. But, of course, I can't do that. I promised Aubrey full honesty. Good, bad, or ugly. In this case, ugly, unfortunately.

As I pull into my driveway, I'm surprised to find Raine already fast asleep in the back. Apparently, that whole experience at the park was exhausting her. For me, too, honestly. I'm wiped.

As I retrieve my daughter's sleeping frame from her car seat and head inside, I practice the speech I'm going to give to Aubrey. The explanation. The excuse, really. But the second I see her worried, surprised face in the living room, my brain flips into fight or flight mode, and I forget everything I've been planning to say.

"What happened?" Aubrey gasps out. "Why are you back so early?"

"Let me get her into bed first," I murmur, as I walk past her with Raine in my arms.

I swiftly head to Raine's bedroom with Aubrey trailing behind and her panic wafting off her body and into my back like a palpable thing.

I get Raine settled onto her bed, march out of her room, and close the door behind Aubrey and me. And the second I'm alone with Aubrey in the hallway, even before I've said a single word, I nearly lose control of my emotions.

"What is it?" Aubrey asks, anxiety overtaking her features. "What happened?"

I can barely speak through the tremble in my voice. "I think maybe I fucked up."

"*How*? Caleb, tell me what happened."

I want to explain it to her, but I can't find the right words. If Aubrey chews me out again, the same way she did in the middle of the street outside her parents' house weeks ago, I'll cry like a baby this time, and I don't want to do that.

"You left without doing the hand-off?" she asks in a worried tone.

"I swear to God, Aubrey, it felt like Raine was channeling Claudia or something. I'm not a big believer in supernatural stuff, but it was like Raine knew she shouldn't be anywhere near that man." In a ramble, I describe the whole thing. And to my extreme relief and surprise, when I'm finished talking, Aubrey isn't mad. In fact, she doesn't even shake her head in disappointment. On the contrary, she pulls on my shirt, guiding me to her, and plants a tender, heartfelt kiss on my lips.

"You did good," she murmurs. "You protected her."

"I violated a court order. What if I've fucked us over?"

"We have to have faith in the social worker. She was there. She saw the situation. She'll back you up."

"But what if she doesn't?" I rub my forehead, feeling stressed. I need to drink, bang on my drums, cry, fight, smoke, or fuck; and since only one of those options is currently available to me in this hallway, the very best one, I pick up Aubrey by her ass and carry her to my bedroom, kissing her passionately as we go.

When I reach my bed, I lay her down, peel off her

clothes and mine, and breathlessly open the drawer of my nightstand to pull out a condom.

"No need," Aubrey whispers hoarsely. "Come here. I want you inside me."

She doesn't need to ask me twice. I don't know if that means Aubrey's on some type of birth control, or if she's saying she's willing to risk getting knocked up by me. But, frankly, it doesn't matter which it is, because, suddenly, other than getting custody of my daughter and living here in LA with both her and Aubrey, I can't think of anything I'd enjoy more than putting a baby inside Aubrey fucking Capshaw.

I sit on the edge of the bed with my hard cock straining toward the ceiling, and Aubrey straddles me and slides herself onto my full length without delay or hesitation.

"You did so good," she whispers, her palms on either side of my face and her eyes boring into mine. "You protected your baby girl today, exactly like a good father should."

I grip her for dear life, praying she's right about that, and Aubrey rides me, kisses me, and coaxes me with whispered words, like I'm a runaway, wild stallion, and she's gently luring me back to the barn.

"Aubrey," I grit out, digging my fingers into her bare back. "*I'm sorry, baby.*"

"You have nothing to be sorry about." She grabs my face, presses her forehead to mine. "*Caleb.*"

Holy fuck. This feels electric. I've never been honest like this. Not completely. I've always doled out half-truths to protect myself. Kept my mouth shut, when speaking wasn't in my best interest. But with Aubrey, complete honesty is the only option. "*Aubrey,*" I whisper tightly, as my pleasure spikes and threatens to shove me over the abyss.

"I've got you, baby," Aubrey whispers, her voice breathless and on the verge of breaking. She's never called me baby before, I don't think. I've called *her* that, countless times; but not the other way around. And for some reason, hearing the word out of her mouth feels like she's electrocuting my nerve endings in the best possible way.

Gasping for air, I touch her clit as she gyrates on top of me, desperate for her to come before I lose control. Thankfully, it doesn't take long before Aubrey grips my shoulders, hard, and unleashes an orgasm that squeezes my hard cock inside her with such blissful force, I'm momentarily blinded by pleasure.

"*Aubrey,*" I grit out, as my release overwhelms me. The word isn't enough, but it's the best I can do for now. A necessary stand-in for what I really want to say in this watershed moment: *I love you, Aubrey Capshaw. And, baby, I'm positive I always will.*

CHAPTER 31
AUBREY

"Ralph is the best guy I know. A real stand-up guy."

This is the testimony of Ralph Beaumont's third character witness of the morning—another ride-or-die of Ralph's who made the trip to LA from Prairie Springs for the hearing. The first guy knew Ralph from church; the second guy was his much older brother; and this third guy worked with Ralph on the police force for years.

It's been easy for me to tell all three witnesses are full of shit. Hopefully, the judge—a no-nonsense Black woman in a black robe—can easily see that, too, since she's the one who'll be making the decision today. Thankfully, the judge blocked all cameras and the public from attending this hearing, so only people directly involved are in attendance. Except, of course, that the little girl at the center of this firestorm isn't here today. Raine is safely tucked away in a small room down the hall, blissfully coloring or watching a cartoon with my mother and a social worker.

For the past fifteen minutes or so, Caleb's attorney, Paula, has been cross-examining Ralph's third character witness, the same way she did his first two. "Ralph promised you financial gain, in exchange for your favorable testimony today, didn't he?" Paula asks with narrowed eyes and a chest full of confidence.

"No, ma'am," the guy says. "I'm here because Ralph's a good friend of mine, and it's my firm belief the child should be with her grandfather."

It's the same exchange, basically, Paula had with Ralph's first two character witnesses, and I don't believe this third guy any more than the others. I glance at Caleb sitting next to me at our table, and, not surprisingly, he looks as disdainful as I feel. Except, in Caleb's case, his disdain is manifesting as downright rage. Indeed, Caleb looks like a volcano on the cusp of erupting.

I covertly tap Caleb's arm, prompting him to look at me. When our eyes meet, I nonverbally remind him, once again, to stop glaring at the witness like he wants to murder him. Both our attorneys instructed us to maintain neutral expressions throughout Ralph's entire presentation this morning, no matter how outlandish the lies might be; and in response to my silent tongue lashing, Caleb somehow manages to erase the glower from his face. Sitting this close to him, however, I can still plainly see the homicidal blaze in his green eyes.

"No more questions," Paula says in an unbothered, clipped voice. She's damned impressive. Through her questioning, she's established that none of Ralph's character witnesses has any idea about his fitness as a father, because none of them, even Ralph's own brother, witnessed Ralph interacting with his daughter, Claudia, except on a few, brief occasions in Prairie Springs, many years ago. Even better, Paula also established none of the men has ever witnessed Ralph interacting with or even speaking about his grandchild, the tiny human at the center of this custody dispute.

As Paula resumes her seat at our table on the other side of Caleb, I write on the notepad between Caleb and me, *The judge isn't buying his BS.*

Caleb glances at the judge before quickly scribbling back, *I hope you're right.*

"Next witness?" the judge asks Ralph's lawyer.

"Ralph Beaumont, your honor."

A shiver runs down my spine as Ralph settles into the hot seat. All I want to do is squeeze Caleb's hand underneath the table to release my anxiety, but I can't do that. According to our attorneys, Caleb and I can't let the judge see us being too handsy or familiar today, because that might make her think Caleb's somehow manipulated my "doe-eyed" testimony. That's the phrase Paula used about me: *doe-eyed.*

After some preliminary questioning, Ralph says, "I didn't even know I had a granddaughter until the police in Seattle called me about my daughter's tragic death."

LIAR, I write on the notepad between Caleb and me. Our lawyers warned us Ralph would lie, lie, *lie* today. But still, hearing him doing it makes my blood boil inside my veins. In truth, Claudia's entire family found out, early on, about her accidental pregnancy, and Ralph and his side of the family cruelly disowned Claudia for being an unwed mother. Only Claudia's mother supported her pregnant daughter, along with me and my parents. But even then, Claudia's mother could only openly support Claudia, without the need to sneak around, once Caleb's monthly deposit enabled her to get her away from her abusive husband for good.

After a few introductory matters, Ralph's lawyer finally

asks him the question I've been dying to know since Claudia's death: "How did you come find out Mr. Baumgarten is your granddaughter's biological father?"

"As next of kin," Ralph replies, "I went to my daughter's house after her death to gather her personal affects." He points at me. "That kidnapper had already taken my grandchild to Montana by then, so I—"

"*Mr. Beaumont*," the judge snaps. "Just give us the facts without embellishment or accusation. We're here to decide what's in the best interest of the child, not to settle personal scores or vendettas."

Ralph's blue eyes blaze with fury. From what I know of this demonic man, he's not a guy who reacts well to being scolded by anyone, but especially not by a woman. Somehow, though, perhaps by reminding himself of the substantial windfall he stands to gain if he wins today, Ralph grits out, "Yes, ma'am."

"*Your honor*," the judge corrects.

Anger is wafting off Ralph's frame like a vapor. But he replies evenly, "Yes, your honor."

On the notepad, Caleb scribbles, *Judge = badass*.

After reading Caleb's note, I don't dare look at him. Instead, I write back, *She takes zero shit*. Hopefully, that will turn out to be a great thing for us, since Ralph is nothing if not full of shit.

"What was the question, again?" Ralph asks his lawyer. And when the guy repeats it, Ralph leans into the microphone and says, "While I was going through my daughter's stuff, I came across a confidential settlement agreement between Claudia and Caleb Baumgarten. That's how I found out. That's when I contacted Caleb with a fair proposal for me to take custody of my granddaughter and for Caleb to work with me the same way he'd always worked with my daughter. But to my shock, he rejected my good-will proposal and instead decided to go to Prairie Springs to buddy up with *her*—the *kidnapper*." He glares angrily at me for emphasis.

The judge reprimands Ralph for his word choice again and warns him he's on thin ice; and he begrudgingly corrects himself.

For another thirty minutes, Ralph continues spewing all manner of bullshit, including stories about his close bond with Claudia as a child and his desperate desire to give his granddaughter a similarly loving, stable, and safe childhood. "My granddaughter should be with blood family," Ralph insists, shooting daggers at me. "Not with an unrelated opportunist who doesn't care about her, beyond the child support payments." He shoots daggers at Caleb. "And certainly not with a drunk, drug-addicted rockstar who only stepped up after he realized hiring a nanny would be cheaper than paying proper child support to a family member—someone with decades of experience as a parent, I should add, unlike both of them." Now, he glares at Caleb and me as a collective.

I shift in my seat, wanting to scream bloody murder. To stand up, flail my arms, and shriek at the judge that this monster is a liar, pedophile, rapist, and wife beater. I fist both hands tightly in my lap, trying to control myself; and when I steal a glimpse of Caleb, it's clear he's experiencing a similar struggle. Although in Caleb's case, he probably wants to leap up there and do something so violent to Ralph, it'd make the slap he gave Trent in Billings look like a love pat.

Finally, it's Paula's turn to cross-examine Ralph; and the minute she rises and stares down her prey, it's clear she intends to rip this motherfucker to shreds.

Get him, Paula, Caleb writes on the notepad.

Succinctly, I dash off three exclamation points at the end of Caleb's note.

"You disowned your daughter when she got pregnant out of wedlock, did you not?"

"That's not how it happened."

"No?"

"No. I *suggested* she marry the father. Or *someone*, at least. But Claudia wouldn't listen to me, because her whole life, her mother told her a pack of lies about me and turned her against me."

Paula perks up. "Is that so? What kinds of lies, Mr. Beaumont?"

Ralph's face turns red. "She implanted false memories that turned Claudia against me."

Paula leans an elbow on the lectern. "Describe the lies and false memories for me, please. In detail."

Genius, I write on the notepad, trying not to smirk. Now that Ralph's stupidly brought up the topic, how will he get out of this, without having to admit his daughter accused him of raping and molesting her? Sadly, Claudia's not here to testify to that truth herself; but at least now, the judge will get to hear about those accusations through Ralph.

"I . . . I don't remember," Ralph stammers, his face turning even redder. Plainly, he's realized his mistake.

Paula persists, at which point Ralph looks at his lawyer for help, prompting the guy to leap up and shout an objection.

"He brought it up himself as fact," Paula argues evenly. "So now, he needs to back up his allegation."

"I'll allow it," the judge says. She stares down Ralph. "Answer the question. What lies and/or false memories do you allege your ex-wife implanted into your daughter's brain to turn her against you?"

Ralph hems and haws and ultimately claims he doesn't remember, exactly. And, eventually, the judge instructs Paula to move on to another line of questioning. The damage is done, though, if you ask me: Ralph now looks like a fucking liar.

Paula asks Ralph a bunch more questions, all of them designed to establish his lack of contact with Claudia and Raine, as well as his lack of parenting skills. And when that's done, Paula returns to our table with a covert wink at Caleb.

"We're done with our presentation, your honor," Ralph's attorney announces.

The judge trains her dark eyes on me. "Miss Capshaw? Your presentation, please."

Shit. While I wring my hands underneath the table, my attorney smoothly rises from our table and checks his notes. He's a smart guy whom I've come to trust. As we've discussed at length, I'm here to support Caleb's bid for full custody of Raine and my own unlimited visitations rights, because that's what I truly think is best for Raine. If I sense things aren't going well for Caleb, however, we're standing at the ready to pivot and ask for full custody for *me* and visitation rights for *Caleb*. Frankly, it'd pain me to do that to Caleb; but the most important thing is keeping Raine out of Ralph's clutches, no matter what.

Someone fetches my first character witness, my mother, from that room down the hallway, and she proceeds to testify that I'm the kindest, sweetest, gentlest person in the whole world and the best possible guardian to Raine. She talks about her own love for Raine. The fact that Raine is part of our family. And when she's asked about Caleb's fitness as a father, my mother confirms he's become a wonderful, caring, and gentle parent. One she wouldn't hesitate to entrust Raine with, as long as our family is always allowed to be involved, too.

My attorney asks Mom a few questions about Ralph. Specifically, about his reputation in Prairie Springs and what she knows of his general character. But Ralph's lawyer successfully shuts down most of the questions as "soliciting hearsay," whatever that means.

Finally, my attorney asks, "What does the child call you, Mrs. Capshaw?"

"Grammy," Mom answers proudly. "Which is perfect, because I certainly think of her as my granddaughter."

"Thank you, Mrs. Capshaw. That's all."

Ralph's attorney says he doesn't wish to cross-examine my mother. Probably, because he's wary of opening Pandora's box on all the bad things my mother has heard about Ralph from living in Prairie Springs her whole life. So, in short order, it's Dad's turn to testify.

Like Mom, my father swears I'm the greatest person who ever lived in the history of the world and a spectacular guardian to Raine. He also repeats Mom's endorsement of Caleb, and similarly gets shut down when trying to say Ralph Beaumont is "well known in Prairie Springs" to be a "really bad guy and a liar." Finally, when it comes time to reveal Raine's nickname for him, Dad answers proudly, "She calls me Pop-Pop, and I wouldn't have it any other way."

As with Mom, Ralph's lawyer chooses not to ask Dad any questions. Which means, ready or not, it's now time for me to take the stand and try to do everything in my power to keep my baby girl away from the man who's evil incarnate.

"How do you know Ralph Beaumont?" my lawyer asks me, after getting some preliminary stuff out of the way.

"He's my best friend's father. Claudia and I used to go over to each other's houses all the time, growing up, when we both lived in Prairie Springs."

"Did a time come when you stopped going over to Claudia's house?"

"Yes. After I witnessed Mr. Beaumont punching and shoving Claudia's mother—" Ralph's attorney bolts up and makes a screaming objection that makes me flinch. There's a big bruhaha, as all the lawyers and the judge squabble about the situation. But, finally, I'm allowed to continue my answer, with the admonishment that I'm only allowed to testify to things I've personally witnessed with my own physical senses, and not about things I might have heard, second-hand, from Claudia or anyone else.

In a trembling voice, I describe exactly how I witnessed Ralph beating the crap out of his wife, and the few people sitting in the audience gasp and titter during my telling. "After that," I say, "my parents wouldn't let me go to Claudia's house anymore. Which was fine, because I didn't want to go back there, ever again."

"Liar!" Ralph shouts at me, slamming his fist on his table.

"*Quiet*," the judge hisses. She glares at Ralph's lawyer. "Control your client, or I'll remove him from the courtroom."

"Did you tell anyone what you witnessed?" my lawyer asks.

"My parents. They reported the incident to the police,

but nothing happened. Ralph was a police officer, and our town is very small, so we figured—"

Ralph's attorney barks out an objection, something about speculation, and after a bit more arguing I don't quite understand, the judge tells my attorney to move on.

"Did you ever talk to Claudia about the abuse you witnessed?"

Another objection. This time, however, I'm told to answer the question.

"She said he did that to her mother all the time." More objections. More waiting. When I'm allowed to continue talking, I figure it's now or never: I have to seize my chance to say the one thing that needs to be said, above all others, or I might not get another opportunity. "Much later," I blurt, "when we were living together in Seattle, we talked about how Ralph Beaumont sexually abused Claudia, countless times, during her childhood and—"

Ralph and his lawyer both flip out, as people in the audience burst into hushed conversation, and the end result is another round of squabbling that leads to the judge personally asking me a question: "Did you have any reason *not* to believe Claudia when she told you these things about her father? Any reason at all?"

"No, your honor. Claudia wasn't a liar, and she was sober at the time. She never, ever would have lied to me about something like that. I'm positive about that, your honor." The moment I get my last words out, I burst into tears.

"Do you need a break?" the judge asks gently.

"Yes, please," I choke out. "Thank you."

"Fifteen minutes, everyone," the judge announces with authority, before disappearing with a whoosh of her black robe through a door behind her.

"What's your relationship to Mr. Baumgarten?" my lawyer asks, once I'm back on the stand and my tears have dried.

I glance at Caleb at our table, and a surge of love and affection for him overwhelms me. "He's my employer." That's my practiced answer. The thing I'm supposed to say. But, suddenly, it feels like a lie to stop there. I'm under oath, after all. So, I add, "He's also become a close friend, as we've navigated co-parenting the child together." We've all been warned not to say Raine's name in these proceedings to protect her identity.

My lawyer asks, "Do you consider yourself the child's parent?"

"I do. Not by blood. But in all other ways that matter, yes."

My attorney smiles, letting me know I'm doing great. "Let's talk about your friendship with Mr. Baumgarten." And off I go, explaining the history of my acquaintance with Caleb, the trust I've slowly developed in him, and the belief I've slowly acquired that Caleb would make a fantastic custodial father.

Unlike my mother earlier, I don't bother to qualify my endorsement of Caleb with, "As long as I'm always in the child's life." Sitting here now, I trust Caleb completely. Enough to know he'd never screw me over in relation to Raine or anything else. Which means that qualifier simply isn't necessary.

When my attorney finally sits down, Ralph's silver-haired attorney gets up and levels me with cold, reptilian eyes. "You're aware Mr. Baumgarten was in rehab until mere weeks ago, correct?"

"Yes. As I said, he employed me as his sobriety coach." I

clear my throat. "He's very committed to his sobriety, and I think that's admirable."

"You know what got him sent to mandatory rehab in lieu of jail?"

"I do." He asks me to explain what I know about the incident in New York, and I tell him what I know, as heat creeps up my neck and into my cheeks. "Caleb was devastated about his mother's death that night. He was overcome by grief."

Ralph's attorney stares at me for a long moment, like he thinks I'm full of shit, before moving on to his next question. For the next few minutes, he tries to get me to admit I've witnessed Caleb falling off the wagon. That I'm covering for him. Lying under oath. But of course, he gets nowhere, since none of it is true. Obviously, he's got nothing and he's simply fishing.

After looking down at his notes for a while, Ralph's attorney switches gears. He asks how much Caleb pays me. Tries to get me to admit the amount is exorbitant. That I'm being paid to lie today. But my attorney prepared me for this tactic, so I'm able to shut him down with facts and figures about the high-end nanny market. Nobody would pay the amount Caleb pays me in Prairie Springs. But in LA, and especially on the "celebrity nanny circuit," my salary, while exceedingly generous, doesn't seem *quite* as insane, thanks to Caleb being a rich, globally beloved celebrity.

With a snarl, Ralph's attorney asks, "Miss Capshaw, are you aware of Mr. Baumgarten's long history of violence?"

Shit. I didn't see this coming. We didn't practice this. "I've seen a couple old videos online of Caleb losing his temper, if that's what you mean. But both incidents seemed justified to me."

The attorney asks for details, and I describe the videos

I've seen. In one, Caleb pushed a paparazzi guy, hard, after the photographer basically assaulted Caleb with a large camera lens. In another video, Caleb tossed a fan clear across the stage, after the guy broke free of security and came running at Red Card Riot's famous front man, Dean Masterson. I try not to smile as I describe the second video, the one where Caleb protected his bandmate; but the attorney's outraged reaction tells me I'm not successful.

"Mr. Baumgarten's violence is *amusing* to you?" he asks righteously.

"That particular video was amusing to me, yes, because Caleb got there before security, and he threw the guy, like, fifteen feet across the stage to protect his best friend from getting tackled. The whole thing was so *Caleb* to me. So, yes, that one particular incident is honestly kind of amusing to me."

Ralph's lawyer quirks an eyebrow. "It was 'so Caleb' to you in what way? You mean, because it was shockingly violent?"

Fuck this guy. "No, because Caleb is incredibly protective of the people he . . . cares about. He doesn't hesitate to go into superhero mode, whenever the situation calls for it." Shit. During that answer, I almost said Caleb is protective of the people he *loves*. But given the time Caleb slapped Trent in Billings for me, that wording would have implied Caleb loves *me*, and I'm not certain of that, especially not under oath.

"Other than in videos, have you *personally* witnessed Mr. Baumgarten being violent?" the lawyer asks.

Fuck, fuck, fuck. Does he know about Caleb slapping the shit out of Trent, or is he fishing again, the same way he did about Caleb falling off the wagon? If you ask me, the incident with Trent only proves Caleb's worthiness as a father, since my own father wanted to beat the crap out of Trent, too, when he found out what my then-boyfriend had done to me. As a matter of fact, my dad stormed out of our house with a baseball bat to look for Trent, after he heard the news. Lucky for Trent, he successfully hid from my father for several days; and not too long after that, he moved to Billings. If Trent hadn't skedaddled, however, what would my father have done with that baseball bat? Surely, something worse than a slap. And yet, there's no doubt in my mind, Joseph Capshaw is the best father in the whole world.

"Miss Capshaw?" the lawyer prompts.

"I'm thinking about my answer," I say. "I want to make sure it's totally truthful and complete." Like Caleb always teases me about, I'm a rule follower, through and through. I don't knowingly lie, especially not when under oath. And yet, when I look into Caleb's pleading eyes, I quickly decide to make an exception to my usual rules. Desperate times call for desperate measures, after all. I'd rather tell a little white lie today on the stand, by conveniently forgetting about a much-deserved, much-appreciated karmic slap, than risk Ralph coming anywhere near our beloved baby girl.

"Yes, I recall seeing Caleb being violent in my presence," I testify, averting my eyes from Caleb. "He was building a deck at his lake house in Montana, and after he'd dropped a tool on his foot, he kicked that tool violently and shouted a string of curse words I shouldn't say in a courtroom." It's a true story. But even so, I know I'm being less than truthful by bringing up this story, rather than the one about the slap in Billings.

"That's not the kind of violence I'm asking about. Have you seen Caleb hit, kick, punch, shove, or otherwise assault another human being, including you, the child, or your parents?"

I glance at my father who's sitting alone in the front row, since my mother must have gone back to be with Raine again. My parents know all about what happened to Trent in Billings. I told them and Miranda that delightful story during Caleb's "rehab is over!" dinner party; and everyone at the table, including my father, busted a gut laughing about it. My father, in particular, praised Caleb up and down for slapping Trent that day. In fact, I'm positive my father appreciated that demonstration of Caleb's character, far more than his generous gift of that new truck.

When my eyes meet my father's, he nods at me, almost imperceptibly, letting me know he approves of my less-than-forthcoming testimony. Emboldened, I lean into the microphone and say, "The Caleb I know has always been gentle and non-violent in my presence. My whole family loves and supports him, completely. If I had any qualms about Caleb as a parent or as a man, if I thought he was a threat in any way, trust me, I'd tell you that. I love the child too much to let her fall into the hands of anyone who'd be anything but a wonderful, gentle parent to her."

I happen to catch Caleb's gaze and quickly look away when it feels like his eyes are screaming "I love you!" I feel the same way, of course. But now isn't the time for anyone to see that truth in my eyes. Now is the time for me to keep a poker face.

Practically rolling his eyes, Ralph's attorney asks, "Does that mean you've never personally witnessed him being violent?"

I take a deep breath. Please, God, let him be fishing right now. "That's correct."

Ralph's attorney exhales and his shoulders sag in resignation. "No further questions, your honor." And just like that, we've reached the end of my presentation.

"We'll take an hour for lunch," the judge declares. "After that, we'll start the afternoon with Mr. Baumgarten's presentation."

CHAPTER 32
CALEB

I'm shitting bricks as my first character witness, my sister, Miranda, takes the witness stand. I know she loves me, but our relationship has been strained at times, as I've pushed her loyalty and patience to the brink. She's also got no filter, this chick. Which, normally, I consider a cool thing. A funny thing. Not in this context, though.

"What's your relation to Caleb?" Paula asks Miranda, once my sister gets settled in the hot seat.

"He's my big brother and my hero. He's four years older than me."

Paula smiles. "You know Caleb well?"

"Very well."

"Why do you consider him to be your hero?"

"Because he's always been my protector. Always had my back."

"Is Caleb a perfect man?"

My sister snorts. "Far from it."

"Even so, would you have any qualms, if your brother were granted full custody of the child?"

"Not a single one. I'm positive he'd be a fantastic father to her." She flashes me a loving smile that makes my heart skip a beat.

"You've seen Caleb with the child?"

"Yes. He's adorable with her. It's the cutest thing, ever."

With prompting, Miranda launches into explaining her recent visit to Prairie Springs, and all the specific things she witnessed that have caused her to conclude her niece would be in good hands with me, as her full-time, custodial parent.

"Aubrey and her family should always be in her life, too, though," Miranda adds, unprompted. "They're family now. That was clear to me when I spent time with everyone in Prairie Springs."

I scribble a note on the pad between Aubrey and me: *So far, so good.*

Honestly, I can't fathom the glowing, unqualified review Miranda is giving of me—under oath, no less—when I know full well I've pissed her off, endlessly, over the years. But then again, I can't imagine my sister would say any of this, if she didn't truly believe it'd be the best thing for Raine. Knowing Miranda, she'd pick Raine's wellbeing over my wishes, any day. And rightly so.

After a while, Ralph's attorney gets the chance to cross-examine my sister. With a smirk, he immediately goes for the jugular. "You've personally witnessed your brother being violent on many occasions, have you not?"

"Several times. But not in a long while."

Jesus. Here we go.

"*Several* times?" Ralph's attorney sneers. "Please, list them all for me."

"*All* of them?" Miranda gasps out, like he's asking her to name every star in the galaxy, and it's all I can do not to palm my fucking forehead. *What the fuck, Miranda? Play some goddamned chess, dude, not simple checkers.*

"Okay, well, when I was about ten, I'd say," Miranda begins, "I witnessed my teenage big brother, Caleb, punching my father in the face for the first, but not the last, time. I believe Caleb punched him twice that time, but it might have been more. Either way, he did it to stop our father from beating the crap out of our mother. That's what Caleb had to do several times over the years. Always for the same reason. Until finally, Caleb's band took off and he got rich, so he was able to get our mother away from our father for good."

Ralph's lawyer shifts his weight and checks his notes on the lectern. Clearly, that wasn't the answer he was expecting.

"Should I go on?" Miranda asks, breaking the thick silence.

"Sure," the lawyer says, sounding a tad less confident than before.

Miranda takes a deep breath. "About ten years ago, Caleb got home from tour and found out this awful boyfriend of mine had gotten a bit rough with me during an argument, so my brother drove over to my apartment and beat the crap out of him. I'd already broken up with the loser by then, so I told Caleb not to bother with him. But he wouldn't listen. He said, 'And what about the next woman he dates? What will he do to her, if he thinks there's never going to be any consequences for his bad behavior?'" Miranda smirks. "So, anyway, he drove me to my ex's place and beat him up, while I waited in the car. And then, he called me inside and made my ex get on his knees in front of me, while his face was all bloody and gross, and apologize to me." She bites back a smile. "Caleb made him apologize and beg for my forgiveness—and he made him do it in a teeny-tiny baby voice."

Really, Miranda? She seriously thinks that cute little detail is helpful here? Fuck me.

I look down at my hands on the table, so the judge won't see whatever's on my face. I'm deeply concerned my sister is unwittingly torpedoing my chances here today. But I'm also, honestly, kind of proud of that moment, and I don't want the judge—or Paula—to see my face, in case I'm involuntarily smiling at the delicious memory.

"I should also mention," Miranda continues, "that my brother also made that guy promise not to do anything like that, ever again, to anyone else. Or Caleb said he'd find out and come back and do much worse to the guy. Honestly, I'm not sure how Caleb would have been able to deliver on that threat, but he seemed pretty convincing at the time, and the guy swore up and down he'd never, ever lay a pinky on anyone else."

Ralph's attorney sighs. "Is that everything?"

Miranda considers. "No. But I think that's enough for you to get the gist, right?"

"No, I want you to tell me *everything*."

With a long, put-upon sigh, Miranda leans back in her chair. "If you insist." She pauses. "Okay, well, around five years ago, some guy in a bar grabbed my ass—sorry, your honor, my *bottom*—and my brother knocked the jerk out cold with one punch." Miranda smiles at me. "The whole bar cheered him on, and a female bartender sent my brother a big bottle of champagne to thank him. Apparently, the guy was a known menace at that bar, a friend of the owner's, apparently, who couldn't be banned; and the whole bar was thrilled to watch him go down."

"Was he badly hurt?"

"Nah. He was fine. His ego was bruised more than anything, I think." Miranda taps her chin. "Another time, not sure when, exactly, years ago, this guy in Paris grabbed my mother's arm, really hard, and insisted she convince Caleb to take a selfie with him. My mother and I had joined Caleb for the European leg of his tour, so we were traveling with him and the band. So, anyway, this guy grabbed my mother with such a hard and scary grip, she screamed really loudly. So, Caleb flew into action and pushed the guy away from our mother. The guy wound up falling back and hitting his head on the sidewalk and going to the hospital. Apparently, he filed a lawsuit against Caleb later, but it was thrown out because the whole thing was caught on video and the judge declared Caleb's actions 'totally justified in defense of his mother.'"

With a smirk, Miranda takes a long drink of water. As she does that, it feels like everyone in the courtroom, including the judge, is waiting with bated breath for her next stomach-churning story about me.

"Another time," my sister finally says, replacing her cup, "I was dating this guy in LA who'd get super sloppy and offensive when he was drunk." She looks at the judge. "Yeah, I really know how to pick 'em, your honor." She returns to Ralph's attorney. "So, anyway, he said something outrageously horrible about me while playing pool in a bar, and, unfortunately for him, my brother overheard him, even though I didn't. And the next thing I knew, my brother was dragging my boyfriend into the bathroom and washing his mouth out with soap." Miranda snickers and bites back a smile. "Everyone in the bar who'd heard the comment said it was really gross and Caleb was totally justified. One person even told me Caleb let the guy off easy. I never found out exactly what he'd said, though, so ..

. " She shrugs. "I wish I knew, honestly. Sounds like it was juicy."

I hang my head, feeling sick. All these stories, told in rapid succession, make me sound like a goddamned, unhinged lunatic. I don't think my sister is making it clear enough all these stories happened *years* apart. Also, I haven't done that kind of shit in a very long time, other than when I slapped Trent, of course. But besides that, the last time I hit someone was when I punched Violet's now-husband, Dax Morgan, years ago, in the face. Thanks to Miranda, however, I'm sure the judge thinks this kind of violent behavior is a daily thing for me.

"Anything else?" Ralph's attorney asks. "Anything at all?"

"That I've *personally* witnessed? No, that's it, I think."

Shit. The way Miranda said *personally*, it's going to make Ralph's attorney ask—

"Does that mean you have *second-hand* knowledge about even more violence perpetrated by Caleb?"

Yep. That.

Paula objects before Miranda responds, thankfully, and much to my relief, the judge sustains the objection and instructs Ralph's lawyer to move on.

"Your honor," Ralph's attorney whines. "Miss Baumgarten is well known to be close friends with a woman whose husband got punched in the face by Mr. Baumgarten—"

"*Move on*," the judge says firmly. "Mr. Baumgarten's propensity to play superhero is now clear and well-documented. I've got the gist."

"No further questions," Ralph's lawyer says, looking annoyed.

As Miranda leaves the stand, I look down at my hands

on the table again, rather than making eye contact her. That was rough, dude. But, hey, at least, Miranda won't be forced to yammer on about me punching Violet's then-boyfriend/now-husband, Dax. So, I guess that's a good thing. Unlike the other stories Miranda told about me, I can't honestly say that punch to Dax's face was justified. In fact, I was dead wrong to do that, as Miranda emphatically told me at the time. In fact, my sister was so furious with me about that punch to her best friend's boyfriend's face, she wouldn't speak to me for weeks.

"Our next character witness is Amy Beretta," Paula announces.

I take a deep breath. *Come on, Amy.* After Miranda's so-called support, I'm going to need Amy to do some serious damage control. She's my only character witness today, other than Miranda. Amy's husband, my good friend, Colin, the drummer for 22 Goats, also wanted to testify; but Paula said having a musician from a hugely popular band on the stand would make it seem like I'm throwing my celebrity weight around. Not to mention, Colin was there, personally, unlike Miranda, when I stupidly punched his bandmate, Dax, so putting Colin on the stand and subjecting him to cross-examination about that would be a big mistake for that reason, as well.

My three bandmates, Dean, Emmitt, and Clay, also wanted to testify today, by the way. But they're even more famous than Colin, so Paula said no way. Plus, they've all personally witnessed me being a hotheaded prick too times to count over the years, so whatever good things they might have to say about me probably wouldn't have been worth it in the end.

"How do you know Mr. Baumgarten?" Paula asks Amy.

"We met when I was assigned to Caleb as his personal

assistant during Red Card Riot's world tour, about six years ago. We've been close friends, ever since."

Under questioning, Amy describes me as loyal, kind, protective, and generous. Someone she knows she can turn to for anything. Someone she trusts completely.

"Have you seen Caleb interacting with his daughter?"

"No, not yet. But I've got no doubt Caleb is a wonderful father to her, given how great he is with my son, Rocco, who's the same age. They were born about a week apart."

"You mentioned Caleb is protective," Paula prompts. "Can you elaborate on that?"

"During the time I worked for Caleb, some crew guys got out of line with me, and, unbeknownst to me at the time—I found out later—Caleb came to my rescue and made sure nobody harassed me in any way for the rest of the tour." On and on, Amy goes, alternately making me sound like her white knight and the second coming of Mr. Rogers. Seriously, it's all I can do not to stand and shout, "Don't overdo it, Amy! For fuck's sake, we have to make this sound believable!" Man, if she truly believes even a fraction of the shit she's saying about me today, then I guess I've been doing something right as a friend, unbeknownst to me.

"No further questions," Paula says, and surprisingly, Ralph's lawyer decides not to question Amy himself. Probably, he realizes he can't dim or besmirch the human ray of sunshine sitting on that witness stand, so why even try?

"Our final witness is Caleb Baumgarten himself," Paula announces.

"Mr. Baumgarten," the judge says, gesturing for me to take the stand. And so, after inhaling deeply and sharing a pointed "here we go" look with Aubrey, I rise from the table, button, unbutton, and then button again my sport coat, and stride to the witness stand with confident, long strides designed to camouflage the current of anxiety throttling every inch of my body.

So far, all Paula's questions have been softballs, as expected. The same ones we've practiced. So, naturally, I feel like I'm killing it.

"What's your goal here, Mr. Baumgarten?" Paula asks.

We've practiced this. "I want custody of my daughter, so I can be the father she deserves." It's all I'm supposed to say in response to that question. But in light of the long list of violent episodes Miranda recounted about me, I feel the need to improvise and add something else. "But even more than that," I add, much to Paula's visible surprise, "I want my daughter to be safe, happy, and loved." I look at the judge. "Your honor, if you decide I'm not a fit father for her, then I beg you to give full custody to Aubrey." I swallow hard. "To be clear, I very much want full custody for myself. So, so much. But I want what's best for my daughter, even more than that, and there's no better person in this entire world than Aubrey Capshaw."

"Thank you, Mr. Baumgarten," the judge says.

"I'm done with my questions," Paula says, before turning toward the table again.

"One more thing," I say, halting Paula's movement. "Sorry." I look at the judge again. "I feel like I need to add something to one of my prior answers. Remember when I said Aubrey is my nanny and friend? That wasn't the whole truth. Since I'm under oath, I feel like I should admit that . . ." I exhale. "I'm in love with Aubrey. Madly in love with her." I peek at Aubrey and her mouth is hanging open. Same with Paula's. "I haven't told her that yet. I haven't told anyone. But I feel like you need to know that, your honor, to understand just how highly I think of her. Aubrey's the best thing that's ever happened to me. The great love of my life. If something happened to me, she's the only person I'd ever want to take care of my daughter." I look at my sister in the audience. "Sorry, Miranda." Miranda smiles. "So, please, if you decide against me having full custody of my daughter, then Aubrey is one hundred percent where my daughter should be placed."

I peek at Aubrey again, and the look on her face makes my heart explode in my chest. *She loves me.* That's what Aubrey's dark, glistening eyes are confirming in this moment. And, man, it feels fucking incredible.

"Thank you, Mr. Baumgarten," the judge says softly, forcing me to wrench my eyes off the great love of my life. "Are you finished and ready for cross-examination now?"

"Yes, your honor," Paula says. "Thank you."

Ralph's attorney gets up and clears his throat. "You had zero interest in meeting your child before six weeks ago, correct? In fact, you only stepped up to avoid paying child support to Ralph Beaumont."

"Not true. I admit I dragged my feet as a father for six months. But then, I emailed Claudia and expressed extreme regret for my prior lack of involvement in my child's life. I begged Claudia to let me meet my baby, but Claudia refused."

Ralph's attorney looks flabbergasted. Thoroughly shocked. "There's . . . zero evidence of any of that," he stammers out.

"I've got the email exchange on my phone to prove it, if you want to see it."

"Yes, please," the judge interjects, as Ralph's attorney chokes on his words.

I bring up the emails and hand over my phone to the judge, who studies the messages with great interest. Once she's done reading, she hands my phone to a bailiff and asks him to show it to all attorneys and parties, which he does. And, finally, when the phone comes back to me on the witness stand, the judge instructs me to read the whole email exchange, word for word, out loud, for the court reporter to take down.

I do as I'm told, and when I'm done reading, I address the judge. "I found out recently Claudia didn't write that reply to me, even though it came from her account. In fact, it turns out Claudia never even saw my email."

Ralph's attorney is beet-red. "And you base that conclusion on *what*, exactly?"

I share a secret smile with Paula, the best, most kick-ass attorney and friend who ever fucking lived, before replying with, "I base it on what Claudia's ex-boyfriend, Ricky Schaeffer, confessed to my attorney about a week ago."

"Yep. It's true. Claudia never saw C-Bomb's email."

That's what Claudia's ex-boyfriend, Ricky, testifies, when he gets on the stand, and, thank God, tells the fucking truth.

"How do you know?" Paula asks calmly, even though her heart is probably beating a mile a minute underneath her cool exterior, the same as mine.

"'Cause I'm the one who replied to C-Bomb's email," Ricky answers. "After I replied, I deleted the email, so Claudia would never know about it. And then, I went ahead and blocked C-Bomb's email address and social media accounts, too, so Claudia wouldn't get another message from him."

"How certain are you that Claudia never saw Mr. Baumgarten's email?"

"One hundred percent. Trust me, if she'd seen it, she would have been on the first plane to LA. Not to mention, she would have let me have it for answering that email for her."

A low din erupts in the courtroom among the few people in the gallery, and the judge tells everyone to be quiet.

"Why did you hide that email from Claudia?"

Ricky shrugs. "Jealousy, I guess. I'd been pretty obsessed with the idea of Claudia cheating on me for months by then—which she never did, by the way; so I watched her putting in her password on her phone one night, and then I started checking her phone every night, after she fell asleep." He looks at me apologetically. "When C-Bomb's email came in, I happened to be on Claudia's phone at that moment; so while Claudia slept next to me, I replied and blocked him."

"Why didn't you want Claudia to receive that email, Mr. Schaeffer?"

Ricky motions to me. "Look at him. He's rich and famous and looks like a tattooed god, and I'm just a regular guy. I knew C-Bomb was Claudia's celebrity crush and she'd already had sex with him once. Now, he wanted to fly her and her baby to his fancy mansion in LA for a family reunion? Hell no. I knew the chances were high Claudia would fall in love with him in California. And what guy wouldn't fall in love with Claudia in return? She was a dream girl. Sweet and pretty and super smart. And let's not forget, she already had a baby with C-Bomb, so why wouldn't he give her a real shot, if she came to California?" He shrugs. "So, I answered the email, blocked him every which way, and never looked back."

"Meaning you never told Claudia about the email?"

"That's right."

Paula sighs, as I do the same behind her. We've struck gold here, thanks to Paula's dogged persistence at finding this guy, and I'll never be able to thank her enough.

"Thank you, Mr. Schaeffer," Paula says somberly. "I've got nothing further."

At the judge's invitation, Ralph's attorney gets up. "Mr. Baumgarten has promised to pay you a whole lot of money, if he gets custody here, hasn't he?"

"Nope. C-Bomb didn't promise me anything. I mean, yeah, he paid for my flight and hotel to come here. But that's it. I came here to do the right thing, that's all."

"Why now?"

Ricky twists his mouth. "When Claudia died, I started feeling guilty about what I did. Claudia told me about how her dad repeatedly raped her as a kid, so I knew—"

"Your honor!" Ralph's attorney screams, along with whatever his client is simultaneously shouting. Mayhem ensues, during which a bailiff steps in to keep Ralph at bay. In the end, however, even after Ralph's lawyer continues his questioning, he only winds up giving Claudia's ex-boyfriend yet another opportunity to repeat his firm belief that Claudia's child shouldn't go anywhere near Ralph Beaumont because of "the bad stuff" Claudia told him about her father.

"The kid should go to Aubrey or C-Bomb," Ricky insists. He looks at Aubrey. "More so, Aubrey, probably, since I personally witnessed her being a really good auntie." He shrugs. "I mean, if Aubrey thinks C-Bomb is up to the job, then I trust her judgment, and I know Claudia did, too. But my vote would be Aubrey. She's a solid citizen, that one."

"I have nothing further," Ralph's lawyer says, his shoulders drooping and his tone dejected.

I glance at the judge, my heart thumping. She's stone-faced, but I feel like we landed a strong punch with this guy. The only question is whether it was a *knockout* punch or merely a flesh wound.

"Let's take a fifteen-minute break," the judge says. "When we return, we'll hear from the court-appointed experts."

CHAPTER 33
CALEB

I slowly let out the breath it feels like I've been holding for five minutes, as it becomes clearer and clearer the first court-appointed witness of the afternoon, a psychiatrist, thinks I'm minimally fit to be Raine's father. I'm not perfect, the guy makes clear. Not going to win Father of the Year. I've got a "short fuse." Could use some anger management counseling to help me learn some "coping strategies." But, hey, considering all the shit my sister said about me during her testimony, I feel like the negative stuff the doctor says about me a) doesn't outweigh his ultimate rubber stamp; and b) most likely doesn't come as a big surprise to the judge, anyway.

When the psychiatrist gets to talking about Aubrey, however, it's a totally different story. She's well adjusted. Caring and kind. "Even-keeled and patient." In fact, according to him, Aubrey Capshaw's got a temperament that's "highly conducive" to being a "loving, rock-solid custodial guardian" for Raine. Of course, every word he says about her matches my own assessment. I wasn't exaggerating when I told the judge Aubrey's the best person I know.

The doctor finally gets around to providing his expert opinion regarding Ralph Beaumont, and the second he starts talking, I feel like the weight of the world has been lifted off my shoulders. In fact, on the notepad between Aubrey and me on the table, I scribble the words, *Pay dirt*.

In summary, the fine doctor testifies that Ralph "appears to check several boxes on the PCL-R"—the test for "all forms of psychopathy;" and therefore, according to the doc, it's "highly possible" Ralph is a narcissist. "I'd need further time and some more information to form a firm diagnosis about that, however," the doctor adds, much to my chagrin. "I am, however, willing to testify that Mr. Beaumont most certainly displays antisocial behaviors and a callous lack of concern for others."

"You're a quack!" Ralph shouts.

Aubrey begins furiously writing something on the notepad, but she stops when the judge declares, "I warned you, Mr. Beaumont, that another outburst wouldn't be tolerated." She motions to a nearby bailiff, a brawny guy with a porn mustache. "Remove him, please, Officer Frank."

"Yes, your honor."

Another bailiff joins the first in descending upon Ralph; and a moment later, he's removed from the courtroom, practically kicking and screaming, while pretty much everyone in the courtroom looks on at the spectacle with brazen satisfaction.

When the three men have disappeared through the big door at the back of the courtroom, and the somber room has fallen silent again, the judge returns calmly to the psychiatrist on the witness stand and prompts him to continue, which he does. I'm not listening closely to rest, though. I'm buzzing way too much about what just happened to concentrate. From what I pick up, here and there, though, it seems like this guy's remaining testimony is a ringing endorsement of Aubrey and an "I guess so" endorsement of me.

Next up, the court-appointed social worker takes the stand—the woman I've been shitting my pants over, ever since I spirited Raine away from that duck pond meetup in violation of the court's order. But to my intense relief, it quickly becomes clear I've got nothing to worry about with this stern woman. That in fact, much to my surprise, she's very much in my corner.

"Mr. Baumgarten's bond with the child appeared to me to be warm, loving, and stable," the social worker says. "Same with Miss Capshaw's bond with the child. It's worth noting that, during my alone-time with the child, she expressed love for both of them."

Aubrey and I exchange a smile, not even trying to hide our mutual affection and excitement about this particular testimony.

"Please provide further details about what happened during your alone-time with the child," the judge directs.

The social worker checks her notes and says, "I played dolls with her, during which I asked her to place dolls and stuffed animals at a table for a tea party, with each doll representing a family member. And after that, someone she loves." She looks at the judge. "This was after she said she loves her 'Dadda' and her 'Aubbey.' She said that, on her own, unprompted, while I was asking her if she likes living in her new home." As the judge makes a note, the social worker continues, her eyes forward, once again, "In both scenarios—family and people she loves—the child set up the same array of dolls and animals: ones representing her mother, Mr. Baumgarten—'Dadda;' Miss Capshaw—'Aubbey;' and both Miss Capshaw's parents—'Grammy and Pop-Pop.'" She shifts in her chair. "After that, I widened the net. Told the child to invite everyone she *likes* to our tea party, which then included her Auntie Miranda and several cartoon characters. After that, I asked for everyone the child *knows*. But no matter my prompt, the child never mentioned Mr. Beaumont. I therefore feel confident in concluding the child doesn't know Mr. Beaumont and is wholly unaware of his existence."

Boom, I scribble on the notepad between Aubrey and me.

That's our girl, taking care of biz-nass, Aubrey writes in reply.

Like her kickass Aubbey.

And her kickass Dadda.

We're not supposed to smile in court, and we know that; but we flash each other beaming smiles, anyway, if only for a moment.

"To be clear, this exchange happened *before* the court-ordered meetup at the park," the social worker adds, and our smiles vanish.

Fuck, I write. *Here we go.*

"Tell me exactly what happened at that meetup," the judge says. "I have your declaration in the paperwork but tell me the events leading up to Mr. Baumgarten refusing to hand over the child for the evaluation."

Shit, shit, shit. I hold my breath, as dread overtakes me and the woman sets the stage. But soon, it's clear I've got nothing to worry about on this topic, either.

"Ralph Beaumont became combative during the interaction, your honor, and the child became increasingly hysterical and terrified. Mr. Baumgarten had a difficult decision to make that day, and it's my opinion he made the one that was in his child's best interest—the one a loving, fit father would make."

The social worker looks at me with a neutral poker face; but if I'm not mistaken, her eyes are smiling at me.

The social worker continues, "I recognize that Mr. Baumgarten violated your order, your honor, and therefore did something wrong; but he also did something very right, in terms of safeguarding his child's safety and wellbeing. I was honestly impressed by his decision that day, your honor. Also, by the commitment he's showed to making his child's new home as happy and welcoming, as possible."

Aubrey places her hand on my forearm, as I hang my head to hide my tears of relief. Ever since that interview at my house, and then, even more so, after that day at the duck pond, I've been losing sleep about what happened. Lying awake, second-guessing my choices on a running loop. And now, it turns out what I did is exactly what a good father would do?

Aubrey scratches on the notepad, and when I glance at it while still stuffing down tears, a massive lump rises in my throat.

I love you so much.

That's what Aubrey's note says, so, of course, I quickly scribble the same words back to her. I admitted my feelings for Aubrey on the stand earlier, but she couldn't say it back to me then. So now, given my precarious mental state, the written exchange causes big, fat tears to well in my eyes through my beaming smile.

As the social worker leaves the stand, I flash her a grateful nod. And to my surprise, she flashes me a small smile. It's almost imperceptible. Barely there. But I'm definitely not imagining it.

"Let's take a thirty-minute break," the judge says with authority. "When we come back, I'll issue my ruling."

After the break, Ralph Beaumont is permitted back into the courtroom to hear the court's ruling. So, the three of us and our lawyers are now seated at our respective tables, intently staring at the judge as she rustles papers and languidly checks her notes.

I know I'm not supposed to touch Aubrey in front of the judge, but I can't help myself. The hearing's over, anyway. What harm can come from it now? I grab Aubrey's hand and squeeze tightly, and Aubrey squeezes right back. She looks every bit as stressed as I feel.

Finally, after what feels like an eternity, the judge looks up, clears her throat, and states, "My ruling is as follows: this court *temporarily* grants Aubrey Capshaw legal and physical custody of the child, with full, uninhibited visitation rights granted to Mr. Baumgarten. This court also *permanently* denies the cross-petition of Ralph Beaumont. As the child's sole, temporary guardian, Miss Capshaw has full discretion to decide who's allowed access to the child, except, of course, she may not deny Mr. Baumgarten his visitation rights."

"Are you fucking kidding me?" Ralph screams, so the brawny bailiff with the porn mustache swiftly escorts him out of the courtroom, once again.

With Ralph gone, the judge continues, "The period of my temporary order shall be six months. During that time, Mr. Baumgarten is hereby ordered to maintain his sobriety, to attend twice-weekly, mandatory sobriety meetings with a qualified rehab provider, and to attend once-weekly anger management classes." She looks at me sternly. "I'd strongly recommend some parenting classes and personal therapy, too, given all your superhero antics, Mr. Baumgarten, but I'm not making either of those things part of my official ruling at this time."

"Yes, your honor. Thank you. I'll do whatever it takes to be the best father possible."

The judge's features soften. "*Fit* parents aren't *perfect*, Mr. Baumgarten. There's no such thing as a perfect parent or person. Which is why this court also hereby orders the following: if Mr. Baumgarten remains in full compliance with my temporary order for the full six months, legal and physical custody shall transfer to him, with full and unlimited visitation rights then granted to Miss Capshaw. If Mr. Baumgarten has *not* met all the requirements of my temporary order by the end of the six-month period, however, then Miss Capshaw shall maintain sole legal and physical custody, with *supervised* visitation rights for Mr. Baumgarten, until he's able to establish full compliance, at which point the clock will reset for another six-month trial period. Do you understand, Mr. Baumgarten?"

Tears are streaking down my cheeks, but I don't bother to wipe them. "Yes, your honor," I squeeze out. "I won't let you down. I won't let my daughter down."

"That's my firm hope." She looks at Aubrey with sympathy. "I'm sorry for your loss. Wherever Claudia is, I'm sure she feels lucky to have you caring so deeply for her baby in her absence, the same way she would have done herself."

Aubrey sniffles. "Thank you, your honor."

The judge nods. "Best of luck to all. This hearing is adjourned."

With my hand clasped in Aubrey's, I pull her up and

bear hug her; and for the next several minutes, we cry, rejoice, and whisper softly in each other's arms.

"I love you, baby," I choke out, thrilled to say the words I've been dying to say out loud for so long. "I couldn't have done this without you."

"I love you, too. I'm so happy."

Aubrey's parents, my sister, and Amy appear, and we break apart and gratefully accept their warm hugs and congratulations. When all combination of hugs have been administered, we tearfully head out of the courtroom as a group, with Aubrey and I leading the way with our hands firmly joined.

"Let's go to a restaurant and celebrate," I suggest, and everyone in our group expresses enthusiasm about the idea.

"Which room is Raine in?" Aubrey asks her mother, since Raine's apparently been watching *Monster's Inc.* with a kind-hearted court clerk for the past hour.

Barbara opens her mouth to respond to her daughter, but before she gets a word out, Ralph appears in front of me, glaring and wagging his finger in my face. "I'd watch my fucking back, if I were you, *C-Bomb*," Ralph hisses. "Nobody disrespects Ralph Beaumont like this and gets away with it."

I push Aubrey behind me to protect her from whatever's about to go down. But before I've wrapped my hands around the old man's neck, Ralph is dragged away by that same brawny bailiff from the court room.

"Go get your daughter, C-Bomb!" the officer calls to me, after he puts a chokehold on Ralph. "I've got him. Go enjoy your family and forget this piece of shit ever existed."

CHAPTER 34
AUBREY

"I've been waiting all day to do this," Caleb murmurs, as he closes his bedroom door behind him and starts stripping off my clothes like they're on fire.

"I love you so much," I gasp out breathlessly, right before Caleb takes my face in his large palms and kisses me with such passion, with such intimacy and *love*, my knees buckle in response.

"I love you so fucking much," he whispers into my lips.

We've been saying those magical words to each other on a running loop, all afternoon and evening. First, when we hugged in celebration of the judge's ruling. And then, repeatedly, during our celebratory dinner with family and friends. Somehow, Caleb quickly managed to arrange a private room at his favorite restaurant in Beverly Hills at the spur of the moment, and we wound up having an incredible, joyful dinner party with an enthusiastic, celebratory group.

Everyone who made today's victory possible was in attendance, plus Amy's husband, Colin, who drove right over after his wife called him with the good news. Caleb's three bandmates, Dean, Clay, and Emmitt, also came straight over, even though Dean was in some important business meeting when he got the news. As we ate incredible food, we replayed the day's events for everyone, soliciting raucous reactions to all of it. And of course, everyone who hadn't yet met Raine before the dinner party fell under her adorable spell.

Not gonna lie, I felt starstruck when Caleb's famous friends first showed up at the restaurant. 22 Goats is one of my all-time favorite bands, and seeing the rest of Red Card Riot made my brain melt. Not to mention, seeing those three with Caleb, like I've seen countless times online, made me remember just how world-famous Caleb is, and that kind of messed with my head for a minute. Eventually, however, when conversation started flowing and it was clear all the rockstars at the table put their pants on, one leg at a time, I was finally able to settle down and start feeling like myself again. And from that point on, the celebration dinner was nothing but magical for me.

Toward the end of the party, Raine fell fast asleep against her handsome Dadda's strong chest, and it was the cutest thing, ever. Of course, I snapped a heart-melting photo of the vignette for Caleb's family photos shelf and Raine's bedroom wall. Today's a momentous day, after all. Another first. But when I told Caleb my intention for the one-of-a-kind photo, he insisted on taking some more with "our whole family." First off, a photo including Miranda, my parents, and me, along with Caleb and his girl. And then, another one featuring only Caleb, Raine, and me. *Be still my heart.*

While posing for that second "family" photo, the one featuring only the three of us, I almost cried. Posing for that photo somehow made today's victory feel real to me. I realized the past is finally put to rest. The future, a blank page we'll fill in together. No more looking back. No more stressing and worrying about what's going to happen at the hearing. No more wondering if our feelings are real and mutual. We're officially a family now, and deeply committed to each other and our future together.

Back in the present, Caleb lays me on his bed with a hungry look in his eyes. But he doesn't jump right to ravishing me. Instead, he fires up a tune on his phone: Led Zeppelin's "All of My Love."

When I visibly swoon at the song, Caleb flashes a crooked smile and says, "My daughter's got her own Zepp song. My lady should have one, too."

A shiver of desire courses through me. "I've never been someone's 'lady' before."

He laughs. "Good. 'Cause you're mine."

"I want to feel you inside me, Caleb," I whisper. "I want you to tell me you love me while Robert Plant says it for you, too."

"Coming right up, baby." As the song serenades me, he crawls on top of me, presses his steely hard-on into my center, and kisses me deeply. "I'd die for you, baby," he coos into my ear. "I'd kill for you. Move mountains for you. I've never loved like this before. You own me, baby. My *lady*. My *woman*."

"I love you so much," I choke out, feeling physically dizzy. "I love you so much."

With a heaving chest, Caleb crouches between my legs, spreads my thighs wide, and proceeds to eat me out with so much enthusiasm, the eventual orgasm that comes is so strong and overwhelming, it feels every bit as spiritual as physical.

When I recover from the waves of pleasure and look into Caleb's feral eyes looking up at me, I pull on his hair and beg him to make love to me. Today has been the best day of my life, and I can't wait to finish it off by feeling my man come inside me.

A moment later, Caleb's thick tip is lodged at my entrance. As his girth stretches me out and his length burrows all the way inside me, a deep groan escapes me—one that mirrors Caleb's deep growl. When Caleb begins slowly thrusting while whispering the words I'm dying to hear—"I love you"—I'm rapidly transported to the brink of sheer ecstasy.

"You're hotter than an atomic bomb, A-Bomb," he pants out hoarsely, as our pleasure spirals into the ethers.

As my body releases, it shatters and turns into a million stars. "I love you," I croak out, once again, as waves of bliss consume me. And much to my elation, Caleb returns the sentiment, as his body follows mine in releasing forcefully.

When his body stops bucking and shuddering, Caleb kisses me so passionately, he curls my toes. "Thank you," he whispers into my lips. "I know what you did for me today. What you didn't say on the stand. I'll never forget it, Aubrey. Never make you regret it."

He doesn't need to tell me what he's referring to; I know he's talking about me conveniently forgetting that slap in Billings. And you know what? Even before Caleb made those promises to me just now, I never once thought he'd make me regret my decision on the witness stand. In fact, I'm more certain than ever that was the right thing to do. The wrong thing, yes. Technically. The same way Caleb violating the court's order about the duck pond meeting was wrong. But sometimes right and wrong aren't mutually exclusive, it turns out. Sometimes, you've got to break a rule to do the right thing by someone you love with all your heart and soul.

When our lips break apart, Caleb slides off me and onto his back next to me on the bed, breathing hard, so I press my body into the side of him and snuggle close.

"Today is the best day of my life," he murmurs.

"Better than playing for a sold-out stadium?" I tease.

"Way better."

"Better than winning a Grammy?"

He scoffs. "That's not even in my top ten." He strokes my naked back. "Actually, moments with you and Raine fill out my entire top ten now. That's the truth. Everything else is in slots eleven through twenty."

I kiss his bare shoulder. The man doesn't even realize how swoony he is. How romantic. But when he says stuff like that, I feel physically dizzy with love for him.

"I need to confess something to you," I whisper. "I don't want there to be any secrets between us, no matter how small." I pause for dramatic effect. "I was secretly thrilled when you slapped the shit out of Trent."

Caleb laughs. "*Secretly*? Aubrey, I already know that."

"Honestly, I think that's the moment I fell in love with you, without even realizing it."

Caleb snickers. "You talked a good game about not condoning violence at the time, but your face gave you away, sweetheart." He kisses the top of my head. "Even if it hadn't, when you told the story at my 'rehab is over party,' it was clear enough you were thrilled about what I did."

"Oh. Well, okay. I just wanted to be sure there are no secrets between us. None at all."

"None at all. Ever. Good, bad, ugly. I promise."

His comment makes me raise my head for a kiss to seal

the deal, and we wind up doing much more than kissing—we begin fully making out.

It's an amazing feeling to trust him, wholeheartedly. Whatever trouble he had being a faithful partner in his only other relationship fifteen years ago, that feels like ancient history now. In fact, there's no doubt in my mind Caleb in the present has learned from all his past mistakes, big and small. He's grown and learned and is now determined never to repeat them. What more could I ask of him? Like the judge said today, nobody is perfect. Lucky for me, though, Caleb is imperfectly perfect for *me*.

"So, hey," Caleb says. "You know how Amy and Miranda suggested we throw a small party at the house to introduce Raine to my closest friends?" The two ladies put forth the idea during our dinner party at the restaurant tonight, and I agreed it sounded like fun, even as Caleb expressed indecision.

"You've warmed to the idea?" I ask hopefully.

Caleb smiles. "Yeah, I think we should do it."

I whoop. "I can't wait to meet all your friends. I'm especially excited for Raine to meet Rocco."

"Me, too." Caleb bites his lip. "I'm also thinking . . . maybe we should invite Dax and Violet to the party, if that'd be okay with you."

My breathing hitches. *This is big.* "Of course, it's okay with me. I think it's a great idea."

"You do?"

"Why wouldn't I?"

Caleb shrugs. "You don't think it might be awkward for you to be around Violet, given my history with her?"

"Not at all. She's been happily married with a kid for years now, and you're with me, so I think it's fair to say you've both moved on and everything that happened was for the best."

"That's my thinking, too."

"Amy and Miranda are both really close friends with Violet, right?"

"Super close."

At dinner tonight, Amy mentioned she works for Violet as her righthand woman on a couple fronts. For one thing, she helps Violet with a charity she started to help kids with cancer. And for another, she helps Violet with the administrative side of her wedding-dress design company.

"Honestly, the stuff Amy told me about Violet at dinner tonight only made me curious to get to know her. She sounds like a fascinating person. Plus, who wouldn't want to meet the famous lead singer of 22 Goats?"

Caleb pauses briefly. And then: "Okay, let's do it." His naked body next to mine practically vibrates with his decision. "I didn't feel like I could take this step before now. But being in love and happy myself, I feel like it won't be weird now. They won't question my motives."

My heart soars. "I think it's a brilliant idea."

Caleb slides a large, warm palm across my back and pulls me close. "I'm so happy. This house finally feels like a home with you and Raine living in it."

Fuck. Shit. And we were on such a roll, too. I know Caleb's intending his words as a massive compliment, but they're causing me to feel some conflicting emotions. Does this mean there's no chance of us moving to the lake house as our primary residence? That's what I'd prefer to do. Actually, that's what I'm yearning to do. But, clearly, Caleb isn't on the same page about that.

With the judge giving me temporary legal and physical

custody of Raine, and Caleb mere visitation rights, I suppose I could *theoretically* take Raine back to Prairie Springs, any time I want, whether Caleb likes it or not. Technically. Legally. But I'd never do that to Caleb. Or to Raine. Caleb is Raine's daddy now, and we're a team. A family. Whatever happens next, I'm committed to deciding it together.

Surely, the time will come, sooner rather than later, for me to express my personal desire to make Prairie Springs our permanent home. I can't imagine Caleb leaping at the idea, though, considering all his connections and business dealings in LA. Regardless, either way, I'm certain now isn't the time to broach the subject.

"Home is where the heart is," I say lamely, more for my own benefit than for Caleb's. I mean, really, if it turns out I'm here in LA to stay, is that really such an awful fate? No. It's not. I'll be with Caleb and Raine, in a gorgeous, luxury home, right on the beach. As far as second choices go, that ain't too shabby.

"Absolutely," Caleb replies softly with another kiss to the top of my head. "You and Raine are my home now, wherever we are."

Oooh, that was promising. Maybe I should broach the subject of moving to the lake house now, after all?

"Guess what?" Caleb says, before I've mustered the courage to open that can of worms.

"What?"

Caleb lifts the sheet, revealing his straining hard-on. "I'm hard for you again."

I chuckle. "In world-record speed."

Caleb waggles his eyebrows, making me giggle. "That's what happens when a guy is madly in love, happier than he's ever been, and lying naked next to the human equivalent of an atomic bomb."

CHAPTER 35
CALEB

"Amy was easily the worst PA I'd ever had," I say to the assembled group standing around me, much to Amy's giggling delight. It's my "Meet My Daughter!" party at my house. A small gathering, by design. Only about fifteen guests have been invited, not counting the three toddlers, including Raine, who are now fast asleep in Raine's frilly bedroom in the back of the house.

Aubrey's parents schmoozed at the party earlier, mostly to help us keep track of Raine. But when our baby girl got tired and started melting down, they took her and the other two toddlers in attendance tonight—Amy and Colin's two-year-old, Rocco, and Fish and Ally's small son, Winston—into Raine's bedroom. Somehow, not sure how, the Capshaws masterfully managed to put all three little ones to bed before crashing themselves across the hall with a baby monitor.

The only people still not here? Dax and Violet. Thankfully, they accepted my invitation last week; but they warned they might be "a little late," due to some event with their kid, Jackson. This feels like more than "a little late," though. Did they change their minds about coming? I wouldn't be surprised. If I were them, I wouldn't give me a second chance, either.

"Yep, I was a hot mess wrapped inside a shit sandwich," Amy says adorably, agreeing with my assessment of her early performance as my PA.

"A human festival of feces," I agree.

"*Caleb*," Aubrey murmurs, her features aghast. When Amy giggles at my latest insult, Aubrey adds, "Don't let him be so mean to you, Amy. My gosh, Caleb."

"No, no, he's right," Amy interjects. "I was so nervous around Caleb at first, I spilled scalding hot coffee all over his crotch on the first day." She snorts. "I thought for sure Caleb was going to fire me before the first week was done."

"I would have, if not for my loyalty to Colin."

I grip Colin's shoulder next to me to emphasize the point, and Colin does what he always does at this point in our storytelling. He murmurs, "I'm thankful to you for that, my brother. If not for you, I wouldn't be standing here with Amy now."

It's our usual party trick, Amy's and mine: telling this funny story. Sometimes, with an assist from Colin. Tonight, we're telling it mostly for the benefit of Aubrey, since pretty much everyone else standing around us—22 Goats' bass player, Fish; Fish's wife, Alessandra; my three bandmates; my sister; and a couple members of the band, Fugitive Summer—have already heard this story. Multiple times, probably. Although, come to think of it, some of them have likely heard it while shitfaced or high, so this might as well be their first time hearing it.

As Amy continues the usual highlights of our story, I glance at the front door, once again. When it shows no signs of opening any time soon, I return to the conversation.

"That's why Caleb initially nicknamed me 'unicorn,'" Amy says. "Because of that huge welt on my forehead."

Everyone laughs.

I missed the lead-up to that comment, due to my wandering attention, but I know what she's talking about. On day one or two of the tour, Amy walked into a backstage dressing room and happened upon Reed Rivers, the founder of my record label, voraciously eating a journalist's pussy on a couch. Amy being Amy, she turned and fled . . . and smacked straight into a wall in her agitation, immediately causing a welt the size of a unicorn horn to grow out her forehead.

"The horn was the reason for the nickname at first," I contribute. "But I *kept* calling her that throughout the tour, when it became clear she'd somehow morphed into the best damned PA I'd ever had."

"Aw," Amy says, as Aubrey says the same.

"Was Reed Rivers mad at you for walking in on him?" Aubrey asks.

Amy snorts. "Actually, I think he was nothing but deeply amused. It certainly helps that he wound up marrying that journalist."

Aubrey asks another question, which Amy answers, but I don't hear a word of the exchange. For some reason, being reminded that Reed Rivers of all people took the plunge and got married—I mean, that guy used to be the biggest player this side of the sun—suddenly makes me realize something shocking. Undeniable. Amazing. *I want to marry Aubrey.* Not only that, I want to do it, as soon as possible. Why wait? We love each other, and we love Raine. I never want to spend a single day away from her, so what's the point in dragging things out?

"Uh, excuse me," I say, my heart thumping in my ears. "Bathroom."

I spot my sister chatting flirtatiously with one of the members of Fugitive Summer—their bass player, Kai. But when I catch Miranda's eye and flash her a look, she says something to Kai and follows me into a hallway.

"What's up?" Miranda whispers, her eyebrows raised.

"I need to get an engagement ring for Aubrey. I want to propose, as soon as possible."

Miranda gasps. "Oh my gosh. When?"

"Not sure yet. Will you help me pick one out?"

"Of course! Oh my gosh, Caleb. Do you want my help to plan the perfect proposal?" If there's one thing my sister loves more than shopping and club hopping and traveling, it's jewelry shopping and party planning. Add to that the recipient of my proposal is Aubrey, the best woman in the world, and I'm sure this entire conversation is making my sister blow a gasket.

We hurriedly talk details in excited, hushed tones and quickly decide we'll go shopping in person, rather than online, on this coming Thursday. Which, unfortunately, is five days from now.

"You can't do it any sooner than that?" I ask, flashing Miranda my patented "pretty please" face.

With a sigh, my sister looks down at her phone. "Sorry, I'm slammed with work stuff till then. Thursday is the earliest I can do it."

Shit. Now that I've made my decision, I'm antsy to get the ball rolling and make Aubrey my fiancée *right now*. Logically, though, I know Thursday will work just fine, since we're not leaving for the end-of-summer festival in Prairie

Springs until a few days after that. "Okay, it's a plan," I say. "I'll ask Amy to invite Aubrey and Raine over for a playdate that day, so Aubrey won't get suspicious that I've headed off for the day without explanation."

"*Perfect*. Love it." Miranda squeals. "This is so exciting. I'm so happy for you. And for me. I've always wanted a sister, instead of a stupid caveman of a brother."

She hugs me and squeals again, and I hold her tight, laughing and feeling electrified.

"Okay," I say. "When we go back out there, act natural. Aubrey's really smart. We don't want her sniffing me out."

Before Miranda replies, Fish, the bass player from 22 Goats, ambles into the hallway, heading toward the bathroom.

"Hey there, Baumgarten One and Baumgarten Two," Fish says jovially. "Dax and Violet just got here. They were asking about you."

"Holy shit. Thanks, Fish Taco."

As Fish enters the bathroom, my sister squeezes my hand and pecks my cheek. "You've got this. I'm so proud of you for inviting them."

"Inviting them was the easy part," I whisper, rubbing my sweaty palms on my pants. "They're the ones who did the hard part and actually came."

"Of course, they did. Caleb, they've both been wanting to mend fences with you for a very long time, you big dummy." She pats my shoulder. "Now go on, honey. Put on a big smile and welcome your honored guests."

CHAPTER 36
CALEB

As I enter my living room, there's a crowd gathered around the latest arrivals, Dax and Violet, so I head over to Aubrey and grab her hand while waiting for the dust to settle.

When the crowd around Dax and Violet finally dissipates, I head over with Aubrey and we welcome the much-anticipated duo to our little party. To my relief, both Dax and Violet greet me warmly and thank me for the invitation. They congratulate me on Raine and offer a warm hug to Aubrey, too, after I've introduced her as my girlfriend.

Holy shit. Now that I've made the decision to propose, I'm wishing I could introduce Aubrey as my fiancée to them tonight. Better yet, as my wife. But I suppose girlfriend will have to do for now.

Small talk ensues, and soon, Aubrey and I are engaged in a pleasant conversation with Dax and Violet about Raine and their son, Jackson, who's currently being babysat by Dax's big brother and his brother's wife across town.

"Are we too late to meet Raine?" Violet asks, looking around.

"Yeah, sorry," I say. "She was here earlier, but she's already crashed."

"I'm sure meeting so many people was highly stimulating for her," Violet says.

"Yeah. Definitely."

Dax smiles. "Hopefully, we'll meet her next time."

Next time.

Aubrey flashes me a look that says, *Oh my god,* before replying, "Absolutely. Yes." She turns to Violet. "How old is Jackson?"

"Almost nine. He's Dax's spitting image. I honestly haven't seen a lick of proof my child got any of my genes, whatsoever."

We all laugh.

"Can I see a photo?" Aubrey asks. And for the next several minutes, we check out photos and videos of both kids, with Dax proudly showing us a short video of his young son wailing confidently on an electric guitar.

"Damn, he's really good," I say.

"That's my boy."

I can't resist teasing Dax a bit. "I do think it's a bit strange you're teaching him to play the second-coolest instrument in the world, instead of the coolest."

Dax snorts. "Teach your own kid to bang on drums, if you want. My son is gonna play the coolest instrument. *Guitar.* Just like his old man."

We all laugh again, and, suddenly, it feels just like old times. Easy and comfortable. Like no time has passed. I thought it'd feel awkward to stand face-to-face with Dax again, and even weirder to face him with Violet on his arm. But if these first few minutes of this reunion are any indication, we're going to be able to patch things up and move on from the past in record speed.

Aubrey says, "Caleb has already started giving Raine drum lessons."

"Not surprised at all," Dax retorts with a smile.

"She mostly likes playing along to 'our song,'" I offer proudly. "'Fool in the Rain.'"

"Nice," Dax says with a chuckle.

"To be clear," I add, "*I'm* the *fool* in the song title. The big, stupid fool."

Dax's blue eyes warm and soften. "We can all be big, stupid fools, on occasion. Nobody's perfect."

Endorphins flood me. Seriously, why didn't I do this years ago?

Violet looks at her husband and shoots him a look that reminds me of the one Aubrey flashed me a moment ago. One that silently screams, *Isn't this going great?* But what she says out loud is, "Your daughter is adorable, Caleb. I can't wait to meet her one day soon."

Dax clears his throat and smiles at Aubrey. "It's great to finally meet you, Aubrey. Miranda speaks really highly of you."

Violet interjects, "Miranda said she's thrilled you came into Caleb's life and finally turned her brother into an actual adult."

I give Aubrey's hand a squeeze. "That she did. Aubrey's been a godsend."

"No, you did that for yourself," Aubrey coos, and the look of unadulterated adoration she flashes me damn-near brings tears to my eyes.

Violet noticeably looks between her husband me, her lips twisted, before motioning toward my sister on the couch. "Speaking of Miranda, I think she's beckoning to me. Do you want to come with me, Aubrey?"

"I'd love to." In parting, Aubrey flashes me a pointed

look, this one encouraging me to get everything off my chest with Dax, once and for all—to leave nothing unsaid, like I told her I want to do tonight. I stumbled and stammered my way through a less-than stellar apology five years ago at Reed Rivers' wedding, but I've learned a thing or two, since then—things I very much wish to make clear to Dax now.

When the ladies have left and I find myself standing alone with Dax, I take a deep breath and speak on my exhale. "So, hey, Daxy, I owe you an apology. A good one this time."

Dax looks genuinely confused. "You already apologized to me, remember? At Reed's wedding. There's no need to do it again."

"No, there is. Hear me out. It's gonna be hard to get this out." I take another deep breath. "Back at Reed's wedding, I didn't have the capacity to fully appreciate the position you were in during our tour together." I look across the room at Aubrey, who's now chatting happily with my sister, Violet, and several other women. "But thanks to Aubrey and Raine, I finally understand the meaning of true, unconditional love. What it feels like to love someone so fucking much, you don't have a choice in the matter."

Dax nods, looking at me intensely.

"What I know now, but didn't back then, is that I would have done the exact same thing in your shoes. If you'd dated Aubrey years before me, and then I happened to meet Aubrey at a party later on and fall hard for her, then I'm certain nothing and nobody could have stopped me from making Aubrey mine. Not even my friendship with you, even though I genuinely loved you like a brother."

Dax's Adam's apple bobs. "Thanks for saying that,

Caleb. But we both know I handled things badly. I should have spoken up sooner. I should have—"

"No. You couldn't do that." I shake my head. "You were the opener for my band on your very first world tour, and you knew I was a hotheaded prick with anger management issues. Was it realistic to expect you to come to me, right away, and possibly risk everything for your band?" I scoff. "No fucking way. You had a skyrocketing career to consider and two bandmates who were counting on you, along with a girl you couldn't possibly give up for the sake of our friendship. In the end, you decided our friendship wasn't the most important consideration—and rightfully so." I exhale. "I'm sorry it took me so long to realize all this. I hope it's not too late for you to accept my full and sincere apology, so we can put the past behind us, for real this time, and start our friendship back up."

Dax takes a deep inhale. "I'd love that." He puts out his hand, but I pull him into a bear hug. And mere seconds later, even before we've pulled apart, we're swarmed by our respective bandmates, all of whom must have been watching our conversation from afar with bated breath.

For a while, both bands—all three members of 22 Goats and all four members of Red Card Riot—mix and match hugs and chatter about what a dumbfuck I've been. That it's been far too long since we all hung out together, like we used to do. Clearly, we're all excited to put this beef to rest, for good.

When the conversations between our two bands have run their course, I drift over to Aubrey across the room and pull her into a corner, where I give her a quick update about the outcome of my conversation with Dax.

"I'm so thrilled for you," Aubrey says. "Things are going

really well with Violet, too. She's being so nice and welcoming to me, and I really feel like it's genuine."

"Of course, it is. She's a sweetheart."

Aubrey's faces catches fire. "*Guess what?* Miranda told Violet and the other women about the Summer Festival, and they're all going to talk to every famous person they know to get amazing donations for the auction!"

"Oh, man, that's huge. Everyone here, especially Violet, is super well connected. Violet's brother owns my label, remember? If she gets him involved, it's game over, baby. You'll have more cool shit than you know what to do with."

Aubrey grips my arm with white knuckles and wide eyes. "*Violet said she'd call her bestie, Aloha Carmichael, to ask for a donation!* Can you believe it? I almost passed out."

I laugh. "That's awesome, babe."

"My mom's going to die. Raine's going to die. I'm going to die. Oh my god. This year's festival is going to be *incredible.*"

Boom.

The blaze in Aubrey's dark eyes suddenly makes me realize the obvious: I should propose to her at the Summer Festival, in front of her family and friends and everyone who knows and loves her the most.

Aubrey fans herself and giggles. "I was a little anxious a small-town girl like me wouldn't fit in with all your fabulous, famous friends, but they've all made me feel right at home."

"They're just people, baby. Same as you and me." I take her hand. "Speaking of your small town . . . I've been thinking about the lake house. You know, what to do with it."

Aubrey visibly holds her breath.

"And I think . . . if it's okay with you . . . we should make

Prairie Springs our home base and this place our second home."

Aubrey clutches her heart and whimpers. "Seriously?"

"If that's okay with you."

"It's all I want! Yes! Thank you so much." She throws her arms around me. "I've loved being here, and I know Raine has, too; but it's not our home. I've been so homesick, and I think Raine has been, too."

Now that she's saying the word—*homesick*—I realize it's exactly how I've been feeling, too, ever since we got to LA. Frankly, that's a bizarre thing for me to feel, since this place has been my home for over a decade. But the fact remains, I felt more at home at the lake house with Aubrey and Raine, than I've ever once felt here in LA.

Aubrey wipes a tear. "I didn't want to drag you back to Prairie Springs, if that's not where you wanted to be. But I've been aching to go back home."

"Aw, baby. Don't cry. We'll go home soon." I put my finger underneath Aubrey's chin and kiss her gently. "I wish you'd told me."

She shrugs off the comment with a wipe of her eyes. "What about all the band and business stuff you've got going on here?"

"Prairie Springs isn't Mars, baby. It's an easy flight back and forth."

Aubrey sniffles. "What about tours? What will happen when you start doing those again?"

I smile. "We'll figure it out, whenever the time comes. For now, let's get back home to Prairie Springs and start building our life there together."

"Without the custody hearing hanging over our heads."

"Exactly."

"I can't wait." She smiles broadly. "I'm so happy."

"Me, too. Happier than ever." I kiss her again. "Wherever you want to be, that's where I want to be, too. You and Raine are my home now, okay?"

"I love you so much."

"I love you, too."

Aubrey bites her lower lip. "I know we're planning to go home next week, but can we go sooner? When my parents go on Wednesday? I'm feeling so homesick, I think I'll melt down if I have to say goodbye to them."

Shit. Wednesday is the day *before* my sister is available to go engagement ring shopping with me. But what choice do I have, when I'm looking into Aubrey's big, brown, doe eyes? This glorious woman owns me, heart and soul. Her wish is my command. Which means my sister's just going to have to cancel all her silly plans and help me, earlier than anticipated.

"Wednesday, it is," I say with more confidence than I feel. My sister can be awfully strong-willed and stubborn, when I least expect it. But something tells me this one time, she'll bend to my wishes. She'd better. Because the perfect place and time to propose to Aubrey is now perfectly clear to me, and there's no turning back.

CHAPTER 37
AUBREY

Raine is fast asleep by the time we arrive at the lake house in the dark of night. Our Uber from the airport stopped at my parents' place first to drop them off, at which point Caleb and I loaded up Big Betty to come here with Raine. Along the way, we made a quick stop at a convenience store for bread, milk, and cereal. Enough to tide us over before we can get into town to do some proper grocery shopping tomorrow. But even with only the barest supplies for our cupboards, I nonetheless feel the forceful, unmistakable sensation of coming home, the second we cross the threshold into the house.

"I'll get her into bed," Caleb whispers, jutting his chin at the sleeping Munchkin in his muscular arms. "Don't worry about the luggage. I'll go back out and get it, after I get her settled."

"I'll get her into her pajamas and pull-up, while you unload the truck."

"Deal."

I follow Caleb into Raine's bedroom—the room that

used to be mine—where Caleb gently lays his daughter down. When his arms are free, I hug him and sigh happily against his hard chest.

"It's good to be home," I whisper.

"Best feeling in the world."

With a kiss to my head, Caleb heads off to deal with the suitcases outside, while I start getting Raine dressed for bed. When I'm done with my side of our bargain, I head into the living room, expecting to see our suitcases lined up in a row. But they're not here, which means Caleb must have brought everything into our bedroom already.

I head into our room—Caleb's bedroom. But there are no suitcases there, either, and no sign of Caleb. "Caleb?" I whisper-shout, so as not to wake Raine across the hallway. When he doesn't answer, my stomach twists. Caleb had a state-of-the-art security system in Santa Monica, so I never worried too much about Ralph's ominous warning at the courthouse. But now that we're here, in a house with no fancy security system, I'm suddenly realizing we're vulnerable and exposed. Ralph knows where we live, after all. And the trial proved he's got no shortage of lackeys, willing to do his bidding.

"Caleb?" I call out again, this time, while standing in the living room. When he doesn't reply again, I head to the front door and reach for the doorknob... just as Caleb flings the door open from outside.

"Oh!" I clutch my heart in surprise, making him laugh. "You scared me."

Caleb bites back a smile. "Sorry. You okay?"

"Yeah, fine. I got paranoid when I couldn't find you. Where have you been?"

A grin breaks out on his handsome face. "I got

distracted doing something outside." He puts out his hand. "Come with me, A-Bomb. There's something I need to show you."

"I love it," I gasp out, when the light on Caleb's phone illuminates the brand-new carvings he's added to the old black cottonwood tree on the side of the house. "It's so romantic."

"Orgasms *and* romance, baby," he says with a wink. "You wanted both? Well, now, you've got 'em."

Swoon.

Next to the "C-Bomb" symbol carved by Caleb into this tree trunk as a kid, he's now added two additional "bomb" letters next to it, both with lit fuses on top. An "A" for me; an "R" for Raine. And the best part? All three lit-fuse letters are enclosed inside an old-fashioned heart.

Feeling overwhelmed with love for Caleb, I slide my arms around his neck and kiss him deeply. My man's not the marrying kind. I know that. So, I feel like this grand gesture is his way of promising to love me forever. I mean, what more eternal promise can a man make than carving his family's initials into a tree that will likely live longer than all of us?

"I want to get Raine's name legally changed," Caleb whispers. "To Raine Claudia Baumgarten."

My heart explodes in my chest. "I love it."

"You do?"

"I think it's an amazing idea. Do it."

Caleb exhales with relief. "Okay, I'll tell Paula to get the paperwork going."

I tug on his beard. "As long as you're making a To Do

List, can you also get a security system installed? Something really good, like what you have in LA."

Caleb winks. "It's already in progress, baby. A crew is coming to make our house as secure as Fort Knox on Monday."

CHAPTER 38
AUBREY

We all slept like rocks last night. Caleb and me, while snuggled up in his bed all night; Raine, all by herself like a big girl across the hallway.

After everyone finally got moving this morning, we ate breakfast from the few supplies we'd picked up on our way home from the airport last night. And now, we're happily strolling down Main Street, heading toward Big Betty with some grocery bags, after a trip the store.

"Hey, Aubrey," a jovial male voice calls out. It's none other than my father's oldest and dearest friend, Bob—a man who's a beloved Prairie Springs institution.

I greet Bob warmly and introduce him to Caleb and Raine, and he dotes on Raine before falling into enthusiastic conversation with Caleb about his new deck. As the men talk, Raine squats down to examine a pill bug on the sidewalk, at which point my attention drifts to a parked police car across the street. The officer in the driver's seat seems to be watching us. Am I imagining that? If not, is he staring at Caleb, because he's a fan of Red Card Riot, or is he staring because he's friends with Ralph Beaumont? I swear, until we get that security system installed, I'm going to be on tenterhooks at all times. Once again, Ralph's ominous warning at the courthouse slams into me: *Watch your back.*

Thankfully, the officer looks away when our eyes meet, which gives me some reassurance. And a moment after that, Bob and Caleb finish their conversation.

After Bob leaves, when I'm alone with Caleb and Raine again, I ask Caleb about that police officer across the street —if anything seems off with him, or if Caleb thinks I'm simply being paranoid. And not surprisingly, I've no sooner asked the question than my boyfriend sets down the grocery bags he's carrying and strides across the street.

"Take Raine to the ice cream place, babe," he calls over his shoulder. "I'll meet you there."

"Wait, what are you going to do?"

When Caleb doesn't answer me, I stay put and watch him, despite what he instructed me to do.

"Do we have a problem here, Officer?" Caleb asks, as he closes in on the police car. True to form, my boyfriend isn't handling the situation with kid gloves; he's jumping right in with the subtlety of a sledgehammer.

I can't hear what the police officer replies, unfortunately. I can't even see the guy's face, thanks to Caleb's big ol' back blocking it from my view, so I can't try to read the officer's lips or body language. I know Caleb told me to leave, but I'm not going anywhere. If this man is doing Ralph's bidding, then I'm not leaving Caleb alone with him.

As Raine continues examining the bug on the sidewalk, I stand, stock-still, watching the men talk. After a moment, Caleb crosses his arms and says something that sounds fairly amiable in tone, though I can't make it out. And a second after that, the police car starts up and drives away, punctuated by a cheerful little *toot-toot* of the officer's horn and a friendly wave to me.

When the guy is gone, Caleb returns to Raine and me, a scowl on his face. "Why didn't you take her for ice cream?"

I brush off the question. "What'd he say?"

"He admitted he was staring over here, but he said it was because Red Card Riot is his favorite band, and he wasn't sure if I was C-Bomb or a guy who looks exactly like him."

I roll my eyes. "Everybody already knows C-Bomb from Red Card Riot is here in Prairie Springs."

"That was my thinking, too." His eyes narrow. "I think maybe he was playing to my ego to throw me off the scent."

The hairs on the back of my neck stand up. "*What* scent, though?"

Caleb's jaw muscles pulse, as he looks down at Raine at our feet. "Take her for that ice cream cone now, babe. Please. I need to run a quick errand down the street."

"What errand, Caleb?"

"We'll talk about it later, at home."

"Where are you going?"

He motions with his chin down the block; and when I follow his motion, I notice a hardware store. Also, a liquor store, right next door. I can't imagine Caleb even noticed the liquor store, though. Surely, he meant to draw my attention to the hardware store... Right?

Crap.

Now, I'm having crazy, paranoid thoughts. I haven't worried about Caleb falling off the wagon in a long while, but I know from Claudia's journey that sobriety can be a constant struggle.

"Go on, baby," Caleb insists gently. This time, his voice soft and coaxing. "I'll meet you at the ice cream place, and we'll talk at home." He motions to Raine at my feet. "She's getting impatient."

I glance down at Raine to find her showing exactly zero signs of impatience. On the contrary, she still seems hyperfixated on that pill bug.

Something's up. But what? "Okay," I say begrudgingly. "I'll see you at the ice cream place."

"Great. See you soon."

"You're okay?"

"I'm great."

I touch his tattooed forearm and stare into his eyes. "Good, bad, or ugly, remember?"

His features soften. "I know, baby. Don't worry. We'll talk later. I promise." He pecks me on the cheek and rustles Raine's blonde curls, but I can't help noticing he's waiting for me to start walking up the street with Raine before he starts his own journey down the street in the other direction.

Slowly, I walk with Raine toward the direction of the ice cream place. But when Caleb isn't looking, I dart into an alcove in front of the sewing store, pulling Raine with me, and covertly peek at my man as he makes his way down the street.

From my hiding spot, I watch Caleb pass the hardware store. And then, the liquor store, too. A couple storefronts after that, he looks both ways and crosses the street, before finally entering an establishment I hadn't noticed down there earlier. *The gun store.*

CHAPTER 39
CALEB

I listen to the soothing sounds of Aubrey's rhythmic breathing next to me, willing my own breathing to fall into lock-step with hers. But I can't do it. Can't relax. Can't fall asleep, no matter how hard I try.

Partly, I'm feeling impatient and excited to give Aubrey the engagement ring I bought her in LA with my sister's help. Mostly, however, my mind is racing with thoughts of Ralph Beaumont. Whenever I close my eyes, I see the inhuman look in his eyes, when he told me to "watch my back" at the courthouse. Something about that cop staring at my family the other day spooked me. Got my hackles up.

Something dark is brewing.

I can feel it.

Unfortunately, that security service can't make it out here for two more days, so I'm my family's only security system until then. I don't take that responsibility lightly.

A rustling sound jerks me from my wandering thoughts and makes me sit up in bed and listen intently. That didn't sound like an animal or the rustling of trees in the breeze.

No, it sounded like human footsteps clomping on dried pine needles and leaves.

I unravel myself from Aubrey and slide out of bed. Peer outside my bedroom window. And sure enough, a darkly clad *human* figure just turned the corner of the house, heading toward the back façade. *Fuck!*

I throw on sweats, shoes, and a hoodie and quickly grab my new, fully loaded handgun from the locked cabinet. With my firearm in hand, I grab a flashlight from the kitchen counter and step outside into the cool night air and onto the deck.

Nothing.

Nobody.

I head around the house, past The Family Tree, as we now call it—the black cottonwood with my family's three initials carved into its bark—and then cut through a cluster of high bushes, as a shortcut to the back façade. When the back of the house is in view, I stop and peer into the darkness, trying to discern any kind of movement.

I hear a crack of a twig, or maybe the crunch of dried leaves or pine needles. And that's when my flashlight beam engulfs a dark figure, dressed in black from head to toe, trying to open my goddamned back window with a crowbar.

"Freeze!" I shout, and the figure instantly turns to look at me with wide eyes.

Fuck me. It's Ralph Beaumont. His face is smudged with black paint, and his silver hair is hidden underneath a black cap; but I'd recognize those deadly, evil eyes and that sneering mouth anywhere.

"Drop the crowbar and hold up both hands—*right fucking now*," I grit out, pointing the gun between his vacant eyes. He's retired law enforcement, so I'm assuming he's armed. But when he begrudgingly drops the crowbar to the ground—right next to a black duffel bag at his feet—and raises both arms, my assumption is immediately proved correct: the butt of a handgun is peeking out of his belt.

"What's your plan tonight, Ralph?" I shout, jerking my chin at the duffel bag on the ground. "Did you come here to rape my daughter, the same way you raped your own?"

"Fuck you, you piece of shit kidnapper."

I scoff. "Excuse me if I don't give two shits what a wife-beater/pedo-rapist thinks of me."

I take careful aim at Ralph's forehead, squinting one eye to lock in my aim. I'm itching to pull the trigger and end this motherfucker now; but if I do that while his hands are in the air, that'd be a tough sell as self-defense. They've got forensics for this kind of thing, right? Plus, as much as I want him dead, I'm not sure I'm capable of cold-blooded murder. That's what this would be, if I were to pull the trigger now, right?

I take a deep breath to steady myself. "Apologize for what you did to Claudia," I say evenly, the gun still aimed at his forehead. I don't expect him to do it. Don't care if he does. I'm actually toying with him. Egging him on to do something, say something—*anything*—to inspire me to squeeze this fucking trigger and put an end to this nightmare, once and for all.

"Fuck Claudia," Ralph spits out. "She was an even bigger liar than she was a slut. All I can hope is Raine doesn't take after her slutty, lying mother."

Oh, fuck no. Gunfire splits the quiet night, and Ralph immediately drops like a stone into a clump of bushes behind him. My heart hammering, I whisper, "Keep my daughter's name out of your goddamned fucking mouth."

As the gunshot echoes, I realize what I've just done, and

my breathing turns shallow and erratic. My heart stampeding in my chest, I shuffle through the brush toward Ralph's unmoving body, barely able to breath, and when I reach my destination, it's clear as can be Ralph Beaumont is no longer among the living. The man's "taking an eternal dirt nap," as my grandfather used to say. In fact, Ralph's forehead would make a mighty fine pencil holder.

I'm shocked to discover I got the fucker right between his reptilian eyes, exactly as I was aiming to do. I've never been a great shot. Not terrible, but not a sure thing. Plus, I haven't been out shooting in forever, so it's honestly a miracle I got off a perfect shot when I needed it most. Shit. Maybe that's not such a good thing for a claim of self-defense?

As I'm having the thought, a light flickers on in my peripheral vision. I jerk my head toward the source of the illumination, my eyes as big as saucers. It's coming from my closest neighbor's house. Obviously, the gunshot woke somebody up over there. *Fuck.* If I don't alter this scene to fit a better narrative than what actually happened, I'll be fucked.

Covering my hand with my sweatshirt sleeve, I slowly pull Ralph's gun from his belt and carefully lay it into his lifeless, opened palm. When that task is done, I unzip Ralph's duffel bag with my covered hand and peek inside. *Jesus.* It's stuffed with some spine-chilling, serial-killer shit: duct tape, rope, a hunting knife, and a box of bullets.

"Holy shit, what happened?" a male voice calls out. It's my neighbor, an older guy in a bathrobe with a rifle in his hand.

Before I've replied to him, Aubrey suddenly appears at the back door, wide-eyed and frantic, asking what's going on.

With my heart lodged in my throat, I look back and forth between Aubrey's terrified face and my next-door neighbor's smug one and realize I've got no choice but to lie to Aubrey in this moment. At least, for now, while this neighbor is in our presence, I've got to tell the same story I'm going to tell the police.

"I-I heard a noise while I was in bed. I had insomnia," I choke out. "So I-I got my gun and came outside and found this guy, dressed in black, trying to break into my back window with a fucking crowbar."

"Jesus, Mary, and Joseph," the neighbor murmurs, punctuated by a whistle.

I look at Aubrey. She's sheet-white and gripping a vertical wooden beam on the back porch to keep herself steady.

"Well, he's worm food now," my neighbor says, nudging the dead body with his boot. "You hit him, square on his forehead, C-Bomb. *Damn.*"

I take a deep breath. "I shouted at him to freeze and put his hands up, but he pointed a handgun at me, instead."

The neighbor shrugs. "Classic kill-or-be-killed situation. Don't feel bad about it for a second, son. You did exactly the right thing."

I look at Aubrey again. She's holding her stomach. From where she's standing, Ralph's body is too far away for her to identify his face, surely, especially given the darkness of the night and the way Ralph landed when he fell back. But her body language suggests, pretty damned clearly, she's got a strong hunch about the identity of the body.

"Is he . . . ?" Aubrey begins.

"*Dead?*" the neighbor supplies, unaware what she's actually asking me. "Yes, darlin'," he continues reassuringly.

"Don't you worry, that bad man can't hurt you or anyone else, ever again."

As the neighbor bends down to check out the duffel bag, Aubrey mouths to me: *Ralph?*

I nod slowly, and her entire body visibly shudders.

"My god," the neighbor says, his attention fixed on Ralph's duffel bag. "Looks like this mofo planned to do something pretty horrific." He identifies the full contents of the bag—all the shit I've already seen for myself—and poor Aubrey bursts into tears, even before he finishes his list.

Thanks, asshole. If I'd wanted Aubrey to know about all that serial-killer shit, I'd have told her myself.

As Aubrey shudders and cries on the porch, I beeline over to her and hold her close. "It's okay, baby. We're safe now." I don't want to hurry her along, when she's sobbing like this; but I also know I've got to call the police and play my part, in order to secure my freedom and my future with my family. "Baby, go inside and check on Raine, okay? I need to call the police and report what happened. Go on now, baby. The gunshot might have woken Raine up. She might be awake and scared."

I've said the magic words. *Raine* and *scared*. Instantly, Aubrey flips into parenting mode. Enough, anyway, to drag herself across the porch and into the back doorframe. In the doorway, though, she stops and turns around.

"Make sure you tell the police about how he pointed a gun at you, Caleb."

"I will, baby. Go on."

"Tell them you had no choice. Tell them what's in the duffel bag."

"I will. It's gonna be okay."

"The judge said you can't get into any more trouble. She said if you do anything violent—"

"It was self-defense," I reassure her. "Plain and simple."

"Classic case of it,'" the neighbor agrees. "Nobody's gonna blame C-Bomb for a minute, darlin'. In fact, all anyone's gonna do is pat him on the back and tell him 'good job.'"

With a trembling chin that breaks my heart, Aubrey drags herself into the house, and the moment she's gone, I press the button to call the police. When the 911 operator answers, I tell her my story again—the same one I told the neighbor and Aubrey, while my neighbor shouts things in the background like, "He had no choice!"

"Stay put and don't touch anything," the dispatcher says. "Officers are on the way."

I hang up and sit on my back stoop, physically quaking with stress and adrenaline. If I've fucked up here, if I've forgotten some important detail that's going to give me away, I'll never fucking forgive myself. It felt so right in the moment to pull that trigger, when he mentioned Raine's name. It felt like a no-brainer. Otherwise, I knew we'd never get a moment's peace again. I mean, really, how long would they have detained Ralph for simple trespassing? But now, as I await the sound of sirens and flashing lights, I'm second-guessing if I made the right call.

"Don't you worry for a second about this," my neighbor reassures me. "This ain't California, C-Bomb. In Montana, when a fucker tries to break into your house to do God knows what to your family with his bag of torture, nobody's gonna bat an eyelash at you for putting a bullet between his eyes."

God, I hope he's right about that . . . even when the fucker in question is my known mortal enemy who publicly threatened my family and me only a week ago . . . and the whole world knows I'm not the type of man who lets bygones be bygones.

CHAPTER 40
AUBREY

As Caleb and I stride out of the police station, hand in hand, in the cool, early-morning sunshine, we're both exhausted, sleep-deprived, and ravenously hungry. But mostly, relieved.

Thankfully, Paula quickly located a Montana lawyer for Caleb last night, a guy in classic cowboy boots and a Stetson hat who sped in from Billings on a moment's notice to save the day.

"Don't say a word till I get there," the lawyer growled at Caleb over the phone. "Not even to ask for a fucking cup of coffee."

Once the Billings lawyer arrived at the Prairie Springs police station and he'd had the opportunity to confer with his famous client, he gave Caleb the green light to give a detailed statement in a small back room. And while Caleb did that, I sat nervously on an orange, rickety chair in a tiny waiting room, rocking back and forth to keep myself from puking from stress.

I didn't want to have worst-case scenario thoughts

while sitting alone in that claustrophobic room on a plastic chair. But I couldn't help myself. I imagined the judge reversing her prior order and ruling that Caleb henceforth couldn't interact with his daughter unless supervised. I imagined Caleb being hauled away for murder, and Raine spending her formative years visiting her daddy in prison. But to my relief, after only about an hour in that back room, Caleb and his Montana lawyer emerged, trailed by two detectives—and all of them were smiling and looking downright chummy.

"I'm free to go," Caleb announced on an exhale, opening his arms to me, and I leaped up from my orange chair and hurtled into them.

"No charges will be filed," the Montana lawyer confirmed. "We all agree it was a classic case of self-defense."

"Thank you, thank you," I said to the Billings lawyer, lurching at him for a hug. Hell, I was so damned relieved and grateful, I even hugged the two detectives, rather than shaking their offered hands. And now, as the sun comes up, Caleb and I are walking toward Big Betty, eager to get home and into bed and put this crazy night behind us forever.

I've got the car keys in my pocket, since I drove the truck here, while Caleb drove with the responding officer; so I pull them out and slide into the driver's side, while Caleb wordlessly slumps into the seat across from me. Normally, whenever we're driving somewhere together, Caleb gets behind Big Betty's wheel, which suits me fine. I don't like to drive all that much. But after the long, stressful night Caleb's endured, we don't even need to talk about who's taking the wheel this time.

"Man, I could use a stiff drink," Caleb grumbles, leaning

against the head rest of the passenger seat with his eyes closed.

My heart stops. "I'll arrange an emergency Zoom call with Gina for this afternoon, while you catch up on sleep."

Caleb opens his eyes and looks at me blankly.

"You said you want to drink."

"No, I said I could *use* a drink. It's a figure of speech. All I meant is it's been a long fucking night and *if* I were still drinking, which I'm not, this would be one of the times I'd throw back a tall one." He pats my arm. "I'm not in any danger of falling off the wagon, babe. Don't worry about that."

"You're sure?"

"I'm sure."

"You'd tell me, right?"

"I would. But don't worry. I'm fine."

"If that changes, you'll tell me, right? You'll come straight to me and confess and never, ever hide it, so I can help you?"

Caleb sighs. "Of course. Please, Aubrey. I'm tired. Can we just go home now?"

I exhale. "Lemme call my parents real quick to tell them the good news." I pull out my phone to make the call, but Caleb touches my arm to stop me.

"Hang on. Come to think of it, there's something I should tell you, before we do anything else."

I lower my phone to my lap and hold his gaze, my heart thumping.

Caleb murmurs, "Good, bad, ugly. That's what I promised you."

"Ralph didn't aim his gun at you," I blurt. It's what I've been suspecting, since the moment I saw his dead body in the bushes. If I know my man, he didn't wait for Ralph to aim a gun at him before firing. No, I'd bet anything Caleb took his shot before letting that happen.

Caleb nods slowly. "Ralph wasn't even holding his gun when I shot him. It was stuffed in his belt, because he had both hands on the crowbar."

I take a shallow breath. "I had a feeling."

His nostrils flare. "After I shot him, I used my sleeve to lift his gun out of his belt and place it in his dead hand."

I process for a brief moment, and then take Caleb's hand. Suspecting Caleb took his shot was one thing; but knowing it for a fact, knowing my man didn't hesitate to protect his family, is another. Indeed, this electrifying news only makes me love and respect Caleb, all the more.

"What about the duffel bag?" I ask, barely breathing.

Caleb shakes his head. "I didn't plant that or anything in it. That was all Ralph."

I exhale. "Thank you for telling me the truth."

"I couldn't tell you last night because our neighbor was there. And then the police. But I want you to know, I think of my promise to tell you everything—good, bad, and ugly—as a sacred vow."

My chest heaves. "It's a vow for me, too." I touch his cheek and he closes his eyes at my touch. "What you did was nothing but *good*, baby. Not bad or ugly at all."

Caleb opens his exhausted eyes. "You're not scared of me now?"

"*Scared* of you? Caleb, I'm nothing but proud of you. Grateful for what you did to protect us."

"I knew we'd always live in fear, if I didn't seize my chance."

"No doubt about it. They wouldn't have kept him long, and he would have kept coming at us, again and again."

"That was my thinking. At first, anyway. When I pulled

the trigger, I don't think I was thinking at all, honestly." He takes a deep breath. "Ralph said something horrible about Claudia. And then, he mentioned Raine. And the second Raine's name left his mouth, I saw him doing to her what he used to do to Claudia. And I just . . . snapped. My body took over and my brain went into a trance."

I nod. "If I'd been in your shoes, I can only hope I would have been brave enough—and a good enough shot—to do exactly what you did."

"I was so scared you wouldn't understand."

"I do. And I couldn't love you more than I do right now." A tidal wave of emotion slams into me. Love for Caleb and Raine. Grief and love for Claudia.

"I'm so relieved," he whispers.

"Honey, you should talk about this with a counselor. The stuff you can, anyway. You know, so you don't get PTSD."

He scoffs. "Trust me, I won't lose a minute's sleep over this. Not now that I know you support me."

"I don't think a lack of regret is the only factor in terms of PTSD. I think it's complicated."

Caleb shrugs. "You heard our neighbor. That fucker came after my family with obviously lethal intentions, and I did what I had to do to protect what's mine. Honestly, I'd do it again, a thousand times over, without a single regret."

My heart is exploding with love for him. I don't know what to say, so I simply whisper, "I love you."

"I love you, too." He pulls me to him for a tender kiss. And when he releases me, he presses his forehead against mine. "I'll always protect you and Raine. Please, never doubt that."

"I never will." I kiss his cheek. "Come on. Let's get you home and to bed. I'm sure you're going to sleep for hours."

FINDING HOME

When we got home from the police station, Caleb and I crawl into bed, both of us intending to crash after our long, sleepless night.

But when we're lying nose to nose, I kiss him. And he kisses me back.

And the next thing I know, we're both naked and Caleb is on top of me, sinking himself inside me. As he thrusts, I wrap myself around his torso and inhale his masculine scent. Sink my fingernails into his bare back. Revel in his strength. His courage. His *love*.

Caleb's thrusts are greedy and animalistic now, my mouth ravenous as it devours his. I caress his hair, back, and shoulders, as he claims me without holding back.

Our walls are non-existent now. There are no secrets left to keep. He's got me. All of me. And I've got him the exact same way. Good, bad, ugly. Although, when it comes to Caleb, I don't think there's an ugly bone in his beautiful body.

"*Aubrey*," Caleb grits out, as he moves his body in and out. "I love you, baby."

"I love you so much," I choke out, my voice stretched and desperate.

A current of electricity explodes between our bodies, as our souls fuse and an eternal commitment is forged. I thought those romantic carvings on the tree outside were the perfect testament of Caleb's eternal love and devotion. The biggest grand gesture possible. But now that he's gone and done that primal, secret *thing* to protect our family from harm, forever, I feel like my very soul has joined with his. We're in this together now. Forever.

Caleb loves me, and his daughter, with every ounce of

him, including the most primal parts. The wildest, most untamed parts that shouldn't be named, unless it's in secret, hushed whispers. And now, Caleb knows I love him back, every part of him, the exact same way.

He's mine. I'm his. We're a family now.

Forever.

CHAPTER 41
AUBREY

A week later

I rap on the door of the bathroom stall and call out to Raine, "You okay in there, Boo?"

"Mm hm. I go potty like a big girl."

"Good girl. But are you maybe all done now and sitting there watching a bug?"

"No, I go potty *and* watcha da bug."

My mother said it's normal for kids during potty training to have false alarms that consume ungodly amounts of time. Also, real alarms that take forever, too. She said patience is the most important thing, letting them know they're doing great, so they don't get self-conscious and get their wires crossed and start to regress.

"Did you turn into an Italian New Yorker in there?" I tease, chuckling at my own joke. When she doesn't reply, I explain, "*Watcha da bug* sounded right out of *The Godfather*."

"No, I *Rainey*."

I giggle. Amusing myself at times like these, sometimes at Raine's expense, is a must to preserve my sanity. "Yes, you are. Take your time in there, Pooh Bear. You're doing great."

I look at my watch. The live band started playing their second set right before we walked into the bathroom. So, according to the festival schedule, we still have plenty of time before the live auction begins. I don't want to miss any portion of that. It's always my favorite part of the festival, but with all the amazing donations Caleb's sister and friends gathered for us this year, it's going to be one for the record books.

Raine starts humming "Pretty Girl" by Aloha Carmichael on the other side of the stall door, so I reflexively start doing the hand movements from the music video on my side.

"I'm doing the dance," I announce to Raine, before returning to humming along with her.

"Me, too," Raine says with a giggle.

I laugh. "Less dancing, more pooping, dude."

Raine giggles again.

"Also, less 'watching da bug.'"

"He my friend."

"Did you name him?"

"Buggy."

"Naturally." It's totally on-brand for her. Her stuffed pig is Piggy. Her stuffed horse is Horsey, and so on.

My phone buzzes in my pocket, so I stop dancing and check it, thinking Caleb or my mother is texting to ask if Raine fell into the toilet or what. But to my surprise, it's a text from an unknown number, claiming to be from my ex-boyfriend, Trent; presumably, because I've blocked his old number.

Hey, Aubrey. It's Trent. I won't bother you again after this. Just wanted to say I'm sorry for what I did to you and I'm glad you found a good guy to take care of you right. I saw the news about C-Bomb shooting Claudia's father. So fucking wild! When I saw that, I thought, "Damn, C-Bomb let me off easy!" Haha. Honestly, getting slapped on the street by the best drummer in the world was pretty cool. Plus, he knew my name? AWESOME! It's too bad I can't tell the story to anyone, cuz then I'd have to admit the awful thing I did to deserve it. It's a bummer, but I deserve the punishment. At least, I'll always have a cool memory. Anyhoo, just wanted to wish you and C-Bomb the best and tell you I'll always be sorry and ashamed of what I did. Take care, Aubs. I really blew it with you. PS I swear I'll never contact you again, so tell C-Bomb not to hunt me down and do to me what he did to Ralph! Haha! Damn.

I can't believe my eyes, so I start reading the whole thing again. But midway through, Raine proudly shouts on the other side of the stall door, "All done!"

As the toilet flushes, my mind races. Should I delete this unexpected text from Trent? No. *Good, bad, ugly.* That's my deal with Caleb. One I plan to honor forever. Surely, when I show him this text later tonight, he'll laugh about it, anyway. But even if he doesn't, I've got to tell him. Caleb's always going to tell me all his deep, dark secrets; so I'm never going to hide anything from him in return.

"Hey, you!" a female voice says brightly, just as the door to the stall swings open and Raine emerges.

I turn to look at the source of the voice, and to my happy surprise, it's Caleb's sister, Miranda, bounding into the bathroom in a cowgirl get-up: denim shorts, boots, and a hat.

"Miranda!" I shout, rushing to her to hug her, as Raine shouts, "Auntie Manda!"

We both head over to her, with Raine toddling in front of me; and of course, Miranda hugs Raine first. "Rainey!" she shrieks, scooping up her niece, and then we all squeeze each other in a squealing three-way hug.

"What are you doing here?" I gasp out.

"You made the Summer Festival sound better than a club in Ibiza, so I decided to see it for myself."

I snort. "Well, Ibiza, it ain't." *Not that I've been there.* "But it's definitely a fun time." I look her up and down, as Raine dances around excitedly about her glamorous presence. "I'm loving the fit, girl. You definitely dressed the part." Miranda normally dresses in designer clothes. Or at least, everything she wears looks designer to me. So, this cowgirl get-up is a new look for her.

Miranda looks down at herself. "You don't think I overdid it?"

I laugh. "Not at all. You're perfect." I turn to Raine. "Did you wash your hands?" I know the answer to my question. I just want to hear her say it.

"I fo-got."

"I don't blame you. Auntie Miranda is a pretty exciting distraction." I guide Raine to the sink and cue her to wash her hands for the length of the usual song; and as she does that, I tell Miranda all the fun stuff she should do at the festival—the carnival games, the cake walk, the contests, and so on; and Miranda looks genuinely thrilled by all of it.

"The auction will be starting any minute now, but you

can do everything, right after that. The festival games stay open for a couple hours after the auction is done."

Raine calls to me that she's done washing her hands, and then holds up her tiny, clean palms as proof.

"Good girl. Now, let's get back out there and dance with Auntie Miranda before the auction starts."

Miranda leads the way, texting someone as she goes. And suddenly, the band abruptly stops playing its current tune, "Brown Eyed Girl," mere seconds before they get to my favorite part: the sha-la-la-las.

"Why'd they stop?" I ask, as we step outside the bathroom into the evening air. But I've no sooner asked the question than the band starts playing a new song. One I think I recognize by its instrumental introduction alone.

When the singer begins the first verse, my hunch morphs into certainty, and I throw my hand over my mouth. The song the band is playing is "All of My Love" by Led Zeppelin. The one Caleb named as *mine*. What are the odds?

I look around eagerly for my man, excited to drag him onto the dance floor, whether he likes it or not. But, damn it, Caleb is nowhere to be found. I spot my parents on the dance floor, having a blast. Plainly, my father is enjoying his newfound freedom in his walking boot. *But where's Caleb?*

"Let's dance," Miranda chirps to Raine, taking her hand. And of course, Raine expresses unadulterated excitement.

I follow the giddy pair, still scanning the faces for Caleb's. But no dice. That's weird. With Caleb's height and brawn, he's normally easy to spot in a crowd.

"Dadda!" Raine squeals.

"Where?" I ask, eager to find him before the song ends.

"Dere!" Raine points toward the stage, which makes no sense. But when I follow the trajectory of her tiny, raised finger, I see him. To my surprise, Caleb is sitting behind the band's drum kit, joining in on the iconic song. *Oh my god.* The band must have begged Caleb to play on a song, and my romantic, swoony man suggested *this* one!

I can't believe this man. His grand gestures and declarations of love never cease to amaze me. Nobody else at the festival will understand the sentimental meaning of this song to me. But it doesn't matter because *I* know what it means, and I'm swooning like crazy.

When Miranda, Raine and I reach the dance floor, Caleb's eyes find mine. As our gazes mingle, he winks and beams a glorious, radiant smile at me, without missing a beat in his drumming.

"All of my love," Caleb mouths, inaudibly, as the lead singer delivers those same words into his microphone for the crowd.

I clutch my chest, letting Caleb know I've received his message, loud and clear, and that I send him all of my love in return.

A firm poke on my shoulder wrenches my attention away from Caleb. I turn to look at whoever's nudged me, intending to simply glance and return to Caleb again; but to my shock, I've got another surprise awaiting me. One that commands my full attention.

It's Amy and her husband, Colin, standing before me, flanked by none other than Violet and her husband, Dax, and both couples' respective sons—two-year-old Rocco and eight-year-old Jackson.

"What the . . . ?" I gasp out, too flabbergasted to finish the sentence.

All four adults, now joined by Miranda, cackle with glee at my reaction, as Raine beelines excitedly to Rocco and hugs him. The pair were instantly inseparable, like peanut butter and jelly, at Caleb's party in Santa Monica less than two weeks ago, so I'm not surprised she remembers him.

Amy wraps my short-circuiting body in her arms and says, "Miranda made this party sound like *the* place to be, so we all came to check it out!"

I stammer while greeting everyone, and they guffaw at my astonished reaction, once again. My parents appear and greet everyone warmly. They already met all these fancy people, briefly, at Caleb's party, before they spirited the toddlers away and retired themselves. But once their greetings have been administered, the whole group, including me, turns its collective attention back to Caleb onstage.

When I catch my boyfriend's eyes this time, I motion excitedly to our unexpected group of visitors; but nothing but smug satisfaction graces Caleb's handsome face, making it clear this group's arrival isn't a shock to him, like it is for me. I mean, Caleb looks overjoyed to see everyone. Also, to see my reaction. But he's definitely not *surprised*. Indeed, his expression is like he's just pulled off the bank heist of the century.

The iconic song ends, sadly, and the lead singer bellows, "Let's hear it for our guest drummer, C-Bomb!"

As the crowd roars, Caleb waves a drumstick in the air.

"Thank you, Caleb. That was a dream come true for all of us. We're honored you've made our little hometown your new home." The singer returns to the crowd with a big grin. "Now, who's ready for the *auctionnnnnnn*?"

The crowd cheers and whoops its enthusiastic reply.

"It's gonna be a good one," the singer declares. "But before that, C-Bomb has asked to say a few words to you."

He has? Caleb didn't mention wanting to do that to me; but then again, he also didn't mention playing with the band, or the fact that his sister and friends would be here today. *What's going on?*

I look at my mother, since she's the festival czar who's meticulously planned everything on today's schedule, and she shoots me a look of such over-the-top joy, such intense expectation and glee, I suddenly realize what's going on here: Miranda must have lobbied all our friends to come here today, specifically to maximize bidding on all the amazing donations they secured for the event. My god, Miranda is a force of nature. Not to mention, I'm thoroughly impressed with Dax, too. When Dax agreed to become real friends with Caleb going forward, the dude wasn't kidding. Obviously, both he and his wife, Violet, genuinely want to forge a genuine bond here. Talk about two people walking the walk!

Caleb comes to the front of the stage and takes the mic from the singer, while the crowd goes crazy. "Hey, everyone," Caleb says, his low, sexy voice sending goosebumps across my skin. "I want to thank you for welcoming me with such open arms into your community. I feel like I'm home, and that's partly thanks to all of you."

More cheers.

"To express my gratitude to this community, I'm going to match, by a multiple of five, whatever total is raised in this auction today. So, please, be as generous as you can afford to be."

As everyone cheers and claps, I look at Mom again, and this time, the near-euphoria on her face verges on mania. *Aw, Mom.* She works so hard to make this festival a success, every year; and, now, she's about to throw her best event yet. *Good for her.* I mean, good for Prairie Springs, of course. But I love watching Mom geek out about the money we're about to raise for some good causes.

I hug Mom and she practically vibrates in my arms. "This is so exciting!" I shout into her ear, above the din; but to my surprise, she simply waves me off and gestures for me to pay attention to Caleb onstage again.

When my eyes return to Caleb's, he continues into his microphone, "Okay, now that we've got the auction stuff out of the way, let me tell you the other big reason, besides all of you, that Prairie Springs feels like home to me now." He points to me. "That woman right there. The amazing, beautiful, brilliant Aubrey Capshaw. Or, as I like to call her, A-Bomb."

I shake my head, laughing and blushing. Goddammit, Caleb. Doesn't he know the whole town is going to start calling me that now, every bit as much as they call him C-Bomb?

Caleb chuckles at whatever he's seeing on my face. "Aubrey, baby. My love." His smile fades. Suddenly, he looks incredibly earnest up there. Like he's gearing up to say something deeply important. He clears his throat. Takes a deep breath. "Aubrey, my love, you're the great love of my life. My family, my forever, my home; and I can't wait to spend the rest of my life with you, as your husband, if you'll let me."

I gasp, and the crowd goes batshit around me; and a second later, Caleb jumps off the lip of the stage and bounds toward me like a bull in a rodeo ring. When he reaches me, he kneels, raises an opened ring box to me, revealing a massive, sparkling diamond nestled in black velvet, and chokes out, "Aubrey Capshaw, will you marry me?"

I can't function. I'm too overwhelmed. But when I realize he's waiting for an answer before sliding that jaw-dropping rock onto my finger, I scream, *"Yes, yes, yes!* A thousand times, yes!"

Laughing, Caleb puts the ring on; and with the dazzling diamond on my hand, my man—my future husband—rises and wraps me in a hug that takes my breath away, while the crowd surrounding us cheers and applauds wildly.

"Ladies and gentlemen," a booming, amplified voice says. It's the lead singer of the band again, resuming his duties at the mic. "Before we start the auction, Caleb's arranged a special guest performer as an engagement gift for his fiancée and daughter. Ladies and gentlemen, please, give it up for . . . *Aloha Carmichael!*"

"*What?*" I shriek. "No. *What?*" I'll be damned, Aloha Carmichael herself suddenly bursts out of a makeshift tent near the stage and struts onstage to thunderous applause.

Shrieking and freaking out, I swivel my head toward Caleb, and he's practically doubled over with laughter at my maniacal reaction. I quickly find Raine, who's screaming and jumping up and down next to my mother, and we proceed to freak out and cry together.

Predictably, phones come out everywhere, as Aloha saunters onstage, waving and laughing as she goes. "Hello, Prairie Springs!" the world-famous pop star shouts into the microphone at center stage. "And congratulations to Caleb, Aubrey, and Raine!" She finds me in the crowd. "Caleb told me 'Pretty Girl' is a favorite of yours and Raine's. So this one goes out to both of you, pretty girls."

I blow enthusiastic kisses at Aloha, as tears stream down my face, while Raine screams and grips her little cheeks next to me, like one of those teenagers in old black and white footage of the Beatles. My god, Raine reminds me so much of her mommy in this moment, my heart physically hurts. Claudia loved music, and she absolutely reveled in being the ultimate fangirl for her favorites.

The intro to the song blares from overhead speakers, and Aloha calls out, "Sing and dance with me, Prairie Springs!"

The cue arrives for the first verse, and Aloha launches into singing it expertly. And of course, every man, woman, and child in the crowd—it's the kind of song everyone knows, whether they like it or not—joins in singing and dancing without holding back.

A group on the dance floor spontaneously starts performing the famous choreography from the music video; so, of course, our small group, even Caleb, join in dancing, too, with varying degrees of aptitude. When the song ends, Caleb takes me into his arms and kisses me, laughing against my lips. And by the time our kiss is done, Aloha has already been quickly shuttled off-stage by a cadre of bodyguards.

"Don't worry," Caleb says into my ear. "You'll get to meet Aloha at our engagement party tomorrow tonight. I rented out a restaurant in Billings for the occasion."

"What? Oh my god!"

"I also rented out an entire floor of a hotel, so we can all hang out together after the dinner."

"I can't believe you did all this. I'm blown away."

Caleb smirks and winks. "Orgasms and romance, baby. You said you wanted both, and your wish is my command."

"I love you so much. *Thank you.*" I look at the ring on my hand. "Holy shit, Caleb."

He laughs. "You like it? Miranda helped me pick it out."

"I *love* it. It's perfect. Beyond generous." Tears form in my eyes, and I wipe them. "I need to sit down. I'm seriously dizzy."

"Come on. I feel a bit dizzy myself." He leads me to a bench on the fringes of the buzzing festival, and we sit for a moment to catch our mutual breath. As we talk, kiss, and giggle happily, the auction starts in the near distance, led by our town's legendary auctioneer, my dad's good friend, Bob Warner.

"So, listen, baby," Caleb says midway through the auction. "I don't know what the future holds for my band, in terms of tours and commitments, but I don't think we'll ever hang it up completely and stop performing."

"Of course, you won't. I'd never expect or want you to stop." I touch his arm. "You're only thirty-five, babe. Hopefully, your band will perform for another fifty years."

Caleb chuckles. "*Fifty*? I'll take twenty or thirty." He gathers his thoughts. "I just want you to understand that I love you and Raine more than I love my band. More than I love making music. More than I love performing. I love all that stuff. So much. It makes me *me*. But you're both my *why* now, my reason for being—my reason for staying sober—to keep growing and becoming a better man. I want you to know I'm never going to do anything to fuck up my relationship with you or our family. Please, believe that, Aubrey."

I touch his cheek. "Baby, I know that. Doing what you love will never, ever fuck anything up."

He bites his lip. "Do you think you and Raine might join me on the road sometimes? We could make future tours and performances a family affair."

"Sounds fun. But don't worry, okay? We'll figure it out."

He sighs with relief. "Lots of musicians I know, some in really popular bands, have families now, and they're making it work. I've asked a bunch of them how they do it, and I think I understand how to balance it all. Mostly, everyone told me to make tours short and always take the fam with me, whenever possible, or create plenty of breaks in the schedule, so you can fly back and forth between home and shows."

"Whatever it takes, we'll do it."

"You're willing to work with me?"

"Caleb, I'd follow you to the ends of the earth."

He kisses the top of my hand. "I love you so fucking much, A-Bomb."

My smile turns into a mock glare. "You know the whole town is gonna start calling me that now, thanks to you."

He chuckles. "That's why I did it. If I'm C-Bomb, then you've gotta be my A-Bomb."

As I laugh with him, Bob the Auctioneer bellows into his microphone, "Next up, let's start the bidding on the amazing package donated by our very own C-Bomb! C-Bomb? Where are you, man?"

"You should go back over there."

He squeezes my hand. "I'd rather sit here with you—my fiancée."

Bob says, "Hmm, I don't see C-Bomb anywhere, so let's get into it. Let me check my notes." He looks down at the paper in his hand. "If you have the winning bid for this one, here's what you'll win." He lists a dizzying array of RCR merch, VIP tickets, and memorabilia. A Zoom call with the entire band for thirty minutes. A top-of-the-line drum kit supplied by Caleb, its toms and several sets of drumsticks signed by him. "And if you don't know how to play," Bob says in wrap-up. "Never fear! The winner will get *three* one-on-one drum lessons from C-Bomb himself—one of the greatest drummers in the history of music, and the greatest living drummer of our time, so you can learn to play your new drum kit like the man himself."

Bob opens the floor for bidding, and the moment he does, the crowd reacts like ants pouncing on a runaway drop of maple syrup, which makes both Caleb and me belly laugh with glee.

"I'm surprised you threw in drum lessons. You seemed skittish about that, when Miranda suggested it."

Caleb shrugs. "I'm home now and not going anywhere, so why not?"

I suddenly remember Trent's text and show it to him. And, thankfully, Caleb guffaws while reading it.

"I told you Trent knew he had it coming," Caleb says. He returns the phone to me and taps his temple. "I've got a sixth sense about that kind of thing. If they skitter away like a cockroach, you're golden."

His words make me think about Ralph Beaumont, since he was a man who probably never once skittered away like a cockroach in his entire life. As it's turned out, Caleb hasn't lost a moment of sleep over what he did a week ago, and neither have I. On the contrary, the only after-effect from the shooting, as far as I can tell, is our bond has only deepened and strengthened.

"I can't wait to marry you," Caleb whispers, touching my cheek.

"Let's do it really soon," I say.

"How about tomorrow? I can't wait to call you my wife."

I laugh. "Tomorrow is our *engagement* party, remember? Not our wedding. But, yes, I agree we should do it, as soon as we can arrange it."

"Or we could turn our engagement party into a wedding."

I laugh, thinking Caleb is joking. And when he doesn't

laugh, I shrug my shoulders and say, "Okay, fuck it. Why not? Let's do it."

"Seriously?"

"Seriously."

He whoops.

Granted, I could spend lots of time picking out the perfect dress and flowers and the rest. But as long as my parents and Raine are there—and Caleb's sister and closest friends—the details really don't matter to me. We can throw a big party to celebrate in LA later, whenever we return there for a visit. For now, the most important thing, above everything else, is I'll get to call Caleb Baumgarten my husband, as soon as possible.

We kiss to seal the deal.

"God, I love you, A-Bomb."

"I love you, too, Caleb."

"And I promise I always will."

EPILOGUE

AUBREY

Music is blaring. It's my playlist, this time. As the czar of our seventh annual Fourth of July party, I always get to pick the music, along with planning the food and everybody's accommodations. Caleb and all the other rock lovers in attendance needn't worry, though: I always make sure there's something for everyone on my party playlist, given the wide age ranges and musical preferences of those in attendance every year.

There's a whole lot of star power at this party, as usual, but someone passing by on a boat wouldn't realize that, thanks to the downhome, family-friendly vibe. Also, thanks to the gaggle of kids splashing around in the lake and running around on our extra-long stretch of shoreline.

Thanks to Caleb buying the house next door three years ago, our shoreline feels like a private beach club these days. I thought it was excessive when Caleb bought the adjacent house for family and friends to have an easy, convenient to place to stay while visiting. But I must admit, the idea turned out to be a great one. In fact, between our visiting friends, family, and my parents, the guest house, as we now call it, is rarely empty.

"A-Bomb!" Caleb calls out from the lake. My husband is standing in waist-deep water with our two-year-old son, Bonham, in one arm, while our four-year-old daughter, Page, uses Caleb's body as her own personal jungle gym. Somehow, even in the midst of the chaos wrought by the children clinging to him, Caleb is managing to calmly chat with the two men standing near him in the lake: Dax Morgan and Reed Rivers.

"Babe!" Caleb calls to me again. "Bonzo's had a huge blowout in his swim diaper, and Page the Maniac won't let me leave to change it!"

"A likely story," I call to him, and Caleb laughs. He's changed more than his fair share of diapers over the years, first with Raine back in the day, and then with Page and Bonham in rapid succession. But that doesn't mean my husband *likes* to do it, especially when he's happily catching up with close friends.

I motion to Caleb that I'm coming and then strip off my cover-up and wade toward him through the water in my bikini. "You owe me one," I tease, when I reach Caleb. By now, it's a running gag between us: taking on the task of changing a diaper and then claiming to be "owed one," even though neither of us ever collects on the purported debt. As we've come to learn, our imaginary balance sheet always corrects itself, without either of us ever needing to keep score in earnest.

"How can I owe you 'one,' when I already owe you *everything*?" Caleb quips, as I take our poopie son from him with rigid arms and a scrunched nose.

"Oh, I'll find a way to let you pay me back," I tease. To Bonham, I mutter, "Come on, Bonzo. Let's get you all cleaned up." I can already tell it's going to be a bad one—a blowout that went *everywhere*. "Bio-hazard coming through!" I call out, as I make my way toward the house, and all our friends part like the Red Sea.

Inside, I find Reed Rivers' wife, Georgina, changing their infant son's diaper on the living room floor. So, I grab a nearby changing pad and throw it down next to Georgina. As we're both chatting and working on our similar tasks, my sister-in-law, Miranda waltzes through the front door of the house and makes a silly "pee-yew" sound at the sight of Georgina and me surrounded by dirty diapers on the floor.

"How *delightful*," Miranda deadpans. "I'm loving this for you ladies."

"Yep, we're living the dream," I reply, and Georgina chuckles. In Georgie's case, she really is living the dream, though. I mean, so am I. But I've managed to get pregnant easily, every time we've tried. From what I understand, Georgina and Reed had to work pretty hard to make their baby dreams a reality, so I'm quite certain she's savoring every moment of this journey, even changing poopie diapers.

"Can I use a back room to breastfeed him?" Georgina asks. And when I say, of course, yes, she bids a temporary farewell to Miranda and me and heads off.

With my own son's fresh diaper secured, I stand him up, pat his little bottom, and ask, "You want a snack before you go back out, Bubba?"

Bonham shakes his little head. "*Dadda.*" He begins toddling toward the front door, but I stop him. "Hold up. I have to watch you go to Dadda to make sure you make it to him safely. Lemme wash my hands first, and then we'll go." As Bonham grumbles, I wash my hands, while Miranda grabs a cold drink from the fridge. Hence, the reason she came inside, apparently. And then, we head out the front door as a trio, at which point, Bonham toddles at full speed toward his beloved father in the lake.

When Caleb sees his drummer boy racing toward him, he eggs him on and scoops him up at the shoreline with a loud whoop. I glance around for Page, our four-year-old, and find her nearby with some other kids, being watched over by my mother. But when I hear a happy squeal in the water, I turn toward Caleb again, just in time to watch him dragging Bonham around by his little hands, exactly like he used to do with Raine back in the day.

"Aw," I coo. "That makes my heart go pitter pat."

"He's so cute with him," Miranda murmurs.

"He's cute with all his kids." I absently touch my belly, even though I'm not showing yet. Caleb doesn't know this, but the phrase "all his kids" will soon refer to *four* of them, rather than the three he knows about.

"Have you seen Raine anywhere?" Miranda asks. "She's supposed to give me a pedicure."

"Last I saw her, she was playing horseshoes with Rocco near the guest house."

We both look over at the shoreline next door, just in time to catch Raine, slack jawed and frozen, with a horseshoe in her hand, staring in awe at Jackson Morgan—the teenage son of Dax and Violet. At the moment, he happens to be striding past Raine and Rocco, on his way to the lake, alongside Paula's gorgeous, vivacious, teenage daughter, Zelda. Not surprisingly, Zelda is commanding Jackson's full attention. So much so, he's not registering ten-year-old Raine's existence in the slightest.

"Crap," I say. "I know that look."

Miranda giggles. "Can't say I blame her for having a

crush on him. Jackson looks exactly like his father, and Dax isn't a worldwide sex symbol for nothing."

"I'm not ready for this, Miranda. She's ten."

"The perfect age to have her first crush."

I flap my lips together. "Jackson doesn't know she exists, right?"

"Not at all. She's totally invisible to him."

"Thank god." I rub my forehead. "Damn. I was hoping my kids would turn out to be late bloomers, like me. I didn't have a crush till I was fifteen. But it looks like maybe Raine got Claudia's boy-crazy gene."

"I've got the same gene, unfortunately, so she probably got it from her daddy's side of the gene pool, too."

"When did crushes start for you?"

Miranda grimaces. "Around Raine's age. Sorry."

"Same as Claudia. In sixth grade, she wanted to marry this boy named James." Once again, I find myself thinking how much my sister-in-law reminds me of Claudia. I thought that the first time I met Miranda, and the resemblance has only grown and crystallized, since then, the more I've gotten to know my sister-in-law over the years.

"I think I'll let Raine off the hook for that pedicure," Miranda says. "If she happens to be looking for me later, let her know I'm over there." She motions toward a group that includes Aloha Carmichael, Aloha's adorable husband, Zander, and their two closest friends, Keane and Maddy Morgan—Dax's older brother and his wife. And off Miranda goes, slithering past me in her bikini, smelling of coconuts and confidence.

"A-Bomb!" Caleb shouts from the lake, drawing my attention. "Look at Bonzo! He's ready for the Olympics!"

Caleb leans down to whisper something to our son, and

a moment later, he swims, on his own, about ten yards, from Caleb to Dax's outstretched hands.

"Woohoo!" I call out. "Go, Bonzo, go!" I race down to the shoreline to cheer from a closer distance, and Bonham repeats the feat by returning to his father.

When Bonham reaches him, Caleb scoops up his son and high-fives him, and our sweet little water-logged boy smiles proudly.

"You want to go a third time?" Caleb asks excitedly.

"All done!" Bonham chokes out. "Sand."

"You sure? Okay." He calls to me. "He wants to play with his sand toys, babe."

"I'll get him settled!"

Caleb brings Bonham to me, and I get him settled with my father and some sand toys on the shore, at which point I accept my husband's sexy invitation to return to the water with him for some "alone-time." It's a no-brainer to say yes. My husband's only become sexier to me over the years, as we've settled into our happy life here on the lake. I've seen the whole world with this man by now, always with our family in tow, usually during short summer tours with the band. But those experiences never feel like real life to me. They always feel like a grand adventure. A vacation. While this place here on Lake Lucille always feels like home.

When we're all the way to our chests in the cool water, and finally acclimated to the temperature, I straddle Caleb's torso with my legs, slide my arms around his neck, and press my center into his bulging hard-on. For several minutes, we make out like horny teenagers, our lust consuming us.

"I was thinking we really should buy that house," Caleb says. He doesn't need to explain. The owner of the house on the other side of the guest house mentioned he was thinking about selling the other day, when we ran into him in town while shopping for party supplies.

"Oh, yeah?"

"This party is only going to get bigger every year, right? And as our friends' kids get older, we'll need more and more room for everyone. We're home for good, right? We're never leaving. So, why not make this whole place into a Baumgarten Family Compound?"

I laugh. He's so cute. "You mean, like we're a cult?"

"Exactly."

I laugh again. The truth is, I already know he's going to do it, no matter what we talk about today. But I'm happy to play along. "How much are they asking for the place?"

Caleb tells me the number, and I whistle. "That's a lot of money," I murmur. Again, I'm playing along. Caleb's always done fabulously well with his band, of course. But after the Ralph Beaumont incident made worldwide news, his personal "brand" took off, without any intention or effort on Caleb's part. Suddenly, even more money started rolling in from all sorts of licensing and sponsorship deals, in addition to all the usual income streams. At this point, it's seriously like money grows on trees for this man.

"Seems kind of excessive," I tease, even though I know it's chump change to Caleb. I brush a lock of wet hair off his forehead and grin. "Although, I mean, I guess it might be kind of nice to know all four of our kids will always have a place to stay with us."

"Well, maybe we shouldn't do it, then," he jokes. But he's no sooner said the words, then his brain processes what I just said. "Wait. All *four* of our kids?"

I let my husband hold his breath and wait for confirmation for a long beat, just for the sheer fun of it. But when Caleb looks too cute to torture any longer, I laugh and say,

"Sorry to tell you, babe, but you're going to need to find yet *another* open spot on your neck." After our wedding in Billings eight years ago, Caleb got an "A" and an "R" inked onto his neck, both tattoos topped with lit fuses like the "C" that was already inked there. And then, with Page's and Bonham's births, Caleb added two more letters to his collection, the same way he'd added to the carvings on The Family Tree.

"Oh my fucking god," Caleb blurts excitedly. "You're sure?"

"I'm sure. I took three tests this morning. All positive. Get ready to change even more poopie diapers, Dadda."

He kisses me. "Can't wait."

"Also, you'll need to carve another initial into The Family Tree. Let's not forget about that."

"Of course. Oh my god." With a laugh, he kisses me deeply, as I press myself into his hard bulge again and enjoy the waves of euphoria rocketing through me.

"What's another good Zeppelin-inspired name?" Caleb asks, nuzzling his nose to mine.

"I feel like we've reached the end of that particular road," I say. "I mean, I don't really want to name my child Robert, Roberta, or any variation of Plant, John Paul, or Jones. Do you?"

Caleb guffaws and agrees none of those options sound appealing to him, either.

Fun fact: the name of our four-year-old, Page, wasn't actually inspired by Led Zeppelin's famous guitarist, Jimmy Page. Everyone thinks that, but it's not true. We both simply liked the name, for whatever reason—although maybe it was subliminal—and we went with it. But then, once Caleb's musician friends, many of whom are also obsessed with Led Zeppelin, started assuming Page had been named for the famed guitarist of Caleb's all-time favorite band, we just sort of adopted that revisionist version of history and rolled with it. Which is why, when our son came along two years later, it felt natural and right to name him after John Bonham, Zepp's legendary drummer and Caleb's biggest inspiration.

"I actually have a couple name ideas," I say, biting my lower lip flirtatiously.

He pinches my ass underneath the water. "Lay 'em on me, baby."

"So, if it's a girl, I'm thinking *Adele*." True, that's the name of one of my all-time favorite pop girlies; but she's not my inspiration. Which is why, in case my intentions aren't clear to Caleb, I add quickly, "After your mother."

Caleb's green eyes widen and prick with moisture. "That's perfect. Thank you for thinking of that."

"And if it's a boy, I was thinking Hayes." That's Caleb's mother's maiden name. And not surprisingly, this next suggestion causes the moisture in Caleb's eyes to morph into full-blown tears.

"I love you so much," he murmurs, pressing his forehead to mine. "Thank you, Aubrey."

"I love you, too. Thank you for our beautiful life."

"That's all thanks to you, momma." He kisses me tenderly. But after a moment, he breaks free of my lips and smiles broadly. "I have a confession to make."

"You want to fuck me," I deadpan. It's a safe bet, given the way his hard dick is currently poking urgently against me underneath the water.

"Well, yes. Always. Endlessly. Forever. But that's not what I was going to say."

I grip the wet hair at the back of Caleb's head and gaze into his green eyes with intensity, making a big show of being ready for whatever silly confession he's going to make this time. Caleb does this often: he "confesses" something that always turns out to be wonderful.

"I already bought the house. Yesterday. Escrow closes in two weeks."

I snort. "*Caleb.*"

He laughs. "The thing is, I was talking to the owner, and he mentioned he was going to put it up for sale *today*, so I had to act fast. We can't let some stranger move in there. This whole beach is *ours.*"

"Well, gosh. It sounds like you had no choice, when you put it like that."

"Right? I knew you'd understand."

"I do."

Laughing, he runs his thumb against my cheek. "I think we should invite your parents to move in there, full-time. Wouldn't that be fun?"

I melt. "That would be amazing." *And I know they'd fucking love it.* Yes, my parents only live twenty-five minutes away, but I can't deny we all have a blast whenever they stay the night next door at the guest house. In fact, the thought of my kids being able to wander over to Grammy and Pop-Pop's house, any ol' time they like, makes my entire body tingle with joy.

"Thank you for doing that," I whisper, nuzzling my husband's nose, yet again. "I love you so much, you sweet, romantic fool."

"I love you, too, baby. You know that, right?"

"I sure do."

Caleb grins. "Good. Because, baby, I always will."

THE END

Want more of Caleb and Aubrey's story? Visit www.laurenrowebooks.com/bonus-scenes to read more of them and also explore the River Records tab on Lauren's site while you're there, too, for more bonus material about Caleb and Dax Morgan and more.

If you want to listen to Dax and Violet's love story, *Rockstar*, or Amy and Colin's, *Swoon*, you can find details about them on Lauren Rowe's website, too.

If you loved Caleb, Aubrey, and Raine in *Finding Home*, I'd be grateful for a review. Thank you for reading!

ACKNOWLEDGMENTS

Thank you to Brad, Sophie, and Chloe; to Sarah, Lizette, and Sophie (the other one). All of you contribute so meaningfully to my books and life, and I can't thank you enough. Special thanks to my dear friends, Marnie and Amy—the kickass family law attorney who gave me indispensable advice and information for this book, and the brilliant romance author who helped me figure out what the heck I wanted to do with this sprawling idea for a story. (She's AL Jackson, folks. Read her now, if you haven't already.) I truly couldn't have written this particular book without both of your amazing input, ideas, brainstorming, and friendship.

Thank you also to Heather aka Parrot aka My Montana Connection for this particular book. Thank you for helping me make fictitious Prairie Springs as Montana-accurate as possible. Thank you also to Shannon Passmore of Shanoff Designs for sticking with me through the back-and-forth design process for the covers. Once I finally homed in on what I truly wanted, you took my vision to the next level and created something far better than what my own pea brain could have imagined. And finally, thank you, dearest reader, for giving me and this book a shot. I love writing the stories in my head, even if only for myself; but I must admit it's a whole lot more fun when there's someone else willing to read them and love them, too. Thank you.

BOOKS BY LAUREN ROWE

Finding Home

I'm Caleb Baumgarten, the "bad boy" drummer of Red Card Riot.

After tragedy strikes and the toddler with half my DNA inside her loses her beloved mommy, I get the

bright idea to hire my daughter's remaining lifeline, her "Auntie Aubrey," as my live-in nanny. Also,

embarrassingly, as my sobriety coach, so I can fulfill the terms of my mandatory rehab.

Going into my forced living arrangement with Aubrey in her small town, I'm determined not to give in to

my growing, thumping, white-hot attraction. There's only a month before the custody hearing that will

decide my fate as a father, and I'll need Aubrey to testify on my behalf. Well, you know what they say

about best laid plans, right? Yeah. My bad.

The Morgan Brothers

Read these standalones in any order. Chronological reading order is below, but they are all complete stories. Note: you do not need to read any other books or series before jumping straight into reading about the Morgan boys.

Hero

The story of heroic firefighter, Colby Morgan. When catastrophe strikes Colby Morgan, will physical therapist Lydia save him . . . or will he save her?

Captain

The insta-love-to-enemies-to-lovers story of tattooed sex god, Ryan Morgan, and the woman he'd move heaven and earth to claim.

Ball Peen Hammer

A steamy, hilarious, friends-to-lovers romantic comedy about cocky-as-hell male stripper, Keane Morgan, and the sassy, smart young woman who brings him to his knees during a road trip.

Mister Bodyguard

The Morgans' beloved honorary brother, Zander Shaw, meets his match in the feisty pop star he's assigned to protect on tour.

ROCKSTAR

When the youngest Morgan brother, Dax Morgan, meets a mysterious woman who rocks his world, he must decide if pursuing her is worth risking it all. Be sure to check out four of Dax's original songs from ROCKSTAR, written and produced by Lauren, along with full music videos for the songs, on her website (www.laurenrowebooks.com) under the tab MUSIC FROM ROCKSTAR.

Dive into Lauren's universe of interconnected trilogies and duets, all books available individually and as a bundle, in any order.

A full suggested reading order can be found here!

The Josh & Kat Trilogy

It's a war of wills between stubborn and sexy Josh Faraday and Kat Morgan. A fight to the bed. Arrogant, wealthy playboy Josh is used to getting what he wants. And what he wants is Kat Morgan. The books are to be read in order:

Infatuation

Revelation

Consummation

The Club Trilogy

When wealthy playboy Jonas Faraday receives an anonymous note from Sarah Cruz, a law student working part-time processing online applications for an exclusive club, he becomes obsessed with hunting her down and giving her the satisfaction she claims has always eluded her. Thus begins a sweeping tale of obsession, passion, desperation, and ultimately, everlasting love and individual redemption. Find out why scores of readers all over the world, in multiple languages, call The Club Trilogy "my favorite trilogy ever" and "the greatest love story I've ever read." As Jonas Faraday says to Sarah Cruz: "There's never been a love like ours and there never will be again... Our love is so pure and true, we're the amazement of the gods."

The Club: Obsession

The Club: Reclamation

The Club: Redemption

The fourth book for Jonas and Sarah is a full-length epilogue with incredible heart-stopping twists and turns and feels. Read The Club: Culmination (A Full-Length Epilogue Novel) after finishing The Club Trilogy or, if you prefer, after reading The Josh and Kat Trilogy.

The Reed Rivers Trilogy

Reed Rivers has met his match in the most unlikely of women—aspiring journalist and spitfire, Georgina Ricci. She's much younger than the women Reed normally pursues, but he can't resist her fiery personality and drop-dead gorgeous looks. But in this game of cat and mouse, who's chasing whom? With each passing day of this wild ride, Reed's not so sure. The books of this trilogy are to be read in order:

Bad Liar

Beautiful Liar

Beloved Liar

The Hate Love Duet

An addicting, enemies-to-lovers romance with humor, heat, angst, and banter. Music artists Savage of Fugitive Summer and Laila Fitzgerald are stuck together on tour. And convinced they can't stand each other. What they don't know is that they're absolutely made for each other, whether they realize it or not. The books of this duet are to be read in order:

Falling Out of Hate with You

Falling Into Love with You

Interconnected Standalones within the same universe as above

Hacker in Love

When world-class hacker Peter "Henn" Hennessey meets Hannah Milliken, he moves heaven and earth, including doing some questionable things, to win his dream girl over. But when catastrophe strikes, will Henn lose Hannah forever, or is there still a chance for him to chase their happily ever after? *Hacker in Love* is a steamy, funny, heart-pounding, **standalone** contemporary romance with a whole lot of feels, laughs, spice, and swoons.

Smitten

When aspiring singer-songwriter, Alessandra, meets Fish, the funny, adorable bass player of 22 Goats, sparks fly between the awkward pair. Fish tells Alessandra he's a "Goat called Fish who's hung like a bull. But not really. I'm actually really average." And Alessandra tells Fish, "There's nothing like a girl's first love." Alessandra thinks she's talking about a song when she makes her comment to Fish—the first song she'd ever heard by 22 Goats, in fact. As she'll later find out, though, her "first love" was actually Fish. The Goat called Fish who, after that night, vowed to do anything to win her heart. SMITTEN is a true standalone romance.

Swoon

When Colin Beretta, the drummer of 22 Goats, is a groomsman at the wedding of his childhood best friend, Logan, he discovers Logan's kid sister, Amy, is all grown up. Colin tries to resist his attraction to Amy, but after a drunken kiss at the wedding reception, that's easier said than done. Swoon is a true standalone romance.

Meet Me At Captain's Series of Standalone Romantic comedies

Who's Your Daddy?

When thirty-year-old patent attorney, Maximillian Vaughn, meets a sassy, charismatic older woman in a bar, he invites her back to his place for one night of no-strings fun. It's all Max can offer, given his busy career; but, luckily, it's all Marnie wants, too. But when Max's chemistry with Marnie is so combustible, it threatens to burn down his bedroom, he does the unthinkable the next morning: he asks Marnie out on a dinner date.

Mere minutes after saying yes, however, Marnie bolts like her hair is on fire with no explanation. What happened? Max doesn't know, but he's determined to find out and convince Marnie to pick up where they left off.

Textual Relations

When Grayson McKnight unknowingly gets a fake number from a woman in a bar, he winds up embroiled in a sexy text exchange with the actual owner of the number—a confident, sensual older woman who knows exactly who she is . . . and what she wants.

No strings attached.

But as sparks fly and real feelings develop, will Grayson get his way and tempt her to give him more than their original bargain?

My Neighbor's Secret

When Charlotte gets into her new dilapidated condo to start fixing it up for resale, she finds out the infuriating stranger who's thoroughly messed up her life is her new next-door neighbor.

Also, that he's got a big secret.

She confronts him and proposes they work together to get themselves out of their respective jams, even though they both admittedly can't stand each other. Yes, he's let it slip he thinks she's pretty. And, okay, she begrudgingly thinks he's kind of cute. But whatever. They hate each other and this is nothing but a business partnership. What could go wrong?

The Secret Note: A Spicy Standalone Novella with HEA

He's a hot Aussie. I'm a girl who isn't shy about getting what she wants. The problem? Ben is my little brother's best friend. An exchange student who's heading back Down Under any day now. But I can't help myself. He's too hot to resist.

Misadventures Standalones (unrelated standalones not within the above universe):

- ***Misadventures on the Night Shift*** –A hotel night shift clerk encounters her teenage fantasy: rock star Lucas Ford. And combustion ensues.

- ***Misadventures of a College Girl***—A spunky, virginal theater major meets a cocky football player at her first college party . . . and absolutely nothing goes according to plan for either of them.

- ***Misadventures on the Rebound***—A spunky woman on the rebound meets a hot, mysterious stranger in a bar on her way to her five-year high school reunion in Las Vegas and what follows is a misadventure neither of them ever imagined.

Lauren's Dark Comedy/Psych Thriller Standalone

Countdown to Killing Kurtis

A young woman with big dreams and skeletons in her closet decides her porno-king husband must die in exactly a year. This is not a traditional romance, but it will most definitely keep you turning the pages and saying "WTF?" If you're looking for something a bit outside the box, with twists and turns, suspense, and dark humor, this is the book for you: a standalone psychological thriller/dark comedy with romantic elements.

AUTHOR BIOGRAPHY

Lauren Rowe writes open-door, spicy romances that will make you laugh out loud, fan yourself, swoon, and occasionally cry, on the way to her characters' happily ever after. When you pick up a Lauren Rowe book, you know you'll always be highly entertained and invested in the characters, you'll laugh at the banter and lovable cast of characters like they're your real-life friends, and of course the heat will be elite!

Be sure to explore all the incredible spoiler-free bonus materials featured on Lauren's website at LaurenRoweBooks.com.

Also, follow Lauren Rowe on all social media platforms at @laurenrowebooks.

Made in the USA
Columbia, SC
27 February 2025

54522626R00243